M000248448

Retribution Dies
Copyright © 2020 by Chloe Szentpeteri

First edition: August 2020

Find me at: chloehodge.com
Instagram: @chloeschapters
Facebook: Chloe Hodge Author

Printed in Australia.

Paperback ISBN: 978-0-6485997-4-6
Hardback ISBN: 978-0-6485997-2-2
E-book ISBN: 978-0-6485997-3-9

Special thanks and acknowledgement to:
Editor; Aidan Curtis,
Paperback cover artist; Erica Timmons at ETC Designs,
Hardcover artist; Niru Sky,
Interior illustrator; Emily Johns,
Formatter; Julia Scott at Evenstar Books.

This book is written in British English.

GUARDIANS OF THE GROVE TRILOGY

Retribution Dies

BOOK TWO

CHLOE HODGE

For Donna and Toni.
You always believed in me ... You always will.

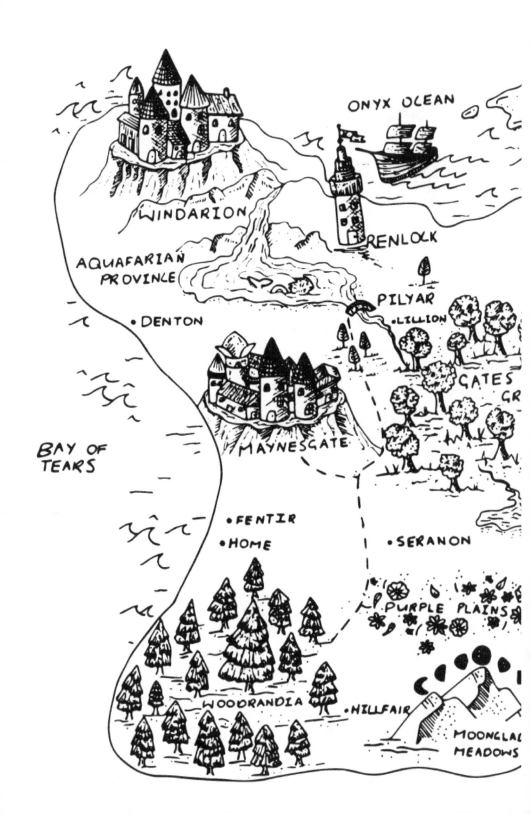

Ashalea Kindaris
Ash-ah-lee-uh Kin-dah-riss

Destiny is a cruel mistress.

1

Leaps and Bounds

ASHALEA

DEATH HAS A WAY OF SHROUDING ONE IN DARKNESS. It dampens the soul, blanketing it like a heavy fog. It lingers in the air with a heady aroma; the stench of misery and decay reminiscent of lives lost. Death came and it conquered; it burnt hope from the hearts of men and elves alike, just as it did to the Academy itself.

The building was now a shadow of its former glory—the bottom an ashen husk, its peaks a glimmer of hope in the morning sun. The battle of Renlock Academy had been waged, but the war for Everosia was far from over. More would fall to the darkness. Many, many more.

Ashalea stood upon the ramparts of the Academy. Her long silver hair framed her face like the feathers of an arrow, and her nose crinkled as she considered the events that had led her to this moment.

From the day she was born, her life had held the promise of death

and destruction. Everywhere she went, misery followed, clutching her hand with a vicelike grip. Her parents were the first to fall—her father was killed at the hands of his own son and her mother survived only long enough to give birth to Ashalea.

She had later perished from her wounds, and Ashalea's life was placed in the loving care of two adoptive parents. It was a life well lived until her sixteenth birthday when the darkness murdered them in their sleep, having returned to finish what he had started—to end the royal line of the Moonglade Elves.

For Ashalea was no ordinary elf, but an heir to the Moonglade Meadows—one of the three Elvish provinces of Everosia. Of course, she hadn't had the faintest idea about any of this at the time. All she had known three years ago was that she would avenge the death of her loved ones ... or die trying.

But it seemed life had other plans. She sighed, her heart aching in earnest. So much death. So much innocent blood spilled. And it was all because of *him*. The darkness. The elf who called himself Crinos— who called himself her brother.

Her lips thinned into a bitter smile as she considered the irony of it all. As fate would have it, Ashalea had more than vengeance on her side. Only months ago, she had discovered she was a Guardian—one of five who were assigned to protect the Guardians of the Grove— Everosia's inner sanctum and gateway to other dimensions.

Its current protectors were dying, and Ashalea and Wezlan had been tasked with finding the next in line to take their place, which had brought them Shara and Denavar—a new best friend and a new boyfriend, coincidentally. But there were still two left to find, and their quest had been waylaid at Renlock Academy, as they fought alongside elves, Onyxonites, and mages, to protect this sacred site.

They had come so close to completing a spell that would seal the

darkness to Everosia, removing the darkness's ability to conjure other portals and wreaking havoc with his otherworldly army. They had come so close to triumph.

The loss felt like a lump in her stomach. It left a bad taste that lingered in her mouth, and she knew she wasn't the only one to chew on this frustration. The fledgling Guardians and their wise leader, Wezlan, all felt the blow to their egos. It was a festering wound that increased in ferocity, weeping pain and sadness in sickening waves. Looking upon the destruction below did little to encourage Ashalea. If anything, it rekindled her desire for vengeance—for her parents, for her royal bloodline, for Shara, and now for the mages of Renlock. The list was growing longer.

She watched men and women hauling the bodies of the fallen into two piles: one for the mages and elves, another for the ensemble of creatures from another realm. The darkness had not deigned to collect his dead. He cared only for himself. As their carcasses were thrown carelessly onto a pile, she grimaced at the sickening angles of their limbs, the fangs and forked tongues jutting from their mouths, open eyes wide and unseeing.

Images of the massacred children flashed before her eyes and bile rose in her throat. The brave boy who swore to protect his flock, the doll-faced girl, so angelic and innocent, covered in a scarlet sheet. She shook her head. Lingering on the dead would help no one. She was alive, and she would use that gift for good.

Her resolve turned to anger as she clenched her fists in silence, gritting her teeth, jaw clamped shut. Power has a way of snuffing out the good in people, and whatever flicker of light left in the darkness was buried deep within. *The darkness ... My brother. My kin. The master of malevolence.*

She felt a presence approaching, and the calloused hands of a

soldier slid over her body to take her fists and gently ease them open. The faint smell of peppermint filled her nose as a stubbled beard grazed her cheek and soft lips planted a kiss along her jaw. A menthol tingle caressed her nerves and fluttered through her system.

"The dead don't wait for your forgiveness, Ashalea. It is time to return to the living."

The elf had an uncanny knack for guessing her thoughts lately. She sighed, melting into his chest and resting her back against him. She crossed her arms, intertwining her fingers with his. Denavar was the one person who had brought her relief these past two days. The one person she could let all her walls down for. The fort was otherwise impenetrable of late.

"They're dead because of us. They died in vain ... because of us."

"Nothing you could have done would have prevented this battle. The darkness was set on revenge with or without your presence here. His way of punishing Wezlan, I think."

Ashalea turned to face Denavar, peering into his icy blue eyes. The breeze stirred his brown hair, and his chiselled arms curved around her body. Even with exhaustion lining his features, he was more handsome than ever. And he was hers. A smile crept across her face and confusion distorted his features.

"Is the joke on me?"

She chuckled, shaking her head. "Despite everything that's happened, and all that is to come, you still manage to guide me out of the deepest storms. You make me want to be better, Denavar. You make me want to fight for what's good in this world, to find a home."

He stroked a hand through her hair and his eyes studied her every feature in admiration. "You are what's good in this world. You are home. You are a warrior, fierce and wild as the sea."

Ashalea wrapped her arms around him and squeezed for a long

minute. She felt the fog lifting from her heart, and the worries retracted their claws. This man wanted to make something more of this life. And she wouldn't let him down. Not today, not ever. The time for mourning was over. *The dead don't wait for your forgiveness.*

Ashalea enjoyed a few moments of comfortable silence before pulling away from his embrace. She smirked at him. "That heart of yours is turning to mush, you know. People are going to suspect you've grown soft."

He placed a hand over his heart, an expression of mock horror plastered on his face. "My reputation! My status as wooer of ladies and breaker of hearts! You're making me a new man, Ashalea."

She rolled her eyes. "I'm sure they'll just see me as your temporary squeeze. You never know, perhaps the ladies will be queuing out the door. People always want what they can't have."

He stroked his beard. "There is a certain appeal to that. Perhaps I should rethink this monogamy thing. Break the tether, so to speak."

Ashalea threw him a dangerous look.

"Yes, you're right. Being with the Queen of Moonglade Meadows is far more interesting."

She huffed and turned to walk inside, pulling on his tunic as she did. "I'm no queen yet. Come on, master of ladies, your wooing and teasing will have to wait. We've got work to do."

Ashalea marched from the ramparts into the Academy, Denavar on her heels. The corridors were empty, and the building was eerily silent. Not even ghosts walked these halls. All mages were either outside tending to the carnage, off to trade for supplies or beginning restorations on the building. Wezlan had given them a day's grace to mourn the dead, but the orders of a gruff, grumpy, and very tired man had been barked out at dawn this day.

The flames of Farah were noticeably absent from his side, and

Ashalea knew Denavar noticed too. She could see her death was a heavy cloak on his shoulders; his posture and expression sagged heavily upon seeing Wezlan, and she had found him wandering aimlessly in the library where he and Farah had spent countless hours poring over the portal puzzles of the Isle of Dread. In her mind's eye, Ashalea could still see Farah's body sprawled out on the battlefield, her face planted in the earth, her red hair fanning around her in stark vibrance compared to the muddy bed she lay upon. Ashalea glanced sideways at him now, regarding the furrowed brows and frostiness to his eyes. She gave his hand a quick squeeze before they entered the council chamber.

Wezlan and Shara were deep in conversation, heads bowed over a map of Everosia. From their tones, she gathered they'd been arguing at length. Wezlan's weathered face was etched with irritation and Shara's arms were crossed in defiance. Flynn stood to the side in silent vigil. Since his twin's revival atop the Academy, he'd been her constant shadow.

Ashalea and Denavar exchanged looks. Tensions were high, and discord was the last thing the group needed. She cleared her throat and both of her friends looked up. Wezlan resumed his full height and Shara gave a weak smile. All eyes were glued to Ashalea.

She gazed upon each of her comrades' faces and a spark of determination jolted through her body. These people were her closest friends and allies. They would die for her, and she them. They were the next Guardians of the Grove. They were Everosia's hope; the knights to shine shields of light upon the shadows of evil. One battle would not define their future. One battle would not end their quest.

"Against the tides of darkness, we fought with a ferocity and courage the mages never knew they had. We defeated his armies and defended Renlock, and though we could not bind the darkness from

opening new portals, we will rise stronger and smarter than before." Ashalea planted her palms on the table, and the fierceness in her face softened. "My friends, let us not look to blame for past events, nor strike a blow when hearts are weak. Now is the hour that friendship shines brighter than all the wrong in the world. Now we must look to the future, strengthen alliances and work together."

Wezlan's lips curved into a smile beneath his beard. "How you have grown since the time we set out. It's not easy, travelling a road never tread. Finding one's place in the world is a fickle thing, and destiny waits for no one. Now we must find the remaining Guardians and lead them to their fate or Everosia will be lost." Wezlan gestured to all in the room and pointed at the map. "Come. A new course must be chosen. We cannot linger too long ... every day the darkness recovers his strength."

They all regarded the withered scroll sprawled lazily across the table, and Shara pinned a finger on three places. "Harrietti said there was a Guardian in the Aquafarian Province, Diodon Mountains and Kingsgareth Mountains. That means we need to find an elf, a Diodonian and a dwarf to complete the circle of all races."

Ashalea shifted her feet. She still hadn't confirmed Denavar's identity as a Guardian with the others. Wezlan was too cunning not to know already, he'd hinted at that, but Shara had remained in the dark. She opened her mouth to speak but Wezlan beat her to it.

"Actually, I've been meaning to talk to you all about that. Our three is down to one." He grinned and Shara threw him a puzzled glance. "We've another Guardian up our sleeve ... and he's standing right here in this room." Wezlan threw one long, burnt orange sleeve over Denavar's back and guffawed in amusement at the elf's bewildered expression.

"You knew?"

7

"My boy, I'd be a blind fool not to have known, and I am neither of those things, thank the Gods. Do you think I haven't combed every inch of Renlock's library? The knowledge you exclaimed so fervently that you read of in ancient texts does not exist within these walls. Only a Guardian would have the Magicka needed to read the dialect back on the Isle of Dread."

Shara's mouth dropped open and she folded her arms accusingly. "Why didn't you tell us sooner?"

Denavar shrugged and raked a hand through his hair. "It was Ashalea's moment, not mine. And since we returned from the Isle of Dread, we haven't had much time to breathe, let alone discuss the formalities of Guardianship."

"You've had time to do other things in the darkest hours of night," Shara smirked, waggling her brows.

Ashalea's cheeks turned a deep scarlet and a wayward thread on her leggings suddenly caught her attention. She darted a shy look at Wezlan, who seemed to find her awkwardness incredibly amusing.

"That's no way to talk about a queen," Denavar reprimanded Shara.

"Call it the perks of being her advisor," Shara said haughtily, "and speaking of, Ashalea, I would be shirking my duty if I didn't insist you stop fooling around with unworthy grunts such as he. It's a bad look for business."

Denavar countered, "My Queen, as your most loyal confidante, I've recently come to learn that your newly-appointed advisor is, in fact, a backstabbing snake. As your grunt, I am a suitable antidote to such poison."

"Children," Wezlan interrupted with a stern look, "perhaps you can join the adults for a grown-up discussion now?"

Ashalea cringed. Of all the things to share amongst the group,

they had to discuss her love life. She planted a palm on her temple and shook her head.

Shara and Denavar elbowed her playfully and everyone resumed their gaze over the map. Their ventures would lead them east towards the Diodon Mountains and Kingsgareth Mountains, and the journey would be their longest yet.

"We will need fresh supplies for the road," Ashalea said. "I vote we pass through Shadowvale; stock up, and then head for Hallow's Pass. It will be quite a ride, but some refreshment and rest with the Onyxonites will do both us and our mounts some good."

Denavar grunted his agreement. "If we keep a steady pace, we should reach Shadowvale within the week by horse. I am hesitant to use Magicka so soon after the battle, but if you think it's necessary…"

Wezlan's weathered face creased like a crumpled page. "No Magicka. We need to restore our strength, and the last spell was taxing on all three of us. Even a wizard needs his rest, and should anything go awry, I would rather have the energy to deal with things accordingly."

Shara glanced at her twin, and unspoken words seemed to pass between her and Flynn. Her brother bowed his head slightly, his face all seriousness and sincerity. "I will journey with you to Shadowvale. It's time we had a talk with our father."

Shara pursed her lips, but the siblings said no more. Flynn opted to lean against the chamber wall, one hand perched lazily on the hilt of his sword. His movement and looks were so akin to Shara, it still shocked Ashalea. *And I thought one Shara was enough …* She returned her attention to the others.

"Then it's settled," Ashalea said. "We head to Shadowvale, then onwards to the mountains to find the Diodonian chief and the next Guardian of the Grove."

"We must be on our guard. The Diodonians do not trust other

races and are loath to be found. It will not be easy to discover their whereabouts," Wezlan said.

"Why do they distance themselves from the other races?" Shara asked.

Wezlan sighed. "Before a treaty was made between the four races of Everosia, it was every race for themselves. In the early days of our world, men and Diodonians fought with equal fervour. Humans wanted to discover the properties and effects of the Magickal abilities of these proud beasts, and under the rule of a cruel king, campaigns were forged to capture them. Experiments were conducted in the bowels of Maynesgate's prisons, the general populace none the wiser."

Shara picked at her nails. "They wanted to dissect them for the sake of Magicka? That's cruel even for Onyxonite standards."

Wezlan shook his head, sadness clouding his eyes. "Magicka cannot be examined like a healer does a wound. It is the very nature of our being. It is in the earth and air, the fabric of our world. Of course, things were quite different back then, and humans with Magickal abilities were few and far between—especially those with psychic abilities. I hate to think how many souls were lost because of these barbaric practices. Nevertheless, despite the peace in this modern age, the Diodonians keep to themselves."

Shara snorted. "Not hard to see why."

Ashalea rubbed her temples in frustration. "Ever the obstacle to overcome."

"Snails crawl in comfort, it's leaps and bounds for us," Denavar nodded.

A wide smile crept across Ashalea's face. "Okay then, let's catch the uncatchable."

Wezlan's face was grim. "Until the catchers are caught."

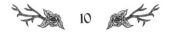

Ashalea moved with deadly precision—her steely intent as sharp as the blade within her hand. Beads of sweat formed in gentle bubbles upon her brow, a braid of silver starlight glittering down her back. She vaulted into a backwards cartwheel, swift and steady as that of an acrobat on a tightrope.

A shuriken whistled past her face, bare inches from embedding itself in the soft flesh of her neck. Her eyes widened in surprise. *Damn that girl is quick.* The assassin closed in with swift feet and extracted two blades from her sleeves in a full-frontal attack. The daggers sparkled with malice before they were jabbed and swiped in smooth motions.

Ashalea turned on her heel and climbed up the wall before arcing over Shara's head and back on her feet. She smirked at the girl as a blade swished in the air before her nose.

"My turn."

The she-elf thrusted with her rapier, blocked by Shara's falchion. A pirouette followed by a steady onslaught of vicious thrusts to Shara's abdomen. And despite the elf's speed and accuracy, Shara blocked them all, her amber eyes glinting with adrenaline. Where Shara was a gifted swordswoman—better than Ashalea—the she-elf had energy, speed, and strength on her side. Time was her ally.

She studied her enemy's feet and the repertoire of her moves. If one observed closely, there was a predictability to Shara's movements. Her stance was adaptable, but she favoured her right foot and fell back into a middle guard. If she could just—

A low kick stole Ashalea's footing and she dropped to the ground with a grunt, the air huffing from her chest. "That's cheating," she wheezed.

Shara grinned. "A shadow army does not care for your honour.

They won't fight fair. Monsters and men do not bow to the politics of the sword."

Ashalea scowled before flipping onto her feet and attacking with renewed vigour. Her rapier thrust to Shara's stomach, and the girl parried and executed a riposte. Using the movement to her advantage, she allowed the falchion to slip past her guard, catching the tip in the intricate swirls of her rapier's pommel. With a sharp twist, she forced the blade from Shara's hands and threw both swords in the air. In a flurry she had Shara's own sword held against the assassin's throat.

With a toss of her braid Ashalea smirked satisfactorily. "Yield."

Her friend chuckled before raising her hands in a gesture of defeat. "Well beat me to the brothel and back. You win this round, queenie."

Ashalea exaggerated a deep bow and found Shara's polished black boots soon replaced with scuffed brown ones. She smiled. "Are you sure you want to play this game?"

A flash of white teeth greeted her when she rose. Twinkling blue eyes, a chiselled jawline. "My love," Denavar said with silky smoothness, "I wouldn't have it any other way."

Ashalea gestured to the far wall which was lined with a small collection of weapons—blunt, barely held together, and which had seen better days in much older times. "Make your choice," she smiled sweetly.

"The sweeter the nectar, the more hidden the poison," he countered.

Denavar approached the racks of weapons, his hands brushing the various hilts and handles with tantalising slowness. His fingers finally settled on an iron mace with a rounded end—perfect for bludgeoning. He equipped his offhand with a crude buckler and strapped it to his forearm with a broad smile.

"Ready when you are, my dear."

Ashalea raised a brow at his choice of weapon before surveying the racks herself. A rusty flail with a particularly brutal looking morning star caught her eye and she grinned devilishly. She selected a round shield for her own defences and slipped the leather strapping through her left forearm.

She marched back into the arena and began circling the flail in menacing waves above her head. His eyes caught the morning star and he scoffed. "The old ball and chain, eh? Blunt enough to scratch an itch."

"And then some."

She positioned herself into an offensive stance, and, running at him with full power, she hurled the flail in a downwards slash. Denavar ducked, circling behind her back and chopping with a grunt.

Unused to the imbalance of weight, Ashalea stumbled to the ground, shifting just in time to raise her shield to the mace. It smashed upon the steel and jarred her arm painfully. Gritting her teeth, she found her feet and swung at his chest. He skilfully deflected the blow with his mace ... but Ashalea was prepared for the momentum. She allowed it to swing her around before upper cutting to his privates, Denavar managing to jump backwards in the nick of time. His eyes widened in shock as he realised, she wasn't playing.

He attacked with gusto, the knock of steel on steel a thunderclap of singing metal. Their pants alternated in short bursts, Shara cheering all the while.

"Rip him to shreds, Ashalea," the girl crowed from the side-lines.

Ashalea answered with an unintelligible grunt, her attention focused wholly on both wanting to win the fight, but also not smashing her beloved's face in. Perhaps maces and morning stars were a bad choice. Her energy was dwindling as she carried the heavy weapon. Riposte, strike, lunge ... Her weapon whistled as it circled above her head.

Their skin was drenched in sweat, Denavar faring better than she as his well-defined arms lifted the mace with ease. His form was impeccable, his footwork near perfect. She would be hard placed to best him. Also, he was so damnably distracting with that saccharine smile and baby blue eyes.

"Knock her silver ass down," Shara whooped again.

Wearily, Ashalea swivelled her gaze in the assassin's direction. "Just whose side are you on anyway?" she snapped.

The break in concentration was enough to throw her accuracy. Her body sagged as she thrust the flail towards Denavar, the morning star sighing as it limply sailed through the air past his head. Denavar swatted it to the ground like a fly, and when the momentum brought the she-elf tumbling forward, he reined her in with the chain, placing his hands firmly upon her waist.

"Do you yield?"

She offered him a tired smile. "To you? Always ... and never." She gave him a half-hearted punch before he planted a victorious kiss on her lips.

"Oh please," Shara snorted. "Just gouge my eyes out now."

Denavar glanced at her in amusement before making a show of rapid kisses upon Ashalea's sweat-riddled face.

"Delicious, I'm sure," Shara drawled.

"Well, my dear," Denavar said as he swept a stray silver lock from Ashalea's face. "You win some, you lose some. Best hedge your bets on the right side."

He grinned at her defiant green eyes as Shara flicked a couple coins his way. He slid them into his pocket and patted them with cocky reassurance.

She gaped at her lover and then her friend. "You made a bet on

who'd win this match?"

Shara shrugged. "I knew he couldn't resist trying his arm, so I made a bet with him at morning meal that I'd beat you and you'd beat him. She shook her ebony hair, the light bouncing softly off her glossy waves. "I lost on both accounts." She frowned. "I don't like losing."

"But there is one who has not yet been tested." A voice boomed from across the wooden floors, and a flash of rusty orange blurred as Wezlan crossed the room in flowing robes. He stood before the trio and smiled expectantly at Ashalea.

"Oh, you can't be serious," Ashalea groaned. She looked back and forth between her comrades. "This is a conspiracy. You're all teaming up against me." She sniffed. "It's all very un-Guardian-like you know."

"Come on, Ashalea, be a good sport." Shara elbowed her in the ribs.

"Just a bit of fun." Denavar mimicked the movement.

They both had her boxed in, teasing relentlessly until she shrugged them off with a huff. Ashalea looked pleadingly at Wezlan, but her old friend was trying hard to hide his amusement.

"All right," she barked, glaring at Shara and Denavar. "You two are trouble. You're as good for me as a dwarf in a gambling den."

"Better, even," Denavar said. "Debtless and unwilling to break legs for money."

Shara's mouth curled up. "Says you. I'll break all your bones if it means reaping the rewards."

Wezlan appraised them both with raised brows. They both snickered before falling silent.

Denavar lowered his head in mock guilt. "Sorry, Wez."

"Don't call me that."

"Wez the Wiz?"

Steely eyes silenced the howls of laughter that followed, and

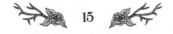

Ashalea looked at Denavar and Shara smugly before turning towards the weapons racks.

"Hold," Wezlan called softly. "It's Magicka for me tonight."

A spark of anticipation fuelled her belly and turning slowly on the spot, she grinned. Snapping her fingers, a ball of flames appeared in a globe above her fist, lapping greedily at the oxygen in the atmosphere. The flames danced a jig in the reflection of her eyes.

"I thought you'd never ask."

Missing Magicka

ASHALEA

SHE WAS GROWING STRONGER EVERY DAY. Her Magicka swelled like overripe berries, circling through her veins, threatening to burst if she let her power lie dormant for too long. Her body felt gloriously charged after training with her team. There was always a lingering adrenaline that overpowered the tiredness of her muscles for a time, but after using Magicka in such an electrified match against Wezlan, her body sang with delightful power.

The wily wizard won, of course. Even with her Magicka in overdrive the man seemed unbeatable at the game. Ashalea nestled into the cot within her chambers, pillows cocooning her as she gazed out the window, arms crossed behind her head.

And why shouldn't he be? He is the world's most powerful wizard after all. The only wizard ... Or is he?

It wasn't a comforting notion, but the darkness's power was unparalleled. He had never passed the test that would declare him a master of wizardry—a councillor worthy of sitting amongst the elite. Wezlan and the other wizards had made sure of that. Yet scorn had bred a more formidable beast. One that could never have been predicted, or even prevented, it seemed.

She wondered what power one would need to master the darkness; to mould it with careful fingers and accurate eyes like that of clay before it takes shape. And if Crinos was the dark ... Ashalea was the light.

She bolted upright. They were the opposite sides of a coin, their goals the currency that divided their causes. Where he bartered in death, destruction and dominion over all living things, Ashalea would see continued peace among the races, the safety of Everosia, and a chance to rebuild her city.

She blanched at that.

My city.

By blood she was Queen of the Moonglade Meadows—a land she had never seen, a people she had never met. They didn't even know she was alive, and from what Wezlan had said, the city had been left to fall into ruination since the devastation Crinos had caused. The day he took her parents.

Her fingers coiled into fists and she rose from the bed, padding over to the window. She leaned a palm against the glass, cool and calming to her heated skin. Looking up, she gazed at the moon. Big and bright, it cast pale white light upon its denizens, aloof to the struggles of mankind, pure and divine in its bed amongst the stars.

Ashalea looked at her reflection in the glass. She appeared almost ethereal. The white gloom crowned her silver hair, casting her skin in a pale glow. Whilst still undeniably youthful, still utterly elvish to the

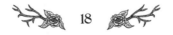

last, she couldn't tell whether the cracks and blueish circles under her eyes was imagined, or whether they were now a permanent feature on her face. She looked ... Weary. Washed out.

Had bringing Shara back to life taken some of her life force gifted by the Goddess Enalia? She sighed. It mattered not. She would do it again and again no matter the price. If she had the ability to heal others, then she would not waste such a precious gift.

But even so, since that night atop Renlock tower her body felt different, alien almost, and utterly frustrating. Reproducing that golden light—that starburst of energy she'd used on the darkness—had been impossible. Try as she might, Ashalea could not summon the force that had erupted from her and triumphed over the shadows.

Her nose scrunched in annoyance as she considered it. Such power ... and yet where had it come from? Had such Magicka always been dormant inside her? She raised her palms upward and studied the fine lines etched into her skin before glancing at the moon again.

Perhaps ...

No. She'd never heard of that being a possibility. A hiss of annoyance escaped her lips. She inspected her reflection again, peering once more at the puffy eyes and bruised flesh. Irritated by this unwelcome addition to her face, she speculated healing herself to make them go away, and guiltily she raised her hands to her cheeks.

Beckoning the Magicka to her fingertips, she withdrew into her mind to connect the nerve responses to the correct spell. She braced for the charge of electricity, feeling the Magicka bounce excitedly under her skin. It raced eagerly to the surface, ready to break free, and then ... nothing.

Frowning, she shook her head, attempting to clear her mind of distracting thoughts. Closing her eyes, she willed the power to come forth, waiting for the soft golden glow to erupt from her palms and

fly free from her—

Bump. She blinked her emerald eyes.

Bump.

It was like the Magicka was hitting an invisible wall within her mind. Try as she might, she could not force it to break free. Seething in aggravation she tried once more, to no avail.

Panicking, she called upon the healing power again and again. No golden light. No release of energy. Had she expended too much in training today? Was this her body's way of telling her *enough*? Uneasiness raked through her, and, with desperation, she called on a fireball. It sparked to life eagerly in her hand, the flames playfully teasing each other.

"Thindarōs," she whispered, and, snapping her fingers, a blue spark sizzled in the air.

She sighed in relief, sagging against the wall. So, her Magicka hadn't eluded her after all. But that meant ...

Ashalea peered at her hands again, sudden horror surging to the surface. A sick realisation jolted in her stomach as if reeling from a hard blow.

Her healing Magicka was completely, utterly, gone.

***

The group reclined in their nightgowns in Renlock's council chamber with sleep crusted eyes, their hair tousled and unkempt from being roused in the middle of the night. Fretful and unable to sleep, Ashalea had snuck down the hall to Denavar's chamber, swinging the door open with a crash and babbling her newfound woes into his ear.

It had taken much prodding and pillows to the head to rouse the sleepy elf, but upon hearing her straight, he had suggested calling a

meeting. "Wezlan will know what to do," he had wisely said.

It turned out Wezlan had no idea what to do.

And though she was aching for a solution to the riddle, she started with the lesser of her problems: the white light used upon the darkness, also inconveniently unresponsive to come forth despite her efforts.

They were now sitting in the wee hours of the morning, tossing ideas around as the group reclined with hot tea in hand. The council chamber had been one of the few places Ashalea could sit in without being bombarded with recurring flashes of death and destruction ... of small bodies and doll faces ...

Ashalea and Shara had made it their mission to make the room a little cosier. Gone were the stiff, steel chairs that surrounded the council room table. An unfortunate victim of the fires, so they'd said, though of course, everyone knew that wasn't true.

Instead they'd dragged in the wing-backed chairs of gold and green velvet from the library, throw rugs in blacks and silvers and purples, and had managed a sneaky trip to the kitchens from which they'd pillaged various tea cakes and pastries. The cook had screeched about a thief earlier that morning, and Ashalea had felt bad for her given the circumstances but ... cakes. They trumped all.

No one had bothered to mention the effort taken to drag excessive furniture up here because no one wanted to be bombarded with questions from the mages, with the stares and whispers, with the sadness that lined their features. Even Wezlan had taken to hiding in this room. Ashalea didn't blame him.

"Perhaps a power relative to your bloodline?" Denavar cut into her thoughts, startling her back to reality.

She sighed, chewing her lip. "Is that even possible? I haven't heard of Magickal properties or abilities being restricted to specific families before, even royal ones."

Wezlan stroked his beard. "It's not a proven theory, but it's not impossible. Elemental Magicka is derived from matter around us. The moisture in the air, the currents in the winds, the soil beneath our feet ... but not all Magicka is developed from natural resources. For example, fire is conducted from gaseous materials within our environment, but it is manmade, too."

He paused to take a sip of his tea, smacking his lips in appreciation. "We draw on what we know and our nerves—our very core—pull on the Magicka within us to create what we produce in our mind's eye."

Shara sighed loudly and all eyes pointed to her. "Look, no offense guys, but was this discussion really necessary at this hour of the morning? If you're going to talk Magicka balls and bright lights, I'm really not your girl."

"Someone's a bit cranky this morning," Denavar said softly.

"I was having a good dream," Shara snapped. Her eyes drifted and a small smile crept along her lips. "A very good dream."

Wezlan cleared his throat and glared at her disapprovingly. "We are a team, and as such, all members must work as a unit. If someone has something important to discuss, I think it prudent we convene. Whatever dreams your filthy mind is concocting can wait."

Ashalea hadn't even heard Shara's outburst, her nose crinkled in thought, the freckles on her bridge bunching together. "When you first rescued me from the darkness, I remember seeing a bright white light before I passed out. Was that the same as what I produced?"

Wezlan put his tea down and steepled his fingers. "What you saw that day was a mild display compared to the power you produced. Light and dark, being the hardest elements to manipulate, require higher energy than that of other elements. To mirror, or to bend light and dark, is extremely taxing on the body. I had barely enough

22

strength to heal you afterwards."

"Okay, let me get this straight," Shara interrupted. "Miss Silver over here managed to fend off the darkness with an explosion of Magickal light unknown to man, then manages to bring my dead arse back to life?"

Ashalea scowled at Shara and the assassin raised her hands with incredulity splattered on her face. "What? I mean … you know I love you but that's just unfair. By all rights you should be—"

"Dead. After using that much Magicka I should be dead," Ashalea said softly.

The room fell silent as her words sank in, dropping like stones to the bottom of a well.

"Now I just feel guilty," Shara mumbled, glancing at the she-elf with an expression that was almost apologetic. Almost.

Ashalea sipped her tea with one hand while Denavar reached out and took the other, his skin warm and smooth like the liquid travelling down her throat. He squeezed it fiercely, so much that it hurt. Her eyes swivelled accusingly to his, but his gaze was nothing but sincere.

The piercing blue eyes said everything spoken words did not: *You're alive, you're here, and I'll never let that happen.*

They held that connection for what felt like a fleeting moment yet forever all at once. One finger grazed her knuckles, tracing small circles. It relaxed her, reminding Ashalea she was not alone. That the Guardians had her back. That Denavar did. She smiled softly, and he winked in return.

A loud huff snapped them from their reverie and Ashalea's eyes flitted to Shara, one immaculate brow raised in amusement. The she-elf gifted her a smirk before re-addressing the group.

"All I know is that I've not been able to replicate that power again.

I feel strong, my mind is wired, and my Magicka ... it's like someone has turned the heat up. But I can't, for the life of me, produce anything close to a ray of sunshine, the light of a star, moonlight, nothing. And now something else has happened. The reason I called this meeting, actually. My healing powers ... they're just—" She trailed off and bit her lip.

Wezlan narrowed his eyes. "They're what?"

Ashalea shifted in her seat, avoiding his stare.

She hadn't wanted to voice it again. Hadn't really wanted to admit not only to herself but to the others that her healing power had packed its bags and just ... left. She'd tried healing Denavar's minor hurts just prior to this meeting to prove her point, but not even the tiniest scratch had endeavoured to close over. Any wound she tried to mend had refused to cooperate. Her curative Magicka was gone.

"Ashalea," Wezlan growled, his gruff tone a warning. "Out with it."

A sigh. "My healing Magicka is gone."

His eyes narrowed and Shara straightened in her chair.

"What do you mean ... gone?" He asked slowly.

"Vanished, disappeared, unwilling to surface. Poof." Ashalea raised her hands with just as much confusion.

Disbelief clouded Wezlan's features. "Poof?"

Recovery

THE DARKNESS

A HOWLING WIND TORE at the wispy tendrils of shadow that enveloped the darkness. Kiletch truly was a miserable place. Its barren grounds stretched aimlessly into the distance, the desert wasteland dry as brittle bone and cold as a lake still thawing from a freeze. The sandy stretch was white as snow; a stark contrast to the sky above it.

The darkness floated on his black cloud, invisible against the dreary void of night sky. It was always dark here. If there was a sun, it had given up its duty long ago, shedding its overwhelming burden of lighting up the dark. Hence, next to nothing grew. Life here was a bleak affair, and with plant matter few and far between, the inhabitants had grown accustomed to one source of food: each other. The desert bore nothing but the bones of its forsaken; picked clean and polished ivory.

Below him, his crooked creatures slithered, crawled, and limped in scores of uneven lines. His red eyes regarded his flock with a greedy hunger, and his tongue pressed against his teeth in frustration. He had offered his sister the chance to prove herself. To join his army and become the bearer of unquenchable power. What a waste. He'd thought she could be swayed, but the stupid girl clung to idiotic ideals of heroism, duty and vengeance.

The last he understood. He'd yearned for that too, once. A long time ago when family and friends seemed like something he should care about. Maybe he did for a time. But the darkness viewed the world from a different point a view. There was no colour. Just black and white and all the delicious shades of grey. He had never been like the other elves. He was not in tune with nature. He was not content to devote his life to the land. He didn't believe the Gods or Goddesses played a part in his life. No, he envied them. He would forge his own path and crush all in his way, proving to all those that had scorned him that he was free from rules and regulations. That he himself could be equal to a God.

Ashalea and her companions had proved tougher than he'd anticipated. They had come so close to blocking his access to this world—removing his portal powers—and he would not make that mistake again. The darkness cursed himself for his carelessness. He'd allowed himself to feel ... To let vengeance and expectations get the better of him. He had hoped ... And hope is a dangerous notion.

The only joy he'd reaped from Renlock was the moment he'd snapped the neck of dear, sweet Shara. The moment her body hit the unforgiving stone of that tower. The moment his sister's eyes lost the defiant fire that had challenged him the day he'd first attempted to blot out her existence in Everosia.

His body reverberated with tingling anticipation at the thought of their next encounter. Ashalea would pay in blood for her insolence. He'd make sure of that.

The darkness descended on his cloud of shadows, approaching his commander for a report. He phased into his elven form and appraised the grunt with silver eyes, the crescent moon scar shimmering, even in the ethereal gloom. The Uulakh was perched on a rock overlooking the vast stretch of bone-white sand now drenched in a wave of black—busy hissing orders at its underlings; yellow slit eyes roving over the horde, forked tongue lashing out with displeasure.

"Massssterrr." It bowed in reverence before cocking an eye at the darkness. A long, ugly red gash ran the length of its scaled face, sealing shut the space where his other orb once sat. A prize won by Shara Silvaren in the battle of Renlock.

"Verosh. Status report," Crinos said lazily.

The Uulakh bobbed its head; the yellow stripe that ran the length of its body snaking down its back. The cretins wore no armour in Kiletch—any being worth its weight in savagery and tenacity to stay alive in this hole was already in the darkness's army. All but one ... and the darkness had plans to change that.

"We lost thousandsss during the mage war, my lord. It's naught but a small dent in your army. The magesss suffered a higher toll."

The darkness nodded. "And the girl?"

"Our spiesss have nothing to report. She has not been sssighted."

Crinos shifted his gaze to the rows of creatures marching before him, his silver eyes narrowed in thought. "What of the Diodonians?"

"They remain elusive. They mount raids on our encampment and pick off our scouts, but we are no closer to finding their base."

"They leave no tracks?"

The Uulakh shifted its clawed feet. "All who follow do not return.

Alive at leassst. Bodies of the fallen have been returned to camp, missing innards, limbs or heads. A warning I think ..."

Crinos offered Verosh a hard glare. "Undoubtedly."

The lizard hissed uncertainly, and the darkness had to restrain himself from removing the forked tongue flickering incessantly from his commander's mouth. Despite his creatures' obedience and lust for blood, there was something to be said for humans. Intelligence was somewhat lacking in his army, and it frustrated him to no end. If only Vera were still alive ...

Her death was considerably inconvenient. Poor, pathetic Vera. His prized pony—plucked from a pleasure house and broken in with the promise of a better life. He snorted. How easy it is to bend something to your will with words dripped in gold and iced with the pretence of love. How easy it is to create a weapon when the subject has such a pliable heart.

The darkness sighed. Not that it mattered anymore. His spy, his plaything, his informant, lay rotting underground ... what was left of her anyway. The wolves and rodents of Everosia would have feasted on her flesh by now. Pity ... Her body was one of the things he enjoyed most.

He turned his attention back to the matter at hand. Verosh hovered at attention, one eye cast downward, his tail flicking through the sand, snaking patterns into fine, white grains.

Madoc Ruins, located in the far-east of the Diodonian mountain range, was housed by a desert, much like Kiletch. Its lands were void of life, bar a few cacti and palm trees. Without a water hole, the only hope of surviving in such a place was by sourcing water from the broad leaves of these trees or digging for nourishment amongst the roots. Rainfall was rare, so the canyons were no such help in storing pockets of water either. Still, the desert was host to a Diodonian tribe, which meant it must be accessible somewhere. If only his beasts could find it.

"Has there been any progress in finding a water supply?"

Commander Verosh shook his head. "The land is much like this one. Barren ... lifeless. What little moisture it receives from the rare rainfall is soaked up almost immediately by the scorching heat. We've charted our investigations but we're yet to find anything."

The darkness rumbled a guttural growl, causing the giant lizard to shrink in fear. "Find the tribe and a water source, or I'll be forced to appoint someone *who can*."

The threat was not lost on Verosh. The Uulakh performed a pathetic bow before darting between the marching creatures. The darkness scowled. *Nothing like fear to get results.* And Verosh certainly had reason to be wary. Crinos had little patience, and it wouldn't be the first time a commander's reign was cut short.

Patience was a virtue Crinos could ill afford. Since his base at the foothills of Hallow's Pass was breached, his preparations for the coming days had been nothing short of challenging. His *sister* had weakened him when last they met. His victory had been an assured thing when out of nowhere she blasted him off the face of Everosia with a ball of light magic as bright as all the stars in the sky combined.

"An interesting turn of events," Crinos mumbled under his breath.

He didn't like surprises. Especially when they burned his darkness to cinders and shrivelled his shadows to nothing. And he wondered where this Magicka had come from. Could it be Wezlan had taught her to master the art of light and darkness? Or was it a birth right from their parents? One that had inexplicably, conveniently, skipped him and been gifted to Ashalea.

He hissed in annoyance. Whatever it was, it stood in the way of his plans. And that just wouldn't do. Until he was strong enough to return to Everosia, his grunts would have to do the legwork, and a base within that land was essential to continue operations. To ready his army for war.

No one would think to search Madoc Ruins as it was desolate and empty of life. The citizens of that city had long since turned to dust. There was no reason for the public to travel to the desert these days, and whilst that provided the perfect place to hide in plain sight, his efforts of establishing a sustainable camp had been marred by raids from the Diodonians, and a constant need to transport foodstuffs and water through portals. An effort that was more frustrating than taxing, but ultimately insufficient, nevertheless.

He needed to find the tribe and convince the chieftain to reconsider their alliances if his mission were to succeed ... The Diodonians had once served darker purposes after all. Long ago when a great battle for Everosia was waged amongst the races. When monsters still roamed the lands and beasts were mightier than men.

It could be that way again. It *would* be that way again. And if the Diodonians rejected his proposal, they would breathe their last breaths.

Ebb and Flow

ASHALEA

ASHALEA FLOATED IN SILENCE in the fifth-floor bathing chamber; the aches of last week ebbing away, forced to sink underwater like a stone thrown in a pond. The steam nibbled at her pores, gently sweating out fatigue, stress, and the symptoms of a girl who'd played at hero ... and lost.

She scratched a nail against the mosaic tiles of the bath. A montage of blue and green that depicted life amongst the corals of the sea, fish of all shapes and colours swimming lazily, trapped forever in the bath. Just as trapped as she felt. Just as lost.

She inhaled the bath oils—vetiver, sage, cedarwood—all scents that reminded her of home. She missed the thick undergrowth of Woodrandia. The way the sunlight caught the canopies, the animals in their burrows and nests, the smell of vegetable soup curling up the spire in her home. In her tree. That magnificent white oak that housed a messy, devious old wizard and his protégé in the making.

A smile curled at her lips. Her life was scarred with death and destruction, but some things—some people—were worth fighting for. And she would not give up.

Her mind drifted to a day spent huddled in Wezlan's study. He'd been lecturing her on the importance of intention and phonetics of ancient dialects for Magicka use. She'd groaned in protest, slumping into her chair with as much defiance as she could muster. Physical training was much more her speed, and lessons of that magnitude were always a bore.

"Was there ever a journey worth taking if the road was straight and narrow?" Wezlan had asked, buried behind towers of books, his nose deep in ancient scrolls.

She'd rolled her eyes and tugged at wayward strands of silver hair. "If the road led to your dreams and desires, then yes?"

The old wizard had chuckled. "Would the reward be so enticing if you didn't work to win it?"

"I suppose all things seem grander if they're not easy to attain. Or if you work hard in the hope of success."

He'd nodded sagely. "Just because something isn't easy, doesn't mean it isn't worthy of your effort. Some plants will grow through all the seasons. They sprout in uncertainty, seeking knowledge and understanding from the earth. As the plants age, they flourish, tested at times by the strength of the sun and the world around it. During winter they battle with forces unforeseen, but in the end, the plants triumph, flourishing anew."

"And what kind of plant am I?" Ashalea had smirked.

Wezlan had furrowed his brows. "You, my dear, are a most rare and exotic flower. Too stubborn to give up, an attitude in need of

 32

a good pruning here and there, but ultimately, one that cannot be denied blooming."

Ashalea had grinned devilishly. "A rose with an old wizard as the thorn in my side."

Wezlan had raised his busy eyebrows in mock horror and the pair of them had laughed, all life lessons temporarily forgotten, and the importance of intention and phonetics abandoned.

It was a simple memory, but one of the best. Just a day in the life of a man and a woman doing boring, mundane things, no cares in the world. But those days were long gone. As she sank beneath the surface, holding her breath in anticipation, Ashalea imagined herself as the flower overcoming life's hurdles. The darkness was her winter, but spring was just around the corner. She needed only to fight for it.

She burst from the water, sucking in the steamy air. Blinking her emerald eyes rapidly, she identified a figure standing in front of her. When her vision came into focus, she was looking right at the manhood of one dastardly elf.

"Denavar!" She laughed, splashing his body in protest, her cheeks somehow heating further.

He stood with hands on hips, a smirk plastered on his face. "I'm not sure if my pride should be wounded or impressed by your reaction."

"Your pride should take a hike or be doused by cold water. We're in a public place you know."

He glanced around the empty chamber and lifted a brow.

Ashalea laughed. "Well you never know who could come in, except, oh, I don't know, any of the female mages?"

Denavar waded into the bath and winced. "You weren't wrong about the water. By all rights you should resemble a prune right now." He settled against the tiling and flicked a lazy fireball into the bath, keeping the flames alive until the water was sufficiently heated.

She swished her hair nonchalantly. "Show off."

He sidled next to her and settled an arm over her shoulder. "So, the adventure continues tomorrow, huh?"

Ashalea pursed her lips. "So it would seem. Three Guardians down, two to go. What do you think they'll be like?"

"Well ... We have a Diodonian and a dwarf. I imagine it'll be like talking to a dog and a very angry short man with a big ego complex."

The she-elf snorted. "How very perceptive of you. Wezlan told me the Diodonians are extremely intelligent beings. They are telepathic in case you weren't aware," she said with a tap to her temple.

"So more like an annoying gnat buzzing in one's brain then?"

She shook her head. Humour was Denavar's armour, and it masked his insecurities and worries better than chainmail and a steel helmet ever could. But it also shielded something deeper. Denavar was a champion of the people, but his behaviour could also be seen as aloof, unreliable, even careless. Ashalea knew better. Beneath his charm and wit was a calculating intelligence and born ability to lead. Denavar was cunning, and he preferred to pretend otherwise. To be underestimated is a dangerous thing.

She sighed. "I know you deal with logic and reason differently, Denavar, but this is important. Without the next Guardians, we have no hope of defeating the darkness. He's too strong. I need to know we can trust these new members ... I need to know they'll be up for the task."

Denavar regarded her with those piercing blue eyes. "Have faith, Ashalea. Remember what Harrietti told us? These people ... or being in the case of our telepathic hound"—Ashalea threw him a glare and he hurried on—"they encourage greatness. They are powerful people, or flock to those in power. This is their destiny, whether they're ready to accept it or not. And given events of late, I should say they'll rush to the job with welcome arms ... or paws."

Ashalea punched him in the arm with a laugh, but her expression quickly sobered. Harrietti Hardov—now there was a woman she'd never forget. The seer who had gifted them her wisdom regarding the next Guardians of the Grove. The rest of her knowledge had died with her not so long ago, and despite knowing Harrietti for but a moment in time, Ashalea had understood her better than most. Fear, pain, misery. Fear of the unknown and the uncontrollable had plagued that woman her whole life. Ashalea knew the feeling well.

"It's not just what lies ahead that worries me. I'm concerned about Shara."

Denavar twirled a finger in the water, creating a mini whirlpool with his Magicka. "Shara has been through the motions, no doubt, but our wily assassin will pull through. She's too stubborn to be bested by a little torture ..." His face twisted, and the last few words came out as a whisper. "Dying and then being revived ..."

A bizarre expression crossed his face, as if recounting the events out loud made it seem more real. A silence hung over them like gathering clouds before a storm.

"All we can do is be there for her," he said at last. "Watch over her carefully and lend our support."

Ashalea snorted. "She's an Onyxonite. They don't play well at hide and seek. Not when they don't want to be found. Not when they'd rather keep their secrets and battle it out alone."

"She's not likely to abandon ship, Ashalea. We've done that once before and it's not an event I care to relive. Besides, you and Shara have grown close. She respects you, admires you. You might well be her first real friend she can rely upon to not slit her throat when the mood suits them."

"Perhaps you're right. I just can't shake the feeling that the darkness has changed her." Ashalea sighed. "I'm not sure she'll ever be the same. And I don't know how I'd be able to live with that."

"You know it's not your fault, right? What happened to Shara could not have been stopped. And if it wasn't her the darkness had taken, it would have been someone else that you love."

A frown crinkled her nose, freckles puckering in indignation. "You're not helping."

She distinctly remembered the moment the darkness had taken her best friend. They had just stepped through a portal from the Isle of Dread into Windarion—one of the three Elvish cities—feeling triumphant after having recovered the tome that was to reveal the spell to bind the darkness from portal travel. *What good that did.* Shara had been the last to step through when the darkness snatched her from Ashalea's reach; hers and Shara's fingers just inches apart. Then the portal had closed, and her friend had disappeared.

It wasn't the only time she'd been inches away from rescuing her friend. The last had been just moments before Shara fell lifeless atop the tower of Renlock. She remembered the bloodshot eyes, the defeated hunch, the apologetic tilt to her lips. And then ... And then a sickening snap ... Her muscles tightened and her eyes found a far-off place as she recalled the memory.

"Hey," Denavar said, concern flashing over his face. "You're shivering. You've got goose bumps." He frowned and repeated his fireball trick until the water was steaming again.

The heat eased the tension in her bones, but her heart still ached at the thought. Ashalea gazed at Denavar. A much more comforting sight than the images bouncing in her head. She studied the planes of his face; the high cheekbones that could cut glass, the slope of his nose, the chiselled jaw and above it the full lips ...

"I only meant to say that it was beyond our control," he said softly, oblivious to her fascination. "But it will be okay, Ashalea, we've got each other. I consider it my personal duty to make sure you are cared for and attended to … in all ways."

He looked her up and down in a very suggestive manner and Ashalea couldn't help but laugh.

She settled back into the crook of his arm with a small smile. "You are going to be the death of me, you know that?"

"Don't say that." His words were so low, so furious, it was almost a snarl. He bolted upright, forcing her to jolt forward. He turned to face her; concern etched on his face … and anger. "Don't ever say that."

"Denavar, I was only—"

"No, Ashalea. All jokes aside, I will always be there for you, as your soldier, your lover, your friend. I would give everything for you, even my life if it comes to it. And I will never let that monster hurt you."

Before she could utter a word, he leaned in and kissed her fiercely, his lips hungry, his need passionate and more electrified than any Magicka either of them could conjure. She welcomed him with equal fervour, her body responding with a delectable shiver.

She could feel the need in the press of Denavar's lips. His need to protect her, to worship her, to feel her.

Heat swelled in Ashalea's core, and as he gently tugged the top of her lip, he proceeded to trail soft kisses down her neck. The near painful nip of his teeth sent a jolt through her with each delicious bite. A soft moan escaped her lips. This was all she needed right now. Everything else was just noise. She gave herself wholly to him, and they sank beneath the depths of bliss, spiralling into their own oblivion.

Uninvited Guests

SHARA

She could see the way people looked at her. Like a wounded dog, left to lick its wounds in solitude. The whispers were worse. They circulated the building in a smog that seemed to stagnate and fester, making it impossible to ignore.

Who did these mages think they were, anyway? Without the Guardians—without the Onyxonites—their precious Renlock Academy would have been razed to the ground, peppered with essence of darkness. How dare they presume to guess at the torture she'd been through? How dare they pity her? She snorted. Gifted or not, these people had a lot to learn. Gratitude ought to be at the top of their list.

Shara gazed at her naked reflection in the mirror. She hated the way she looked now. Not because of what the darkness had done to her physically, but because of how it reflected her misery inside. It

made her feel vulnerable. Weak.

She peered at the hollowed eyes, sallow skin and cracked smile. Her figure was still pleasing enough to look at, sure, but she felt half the woman she was not so long ago. A different shade of sorrow. The darkness had broken her, inside and out.

Turning her body, she eyed off the ugly scars that lined her back with distaste. They lingered in long scratches and short incisions, bright red, as if to mock her still. They would fade in time, but the memory wouldn't. She would always feel the agony that her brother, Flynn, had inflicted. She would always remember the blank look of his eyes, the methodical stroke of every blade ... the pain.

Oh, the pain. Had she not been trained to endure torture and starvation as a young girl, she would be dead by now. Or worse, a creature, witless and crazed, turned insane by the daily rituals the darkness and his minions had inflicted. She laughed bitterly.

There was a locked box she didn't care to open. She had survived through sheer will and the fact her father was a pathetic parent, and instead of showering her with kind words and comforting hugs when she was a child, it had been a game of 'when's the next meal' or 'how much will it hurt'.

Shara shook her head. Better to throw away that key. Better to keep those feelings buried. She thought of the darkness's little pet, Vera, and a small sliver of satisfaction fired in her belly. She was dead at least. That vile woman who had spied for the darkness and taken pleasure in Shara's torture, was dead.

Yes. The woman got what she deserved in the end. Shara never usually took pleasure in her kills—it was just a job—as normal for an Onyxonite assassin as it was for bakers to make bread or farmers to sow seeds in the fields of Everosia. But this woman was a worm. It was only fitting she should rot beneath the dirt, sprawled in the darkness's old base of operations, left to be picked apart by wolves and wild beasts.

With a smirk, Shara shimmied into black leather breaches and boots and a black skin-tight top, cinching her waist with a belt equipped with shurikens, along with some other hidden compartments for weaponry and traps. Standard Onyxonite attire. She flicked her ebony shoulder-length hair and smiled. One could be in the business of killing and still look fabulous.

The finishing touches were two scimitars which she hooked to her belt. Finally, she regarded herself once more in the mirror. Her amber eyes glowed with less ferocity than usual and her clothes clung less tightly since she'd lost weight, but she pulled up all right.

She glared at her mirror image. More than all right. She was Shara Silvaren, the next Guardian of the Grove, Onyxonite, daughter of Lord Harvar Silvaren, Chief of the Shadowvale clan. She was the resurrected.

She puckered her lips and fluffed her hair. "And to hell with anyone who has a problem with that."

Picking up her rucksack of meagre belongings, she shouldered it with a defiant tug and burst from her chambers, earning startled glances from various mages as they walked past. One fierce glare from Shara and they were scrambling on their way, all bowed heads and shifted eyes.

She sucked in a breath of air and nodded her head resolutely, glancing down the hallway. Glad to be rid of this place, she eyed off the various tapestries and paintings that garnished the walls, tipping her head in mock respect for the mages that frowned, smiled or stared broodingly from their gilded cages.

Putting one foot firmly in front of the other, Shara strolled down the polished floors with her usual confident swagger, descending the

flight of stairs from one level to the next with queenly grace. But when she approached the ground floor, her boots failed to find purchase.

This room had the effect of stealing the air from her lungs and causing her heart to thump loudly beneath her ribs. A nervous sweat broke out on her forehead and panic rose in her chest. The foyer was buzzing with activity, but when overlooking it, all she could see was the massacre from the night of the battle. *Flash.* Healers' bodies ripped and defiled. *Flash.* Walls painted red. *Flash.* Children's corpses crumpled together in heaps. *Flash.* Running up the stairs to make the murderers pay. And then ... nothingness.

Her body shook with fear, her palms slick with sweat, one hand sliding along the balustrade as she took another step. Stars threatened to overwhelm her vision and her knees buckled. Her breath hitched in her lungs when a voice said her name.

"Shara?" Wezlan was calling to her from across the room, his brows knitted together, grey eyes piercing her soul as if he knew her secrets. Like studying a specimen under a microscope.

She shook her head, and just like that the moment passed and she was back in the present, the foyer of Renlock Academy having returned to its bustling self. No blood, no bodies, no pain. The room was back to normal. Old wooden floorboards scuffed from time and travel, a sweeping bannister that joined a set of red carpeted stairs— one for each side of the room. Corridors branched off in different directions, and above the foyer was a chandelier of glittering glass droplets.

She breathed deeply. Nothing strange. Perfectly ordinary. Shara straightened, wiped her clammy hands on her breaches and planted a smile on her face, forcing her feet to descend the final step and cross the floor of the foyer.

"I called your name several times." He peered at her; lips pursed

41

beneath his bushy white beard. "Ready to go?"

Shara knew he didn't want to pry, and he was trying his best to keep his concern hidden, but she didn't need a sixth sense to know what he was thinking. What they were all thinking: Ashalea, Denavar, and Flynn as well. Recent events made her a liability, and that meant she would be treated with care and caution. It meant she'd have to face further scrutiny and sympathy. The last thing she wanted—especially from her friends.

Though feeling deflated inside, she offered him her best smile. "Ready as I'll ever be."

He held out an arm with a cheery wink and she couldn't help but melt a little. "Well then," he said, relinquishing a sigh and fondly surveying his beloved Renlock for possibly the last time in a long time, "on our next journey we go."

Shara patted his arm. "Let's make it a good one."

They marched through the doors and into the sunshine. The weather had put on a show today; blue skies greeted them, along with two broad grins from Ashalea and Denavar. They were awfully glowed up. She didn't need to guess much as to why. For once the mages had other gossip to cluck over today. Something about two elves in the top floor bathing chamber. She sniggered. They had been near inseparable the last week, and as much as Shara wanted to be jealous, she just couldn't. How could she?

They were a good match—the two elves brought out the best in each other. Denavar, with his witty charm and humorous nature, seemed to further ignite the passion and drive in Ashalea. He did wonders for her confidence and perhaps would even temper her fire when the flames grew too wild.

Ashalea brought a realness to Denavar. She was the only one who could lower his gates and penetrate his defences, allowing those close to him a glimpse at the real softie behind that muscled exterior. Ashalea could keep all that for herself—Shara enjoyed the banter Denavar provided and, if she were honest, she had come to see him as a good friend in a short time. Quite unusual given how much she'd kept to herself before becoming a Guardian.

But despite all that, a soft pang fired in her heart. Would anyone look at her the way those two ogled each other with lovestruck eyes? Could she ever settle down and leave the problems of the world to someone else? She snorted softly. An investigation for another time, perhaps.

Shara's eyes drifted to Flynn. Her twin—usually a man everyone flocked to because of his easy nature, strength, and reliability—sat quietly upon his horse, a brooding stare clouding his features. His posture was stiff, and he gazed into the distance, an unreadable expression on his face. Once she would have known what he was thinking in a heartbeat, but these days he was a ghost of his former self. And as much as that pained her heart, it hurt to look at him even more. The memories of his puppetry by the darkness were too strong. She could shove them aside when in battle—with a sword in her hand and an enemy to kill—when they moved as one in a dance of death. But to be friendly again? To share a laugh or a smile? Unfathomable. For now, at least.

Shara looked at Ashalea fondly instead. Such a beautiful, gentle creature, despite all the talk of vengeance and justice. When the she-elf got riled up she could be quite scary to the unknowing stranger. Her Magicka was not to be trifled with and most people who met her would be no match with a sword or bow. Except herself of course. Ashalea had a way to go before having any hope of passing her teacher in swordsmanship skills, elf or no.

The woman sat upon her horse now, silver hair shifting in the

breeze, soft lips tugged into a smile at something Denavar said, her emerald eyes twinkling yet still alert. She held herself casually, but there was a sharpness to her body that Shara detected. And her smile was rarely fully free. Her heart knew too well the pain and wretched misery of the darkness.

"Are you going to gawk at us all day or get on the damn horse?" Ashalea called playfully.

Wretched misery be damned, if Ashalea could hold onto that spark then Shara could too.

She flicked her hair. "Just considering how long I'll have to put up with you two lovebirds on the road. Your chirps will undoubtedly get tiring before long," she grinned.

"Lovebirds make the sweetest of songs," Denavar said as Shara walked up to her horse. "You should feel privileged."

Shara rolled her eyes with as much exaggeration as she could muster before attaching her rucksack to the saddlebags. She stroked Fallar's muzzle. "At least I have you. You'll keep me sane." With one foot in the left stirrup she hoisted the other over Fallar's back, sitting gracefully in the saddle. Wezlan mounted up and the four of them cast a final glance at Renlock.

"I shall miss this place," Wezlan uttered affectionately.

"I shan't," Shara mumbled under her breath. "Two mages and a wizard in this group is more than enough."

"What's that?" Wezlan said, scrutinising her with all the intensity his grey eyes could behold.

"Oh nothing. Just looking forward to passing through Shadowvale," she replied a little too cheerfully.

He raised a brow but nodded in satisfaction. "Then let us hope our ride is a smooth one. Onwards!"

With no road running between Renlock and Shadowvale, the party were free to traverse the grassy plains in solitude. Renlock rarely received visitors, and most dared not enter the woods of Shadowvale— lest the trees gobble up their guests. The Onyxonites did not wish to be found, though many had played the seeker. Shara smirked. Mostly young lads trying to prove themselves to their village elders or jostling with mates as they dared the bravest among their troupe to venture into the dark forest.

Of course, the Onyxonites knew the very moment a foreigner stepped into their domain. There were sentries at even perimeters surrounding the outskirts of the forest, hidden among the twisted black branches of the trees. Shara had been posted on guard duty many times, and at first it had felt like a punishment given how boring it was, but she'd soon learned that every now and then an unknowing bunch of idiots would try their luck, and then the fun began.

She'd enjoyed herself thoroughly on many occasions, snaking through the trees, stepping purposefully on a dead branch here, rustling leaves over a fallen log there ... encouraging wide eyes and thumping hearts. She'd even cloaked herself in a tattered shawl and hat, flitting from one tree to another like a ghost: moaning and uttering harmless curses, shrieking false incantations.

If anyone remained at that point, they'd turn on their heels, yelping like little girls and bolting home like spooked chickens, no doubt to cluck tales to their mothers who'd likely clip them around the ears for daring venture to Shadowvale.

Shara cackled openly now, and her companions offered her a few quizzical looks. Flynn rode up beside her, a rare smile on his face. A twang of pain crept into her heart. This was the Flynn she remembered. Chocolate hair with a mind of its own, sweeping across his face, brown eyes twinkling, a lopsided grin. His head was cocked as he searched for answers.

"Just thinking of guard duty in Shadowvale. Ahh, those days were a real treat."

He uttered a small laugh. Half the boisterous guffaw that once would have graced her ears ... but she'd take it all the same. Progress was progress.

"If Father knew what you were really doing on guard duty you would have been whipped and stripped of rations for a week," he said.

"Oh, what's a harmless bit of fun. It stopped them from coming back, and the elders know better than to believe in false curses from 'the ghost of Shadowvale'." She grinned satisfactorily. "Besides, the looks on those boys' faces were priceless. The memories shall keep me warm and cosy in my bed at night whilst they look for witches and hags."

Flynn raised a brow. "If I didn't know you better, I'd think you a heartless wench."

She shrugged and reclined lazily on her horse. "Many do. Makes no difference to me."

He rolled his eyes, chuckling quietly, allowing his horse to stray as it munched on overgrown grass. She kept him in her line of vision and noticed the mirth leave his face, and the regretfully familiar tautness and strained lines return instead.

She sighed, slumping a little deeper in her saddle and taking in her surroundings. *Progress.*

The countryside was lush, the grass strikingly green and plentiful from the recent rain. Blue skies greeted the earth, the odd fluffy cloud sluggishly waving from above. The coastline beckoned from the north and she averted her eyes. The memory of the Onyx Ocean's wrath would only sour her mood. Not that it took much lately. Everyone's temper was high after the events of the last few months.

Shara couldn't help but spiral into the chaos. Just months ago, she'd been searching for the seer, Harrietti Hardov, in the rough and tumble city of Maynesgate—the city of all cities—when she'd come across Ashalea and Wezlan. Little did she know their fates were intertwined from the start. Becoming a Guardian, meeting the elves of the Aquafarian Province, voyaging the black seas of Onyx Ocean and barely making it to the Isle of Dread alive ... she shuddered. Whatever that creature was that had destroyed their ship and almost the entire crew, well, she had no intention of meeting it again. She was happy to stay on land indefinitely. Away from prying tentacles and strange, spiky urchins.

Then there was the Isle of Dread. What a cursed place. She was thankful Denavar had been the one to jump down the chasm to Fari's Dungeon to retrieve the tome. Not that it had helped. She sighed. Were they destined for bad luck? All that effort to find the Magicka spells to seal the darkness's power to portal travel, and yet they were too slow.

That vile creature was still out there, no doubt planning his next attack. She imagined him now as an insect, rubbing its hands together in glee, tainting everything it touched until the world festered under his rule. A sour taste filled her mouth and she shook her head to scramble such thoughts away.

Her eyes found Ashalea, who was riding a little to her left, nose crinkled, and lips pursed. That was the elf's thinking face. Perhaps she, too, was lost in the past. But her posture suddenly straightened. She pulled Kaylin to a halt and practically pricked her ears, eyes darting to Denavar. They both nodded.

"Wezlan," Ashalea hissed, motioning for the party to stop.

Shara strained her own ears, jumped off her horse and pressed an ear to the ground. A low rumbling filled the earth.

"Riders approach," she confirmed.

Shara cursed herself inwardly. Had she not been invested in her own misery she might have heard them coming. She was no elf, but her training meant her senses were keener than most humans. Trained. Her mind and body were a weapon, but the blade had become noticeably blunter of late. *Vulnerable. Weak.*

Denavar perched in his saddle, icy blue eyes staring into the distance. "A small group, no larger than six or so."

Shara followed his gaze straight towards Shadowvale. "Perhaps an escort from my father?" She witnessed Ashalea and Denavar exchange a glance and she scowled. "What? What am I missing?"

"They're riding at speed, Shara. And we gave no word to Harvar that we were passing through," Ashalea said softly.

Wezlan interrupted. "Enough chatter. Stay cautious but remain civil. We aren't sure if they're hostile so let's not stab first and ask questions later."

He gave Shara a sideways glance at the last and she threw her hands up. "What?"

The group waited earnestly and sure enough, a few black specks appeared on the horizon. Shara grinned. "See? Nothing to worry about, just some Onyxonites to escort us through the forest."

A few shoulders visibly drooped and wayward hands loosened grips on swords and staff. Five riders approached and slowed their mounts. They were dressed in standard Onyxonite attire—black tunics and breaches—and their weapons remained attached to their belts.

Shara dipped her head in acknowledgement. "Brothers, sisters."

Three men and two women offered a small bow to Flynn and Shara. "The children of Harvar. It is an honour," said a bronze-skinned

48

woman, her long ebony hair secured in a tight braid down her back. She smiled sweetly. "The chieftain arranged for us to accompany you back to Shadowvale."

Wezlan edged his horse forward, jade staff in hand. "And how did the good lord know to expect us?"

A man with an eyepatch and a sharp nose piped up. "One of your mages thought to inform us ahead of your arrival."

Wezlan eyed them off, his expression unreadable, his response a beat too slow. "Indeed. Let us continue then. We will stop for camp as the sun begins its descent."

The party continued their journey in relative silence for the rest of the day, and as happy as she was to see her comrades, Shara admittedly thought it a little strange there was need for a welcoming party at all. Her father was a practical man. Resources, time, men, were precious. If she were the chieftain, she'd waste no time escorting visitors— blood of her blood present or not—and put her forces to better use by bolstering the village's protection, sending scout parties out to search for spies of the darkness or meeting with potential allies.

In fact, the more she considered it the warier she became. Pleasantries were considered wasted time in Shadowvale, so why the extra protection? Why the show of goodwill towards them now? And after all they'd been through in the battle of Renlock? She narrowed her eyes as she watched the strangers.

She didn't know these Onyxonites—had never seen them in her life. She didn't know every man and woman in Shadowvale, that would be unreasonable given how many warriors the village housed, but she did know those closest to the chieftain ... So had these people replaced the positions of the fallen? Those reserved for the first soldiers, never far from Harvar's side?

Shara eyed off each of the five members. The man with the

eyepatch peered around with one darting eye, a little too shifty for her taste. Another man with a shaved head kept glancing at Ashalea with eyes as dark as night. Sure, she was gorgeous, but the glances were in short nervous bursts. Unusual for an appreciating onlooker. The others behaved in similar ways; their movement, posture, and attention lacking the usual traits of a honed Onyxonite assassin.

She glanced at her brother and found him assessing them in a similar fashion. Their eyes met, his brown orbs narrowed, and she knew he was thinking the same thing.

These are no Onyxonites.

The fire roared happily in a makeshift pit, spitting at the meagre collection of wood gathered earlier that day. There were no forests around—the closest being Shadowvale and the Grove itself—looming to the south, almost crying out to its saviours.

How odd, Shara thought, *that the final destination lies so close to our grasp, and yet we must near circle the entirety of Everosia before we enter its borders.*

The Grove would have to wait. As would the last Guardians within it. For now, she had five play-pretend assassins to deal with. Should it come to it, Shara had no doubt that the group could dispatch them without so much as a bead of sweat upon their brow, but she was hesitant, hungry for answers.

Plus, she was sure the wizard would be all too disapproving if she removed their heads without an interrogation. "*Kill first, questions later?*" She imagined him asking, grey eyes wild as a storm, brows knotted fiercely together.

The question was, how would she go about it? Pretenders have

a habit of keeping their guard up, and she supposed they wouldn't be lining up to have their wrists bound, mouths gagged, and arses spanked by way of punishment if they were found out.

She hunched next to Denavar on one side of the fire, using him as a backrest while she conjured up a plan. All she could imagine was different ways of killing those who dared to mock the Onyxonites, and she dug her elbows into the elf's side as she tried to get comfy.

"If you don't stop wriggling, I'll tie you up and roast you like that poor rabbit in a minute."

"Hmph," she retorted, "you'd be dead before you could blink."

"Ehh you've no meat to you anyway, just gristle and bone. Hardly a meal."

She elbowed him in the ribs, and he uttered a small yelp. She settled into his back again, watching the intruders thoughtfully. Wezlan and Flynn were tending to the rabbit on the spit, and Ashalea was rummaging for vegetarian options in her rucksack. Bread, mushrooms, assorted fruits and cheeses ... *Peasant's fare*, she thought distastefully.

Shara would take grilled, juicy meats any day, even if rabbit meat *was* tiny and their cuteness inflicted a small sliver of guilt when she killed them. Not enough to quit eating meat, of course. Wezlan was now slicing strips from the carcass, offering them to their 'guests'. Ashalea returned with her assortment of food, slumping on the ground in front of the pit. She had her back to the fire, blocking the others from view.

Shara seized the moment. "Psssst."

Her whisper was ignored as Denavar ferociously tore into some bread and Ashalea gulped down a hunk of cheese.

She elbowed Denavar again.

"For crying—"

"Quiet," she hissed.

Sensing her urgency, Ashalea crept forward a little and Denavar's back tightened in anticipation. The movement caught some of the others' eyes, and Shara forced a wide grin to her face.

"Be casual. We're just having a friendly conversation."

Ashalea smirked. "If your grin could be any more strained, you'd look like a constipated duchess at a fancy dinner."

Shara tittered as if Ashalea had shared some grand joke.

"You *sound* like a duchess at a fancy dinner," Denavar said.

"Ha ha." She stuck her tongue out at Ashalea and elbowed Denavar in the back again for good measure. The intruders carried on their conservations without another glance in her direction. "These people are not Onyxonites. I don't know what they're playing at, but it can't be good."

The amusement drained from Ashalea's face. "I expected as much. I've only met your father once but holding hands with allies doesn't seem his style."

Denavar shuffled around to face Shara and Ashalea, nodding his agreement. "I don't trust them. I've been watching and listening all day. Their heartbeats suggest this doesn't end in tea and crumpets."

"Ridding ourselves of them isn't an issue but we need to find out who they are and what they're hoping to achieve here," Shara said.

"What do you suggest?" Ashalea asked.

"When we settle in for the night, you, Flynn, and I will take on the men. Denavar, you take on the women. I think their hearts are in for a rude shock, don't you?"

He shrugged. "I don't know, they might be expecting an attack," he said bluntly.

Shara sighed. "I mean with your lightning fingers, man. You know, thindarōs?"

Ashalea snorted at Denavar's bemused expression. "Try to keep up, will ya?"

"My talents are wasted on you people," Shara said with a grin.

Denavar sighed. "I'd prefer the tea and crumpets."

The three of them kept their charades up until blankets were rolled out and the fire was stoked a final time for the night. Ashalea and Denavar curled up together, Wezlan sprawled out rather decadently over a makeshift mattress of bags and blankets, and Flynn lay opposite Shara.

When the fire dwindled, she would make her move. The stars scattered the sky, merry and bright on the still cloudless canvas above, so she would have to prowl on light feet under their spotlight. She glanced at her brother. He was staring at her with near black eyes; the orange glow reflecting in them, making him look possessed. It reminded her too closely of those lightless eyes back in the darkness's dungeons.

She frowned. *He is not a monster but a man. His blood is mine and my mission is his. He bears my father's chin, the eyes of my mother. He is Flynn Silvaren. And he belongs to no one.*

She forced herself to look at him again and saw the old Flynn. The one who would do anything to protect her, the one with a cheeky attitude, whose mirth came easy. He smiled at her, and it held nothing but goodness. And she smiled back.

Life is fleeting. Perhaps meaningless to many. But small moments are the bookmarks of our memories. And she meant to see this story to the end. One day at a time. She sucked in a deep breath of air and let her regrets, pain, punishments ... all fly away on a breath of wind.

53

Then she closed her eyes and waited.

After what felt like an hour, Shara's eyes opened in a flash. The camp was deadly quiet but for the light breathing of her companions and the odd snore from Wezlan. Not a bird cawed, nor a mouse scurried. It was time.

She saw Flynn's eyes snap open too, and the duo stood in silence, each unsheathing a sword in unison. With bare feet they padded around the encampment, snaking through the various belongings until they reached their targets.

Shara saw Ashalea and Denavar rise and creep towards their marks, the she-elf's hair a stark silver against the night sky, making her appear almost ethereal. When they all reached their target she nodded, and Denavar's Magicka crackled in his hand.

The sound stirred the sleepers, and their guests woke in a start. In a scurry of movement, Ashalea, Shara and Flynn had their blades to the throats of the men, and before the women could say "ambush" they received a small jolt of lightning that had them writhing uncontrollably on the ground.

When the five were sufficiently bound by ropes and gagged, Ashalea shoved them to the ground in a heavy thud, where they all shuffled to huddle with their backs together. She re-stoked the dwindling campfire with her Magicka, and they all peered at the raven-haired woman as she stared at them indignantly.

Shara crouched and snatched the gag from her mouth.

"I think it's time we had a little chat."

A Maiden Among Monsters

ASHALEA

WEZLAN WOKE IN A FIT OF CHOKED SNORTS AND SNORES. His back protested loudly as he creaked upright and stared blankly at the hostages. He yawned. "What have we learned then?"

The others glanced at each other, and Ashalea knew better than to be surprised. "You knew our plan all along then?"

He chuckled. "Not the logistics, but I knew you'd try something. Figured I'd let you all handle it while I got some sorely needed sleep."

Shara cocked her head at the old man. "Figures. Well, we haven't begun interrogations yet." She narrowed her eyes at the captives. "You'd know if I had."

The ungagged woman lifted her head defiantly and spat on the ground in disgust. "I'll never—"

Ashalea slapped her hard across the face, earning surprised looks

from both the woman and the party. "Yes, yes, you'll never reveal your secrets, betray your master's trust and so on. We've heard it before, so let's just skip that part, okay?"

Shara positively beamed at her. "My fledgling has turned rogue. I'm so proud." She sniffed in what looked like a genuine display of emotion.

Ashalea rolled her eyes. "I'm tired of these games. Can't we just do our thing in peace? Is it too much to ask to go one day without some sort of injury, death, interrogation, or night of interrupted sleep?"

She didn't much feel like the torturing type, but she was so exhausted from constantly watching her back and keeping alert that Ashalea felt curiously open to the idea of beating information out of these people. She'd been disgusted once before when Shara had done it, but what's a little blood in the scheme of things? Why did these people deserve any less? Her fingers almost itched to swing the blade again, and it reminded her of the elation she'd felt on the battlefield.

She'd been high on blood; on the power of ending one's life and swinging her sword in defiance. Was it just the adrenaline of the battle that had fired through her? Or something more? Something sinister. Something ... *dark.*

Alarm bells rang in her head and she stepped back involuntarily. The others looked at her curiously and Wezlan placed a hand on her arm.

"Ashalea? Are you all right?"

She took a deep breath to clear unbidden thoughts and shrugged him off with a grim smile. "Fine. Let's get on with it." She moved forward to begin but Shara blocked her path.

The assassin shook her head, clasping Ashalea's arm. "No, my friend. This is not a path for you to walk down. This is my job."

Ashalea looked in Shara's amber eyes, searching for answers the

woman did not have. She found only a reassuring smile on her friend's full lips, and a slight nod that caused her ebony curls to bounce, as if in agreement.

"Okay, Shara. Okay."

Denavar took her hand and they sat a small distance away, observing from the safety of their blankets. She watched as Shara placed a palm on her brother's chest when he approached, offering a similar shake to her head, though a little more forcefully on his part. Her words drifted back to Ashalea's elvish ears. "Not a good idea" and "need to heal" were part of the conversation. And she had to agree. Flynn was in no state to be interrogating again. In fact, it was best he stayed far away from any small, sharp instruments for some time. Who knew what traces, if any, the darkness had left behind in him?

With a huff he skulked into the darkness, leaving the light of the campfire behind. Shara watched him go with her golden eyes before turning back to the woman and shrugging.

"So, what the elf said ... but under threat of *my* blade. And it hasn't known the pleasure of interrogation for a while."

The woman remained tight-lipped and scowling, to no one's surprise. But the other female wriggled eagerly on the ground, almost desperate to get their attention. Her brunette hair was matted and frizzy, a sheen of sweat plastered on her forehead.

Ashalea whispered to Denavar, "I think we have a volunteer."

He leaned in. "There's always a weakling in the pack. Interesting, considering Shara hasn't even thrown a punch yet."

As he said that, Shara's fist connected with the spitter's face. No globs of saliva this time. Just blood.

"Aaaandd there it is. Never mind."

Ashalea smirked and Wezlan looked over at them crossly. "Are we in the habit of enjoying this now? People's lives are not morsels to

play with like a cat would a mouse. You would do well to remember that Ashalea Kindaris, *queen* in waiting, and Denavar Andaro, *mage* of Renlock." His weathered face pinched together to full capacity.

Ashalea and Denavar lowered their heads sheepishly like naughty school children. "Yes, sir," they muttered.

She looked up through her lashes to see the wizard stroking his beard, muttering under his breath as he paced back and forth. As each day passed the weight of the world seemed to further take its toll on him; the shoulders slumping a little lower, the frown lines etching a little deeper. It concerned her to see this powerful, wonderful man beginning to show his age. And she was scared. He was like a father to her—the one who kept her on the right path, who advised her, guided her, believed in her. She loved him dearly. What type of world would Everosia be without him?

A loud crunch snapped her attention back to Shara and her prisoner.

"There goes her nose," she whispered to Denavar.

Shara's voice barked from across the clearing. "All right, let's move on to your friend, shall we? She's just dying to tell me something, I know it."

Shara shoved a dirty cloth back into spitter's mouth before ungagging frizz ball. She sucked in fresh air for a moment before staring pleadingly at Shara, and beneath the dishevelled locks and dirt-caked face, Ashalea noticed the smooth, unmarked skin and the youthful glow of her eyes. She'd barely begun womanhood. *What was she doing with the likes of these people?*

"Please," the lass sobbed, tears trickling down her cheeks. "Please don't hurt me. I'll tell you anything you want to know."

The others began jostling fitfully, mumbling through their gags, earning a frightful glare from Shara. "SILENCE!" The assassin studied

the girl's face with narrowed eyes. "How long ago did you have your first bleed?"

Her captive hunched over, tears now a torrential downpour, her nose snotty and snivelling. "Two—two years ago," she managed between sniffs.

Ashalea noticed Shara's face soften just a touch. "And how did you end up with this rabble?"

The girl glanced at her crew with uncertainty, and Shara gently laid a hand on her shoulder. "They won't hurt you. They won't hurt anyone again."

At the last, the girl seemed to break down all over again and exasperated, Shara threw her hands in the air. "For goodness' sake girl, will you stop crying?"

"This discussion is going nowhere," Ashalea whispered to Denavar. "I think it's time for someone with a little more ... finesse."

"Or just someone who doesn't look like they want to rip your head off?"

Ashalea shrugged. "In this case, they're one and the same." She rose and strolled over to the pair, tapping Shara on the shoulder and nodding towards the hysterical creature. "I think I can take it from here."

Shara gave the so-called rabble a final glance and shrugged. "Be my guest."

Ashalea nodded before kneeling and gently taking the girl's hands. "My name is Ashalea, I'm an elf from the Moonglade Meadows. It goes against my beliefs to cause undue harm to other living creatures, human and animal alike."

Do I really believe that anymore?

She heard a loud snort come from Denavar and Shara's direction and threw them a burning glare over her shoulder before continuing.

"What's your name?"

"Helena." She wiped at her eyes with bound fists and took a shaky breath.

Ashalea studied her. The girl was a petite, crumbled mess who looked incapable of lifting a sword, let alone using the pointy end. She couldn't imagine her harming anyone, though she was smart enough not to assume such dangerous things. Still, she looked so scared and Ashalea couldn't help feeling sorry for her.

"Helena, I'm going to unbind your wrists with my knife, okay? I'm pulling it from the sheathe now ... can I trust you to remain calm and not do anything rash?"

The girl nodded hesitantly.

Ashalea slid a dagger from a strap around her leg and slowly lifted it to the rope. The girl's eyes bulged at the sight of it but Ashalea gently sawed at the binding so as not to hurt Helena. When the rope was free the girl rubbed her wrists and peered at her gratefully. She seemed to calm down after Ashalea gave her a moment to recover.

"Thank you. When I was little, my parents and I lived in the slums of Maynesgate docks. My father was a weak man, having suffered from illnesses most of his life. They never meant to get pregnant, but they couldn't risk aborting me ... Father wouldn't have made it if Mother didn't survive."

Ashalea waited patiently as Helena told her story. She could sense Shara's frustration simmering behind her and felt Wezlan's eyes boring into the back of her skull. But the girl was like a deer amidst a hunt; jumpy and ready to bolt. Patience was the game here.

Helena continued. "They sold me to a brothel long before the bleeds began. The women there trained me in, well, you know." Her cheeks reddened and Ashalea had to stop herself from shaking the girl.

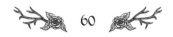

60

Get to the point!

"Anyway, the woman who I spent the most time learning from, her name was Vera."

That name got Ashalea's attention. She had to stop herself from peeking a glance at Shara, whose rage was likely about to reach boiling point.

Helena sighed. "She's dead now but when *he* came along and bought her from the lady of the house, she asked that I be saved too. I don't know why. I always thought she despised me ..." she trailed off, eyes glazing.

"And? What did you do when the man took you in?"

Helena's shoulders wilted. "I became the entertainment. Vera thought she was saving me, but things only grew worse. He took me to some hideout underground. I didn't see the sun for days—weeks—at a time." She shivered and her eyes grew distant. "They were like animals, those men."

A tide of sorrow flooded Ashalea. This poor girl was guilty of nothing but bad luck—of making friends with the wrong people. And she had paid the price many times over. But she couldn't let emotions cloud her judgement. She needed more answers.

"What did you see? In the darkness's hideout? What did you learn of his plans?"

"I ... I don't kn—know," Helena stammered. Her eyes began to well once more. "I was confined mostly to one room. He only let me out on rare occasions to accompany his soldiers on raids. I had to play the helpless maiden and lure in strangers. No one spoke to me but Vera, and she never said a word about *him*."

Now it was Ashalea's turn to seethe. She gritted her teeth to stop from screaming at the girl. "Why are you here then? Why didn't you escape when you had the chance?"

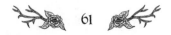

"I didn't have anywhere to go," the girl wailed. "After his hideout was infiltrated, any soldiers who survived or were already out on missions were to report back to the darkness. All I know is that we were to spy on Renlock ... Determine what the mages were doing. Then we were to capture civilians on the ride back."

Ashalea considered this information. It made sense, and the girl seemed to be telling the truth. But one thing niggled at her mind.

"You said you were to capture people? Why?"

Helena erupted in tears once more. "I don't kknnnoowwww."

Ashalea's wits were at the end of her tether. She tied Helena up again, shoved the gag back into her mouth with a mumbled "sorry" and returned to the others to convene. They huddled in a circle.

"I believe her," she stated simply.

Denavar shook his head. "She may be telling the truth, but it doesn't fill the gaps in her story. Why would the darkness want to capture townsfolk?"

There was silence as they contemplated the matter, and then a small, "I think I know why."

All eyes flicked to Shara. She shifted uncomfortably and scanned the camp for any sign of Flynn, but he was nowhere to be seen.

"When I was in ..." she swallowed hard, "in the darkness's dungeon, he would take prisoners from their cells from time to time. He took both innocents and filth—rapists, murderers and the like. I would hear screams echoing down the halls which eventually turned into guttural howls and grunts. Almost like animals. Most of them never returned. The ones that did were ... changed. I never heard them speak, utter any sound for that matter. It was like they were a ghost. When the guards came, they weren't harmed, they acted as if ... as if ..." Her eyes widened and Ashalea could almost see the gears lock into place as Shara's expression changed.

"As if their minds were being controlled," Wezlan finished. He stroked his beard, mouth downturned and hidden behind the grey hair. "We know the effects of this experiment—we've seen it with Flynn. But if the darkness is performing other procedures ... this does not bode well."

Ashalea glanced at Shara and Wezlan in horror. "Please tell me you're not suggesting the darkness is trying to create a new kind of monster. As if he hasn't got enough monsters in his army. But this ... experimenting on humans to make a new breed of twisted is just—"

"Barbaric," Shara said. "I know. But it's exactly what I'd expect from him, Ashalea. He craves power and domination and any means necessary of getting it is just a game for him. A sort of sick challenge that he delights in. He probably finds it humorous to destroy Everosia with its own unwilling subjects."

Wezlan shook his head. "I believed there was still a glimmer of hope. That we could restore some semblance of humanity in him, but I fear there is nothing left. There is only one way to end this now."

"I must kill him, Wezlan," Ashalea whispered. "I must kill my brother."

Shara burst through the chamber doors to Harvar's suite, the others hot on her heels and just as quick to stop in their tracks. Shara turned around with a hand over her eyes and Ashalea averted her gaze in embarrassment, but not before she caught a glimpse of the scene before her.

Lord Harvar Silvaren was stark naked in a bathing tub, arms around two buxom women as they each lathered his hairy—though admittedly well-defined chest—with soaps, the strong smell of oak

moss and musk permeating the air. The women were unperturbed by the interruption, as was the chieftain himself.

"Shara, Flynn." He smiled. "My children. It does me well to see you." He looked past his offspring to find Ashalea and his eyes lit up with glee. "And the she-elf is here, too. Marvellous."

With her back still turned, Shara pulled a squeamish face at Ashalea. "Perhaps we should return when you don't have guests and are suitably dressed, Father."

He rose from the tub and exited, water sloshing over the sides and pooling at everyone's feet. The movement drew Ashalea's attention and she instantly regretted having looked up. He continued to move around oblivious to the stares, however uncomfortable, garnered by all but Shara.

Flynn chucked him a towel and the chieftain fully dried himself, bending over in the process and displaying quite the view.

"Oh, I did not need to see that." Ashalea then also turned around, the tips of her ears a cherry red, and snuck a peek at Wezlan and Denavar. The former looked positively ill whilst Denavar looked nothing short of amused at the chieftain's behaviour.

Wezlan cleared his throat awkwardly. "Perhaps a robe?"

Harvar chuckled. "Mages. Elves. So modest. We were born this way, why should we hide our true forms?"

"Because sons and daughters should never have to see the instrument of their creation," Shara responded with a roll of her eyes. "Please, for the love of all that is bloody, put on a robe so you don't scare away the normal people."

Harvar's laugh boomed off the walls as he picked up a pair of black breaches and a thin cream shirt from a nearby chaise. He shrugged the clothes on and smiled. "Better?"

"Much." Wezlan nodded his head in relief.

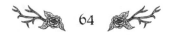

Harvar motioned for the women in the tub to leave, and they got out, all too aware of watchful eyes, laughing as they sauntered out the room. Ashalea noticed the men didn't complain or avert their eyes at the view this time, and she even caught Shara's appreciative gaze at their behinds as they exited.

Ashalea watched curiously as the family offered each other the barest of nods—no embraces or heartfelt words, such was the Onyxonite way. Harvar sat on the chaise and beckoned them to sit opposite on a modest lounge suite, calling a nearby servant to bring food and, of course, wine.

The chieftain leaned forward, folding his fingers together. "So? To what do I owe this pleasure?"

Shara reclined lazily whilst Flynn snapped to attention. It was the most animated Ashalea had seen him since the battle of Renlock and his back was ramrod straight as he began his report.

"It seems the darkness has invented new ways to discover and infiltrate our base. We intercepted soldiers dressed in Onyxonite attire, claiming to be an escort party to bring us home."

Harvar lost his easy smile and a fire lit in his eyes. "I expected him to cower in a dark corner to lick his wounds for a time. Seems he's done anything but. Did you question these imitators?"

"Of course. Though ... it was Ashalea who extracted the information."

Harvar gazed at her appreciatively, eyes scanning the length of her body. "My feisty elf comes through once again," he grinned.

Denavar threw her a questioning look as he noticed the unsubtle rove of the chieftain's gaze.

Ashalea blushed and thrust her chin in the air haughtily. "Before you get too excited, torture was not the right course this time. At least not entirely. One of the captives spoke freely. She had been held against her will by the darkness as a ... a source of entertainment for his soldiers."

"Oh?" Harvar lifted a brow.

She cleared her throat. "Yes. A young woman. Turns out she was taken in by the woman partly responsible for—" She trailed off and looked guiltily at Shara.

"For my holiday retreat at the darkness's villa," the assassin drawled. "Can we all stop making such an effort to skirt around the details? It's becoming quite tiresome."

Feeling abashed, Ashalea nodded. "For the capture and torture of Shara."

The servant returned with platefuls of food and wine—steamed fish with buttered greens, freshly baked bread, fruits, pastries, cheeses, a rack of lamb and an assortment of roasted and spiced vegetables for the elves. After a near week of riding, not to mention night shifts watching their prisoners, the Guardians were positively famished, and they all dug in gracelessly.

Wezlan had not agreed with transporting the prisoners to Shadowvale, but even he had no sway over the decision. Impersonating an Onyxonite was a crime punishable by death in this clan, and the twins were adamant they be dealt with in the Onyxonite way. It had proved most tiresome bringing them here, and the result would be an ugly death Ashalea would wish upon no one.

After she'd gleaned all the information she could from Helena, Shara had followed through with questioning the others. They were bumped and bruised from the ordeal, but small words choked out in pain revealed all they needed to know.

The five of them were to spy on Renlock and assess the damage from the fire and the recuperation efforts of the mage army. Five targets had been specified to watch in particular—a silver-haired elf and her companion, the Onyxonite twins, and an old wizard. If the group moved on, the soldiers were to intercept and 'escort' them back to Shadowvale, where the children of Lord Harvar Silvaren would be welcomed with open arms, no questions asked. After the impersonators had infiltrated the camp, gleaning what information they could, they would slip away under cover of night, reporting they had a new mission if they were questioned upon leaving.

Ashalea conveyed all this to Harvar as they feasted on their meal. By the end of her story, the chieftain's features were dark with rage, though she distinguished he was a dash impressed, too.

"Where are the prisoners now?" he said gravely.

"The guards have been instructed to bring them in when you're ready," Shara said between chews.

Harvar shifted his gaze to Flynn and the young man nodded, promptly leaving the room and returning shortly after with four prisoners in tow, accompanied by two guards. The latter deposited the hostages with a rough shove onto the floor and took their posts by the door.

Harvar gazed at their miserable faces one by one before facing Ashalea with a frown. "I thought you said five. Where is the last?"

Everyone's eyes turned to Ashalea and her cheeks heated. "We, um ... we lost one."

His brow raised. "Two deadly assassins, one of the most powerful wizards of our time, and two elves gifted with strength, speed and honed instincts, and you managed to just *lose* a captive?"

She averted her gaze. "The girl didn't deserve to die. She had no choice but to do as she was bid. The darkness would have—"

"Would have what?" Harvar bellowed, his skin now a beetroot red. "Killed her? Tortured her? Used another to do his dark bidding? We're at war, girl. We need warriors, strategists, miracles even, to

match the darkness, not heroes."

Ashalea seethed, clenching her fists. "You're wrong. Death begets more death. Our power lies not in the weapon but the hand that holds it. We need only choose life instead of taking it."

Wezlan laid a hand on her arm, a proud smile on his face. His assurance gave her confidence and she stood to face the chieftain.

"It is easy to swing the sword, less so to forgive and forget. I know there are some evils that must be cleansed from this world, but there are others whose voices can unite the peoples of this land and lead us to hope. I know which option I'd prefer. What about yours?"

Harvar sighed and the harsh lines of anger softened. "Pretty words—ones that will inspire and conquer the most stubborn of minds ... But you are in Shadowvale she-elf. Our customs are as rock and mortar—well-built and unyielding."

Ashalea crossed her arms, refusing to meet his gaze. "Walls can be brought down and remade into a stronger foundation."

"Do you really expect me to let these people go? Look at them. LOOK AT THEM."

She lifted her eyes to glare first at Harvar before shifting to the prisoners. They looked at her imploringly, as if encouraging her to fight the good fight that would set them free. And even as she argued, she knew it was a losing battle.

"Ashalea, from what you've told me, these soldiers have maimed, murdered, and tricked innocents to their death. They have lied and cheated, impugned the Onyxonite honour. They are a danger to society, to me, to this village, to all of you," he said with a wave. "And they have seen Shadowvale now."

She closed her eyes and tilted her head back. He spoke true. Whatever led these people to this moment—whether they were inherently good or bad by nature—was no longer her concern. Deep

down, she wasn't convinced she cared about their lives at all. So, what then? An attempt to drive off the monster within? The gathering thoughts of bloodlust, of death, of *vengeance*? Was she so different from the Onyxonites?

She felt a presence by her side and opened her eyes. Shara clasped her shoulder. "It is done, Ashalea. Let it go."

Ashalea cast one final look at the frightened faces of the sentenced before meeting Harvar's stare with that of ice and fire.

"So be it."

Death is Art

ASHALEA

THE MOANS AND GURGLES OF THE DYING filled the air as the villagers of Shadowvale observed the final hours of the punished. Three men and one woman were tied to individual wooden racks in the form of an 'x' and strung up for the world to see—their tongues removed from their mouths, so they were forced to choke and splutter their pain in strangled groans.

The prisoners would die at the hands of one executioner, who would perform a death ritual of 100 methodical cuts to their limbs and chest. If they were still breathing after the final slice, they were left to bleed out, tied to their posts in public humiliation, nothing more than meat for carrions to make a meal of.

Ashalea watched in disgust, her stomach churning not from the sight of the blood but the sounds drifting through the otherwise silent air. She could think of only one word to describe the event: barbaric.

Were all men like this? Were all humans this malevolent? This bloodthirsty? She imagined the King of Maynesgate had regulations in place for the most despicable of creatures amongst his dungeons, but this … this was a mutilation of the body that would go beyond death. Some humans believed their bodies had to be whole—organs in place, limbs and head still attached—in order to be reborn or to allow them passage to the afterlife. Elves believed in spirituality, but they shared a unique connection to the land, and upon death, found peace in knowing their souls would return to the earth; the gifts of long life and enhanced physical makeup granted by the Goddess Enalia being restored unto Mother Nature herself.

Ashalea shivered, the cries of the dying piercing her soul like shards of unforgiving ice. Life was morbid enough without thinking about what comes after, much less the empty void she imagined that awaited the maimed and broken who would be denied their spiritual beliefs in death.

She looked at the friends surrounding her. Denavar's brows knit together as he watched the scene before them, and she suspected he was just as uneasy as she. Wezlan stroked his beard with one hand, the other jammed into his forehead, his palm grinding like a pestle in mortar. Then there was Shara and Flynn. The twins stood dutifully at attention, their faces blank and rigid—trained soldiers that they are. Their shoulders were locked, their hands fisted at their sides, but their eyes burned—Shara's with amber fire, Flynn's full of a hatred that threatened to quake the earth and split the world at its seams.

And Ashalea realised in that moment that the crimes of these people went beyond treason, murder, and the mindless actions of fanatics and followers. Flynn's eyes promised punishment for everything the darkness had done to him. For controlling him, abusing him, breaking him until Flynn was little more than a slave at that cruel man's beck and call—for forcing him to carve his sister's flesh as if he were charcoal and she a canvas.

Every cut to these prisoners was a shot at redemption, every drop of their blood a release of Flynn's own pain. And if bloodletting—if this barbaric practice was something his broken heart and twisted mind needed to heal—then Ashalea would welcome the sight. She would drink in every last drop of the scene if it meant he could move on. Her eyes shifted to his twin. If Shara could move on ...

Ashalea's gaze returned to Flynn's face and she studied him closely, carefully. His eyes narrowed as he watched the executioner at work, and still they burned with an icy rage threatening to freeze all in his presence. She could almost see his thoughts, hidden beneath those mirrors of pain, buried within a dark and empty pit ... And as she peered into that fire— the beautiful but broken eyes—her own Elvish orbs saw the carnage in that reflection.

Slice. Repayment for the lives Flynn had been forced to take.

Drip. A raised middle finger for being rendered mindless and unable to control his own body.

Slice. A promise to protect his sister from being harmed by the darkness ever again.

Drip. A string of curses. A crooked smile that promised revenge.

Ashalea continued her assessment of the public, and as she gazed out across the village square, she saw nothing but brown and black hair, all bronzed bodies and toned muscles. They were all dressed in black, some clad from head to toe, others adorned with minimal cloth. From the faces she could see, not a single one found joy in the death of these people, but none looked away either.

Every Onyxonite was in attendance, bar the guards stationed at the forest perimeter. It was a written law that every Onyxonite—even

the children—attend these ceremonies ... if one could call it such. Shara had told Ashalea that it served as a reminder: strength, loyalty, honour, resilience. The highest qualities one could behold in this community.

Treason, defection, and imposters were dealt the harshest punishments. The most severe of all—and even Shara had grimaced at this—was being drawn and quartered. The thought of it made Ashalea's blood feel like it was being pumped and drained all at once. Ashalea hadn't pressed for more information on this practice or to how often it had happened before, and Shara hadn't offered.

"*Death is art,*" she had said last night as they lounged on chaises, taking a rare moment to shrug off responsibilities and enjoy a wine in relative peace. "*The body is a canvas, I the artist. One must wield the brush with precision, the hand steady, the intention true. Each painting is different, but all are a masterpiece.*"

Denavar had elbowed her with a clownish smirk on his face. "Bet you don't get too many volunteers for models, though."

Shara had scowled, leaping at him with a vicious snarl, their wines cascading over the floor, the glasses smashing and sending shards sweeping over the ground. Then the pair of them were soon tumbling on the floor, fists flying wildly, elbows knocking.

Ashalea had rolled her eyes, laughed, and then opened the door of the threshold, kicking that ball of human bodies to send them rolling down the steps of Shadowvale. She'd shut the door and dusted her hands off, the grunts of her friends growing fainter as they bounced down the stairs.

She'd turned to Wezlan and the old man had raised a brow, a wily grin smoothing over leathered cheeks. They'd both burst out laughing and didn't stop until the others had slunk back into the room, guilty expressions on their scraped, bruised faces.

One look at the state of them—and at Denavar's puppy dog eyes—and Ashalea and Wezlan had again burst into raucous laughter, cackling for so long that even Shara and Denavar gave in, their sides soon splitting from a fit of giggles.

Ashalea hadn't laughed like that in a long time. Too long. Maybe ever, she realised. And one look at Denavar and Wezlan casually side-glancing at her told her they knew it, too.

Even last night felt like a distant memory as her eyes now settled once more on the prisoners. Blood dripped in spittle and globs from each, and all but one hung their head dejectedly. The woman with the beautiful black hair glared at them defiantly, not one tear on her face, not one sound uttered from her cracked lips. Her eyes found Ashalea's and they glared with hatred. Beneath her dirt-caked face and blood-spattered body, she looked almost crazed—a frenzy to her like that of a wild animal on the hunt.

The woman attempted to speak, spitting and drooling as her brain tried to do what her mouth could not. Her shortcomings were replaced with eerie grunts and her petite frame started shaking with fitful bursts. Ashalea gaped at the maimed creature before her, the shudders and sounds of this woman a haunting melody.

"She's ..."

"Laughing," said Shara softly. "Her blood pools beneath her feet, yet still she is defiant." The assassin shrugged and an expression akin to admiration passed her face. "You gotta give it to her, the woman goes out with style."

Wezlan glared at her, smoothing his beard like a bird would preen ruffled feathers.

Shara smirked before returning her attention to the execution, and the five of them looked on, each left to their own thoughts.

They stood for several more hours until the sun's light was

waning, and evening shimmered golden rays upon the crowd. It glittered within the ruby red pools within which rivers had wound their way down the stone stairs of the clearing. And as the sun crept beneath the horizon, Ashalea heard a sigh drift on feathered wings as the raven-haired beauty's heart ceased to beat.

The executioner, ever present in his silent vigil beside the looming wooden racks, padded to her feet and laid a spindly finger on her bare throat. After a beat he glanced at Harvar. One nod.

"It is done," the chieftain declared, and as one the Onyxonites bent their heads, hand over heart, and announced:

"In shadows we dwell, in darkness we die."

Harvar ascended the stairs, his boots caressing the puddles of blood as he climbed. Turning at the top, he surveyed his tribe with steely eyes, a hardened stare passing over the brows of the men and women before them. An army of assassins, an elite squad of trained killers. He raised his palms skyward before thrusting one hand pointedly at the dead.

"My brothers and sisters, sons and daughters, children of the dreaded dark ... This is the price you pay for breaking the code. Impersonation is a dangerous weapon that could undo everything we stand for. The uniforms you don, the scars you wear, the tools of destruction you hold, they are the markings of a dealer of death. They are what make you Onyxonite. Should a snake slip through our defences, our secrets would slip like poison through the vein."

The chieftain circled behind the fallen, slowly pacing until he stood before the wooden racks once again. "If Shara and Denavar had not had their wits about them, such vipers would have found our nest."

The square was deathly silent as Harvar paused for dramatic effect. His message was loud and clear: should Shadowvale be infiltrated, the location of the Onyxonites would be revealed to all, most importantly, to the darkness. The tribe would stand no chance against a legion of monsters.

"Let this be clear," Harvar continued. "We deal in death, and in death we are judged. Shadowvale is our mother, the keeper of all secrets. She birthed the Onyxonites, and her blood gave life to those who would take it. Live with honour. Die with grace. And never, *ever*, betray our code, or by my own hand will I feed you to the depths of Onyx Ocean."

The chieftain's dark almond eyes scanned his disciples once more before he nodded curtly. "Guardians, offspring, with me. The rest of you, dismissed."

The crowd dispersed on silent feet and Ashalea watched them with interest as they exited the square. They marched rigidly, shoulders still locked, eyes straight ahead. Trained soldiers to the last. Every man and woman who passed the chieftain nodded or placed a hand over heart before departing. And despite the harsh punishments or the brutal training, Ashalea realised just how much respect this man had garnered. They were loyal to him, loved him.

When the last Onyxonite had exited and the others in her group had departed for the war room, Ashalea found herself alone in the dust and blood, the smell of emptied bowels accosting her sensitive elvish nose. And she found herself wondering: *If I were born into this tribe, would I murder without qualm or question? Would I take pride and joy in the kill?*

"*But you already do*," a little voice countered. "*You have tasted death and found it fitting to your palette.*"

Ashalea started, whirling to find the speaker, searching with hawk eyes as she scanned the square. There was familiarity in the tone. A vagueness that crawled up her spine. Almost like—

"You were born with the tools to dispatch. Despair and destruction bred a beast unwilling and unable to stop the anger and hate flowing through your veins. The desire to avenge those you cared for. Those you never had the pleasure of laughing with, smiling with ... loving."

The voice was like honey, thick with intention, dripping with temptation. Still she found no one in sight, her emerald eyes finding nothing but the husks of the dead. And they would forever be silenced.

"Who are you?"

The voice tutted softly. "I am the voice of reason. Come now, Ashalea, you work so hard to be the saviour the people need, the answer to every riddle. You set off with revenge in your heart, murder in your bones ... and yet here you are trying to save the world instead. Are you not tired of these expectations? Do you not deserve to put yourself first?"

Ashalea found a strange emptiness settle in the air. A cooling calm washing over her. She found herself agreeing with this unknown entity. Her conscience, her logic, escaping her body like a breath upon a breeze. After all, there was truth in its words.

"You must forget the Guardians. The people of this world. Your purpose is to find the darkness. Find Crinos ... Come to an accord. Let nothing and no one get in your way." The voice shifted now, cooing softly, gently, understanding laced on its tongue. "Wouldn't it be nice not to worry about anyone else? To give in to your natural instincts. Peace is an ill-fitting cloak for you Ashalea. You are meant for better things."

Ashalea stood rooted to the ground, transfixed by the words. Lost in the fantasy of it all. "It would be nice to end this suffering. To be my own master again." She sighed, a longing aching in her gut.

The cool breeze surrounding her shifted as if the being nodded with understanding. She felt iciness dig into her shoulders with sharp claws. "Yes. Let go of the past and forget the future. Let your wildness come to the fore. Let your thirst decide the close."

Ashalea stared with unseeing eyes. "Thirsty. So thirsty." She gulped in the nothing, picturing herself on the battlefield, unstoppable and unyielding as her sword cleaved through countless foes. The adrenaline swelled to bursting, her power on a high. She drank in the visions with greed, consuming one after the other, her hand drifting to the sword at her waist as she stood lost in hallucination.

"*That's it,*" the thing hissed with glee. "*More. You deserve so much more.*"

The images shifted, and she was now in a void, standing before a strand of silver. She clutched at the silky string of visions eagerly, walking the length of the thread until she approached the heart, its power throbbing in anticipation, its delight at her presence wavering along the many threads binding her. The entity was buried deep in her mind—a cluster of blackened cells within her brain.

"*Closer. Let me ease your suffering. Let me wash away your fear and sharpen your intent, for you are a weapon forged from darkness.*"

Ashalea paused, lifting a hand painstakingly from the thread. She was gasping now, so overcome with desire, a lust for power driving her body, raking through every fibre of her being. It took every effort not to continue her path, but where her body was near to crumbling her mind screeched in warning.

Darkness? A weapon? Forget everything she stood for. Everything she'd worked and cared for? Something wasn't right. The words were honey, but beneath the sticky mess she'd found herself trapped in lay poison, and just a few more steps and she'd be at the heart of its web. The web within *her* mind.

Panic gripped Ashalea and she turned, racing back the other way. Her legs moved lethargically one in front of the other, her stomach still filled with want. Her breath exhaled in bursts and stars and overwhelming black threatened the front of Ashalea's eyes.

"*Where are you going?*" The voice hissed with frustration. "*Return to the path. Become the monster you were always meant to be.*"

The world blurred as the entity shook her mind with overwhelming rage. She felt it now. Gone was the sincerity, the reasoning, the layer of persuasion. Left was the deceit, the danger, the dark. Ashalea stumbled, her breaths coming in quick gasps now as the black was closing, closing ...

"*Come back,*" it roared. "COME—"

"Ashalea." A voice spoke from faraway. Hands were on her shoulders, shaking. "Ashalea!"

With a gasp her eyes snapped into focus and she was standing in Shadowvale once more. More importantly, Denavar was standing in front of her, her blade taut against his throat. A thin trickle of blood wriggled its way down his neck as she shivered. Her eyes darted to his in shock, the picture of ferocity glaring back in their reflection.

Slowly, with fluid movements, he lowered her hand. The scimitar clanged to the floor, its mirrored tip glinting ruby in the sunlight. Shuddering, she closed her eyes, took a deep breath and tried in vain to slow her heartbeats.

"Denavar, I—I don't know what came over me. I didn't mean to—"

"Shhh." Her lover blotted his sleeve at the cut on his golden flesh before taking her in his arms. He cradled Ashalea in silence as she buried her face into his shoulder, nuzzling into the familiar warmth, the peppermint scent, the place that made most sense in the world.

Casting one final look at the ground, half expecting the scimitar to take flight on its own, she peered at the ruby speck coating its tip. For her to lose touch of reality, to be hearing voices, to see the unseen ...

Something was wrong. Very wrong indeed.

The war room was considerably different than the first time she'd seen it. Once Ashalea had lounged on chaises, lapping wine with reckless abandon and convincing the chieftain of Shadowvale to assemble a recovery team to rescue Shara.

Now the chamber was dominated by a round table, black marble shimmering in the flickering light of the sconces lining the walls. Base wooden chairs surrounded it, occupied by the leaders of the Onyxonite army, the twins, Wezlan, and of course the chieftain himself.

Ashalea recognised a few faces from her last council meeting. Jeelu, the tall, well-built man with ebony skin and dark glittering eyes. The woman with long raven-hair and plump lips, the burly man with a jagged scar over one eye.

Harvar offered quick introductions to the group. Raven-hair was named Amira; scar-face, Neefu. She stared at them in turn, offering a subtle nod in greeting.

Denavar took his place by Wezlan's side, but Ashalea chose to stand. The visions, the hallucination—whatever it was—still haunted her, and she suppressed a shudder as she schooled her features into a smooth mask. She had sworn Denavar to secrecy before they entered. The last thing she wanted was their concern at this hour, and, troubling as it was, now was not the time to discuss her personal terrors. The chieftain would not have called this meeting without a good reason.

She gripped the chair's back with white knuckles before sliding into her seat, Denavar placing a firm hand on her thigh to ground her. Conversation whispered in gentle ebbs and flows until a tray laden with wine goblets was distributed by a young serving girl. She offered Ashalea a shy smile before skittering from the room on feet

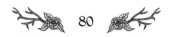

silent as a mouse.

Harvar took his goblet and raised it skyward. "A toast. To my tribe. To the Guardians. To my children. Let today be a reminder to all. Vigilance. Vigilance for our people, for our mission, for our path. The darkness grows cunning. Desperate. Two traits that combined spell a greater danger than we've yet known from this creature."

The chieftain looked to Jeelu, his second, addressing him directly. "After the battle of Renlock, our numbers have declined, and our village is at risk. Our defences need bolstering, our training increasing. The darkness has spies everywhere."

Jeelu nodded slowly, the dim light shining on his shaved head, catching on his high cheekbones and perfect skin. "I shall double the guards on perimeter, send some of our best spies to survey surrounding villages and report back."

The chieftain nodded, seemingly satisfied. "Wezlan, how do the mages fare?"

The old man released a small sigh. "Still reeling from the aftermath. They need leadership, reliability. People they can look up to and take clear orders from. I wish I could stay ... but I am needed elsewhere."

"They need *you*, Wezlan," Ashalea said softly. "Without your guidance they are lost. You, Denavar, Farah ..." At the mention of her name Denavar winced, but she continued, nevertheless. "After Ventiri's betrayal and the loss of its most trusted members, the Academy will fall into ruin."

"You could portal travel and still meet us at a later point," Denavar suggested.

The wizard shook his head. "It's too risky. The energy spent travelling to and from the Academy will be costly, not to mention the constant need to know your current whereabouts. Besides, no one in our party has travelled to the Diodon Mountains before, unless I'm mistaken?" He raised a brow.

The Guardians looked at each other blankly before resting on Wezlan's eyes again.

A harrumph escaped his lips. "As I thought. My knowledge of the area will be useful. The desert is an unforgiving place. It is not to be trusted."

Shara frowned. "What do you mean by 'it'?"

Amira shook her long black locks. "Legend tells of sands that are ever shifting, terrain changing so often that travellers would lose their way, lost to dehydration and the mercy of the Gods. There is no path. No method to the madness."

"Aye," Neefu joined in, "wayfinding instruments like compasses, even the stars themselves, are useless. There is only one species which knows the way of the wastes."

Ashalea pawed at her eyes with frustration. *Diodonians.*

"And we're only just hearing about this now?" Shara drawled. Her eyes stared daggers at Wezlan. "How do you propose we make this journey?"

Wezlan smiled and tapped his nose. "A wizard has his tricks. But back to the matter at hand. Harvar, long have your people been isolated from the outside world. It is time to join forces. The Onyxonites must rally with the other races in this fight. Everosia needs you."

Amira narrowed her eyes. "Shadowvale has always been its own entity. The way of shadows is the way of our people. Lift the fog of our tribe and—"

Harvar raised a hand and the woman quietened, pursing her lips sourly.

"What do you propose, wizard?"

Wezlan took a breath, straightening his shoulders. "Send protection to Renlock. With Onyxonites guarding the ramparts of

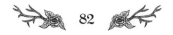

the Academy I shall sleep better knowing the mages are offered some protection. Have some of your best teach them to fight. Equip them with the skills needed to defend themselves."

Harvar stroked his cropped beard, his face contemplative, his relaxed posture suggesting he was open to Wezlan's requests.

"Send missives to negotiate with the other races," Wezlan continued. "Establish an alliance with the elves and the dwarves, and for the love of the Gods, aid me in convincing the king of Maynesgate to open his eyes to this threat."

"My lord," Amira interjected, "I do not think this wise—"

"Silence, woman." The chieftain's eyes glittered at her dangerously and the room went deathly quiet.

Ashalea and Shara exchanged a glance, trying to hide their amusement. *Suck on that lemon.*

Minutes trickled by as the chieftain considered Wezlan's appeals. He continued raking a hand through his short black beard, dark almond eyes squinting in thought. Ashalea studied him, and, as if in response, the man looked up and caught her gaze. A slight frown creased his features before he offered her a charming smile. His eyes shot back to her mentor.

"All right, Wezlan. You have a deal. I will send a party of Onyxonites as a gesture of good will. They will protect your precious Academy and teach the mages to better defend themselves. Neefu will be first commander. All orders will pass through him."

The burly man's surprise registered for a split second before his features returned to their usual gruff neutrality. "As you bid, Chieftain."

The tension in the room visibly deflated as Wezlan uttered a soft sigh. "You have my thanks, Harvar."

The chieftain raised his goblet in answer, taking a large, audible

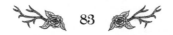

gulp from the cup. "However," he continued, "I am yet to decide on the matter of alliances. You will have my answer before you leave.

"As for today's proceedings, the dead take their secrets to the grave. I give thanks for your action. Your horses have been attended to and your provisions re-stocked. Should you need weaponry or armour, visit the blacksmith." His eyes swept over Wezlan, Denavar, and Ashalea. "You may stay as long as you wish."

They dipped their heads in acknowledgement. With formalities over, Harvar beamed at them, raising his cup once again. "Enjoy our hospitality while you can. All of you may go. I'd like a word with my children."

The party excused themselves at once, Harvar's generals offering small bows to their chieftain, exiting without a word. Ashalea spied their faces as they left, all betraying nothing of their inner thoughts. She suspected more would be said behind closed doors, but of the three only Amira seemed openly against her lord's decision. What would become of that, she had no idea.

She cast a wondering glance over her shoulder at Shara, and the girl offered a small smile in response, but where her lips where genuine, her eyes strained. Whatever conversation lay ahead for her friend, Ashalea suspected it would be all but pleasant.

A Family Reunion

SHARA

THE SILVAREN FAMILY was not your average household of Everosians. The home had its luxuries, sure, but life growing up for Shara and Flynn was as alike to other children as dwarves to elves—as opposite as possible, with a high probability of brawls and backlashes. Instead of hugs and kisses, smiles and laughs, the twins were embraced with blades and bats, whimpers and groans.

Shiny toys and purebred ponies were replaced with shiny shurikens and purebred POMPs—what the twins referred to as Pompous, Obnoxious, Moronic, Pig-heads of society. Only these ones came with an order of execution to whatever crime they'd committed. Usually they revolved around assassination attempts of political ambassadors, the murder of someone who'd stolen their mistress, or something so trivial as an intense dislike for a fellow POMP.

It didn't matter what they had done, Shara and Flynn always did their duty. They never asked questions, never rebelled, never shirked their assignments. Weapons didn't wonder at life's complexities or want for better things; weapons were wielded to destroy, and that's just what the twins did.

Shara couldn't remember the last time they'd sat down together for a meal. Probably when they were little more than toddlers playing pretend with wooden sticks and pot lids, fighting battles as wild and wonderful as a child's mind can conjure. Back when her mother was still alive, she supposed, Goddess bless and keep her.

Her mother had died when they were young. A variety of the pox had taken her, along with a sizeable chunk of the village citizens. It hadn't mattered how much Shara had cried or prayed to any God or Goddess who'd listen. One day she was there, the next she was gone.

Her father had ordered the twins to say their goodbyes before the burning. '*The sickness cares only for the living,*' he had said. '*You are safe,*' he had said as they stood by her bedside, eyes wide and hearts thumping as they gazed upon her body.

Shara remembered her mother still. Blistered pimples all over her face, pustules angry and oozing, her skin reeking with the perfume of death and decay. Red welts had lined her arms and neck, furious lines clawed in the skin where her mother had suffered self-harm, attempting to scratch her sores.

She remembered her at her worst, forgot her at her best. There was a vague memory of long wavy hair, golden eyes, full bow lips that tilted up at the corners. But it was blurred, shrouded in a mist that never quite lifted.

Yes. That was the last time she'd seen her mother. And since that day, Shara had grown harder, stronger, less forgiving. Love was just a concept. An ideology for young women to gush over and romanticise

with their friends. Shara never had those. Never had the time, never wanted the burden. Her shadow had room only for one.

And as she sat here now, eating dinner with her father and brother, feeling as uncomfortable as ever, she realised just how isolated her life had become. What little love they'd really shared as a family. Her closest confidante had always been her brother, but now even that relationship felt as dead and gone as her dearly departed mother. She almost scoffed miserably at the thought.

"Daughter," Harvar smiled. "You do not break bread with us tonight? You haven't touched your meal."

His voice jolted her back to the living. She gave him a sideways glance before ripping a chunk of bread from the loaf and stuffing it into her mouth. She chewed viciously, paused to take a swig from her wine, and then swallowed both down her gullet with a loud gulp.

Look at him smiling, like all is well in the world. As if he's been the perfect father figure all my life. High and mighty and oh so lordly.

Harvar regarded her with amusement, and she felt Flynn's eyes burning holes into her head from across the table. She reached for the roast pheasant, tore its limb from the bird, sloshed it into gravy and then shredded the drumstick with her teeth, gnawing loudly.

She was angry. Unreasonably angry. Not-even-sure-why angry. Her father smiled broadly as if goading her on and she felt rather than saw Flynn stiffen across the table. She slammed her palms on the smooth marble, black as her mood.

"Why are we here, Father? What do you want?"

He regarded her with glee, lips curling in obvious amusement. "Can a parent not simply enjoy a meal with his children?"

"Said parent hasn't broken bread with his children since the day their mother burned from this world," she spat.

Flynn choked on his mouthful, a slight shake of his head a subtle

warning to stop.

Harvar's eyes clouded dangerously. "Careful, girl, don't forget your place."

"And where is that, Chieftain? The dirt has grown ever muddier of late. Where should your broken children kneel before your feet?"

"Shara ..." Flynn tried vainly, but she wasn't having any of it.

"Not once have you asked us how we're doing. Since I was trussed up like a limp doll for some puppeteer to string. Since Flynn was forced to do *his* will. We fight for you, kill for you, bleed for you ... and in the many years since our birth you only now sit down, and attempt to play pretend at happy families?"

"You are my heirs and next in line to lead our people. Happiness is inconsequential. Your lives belong to the shadows," Harvar barked.

"No longer," Shara snapped. "Your pretty wishes are wasted on me. A higher calling has demanded a change of course ... I'm a Guardian now, whether I want it or not."

"Your duty lies with your people!"

"And by becoming a Guardian I am serving them far better than I ever could," Shara argued. "The fabric of our world is stitched well beyond Shadowvale, Father. The darkness threatens all that we are. All that we could become. You said so yourself."

Harvar rose, slammed his own palms on the table. His chair fell violently to the ground and he growled in frustration. "Damn you, Shara, you're stubborn as a mule and cunning as a fox."

Shara scowled at him defiantly, and Flynn buried his face in his hands.

"Just like your mother," Harvar said softly.

The twins started at that. Not once since their mother's death had he mentioned her—spoke her name or recalled a memory. Shara raised a brow and Flynn cocked his head.

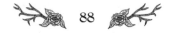

Harvar returned his chair to standing, leaning on it as heavily as the weight he carried in his chest.

"She was the light of my life. The brightness to my dark. Her smile could set fire to my skin, spark a joy in my bones. She had your smile, Shara, your wit. Your stubborn attitude and unwavering ambition." He smiled softly. "Everyone loved her. They flocked to her just as you shepherd the people, Flynn. She made them all laugh, led them without qualms or concern for herself."

He sighed, his smile crumbling into a thin line of weariness. "She gave the best of herself, passed it down to you kids. You remind me so much of her that it hurts just to look at you sometimes. My own flesh and blood." He shook his head. "Her death was a stone in my stomach, dragging me down day after day. We are Onyxonite. We are death's servants, and at her mercy do we carry out her bidding.

"It was easier to hold you at arm's length. To train you, hone you into weapons of the sharpest steel and intent. They say nothing is more painful than the death of your children, but after Olifia passed I just ..."

He turned away, his broad shoulders bunched and knotted as he faced his inner demons in the corner. Harvar's words stung Shara, her heart swelling in painful response. Tears burned in her eyes, threatening to spill down her face. The face that her father could barely stand to look at.

It all made sense now. Why he'd pushed them so hard. Why he was distant, aloof, uncaring and incompetent at being a father. Why he couldn't even look at them without seeing *her*.

"You dishonour her memory." The voice was so small, so quiet and cold, she barely recognised it.

Harvar slowly turned on his feet, shock carved into his face as he gazed upon his son. "What?"

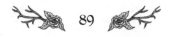

Disbelief drenched in pain. Four words that embedded themselves beneath their father's skin.

"You pushed us away because her absence is too unbearable for you. Because you can't stand to see a reflection—a small sliver—of what she once was. But in doing so you reject the best parts of her. The things that made her shine so bright. The things she loved more than anything in this world," Flynn said.

"She would've wanted you to guide us. To prepare us, sure, but with wisdom and understanding in your heart. You think love is a weakness, but I say it's our strongest asset." He looked to Shara, a sad smile on his face. "Love can break a man, make him bend over backwards, even destroy him. But it also has the power to bring him back to life. To make him find humanity once again."

Flynn's words were thick with emotion. Shara gaped at him in awe. She wasn't ready to tread through these waters. Not now. Not—

"I mean it Shara. Without you I wouldn't be here right now. I could still be a pawn for that *thing*. That *monster*."

"Flynn, don't," Shara warned. Her voice was deadly, her hackles raised in defence.

Harvar's dark eyes flitted between his children. The current in the air had changed from boiling to an icy freeze. He was no longer the subject of debate.

"I need to say this," Flynn pleaded. His chocolate brown eyes widened, face reflective of a deer before an arrow strikes true. "I can't ..." He stumbled, swallowing his words. "I can't apologise enough for what I did."

Images of her brother slicing her, cutting her flesh, carving her like roast meat, flashed before her eyes, as blinding as the sun. Phantom pains scorched her body, her scars suddenly itching, her hollowness opening wider as a chasm of fear re-opened inside.

"I'm so sorry, Shara. I'm so sorry for what I did." Flynn broke down, shudders racking his body, tears leaking from those eyes.

She stared at him, her breaths coming in ragged gasps, renewed anger bubbling to the surface in blood thick with rage. There was no leashing these emotions. Not today.

"Stop! Just stop, Flynn! I can't tell you it's okay. I can't tell you I forgive you. I'm—" She pulled at the ends of her hair before clenching her fists into tight balls. She closed her eyes, still seeing the pain flashing before her eyes. "I am broken!"

Harvar watched on in silence, allowing his children the space they needed to work it out.

Shara opened her eyes accusingly, golden fury beating into melting chocolate brown. "I am plagued with the memory of it. Every night you're in my dreams, torturing me, cutting me open, always ignorant of my pleas, always careless to my screams. I see the shadow in your eyes still. I see ... I see ..."

Her gasps merged into heavy sobs, uninvited tears splattering on olive skin. She despised crying. Anger was always a sharper, more reliable tool to wield. So, she did what Shara always did when she felt cornered. When she felt trapped.

Rising from the chair she grabbed the latticed steel at the back and hurled it at the wall with a scream. Flynn's face crumpled in remorse, and after rising he reached out a tender hand, placing it on her shoulder.

The contact was too much. A bloodcurdling cry of rage escaped her lips and she grasped his forearm, bent double and pulled him over her back, driving him to the ground with such force the breath whooshed from his lungs.

Snarling, she knelt over his body and began pummelling, mashing her fists into a bloodied mess as they cracked his cheeks, split his lip, twisted his nose as a sickening snap clicked in the static air.

And Harvar looked on, watching, waiting, observing, making no move to hold her back or stand in the way, always careful and calculating.

Exhausted, Shara paused her flurry just long enough to utter two words. "Fight back," she spat. No response.

Punch, punch, punch.

Flynn lay there, took every blow, and not once did he raise a hand, cry out in supplication or attempt to block her fist. His face was pulp made into wine juice, the liquid flowing freely from his wounds to begin pooling beside his skull.

"Fight back!" She choked. A soft sob. A keening as she released all her pain, all her regrets, all her suffering into the meat of this man she called brother. And as she let fly her last half-hearted blows she sank into a crumpled heap on his chest, body trembling with pain, with fear, with sorrow.

Tentatively, he placed one hand on her back, left it there gingerly, awaiting permission, letting her know that it was okay. That everything was going to be all right.

Shara buried her face in his chest, sobbing freely now. After all, there were quite a few years of tears gone unshed. Flynn placed both arms around her, and after a time, when Shara had released all she had left to give, she lifted her head, peered into those chocolate brown eyes.

There wasn't much left to look at. Her brother was black and blue and mush all over, blood staining the planes of his cheeks. A garish portrait drawn from a not so talented artist. But there ... A crooked smile to match a crooked nose.

And in that smile that touched the light of his eyes, Shara saw only her brother staring back at her. The man she had always relied

on, could always rely on. The one who had her back, who'd fight, bleed, kill, for her. The twin who would always be by her side.

And for a moment she thought, maybe, just maybe, everything was going to be all right.

More groans. More gurgles. This time from a very black and blue and mushed all over, but still very much alive, Flynn Silvaren. Shara had done a number on him to be sure. One of his eyes glimmered from his purpled face, the other was glued shut and swollen. He was beaten to what some would refer to as *'within an inch of his life'*.

That wasn't really true for Onyxonites though. Most would call it the result of a friendly argument. A tiff. A small disagreement dealt with in true Onyxonite style. A brawl, followed by some banter, followed by a good and solid shot to warm one's innards. And if the lips didn't sting from the cracks, if the liquor didn't burn down the throat, well, you're simply just not doing it right.

And so, as the family sat at the table in a more civilised manner—civilised being a widely debatable term to describe the Silvaren family—Shara tilted her head and downed the shot as duty demanded. Naturally, Flynn's lips stung at the cracks, his throat burned at the downing, and his innards felt worse the wear. All followed by that crooked smile to match the crooked nose.

They downed another for good measure and looked to their chieftain expectantly.

"Now that you've made amends and," he raised a brow, "come to an accord of sorts, I hope?" Harvar let his question waver in the air. The twins glanced at each other, shrugged, and returned their sights to their father.

Shara knew this was just the start of her healing process, of course. A brawl could only do so much for one's state of mind. But she had a feeling that things were about to change. She just didn't know how. And that's where her father came in.

Harvar sighed. Deep. Long. And then a big breath before the exhale. "You were right. I pushed you away. I hardened your bodies, your minds, I created the perfect warriors, the perfect Shadowvale stock. I put duty first, the cause, our way of life. But in doing so I failed you as a father. She wouldn't have wanted that."

Shara stared at him hard. "All Flynn and I had was each other. Thank the Gods or things might have been quite different. You pushed us beyond our limits, you starved us for days, tortured us, listened with deaf ears to the screams of your flesh and blood. What kind of a man ... what kind of a *father* does that?"

Harvar smiled, his eyes remaining stern. "Do you really blame me? Your training was an escape from your mother's death—not just for me, but for both of you. I couldn't give leniency to those next in line to take my place. What would our soldiers say if you were bred weak? If you crowed at the first sign of pain, if you bowed to the will of steel? I made you strong, capable, smart. Had I not trained you as I did, perhaps neither of you would be standing here today."

Sensibility sunk into her bloodstream and she wilted ever so slightly. His words were an injection of truth swimming through her veins, sparking her nerves. She looked at her brother, his brows frowning as he too, mulled over this acknowledgement.

Harvar was right. Without their training, she would likely be dead. Without Flynn's willpower, he might still be a pawn for the darkness. She was a weapon. One of the best. Perhaps *the* best amongst their flock. Would she be a Guardian had she not honed her body and skills to deadly precision? Had she not learnt to be cunning? To be strategic, agile, quick-thinking in battle?

Could she really hate her father for doing what was needed? For creating her into the woman she was meant to be? Perhaps even he had little choice when it came to picking cards from destiny's collection.

"Father," she began, at a loss to find the right words. "You did what you thought you must, and whether it was the right path to take, perhaps we'll never know. But we're here now. All of us. Your honesty today is worth more than you could know ... and it damned well took you long enough to say ... but I will admit that we wouldn't be here without our training."

She took a deep shaky breath and swallowed her pain. "We'll never be a normal family. A small part of me thinks we'll always be broken. But we must try. For *her*. Blood of my blood, honour thy name."

Her family replied as one, "Blood of my blood, honour thy name."

Harvar reached a calloused hand out and placed it upon her own. He gave her knuckles a light squeeze, looking to his son in earnest. "Can you forgive an old man for his wrongs?"

Shara glanced at Flynn, their eyes met, and unspoken words passed between them before they looked upon their father, their chieftain, their blood.

"I can accept an old man for his rights," Flynn said.

"Let the past remain buried. 'Tis the present that paves our future," Shara added.

Harvar beckoned for his children to stand, ushering them close with open palms. His hands found their shoulders and he tugged them into a tight bear hug, the ferocity of his squeeze saying more than words ever could. The first hug they'd shared as a family in years. The first step to amends.

"You're not about to go soft on us are you, Da?" Shara mumbled

into her father's shoulder.

A booming laugh escaped Harvar's lips, his beard mussing the top of her head. "I could grind your bones to butter my bread without batting an eyelid."

"Better be the best baked loaf in all of Everosia," Flynn said with a muffled voice beneath Harvar's meaty arm. He wrestled his way out, peeking at Shara with one open eye.

Shara laughed, gripping her family tighter. Soft or hard, crushed bones or not, she didn't care. About anything. All that mattered was this moment. Every daughter's dream, just to be loved, to be held, to make her parent proud.

She wished it could last forever, but it was gone in an instant. They pulled apart, Flynn and Harvar sharing a few friendly fist bumps, and a couple of pained winces on Flynn's behalf.

The young serving girl from before dashed into the room with another tray of wine goblets, depositing one each in front of the family. Her big doe eyes widened when she spied Flynn, momentary confusion flitting across her face as she realised his beating had taken place sometime between her last departure and now.

He winked at her with his good eye, and her cheeks flamed, that shy smile spreading across her face. She noticed the others staring and averted her eyes before uttering a small squeak of "my lord" and running from the room.

Shara raised a comical brow at her brother. "Ever the charmer I see?"

Shrugging, he grinned wolfishly before taking a long draught from his cup. "As eventful as tonight has been, I'm assuming you didn't bid us eat with you for the pleasure of our company?"

Shara's face swivelled to Harvar. She settled back in her steel chair, threw both boots onto the table and swirled her goblet lazily in

one hand.

This should be interesting.

Her father frowned at the dirt that crumbled from her boots onto the war table, but he said nothing. His face ironed out; any hint of humour died in his eyes as the demeanour of the chieftain returned.

"Recent events have had me thinking long and hard about the future of Shadowvale," he said slowly.

"Look out," Shara smirked, "there's a danger in itself."

Flynn sniggered in response, but the pair quickly quieted at the hard glare from their father.

"With the recent battle at Renlock, the trials you've both been through, I've realised that we don't have the luxury of time to let nature take its course. There are no promises of tomorrow in this world. Just the whisper of war. Blood. Death. It lingers on the horizon."

"And that's different to any other day in the life of an Onyxonite?" Shara said.

Harvar shook his head. "Contracts come at the price of one. War risks the lives of many. The balance shifts, the scales weigh heavier for one side. We will fight. And many will die."

Flynn gazed at his lord warily, dark eyes narrowing. "What are you saying, Father?"

"I may not survive the battles to come, and if I should fall, I need assurances that my affairs are in order. That my line will come to fruition."

Shara considered his words, realisation dawning as she sipped at her wine. It sounded suspiciously like—

"It is time for a new lord of Shadowvale. It is time for you, Flynn Silvaren of the Onyxonites, to take your place as chieftain."

Shara spat her wine all over Flynn's face, the liquid covering his skin in a fresh coat of blood-red.

"Oh shit."

A Darkness was Born

Ashalea

THE FOREST HERE WAS NOT LIKE HOME. The trees stood protective and defiant, blackened trunks steadfast in the soil, spindly fingers clutching towards the heavens as if seeking brighter days. There was a silence to Shadowvale that hung heavy in the air, as though even the animals knew that death waited in dark corners.

The only sound breaking the eerie stillness was the horses' hooves crunching on fallen leaves, and the soft whispers of Shara and Denavar as they plotted together in the rear flank. Ashalea and Wezlan rode side by side in comfortable silence, and a sneaky glance at an absent hand stroking his beard told her he was deep in thought.

Ashalea smiled at the comforting sway of Kaylin beneath her and gave him a gentle scratch behind the ears. He nickered in response; it was his favourite spot after all. The duo had barely spoken since the nightmare at Renlock but Ashalea had been practising her Magicka, pushing the boundaries of her mental tether and reaching out to woodland creatures and unassuming humans alike.

The horse, it seemed, shared the same sentiments as Ashalea about the wooded expanse. He longed for bright skies and open fields, where strange men and women didn't hide amongst the canopies.

Ashalea was well aware sentries laid in wait within the treetops, watchful eyes bearing down on their backs. Had she cared to spy them out, she was sure her elvish eyes could without qualms. Jeelu had certainly made good on his promise to double the perimeter guards. But none of that mattered. Her mind was on other things this day.

On the outskirts of this forest, due east of Shadowvale, the peaks of the Diodon Mountains loomed in the distance, and so too did their quest. Kalanor's Klan was the next piece of the puzzle, their solution to finding the next Guardian.

"Just two left," she whispered.

Wezlan's face snapped to attention as he rode beside her, his staff emitting a familiar jade green glow under the darkened canopies. "Two Guardians to go, but a whole lot of work yet to be done," he said.

Ashalea studied the old man beside her. His long white beard was growing ever wilder of late, and the frown lines had etched deeper into his tanned, weathered skin. His back no longer defied gravity and the demands of old age, and Goddesses, did he look old. Even his customary burnt orange robe had seen better days, but still his eyes twinkled with a cheekiness that none other than Wezlan could possess, and she smiled sadly.

He reached over the divide between their horses and gently took her hand, patting it knowingly. "My bones still weather change, my dear. They've grown accustomed to comforts not found in dark forests or bumpy roads, but they carry me on regardless."

Ashalea's green eyes dove into the calm grey seas of his and she wanted so badly to tell him what happened the other day. To tell him about the visions and the strange voice that had spoken to her. It was dangerous to keep it to herself. But still she could not bear the scrutiny of the others. Even now she sensed Denavar's eyes burning into her back.

She sighed, and Wezlan cocked his head. "What ails you, my dear?"

Ashalea snorted. "Where to start?"

He peered at her beneath bushy brows. "I find the beginning is always a most reasonable choice."

She fidgeted with the reins, thumbing the leather as she considered. "I don't know who I am anymore. I feel changed, and not necessarily for the better."

"Ah. But the world will do that to a person. You are no longer a girl, Ashalea. You are a woman, realising her dreams, fighting for a greater purpose. The seasons change, and so do we."

Ashalea sighed. "There is a natural course to the world around us. It makes sense. It's reliable. But my life feels scattered, unsteady. I don't know ... I don't know what I want anymore. What my purpose is."

Wezlan nodded. "Whether it be the will of the Gods and Goddesses, whether it's a twist of fate, you have been set on a path that was not your choosing. Since the beginning, you were made for a greater purpose, and the price of this calling has been steep."

Ashalea frowned. "Destiny has a funny way of showing me the path. My history is steeped in blood. Wherever I go, bad things follow. I'm afraid for what's to come. I'm afraid the sum of this life is more than I can pay. It seemed much simpler when it was just me and *him*, and the world was not part of the equation."

"Destiny is a cruel mistress, Ashalea, but there is no doubt in my heart that you were meant to be the one to put an end to the darkness, to restore peace to our world and protect the Gates of the Grove. There will always be casualties. It is unavoidable."

"And if the cost of being a Guardian is more than I can give? If the casualty in this scenario is me?"

He stared at her sternly, a frown on his face. "I would never let that happen. I have watched over you since you were but a babe, squalling in your mother's arms. You are like a daughter to me, Ashalea, and vengeance or not, I vowed to protect you. I always will."

A silence hung between them, thick and foggy and full of unpleasant thoughts.

"But," Wezlan continued cheerfully, "if you believed, and I mean truly believed, that you couldn't shoulder this burden, that you weren't willing to try, I don't think we'd be having this conversation."

She raised a brow, crinkling her nose. "You're really not bothered by anything are you?"

"What will be, will be. Life has a way of sorting itself out. All we can do is try to make sense of it and be at peace with our choices. I've lived too long to maintain regrets or to harbour sorrow. That ship has long since sailed. Instead, I'll tackle every obstacle that lies in our path. In *your* path."

Ashalea grinned. "You'd take on a thousand Wyrm-weirs if it meant saving me."

Her old mentor shrugged. "Oh, I don't know if you're worth *that* much effort ..."

Ashalea's brows shot sky high and an affronted 'o' formed on her lips.

A guffaw. "I'd give it my best shot."

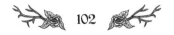

She punched him playfully before her face smoothed out, the hard lines returning. "I mean it though Wezlan ... What if we don't all survive this? I have more to lose now."

He smiled knowingly, looked behind them to the elf and assassin whose conversation now involved decorative gestures and animated voices. Wezlan's gaze fell pointedly on Denavar, a softness on his face as he turned back to his ward.

"You have more to fight for. Love is a powerful tool Ashalea. Use it."

"You don't disapprove?"

Wezlan sighed. "You never had the luxury of a normal childhood. Yours was a life of solitude and simplicity. No friendships, no romances, no harmless dillies in dark corners or wild romps in—"

"Okay, okay!" She stretched a palm out, freckles puckering on her nose.

"My point is you're still learning," he said. "Still discovering parts of yourself. Your friendship with Shara, your bond with Denavar, it shapes you into something new. Love and loyalty are gifts. And those two are wrapped better than any you're likely to find."

Ashalea pursed her lips in amusement. "So, you approve a murderer as my closest friend and a lady's man as my lover?"

"*Do* you love him?"

Ashalea frowned, twirling a strand of hair in one hand as she considered his question. Her brain told her it was stupid to fall for someone so easily, to give in to the charms, free smiles and the fun of it all, but she felt connected to Denavar on a level that defied all reason. At his voice she felt her soul light up with happiness, and his touch would send her heart pounding. Yes. She loved this man with all she had.

She met Wezlan's eyes and offered a determined nod.

"And he loves you?"

That caught her off guard. Denavar had said so many times, but was it sincere? A ruse he said to all his conquests?

Logic waggled a finger at insecurity and told it to crawl back to its corner. No. There was a softness to Denavar that he shared only with her. A deep sincerity, a passion, a promise. When he said he loved her, that he'd die for her, everything else melted into nothing. More than that, their connection was ... inexplicable. More than a feeling, a want or a need. Like one without the other just simply wasn't meant to be.

She nodded almost to herself, smiling as she glanced over her shoulder at her lover, her bonded, her mate. His grin dazzled in the rare sun's ray that crept through the trees, his laughter bouncing off the trunks, transforming the dark and dreary woods. A longing filled her heart, an aching at how perfect he was. Denavar accepted all her flaws. No, didn't just accept them, he cherished them. *Her.*

When she turned around, she found Wezlan staring at her fondly, his grey eyes glittering with that all-knowing look. He knew the way Ashalea and Denavar felt about each other—perhaps could feel the change in the current when the pair were together. Nothing escaped Wezlan. Nothing.

Ashalea beamed at him. "You already know, you wily fox."

Wezlan chuckled. "Naturally. And in answer to your question? Wholeheartedly."

They simultaneously settled back in their saddles with a contended sigh. Some things were right in the world at least. There was still the matter of her visions, but for now she was happy to shove those thoughts into the pit of her mind. They'd no doubt surface later, put on a theatrical show, cause some new chaos with a flourish and a dance.

She caught his eyes back on her, narrowed and side-glancing.

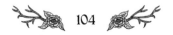

"Whaaaaat?"

Harrumph. "I know you're hiding something from me, Ashalea. But you *will* tell me when you're ready, hmm?"

Wily fox indeed.

"You know I'm always honest with you Wezlan. I just need to sort some things out on my own first." She smoothed out her hair, gave Kaylin another scratch behind the ears. "I can't rely on everyone else to clean up my messes."

Wezlan pulled a flask from beneath his robes and took a noisy slurp, red dregs dribbling into his beard. "And just how messy are we talking?"

Ashalea held out an expectant hand, grabbing the canteen as it was deposited in her palm. She took a long drink, surprised by the taste of a smooth vintage red, a touch of sandalwood lingering on her tongue.

"Delicious." She smacked her lips and tossed the flask back. She contemplated his question, gestured at the flask in his hands. "Well, I'm like a fine wine. I get better with age, but I'll be damned if the cork wasn't lacquered in poison and perfumed in perplexity. What comes once I'm opened is as good a guess as any."

Wezlan stroked his beard. "Basically, you're referring to yourself as damaged goods. And once you reach the point of no return ... good luck to the poor sod who takes a whiff and drinks 'til he's at death's door?"

Ashalea shrugged. "Basically. I'm no good, Wezlan. I might fool others at first glance but once you get a taste there's bound to be some disgruntled palettes and a good chance of a tummy ache." She frowned. "People get hurt around me. Die around me. I'm tainted, Wezlan. There's some serious taintage happening here."

Wezlan looked at her blankly. "Taintage? You do realise there's no language on Everosia wherein that's a word."

She flapped a hand back and forth. "Oh, sod off. You know what I mean."

A few disgruntled mumbles escaped his lips and he flashed her a glance that promised a 'to-be-continued' later. But he let the matter lie.

They sat in comfortable quiet for a time, both left to their own thoughts. Ashalea eyed off the trees in contemplation. Would that she could join them. Forget the worries of the world and stand in ignorant bliss to the passing of time and the troubles of men. Her eyes followed their spindly fingers as they clawed at the sky above.

Perhaps not. Perhaps being lost in shadow, just a hands-breadth away from light and fresh air and freedom was no fate at all. She wouldn't wish that on anyone. She twisted in her seat to peek at her comrades.

Denavar was talking animatedly, a joke involving a beggar, a strumpet, and a tavern full of dwarves drifting on the still air. Shara burst out laughing, white teeth positively beaming as she shook her glossy hair. Ashalea hadn't seen her look so free in some time. The hollows under the eyes were still there, the thinness, the burdens she carried, but there was a fire in her eyes. A spark that burned as melted gold.

Whatever had come to pass between Shara and her family, she was the better for it. Flynn was noticeably absent from her side, but perhaps that was a good thing. After it had been officially announced her brother was to be the next chieftain, he had declared his place was in Shadowvale, preparing for days to come.

She remembered Shara's face had fallen at that, if only for a second. Ashalea knew as well as the twins did that their destinies lay at a crossroads. The proverbial fork in the road meant it would be some time before they met again, and circumstances were unlikely to be good.

Shara was a Guardian now, her brother, the next in line to become lord of Shadowvale. Ashalea shook her head. Just reunited, now dearly departed. *Destiny is a cruel mistress.* Still, she'd be lying if she didn't admit how relieved she was that Shara was continuing this journey. The assassin was resourceful, cunning, and damned near unstoppable with a blade. And she was Ashalea's friend. These days that seemed to count more than anything else.

***

Smoky tendrils wrapped around her form, caressing and clutching at her shoulders. A voice, crooning in her ear, whispering of death and decay and sweet, blissful release. There was no web this time, no cocoon to trap her in place.

Only poison. Dripping from a malevolent tongue, the entity's voice hypnotic, its words compelling. It told her to forgive Crinos, to see reason in his purpose, to forget the past and embrace the future. A new future forged from the blood of the weak and sharpened with the will of the strong.

Violent flashes of innocents dying swam before Ashalea's eyes—of the world on fire; of a darkness so impenetrable it blocked out the sun and left the land in perpetual shadow. She groaned, twisting and turning, pale beads of sweat glistening upon her brow, breaths coming in short gasps.

She was falling into the abyss, clawing at the darkened sky, reaching with strained fingers at the full moon as it smiled upon her. And then it too was burning. Eating its own immolation, spinning and spinning, blinding and oh so bright until nought but a crescent remained.

An image of Crinos's smug face crossed her vision, his crescent moon scar burning a brand into her mind's eye. She could feel his breath on her cheek, his lips rushing frigid air, whispering until her skin crawled. The world tumbled like sand through an hourglass, and she found herself face to face with him, silver eyes glinting dangerously as he regarded her.

"Brother," she hissed.

The phantom smiled with filed teeth, blinked, and regarded her with eyes red as blood. "Join me, Ashalea. Join me and watch as the world bows before us."

With a swish of his hand she was no longer falling, stretching, twisting. Instead she stood beside him upon a clifftop, and below, all the races of Everosia knelt before them. A vast, snaking cloud that blotted out the horizon. Her pulse quickened and her stomach churned at the same time. Such was the extent of their power.

All were chained. All were suffering. Elves, humans, dwarves, and Diodonians alike. Each time her gaze landed on those who looked up in anguish, her heart broke a thousand times over again, and the small sliver of conscience that remained in her mind stepped forward and roared to be obeyed.

Ashalea turned to face the creature at her side.

"This is wrong, Crinos, so very wrong," she said softly. "If this is the world you imagine, the world you seek to rule, then I pity you. I pity the black hole where your heart used to be."

Rage flickered as his eyes turned quicksilver. "This is the power of a king." He gestured to the countless numbers before them. "This is the power of the Gods."

She shook her head. "And when you're seated on your throne, when all are enslaved and bound to your will, what then? When

Everosia falls to decay and ruination? When nothing and no one is left but you?"

He sneered at her. "Then I will stake my claim in the nether realm, contest with the Gods. I will seek out and conquer the other dimensions. I will watch them all burn."

Her heart registered countless emotions in that moment. From disgust and rage, to pity and pain. But all became a blur as she examined his face and landed on sorrow.

"What happened to shape you into such cruelty? What turned you into a tyrant so intent on crushing hope from the souls of this world?"

For the briefest moment she saw a flicker of emotion cloud his eyes, and Ashalea latched on. She didn't know how, but she caught the thread of feeling and dove into it, tugging the line until she landed in a vision. Nay, a memory.

A little boy with tousled hair of ashen silver and joyful grey eyes squinted with mirth as he ran through meadows of lush green, dotted with wildflowers and covered in scores of golden fireflies. It was one of the most beautiful sights she'd ever laid eyes on. A woman's voice called, pretty as a nightingale. The owner chased Crinos through the grasses, both laughing as she scooped him up and they collapsed in a heap.

Ashalea craned her neck, straining her eyes to see the stranger's face, but the vision blurred, re-focused to find the boy again. He was a few years older, backed up against a stone pillar as he was confronted by others of his age. They circled him, voices low and menacing. The tallest of the group swung a punch at Crinos, hitting the lad square in the jaw, and he fell, heavy as a sack of bricks to the ground. The others began punching, kicking, wailing on the youngster until he was left bruised and bloodied and unconscious to the world.

"Stop," Ashalea called, but her voice carried no sound.

Now she was standing before two thrones beneath a bed of stars, its stone surface a rippled marble of black and white. A magnificent archway of carved stone curved elegantly above them. Two fountains in the shape of crescent moons flowed gently on either side of the thrones, trickling down tunnels to rest in two pools that ran the length of the dais.

The boy was a strapping lad now, kneeling before a king and queen, posture rigid and fingers coiled into fists. The faces of his rulers were blurred, fuzzy, hidden from Ashalea's view.

"It's time you took responsibility Crinos," reprimanded a deep baritone voice. "Enough fights, enough parlour tricks. The people whisper about your deeds. You can't treat the common folk like this."

"It's not my fault!" the boy returned. "I never start it. They're lying!"

The conversation grew softer, as though the vision was tampered with, but a few words from the king trickled to her ears. "*Cruel … spiteful … strange …*"

And then soft counters from a woman. "*Just a boy … not his fault … so strong …*"

The world shifted focus again, and this time Ashalea stood within a place she recognised. A circular room bereft of its usual table and uncomfortable chairs, six faces looming above a young man with cropped silver hair, his head bowed in reverence.

She circled the room, studying the men and women present until she found herself rooted to the spot in shock. A mature man with a long grey beard gazed with stern grey eyes at the disciple before him, just a hint of remorse buried within.

"Wezlan," she cried, but her mentor neither saw nor heard Ashalea.

Past Wezlan cleared his throat and the lad awaiting judgement puffed his chest, pride etched across his features. Wezlan shared a quick glance with the councillors before taking a deep breath.

"The Divine Six and I regret to inform that you will not be continuing your studies as a wizard."

The lad's smile faltered, and confusion crossed his face. "Wh– Why? I exceeded all the tests. I–" The young man fumbled, glancing at the wizards with dismay.

Wezlan assessed him gravely. "All but one, young Crinos. You failed the fifth test of Magicka. We examined the properties of your soul–the balance of light and dark, the essence of good and evil–and we found the former wanting."

Ashalea's mentor peered at Crinos with a strange expression on his face: a mixture of awe, concern and ... ever so slight ... fear.

"By Academy law, those who are judged imbalanced of heart and mind are therefore unable to become a wizard. It is our sacred duty to ensure that power is protected from those who would abuse it." Wezlan leaned closer to the elf. "There is a darkness inside you, son, a cloudiness that seems unwilling and unable to lift."

Crinos's eyes narrowed and his body shook to bursting. "What kind of stupid test judges a man like so?" he yelled bitterly. "How is anyone expected to maintain a perfect balance of body and mind?"

Wezlan offered a sad smile. "It is a rare thing to be sure, hence why there are so few wizards who have walked the halls of our great, illustrious Academy. Some of the greatest mages have been turned away from this council for the very same reason."

Crinos's eyes flicked from wizard to wizard, resting on Wezlan's face, his gaze imploring. "Please," he said, desperation creeping into his tone. "This is all I've trained for. If I return home with this news my parents ... I ... I don't know what will become of me."

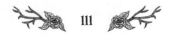

Wezlan crossed the floor and rested a hand upon the lad's shoulder. "I am sorry, Crinos, but the law is absolute. You may continue your studies in Renlock as a mage, or you may return home to the Meadows with an exceptional reference written by my own hand. But sadly, you will never be a wizard."

Wezlan patted his shoulder one last time, nodded to his fellow councilmen and women, and the party departed, leaving Ashalea alone with her then younger brother.

The man collapsed, knees hitting the polished tiles with a thud. Silent tears trickled down his smooth alabaster skin. His silver eyes raised to the heavens as if beseeching someone— anyone—for comfort. But he was utterly alone, unaware of the ghost who was visiting his memory.

Her heart ached for him. He was still but a boy, misunderstood, mistrusted, abused, wanting nothing more than to make something of himself and make his parents proud in the process.

He was a pariah, just like she was for most of her life. Sad, lonely, friendless. She knew what that was like. But she also couldn't forget who made it that way. Crinos.

She gazed at him one last time and saw that angelic face harden into resolve. Saw Crinos's fingers curl into fists, the curve of his lips twist into a sneer, the mysterious eyes take on an expression she fully recognised in the present day.

Rage.

Those eyes promised a reckoning. And just as the vision began to fade, she saw it flash in those silver orbs ever so quick.

Red.

Deep and dark as blood.

Thick and unfeeling.

Hard and unforgiving.

And thus, the darkness was born.

◆◆ ● ◆◆

She started awake with a gasp, lurching upwards and clutching at the heart threatening to rip free from her breast. It was there again, in her dreams, only this time the voice had taken shape. This time she'd seen glimpses of a man unknown to her. When Crinos was still a person who breathed, and bled, and *felt* as she did.

Ashalea peered at the campfire as it crackled lazily in the centre of their bedrolls. She glanced at her friends, checking to see if anyone was awake. Wezlan's soft snores competed with the hiss and spit of the fire, Shara was sprawled face first into her blanket, and Denavar lay silently next to her, the only signs of life the steady rise and fall of his shoulder as he lay on his side.

She exhaled a sigh of relief. Her secret was safe for another day. Ashalea knew it was stupid, risky—even dangerous—but the she-elf didn't know what the visions meant, and for now they had proved harmless enough. Perhaps they would even reveal something useful about Crinos's past that could help their quest.

But how am I seeing them at all? It doesn't make sense unless ... Unless a connection has been established.

Her body stilled, blood running cold at the thought. Ashalea looked at her palms and considered her recent loss of Magicka. Ever since she'd used that light power to blast the darkness off the tower her powers of healing and of light had all but vanished.

Was it possible that when she'd struck him a transferal of sorts had occurred?

Ashalea sighed. Theories and unanswered questions. Her life was full of them. She lay back in her bedroll, shivering from the sweat

that had cooled over her body. Tossing her silver braid out of her face, clever fingers coiled it to rest in a messy knot above her head.

Gazing at the dark canopy overhead, she fancied the moon shining on the other side. Big and bright and mischievous in the night sky. They still had a day's travel before they escaped the confines of Shadowvale, and regardless of her love for nature, of her affinity with it as an elf, she would soon be glad to be rid of the dense, dark forest.

She longed to see her old tree again, its bough wide and inviting, its canopy full of light and the songs of blissful birds. She longed to sit in front of the fire and exchange pleasantries with her old mentor, a bowl of vegetable soup in hand, a book in the other. Hell, she'd even be happy to drape herself over laborious scrolls of history and language under the watchful—and somewhat scrutinising—eyes of Wezlan.

But all that would wait. Perhaps for an eternity until the darkness was stopped. Until Everosia was saved. But for now, she could dream.

And dream she did. Of mysterious glades dotted with wildflowers, tall grasses, endless meadows, and a woman's voice that sounded as hauntingly beautiful as a nightingale.

Little did the she-elf know, now buried in dreams of a better nature, that there was one who did lie awake, witness to her sweat and cries and nightmares from before. He lay on his side, the soft breaths heaving his shoulders up and down. His icy blue eyes were wide with worry, brows furrowed, lips curved into a frown. And the elf prayed to all the Gods who'd listen that his love, his bonded, his mate, would be all right.

10

To Deserts and Danger

ASHALEA

THE KISS OF SUNLIGHT ON HER SKIN had never felt so good. Ashalea revelled in its warm glow, soaking in its glory as she breathed in fresh air. The trees of Shadowvale stood vigilantly behind her, their curling branches and twisted fingers reaching out as if saying a sombre farewell.

It had only been a two-day trek winding through the trunks of the dark forest, but she, Wezlan and Denavar all sighed in collective relief to be under a blue sky once again. The denseness of that place had felt insufferable, clutching their shoulders as if seeking to drag them farther into its depths.

With the forest now behind her, the peaks of Diodon Mountains loomed in front, guarding the passage to the east. Dusty red and rich brown in colour, they stretched in jagged lines for what seemed an

eternity. The terrain would be changing soon, shifting into the rise and fall of rock and stone. Ashalea's elf eyes could make out the rare tree in the distance. Swollen trunks with bare branches that hung defeatedly.

She glanced at the sun burning above and gritted her teeth at what she knew was coming. It was autumn, and despite the cooler temperatures, Ashalea knew the Diodonian desert would be sweltering, dry, and deadly. Already the sunlight held a striking heat as it beat down upon their backs. Unusual for this time of year. Pleasant enough at first, but she was sure a few hours spent under its rays and she would feel differently.

"How many days until we reach the pass, Wezlan?"

She reached into her saddlebags, checked their water supply. Their provisions had been well stocked in Shadowvale, but who knew how long it would last in the wastelands beyond. They could survive without food for a time, but water would be a precious commodity, and in a place so dry and brittle, conjuring it would be no easy feat.

The wizard squinted at the expanse of green that slowly relented to deep browns, and beyond that, sandy reds. He clucked his tongue to the roof of his mouth, muttering to himself as he pulled out a crumpled map from within his robes.

What else the old man stored in there, Ashalea could only guess at.

"It will be a two-day ride at a steady pace. Less if we pushed the horses faster, but once we reach the foothills of Hallow's Pass, the terrain will grow trickier to traverse. I'm afraid beyond that, we'll have to go on foot."

"What?" Shara said indignantly. "You want me to trudge through the desert? Don't you think that will make things considerably slower?"

Wezlan's lips curled in amusement. "The desert heat is arid,

unforgiving. The horses will have no food source, no water. And I doubt they're interested in hauling your arse around, much less roaming the wastes."

Kaylin nickered and Lerian snorted as if in agreement.

A few unintelligible grumbles came from Shara's direction. "They'd make good meat though ..."

Ashalea laughed and gave her mount a reassuring pat. "Don't worry, boy, I wouldn't risk you on some silly trek through the sand. That mean old assassin can get her fill elsewhere."

Shara rolled her eyes. "What about our belongings then? Where will the horses go?"

"Anything that isn't essential we'll leave with the horses," Wezlan said. "I have a contact in Galanor. She'll board them until we return."

"*If* we return," Denavar said with a smirk. "The desert may keep us captive yet."

"Oh aye," Shara said with a roll of her eyes. "Our bones would make a fine prize for the Ruins."

Wezlan frowned. "Let's hope we needn't stray so far. Madoc Ruins is a desolate place. It was once a city amongst the sand, flourishing, peaceful, an architectural wonder for its time. But it was coveted by those who lived there, kept hidden from the world and those who would seek to claim its riches as their own. It was a city of men, and it was men who brought about its destruction."

The old man paused to take a sip from his flask, and Shara shuffled in her seat impatiently.

"And?" the girl demanded. "What happened?"

Wezlan chuckled. "The city's elite maintained a natural divide of factions: the politicians, power hungry and fighting for seats that would sway the minds of sheep; the mages, sacrilegious folk with silvered tongues and cheap tricks to gain their favour; the gangs, well fed and fattened from the coin of their opposing factions' pockets. Then there was the king. A boy of no more than twelve, his parents never returned from a diplomatic voyage across the maiden seas to the east, and thus, he was left in a den of snakes. Not two moons later he was found with his face in a bowl of evening meal."

"They murdered a boy king?" Ashalea said, horror plastered on her face.

Wezlan nodded. "Poisoned by his own advisors no doubt, or someone they'd paid to do it."

Denavar peered at him thoughtfully. "Who ascended the throne?"

Wezlan lifted a brow. "No one, it turns out." At his companions' dumbfounded stares and slack jaws, he laughed grimly. "The city was torn to shreds from the inside out. War erupted amongst the factions. Murder and larceny increased tenfold, bloodbaths spilled to the streets and the townspeople rioted at the murder of their monarch."

Ashalea shook her head in sadness. "Nothing brings out one's true nature more than the allure of greed and lust for power."

"Ain't that the truth," Denavar said. "But how did the city fall?"

The wizard glanced at Denavar thoughtfully, eyes squinting in the midday sun. "After the city was overrun with blood and betrayal, the mages sought to cast a spell that would sink the lower levels of the city beneath the sands. Ultimately, their hunger for power was what doomed them all. They could not control the scale of their Magicka, and their spell did as they bid and more—burying the entire city, drowning all inhabitants in quicksand."

Shara snorted, tossing her raven locks about her shoulders. "The irony of it."

Denavar's shoulders slumped. "All Magicka has a price."

"Aye. And pay the price they did," Wezlan said. "Let that be a lesson to the pair of you," he nodded at Ashalea and Denavar. "Know

your limits. Don't squander your skills, and always, always be prepared to pay the cost."

———————◆◆●◆◆———————

The mouth of Hallow's Pass yawned before them, its teeth filed to sharp points as they rose in staggered peaks and troughs along the passage. The smooth rock shone in brilliant hues of red and orange from age and gradual weathering of the hematite minerals within.

In short order, it was breath-taking. Ashalea had never seen the likes of rock such as this, or truthfully any mountain ranges at all—at least not this close. She gawped at the passage before them as it slithered through the mountain, wide enough for a small group to walk abreast of one another.

Shadows stretched along the winding path, and she sighed in relief after Kaylin stepped into the cool shade—a temporary respite from the scorching sun above. Swinging a leg gracefully over his back, she jumped to the hard earth and smiled at her mount.

"I'm going to miss you, boy," she whispered in his ear, resting her forehead upon his muzzle.

She peered into his deep brown eyes and noted the intelligence shining from them. They seemed to convey his sorrow at being parted. And without tuning into his thoughts, she knew he did feel sad. Ashalea stroked his velvet nose and giggled as he lifted his head and nibbled gently at her fingers.

With a small sigh she unstrapped her weapons; her white oak bow, imbued with Magicka to guide her aim and instil courage in her heart; a quiver full of white-feathered arrows; and her emerald scimitar—all gifted from the Lady Nirandia of Woodrandia. She'd accrued more weapons in Shadowvale, stashing a switch knife in her boot, strapping a vicious looking dagger to her thigh, and slotting some shurikens into her belt.

"And here I was thinking we were on a diplomatic mission," Wezlan said humorously.

Ashalea offered him a sweet smile. "One can never be too careful."

She glanced pointedly at Shara who had donned such a wide assortment of blades she may as well have been a walking weapons rack. Wezlan followed her gaze beneath his bushy brows and guffawed in amusement.

Denavar had his bow and quiver already slung over his back, twin swords sheathed at his sides. He was wearing a cream shirt with cut-off sleeves, brown britches tight but conservatively so. Her eyes raked over his exposed tanned arms, rippling with muscle, his backside positively—

Shara thumped an arm around Ashalea's shoulder, following her gaze and nodding in approval. "Buns of steel that one. Tight as a maiden on her wedding night. Sharp as a knife to slice my bread. Hard as a boy in a brothel. If he was my man, I'd—"

Ashalea shook the assassin's arm off and scowled. "Are you done?"

The olive-skinned beauty raised her hands in peace. "What! Just appreciating the merchandise."

The she-elf bared her teeth and gave Shara a playful shove. "My man."

She stalked over to Denavar, turned his chin, and crushed her lips against his mouth, twisting her tongue against the buttery sweetness of his own. His eyes widened in shock, but he melted against her, one chiselled arm wrapping around her body, the other creeping down to grasp her buttocks.

Shara stared at the display with both hands on her hips. Wezlan on the other hand, busied himself with their gear, his cheeks turning

a pretty shade of pink. When the lovers were done, they pulled apart with a loud smack of their lips, Ashalea turning to her friend before smiling smugly and blowing a kiss.

The assassin laughed. "Point made queenie; I'll keep this memory close at hand when I'm alone at night instead."

Wezlan uttered an appalled grunt before turning around. "If you're quite done with the theatrics, I suggest we get a move on."

Shara looked him up and down with a click of her tongue. "Sounds like someone could use a little loosening up himself. How's the love life, old man? Any mage lasses you've made some Magicka in the chamber with lately?"

Ashalea offered an involuntary gag. "Could we not?"

Wezlan's stormy glare could have drowned all the ships in the Onyx Ocean. "Not now, nor ever, will I discuss my sexual endeavours with you in the bedroom, Shara."

"Well I'd hope not. Would be a little strange to talk about it in your chambers. People might get the wrong idea."

The wizard stiffened, his leathery skin pinching in folds as he frowned at her. "Pah," he threw out a spotted hand and shooed her like one does an annoying gnat.

The party gathered their supplies, choosing to forego everything but their weapons, water skins, and rucksacks. Ashalea caught a glimpse of her usual emerald attire from within her saddlebags and she stroked the material fondly. They had garbed themselves in cotton cream shirts, brown slacks and brown boots, the girls opting to adorn fitted yet practical corsets over the top.

The desert was waiting, and they were dressed for it. And though their weapons weighed them down, Wezlan had warned that the heat wouldn't be the only predator stalking their shadows.

Ashalea looked warily up at the walls boxing them in, the smooth

ridges that ran in undulating lines in tiers above them. Should anything happen, there was only forward and back, and the latter just wasn't an option. Not until they found the Diodonians. Not until they found the next Guardian.

When everyone had gathered their belongings and said their goodbyes to the horses, or rather, in Shara's case, grumbled about trekking on foot, Wezlan gave Lerian a gentle smack on his hindquarters and the nags trotted off towards green pastures, comfortable stables and a good feed. Or so Ashalea hoped. Still, if Wezlan trusted this mystery contact, that was good enough for her.

She watched as Kaylin and the others dwindled into tiny specks in her vision, then disappeared altogether. With a sigh she turned and assessed her crew.

"Ready?"

Denavar gave her a sly grin. "Always."

She led the way into the mouth of the beast, admiring the smooth gradient of the rock, sliding a palm along the rusted surface of the mountain wall. A rugged, steadfast beauty, bowing only to the storm and spit of the Gods and Goddesses above. So different to the wild, sprawling woods she once called home.

The party trekked in silence, Denavar following Ashalea's lead, Wezlan treading after, guarded at the rear by Shara. The mountain trail was quiet, nothing but the soft swish of sand and the occasional pebble as a boot set it rolling.

She wasn't sure how much time had passed since they started out. It was impossible to tell how high the sun had climbed due to the walls overhead caging them in. The heat still lingered despite the shade, creating a hotbox of sweat and stagnancy.

The atmosphere was ominous and eerie. It set Ashalea's teeth on edge, the she-elf wishing to be out in open fields once again. But, if

she listened hard enough, she could hear Denavar's steady breathing and she focused on its rhythm to calm her.

In, out, in, out, in ...

She waited but the exhalation never came. Peering over her shoulder, she saw Denavar stood in his tracks, ears pricked like that of a dog on a hunt. Opening her mouth, she caught his eyes flash in warning. So, she paused, still as the calm before the storm, the predator before the prey. Only they weren't the hunters; they were the hunted.

She strained her ears and looked around with cautious eyes, but she saw nothing. And it wasn't the aforementioned orifices that revealed the threat. No. It was her nose. The scent regaled her nostrils like steam rising a chimney: rotting carcass and putrid leather, an oily tarlike pungency that embedded itself into her very pores. She blanched at the stench, eyes widening as she recalled where she had smelt that before.

Uulakh. They skittered one by one upon the rockface, their long bodies clawing at the stone, tails whipping behind them, jaws snapping. The ridges gave them invitation to stalk from above, peering down at the crew with cocked heads and lashing tongues. The forks in their mouths tasted the air, sampling it for fear.

Ashalea and the others swivelled slowly in the sand, eyes darting left and right as the trap, already set, was about to be sprung. They were surrounded, the vile beasts at their rear descending the precipice and blocking the way they had come. But Ashalea had no intention of turning back. There was only one way out: through sword, sweat, and arrow.

The serpentine creatures drew closer and Ashalea reached for her bow, the Uulakh hissing as her hand neared the weapon. She flicked her crew a questioning gaze, and each offered a slow nod in return.

The only answer she needed. She fired a grin back. Game on.

In a heartbeat she had an arrow nocked to her bow and with a roar, leapt into a forward roll, settling in a crouch before she tugged the string and loosed the reed. It sailed through the air, the lack of breeze sending it shooting straight through the eye of an Uulakh, pinning the beast to the ridge.

Black blood oozed from the wound and the reptile breathed its last. The first move was made, the battle begun. As one the Uulakh hissed in rage, the sounds reverberating off the rock and ringing in Ashalea's ear.

"Run!"

The team sprinted on feathered feet, Ashalea and Denavar dashing through the trail with relative ease, their lithe legs and elvish speed a welcome burst with the horde above and behind them. The duo fired arrows as they ran, their accuracy unwavering, each shaft hitting home.

But the wizard was too slow, and Shara too loyal to leave him behind. Ashalea spun on her heel, gasping as she saw the gap between them begin to close, Uulakh filing down the mountain and blocking her from her friends.

"Denavar," she cried. "There's too many!"

Grunting his assent, he leaped in the air, twisting like a cat as he nocked three arrows and set them free. They embedded themselves in the scales of three Uulakh circling Shara and Wezlan, and Ashalea gaped at him in awe.

He gifted her a quick wink before running towards the fray. "Not just a pretty face, love," he called over his shoulder.

She grinned. "No, dear," she agreed, hot on his heels. "But it doesn't hurt to look at."

They drew their blades, Ashalea favouring her scimitar, Denavar

gripping his twin short swords, and with a roar they joined the gathering dark. With a mighty swing Denavar decapitated the first lizard and punctured the second in the spine.

Ashalea lunged at a tall, particularly broad beast snapping viciously at her old mentor. It scampered to the ground on all fours just as her sword swiped where its head was seconds before. Hissing, it leered at her with one yellow eye and one black, and Ashalea glared at its horrible face. A long, garishly red and pustular incision rent its way down the creature's skull from eye to throat.

And as Ashalea sidestepped left to right, ducking beneath the spear it jabbed at her from clawed fingers, she studied the wound. The line was jagged, the mark similar but not yet accurate enough to be a blade. She ducked again before swiping viciously at the creature, but her blade sawed right through its crude wooden weapon.

It hissed with anger and resorted to using its claws instead. *Claws.*

What manner of creature in the desert would attack a host of the darkness's creatures? What could possibly pose a threat to ... Her eyes lit up and a smile crept across her face.

"Well what do you know," she mumbled between pants, the creature opposing her growing ever more frustrated with each missed swipe of its claws. Its last strike scraped the surface of her arm, shearing through the white fabric and drawing blood.

Ashalea uttered a hiss of her own. "Right, time to go, you ugly mother—"

Her retort was cut short as the creature's legs were removed, and as its significantly shorter body tumbled backwards, Shara's smug face popped into view. *Smirking.*

Ashalea frowned. "Go find your own pet lizard," she snapped.

"Sharing's caring," the assassin called sweetly as she drove her blade into the felled beast's heart.

Ashalea turned her attention to the crew. The beasts were relentless, their numbers undiminished. Grunting in frustration, she called to Wezlan, who was up to his elbows in black gore, swinging his staff and sword with a strength belying of his age.

"There's too many of them, Wezlan." She ducked a blow to her head and responded with a slash in an Uulakh's side. "We need to get out of the passage!"

The wizard cracked the skull of one lizard with his staff, piercing the hide of another with his sword. "Diversion," he managed to gasp between blows.

She surveyed the scales glittering in the sea of sand, followed the cracks and fissures in the rocky walls surrounding them. Magicka was too risky in such close combat; she could burn her friends with fire, risk electrocuting them ... but maybe ... just maybe ...

She forced her way through the thrum, smashing, slashing, stabbing, until she found herself back-to-back with Denavar.

"I need you to make a break for it through the pass. Wezlan isn't fast enough and he'll need the cover." She grunted as she cleaved into an Uulakh's chest, its blood splattering her face. She spat in disgust before shouting: "I'll stay behind, draw them off your tail."

Denavar blocked a blow with guarded swords, responding with a parry. Like dancers they whirled on their feet, switching positions. "What are you ... thinking," he said, narrowly escaping a chomp aimed at his arm.

"M—Magicka," she breathed, deflecting a spear, answering with a riposte. She grasped the creature's weapon and pulled it towards her, using the momentum and snarling as she impaled the beast's stomach with her scimitar.

Her back was soaked in sweat, her silver braid whipping about her like a scorpion's tail. The Uulakh were strong as dwarves and fast as elves and, were it not for the laughable quality of their weapons, Ashalea and the others would probably be dead already. The quarters were too close, the beasts too many. Something had to give.

"We can use the rock to our advantage," she continued, round-housing a reptile that tried to sneak behind Denavar's guard.

She saw understanding register, and he nodded sharply. "Wezlan, Shara, to the fore," he barked at his comrades.

The wizard and assassin were a hurricane as they whirled through the mass. A flicker of a long beard, a glimpse of amber eyes, and together they churned through the reptiles in a flash of silver and staff. They reached Ashalea and Denavar, forming a circle as they guarded each other's backs.

"What now?" Shara panted, black cropped hair plastered in wavy strands to her face.

"Behind me," Denavar said, and as the group pushed forwards through the pass, the elf ran towards the Uulakh horde, not looking back, not faltering for an instant. "Run!"

With a whispered word, a blast of Magicka erupted from Wezlan's palm, a gale-force wind knocking the remaining foes off their feet and clearing a narrow path ahead. "Now," the old man roared, and with a tug of Shara's hand on her own, Ashalea was jolted into movement.

The women bellowed as they cleaved their way through the throng, shearing limbs off any Uulakh who stood in their way or attacked from the side-lines. And with one last look of dismay, she cast her eyes over her shoulder to see the love of her life jump off a reptile and soar, wingless, glorious, perfect, before the fall. And as he hit the ground his body was blotted out. Overcome by the writhing mass of tails and talons and teeth.

She cried out in panic, her heart thudded in her chest and the world seemed to still as she tried desperately, vainly, to see him rise

again. And then it hit her. A physical tremor that shook the earth and cracked the stone, demanding to be heard. To be felt.

Her eyes lifted in hope, and an unseen force rebounded from the sand, sending all Uulakh within a twenty-foot radius of the blast flying, tumbling into each other or cracking skulls upon the mountain walls.

And there, crouched on the ground, bloodied and battered and covered in gore, was Denavar, hands splayed on the earth, face flushed with power. And at the calling of his name his eyes rose, the bottomless blue piercing her emerald green as he stood. And he ran; ran as the ground began to fissure; ran as the sands spilled through cracks in the hard earth; ran as the walls began to crumble and the passage began to collapse in on itself.

It tumbled down, red rock angry and unforgiving as it tore itself asunder, threatening to crush the insects beneath it.

"Ashalea, *move!*" Shara demanded.

The girl pulled her along, their legs like pinwheels as their boots pounded the sand. Wezlan was up ahead, nearing the yawning mouth that opened unto endless desert. Just a little farther. Ashalea's instincts spurred her on, and while her heart ached and her mind demanded her to turn around and ensure his safety, every instinct in her body pulled her to the clearing ahead.

The ground rumbled its discontent, and still they sprinted, Ashalea leading Shara now, pulling the girl just that little bit faster, just that little bit farther past the mouth threatening to swallow them whole. And as they cleared the shadows and burst forth into the sunlight, Shara collapsed to the ground, joining a wheezing Wezlan.

Ashalea turned on her heel, oblivious to the lack of oxygen in her lungs. Her eyes pierced the building dust storm, seeking out the man she loved, making sure he would make it. He was so close now, but

the rocks fell faster, the cloud grew larger, and as his hand stretched towards her, blue eyes wide, the dust swallowed him ... and he was gone.

"No ..." A whisper on the wind. A heart shuddering, collapsing, caving like the passage before her. Tears stung her eyes, welling, threatening to take shape. She stumbled to the ground, wishing she could sink into the sand. This can't be it. This can't be the end.

The world turned to silence, nothing but the remnants of the dead beneath the earth, a soft breeze sighing as the dust began to clear. Even Shara and Wezlan held their breath as they waited anxiously. Ashalea clenched at the sand, feeling the grains slip through her fingers. She couldn't—wouldn't—let him go. Too many times had she been close yet oh so far from saving the ones she loved.

She closed her eyes, hysteria climbing her throat, snaking into the pit of her stomach. She forced her mind to slow, her heart to settle. And she sank into stillness. There was nothing, no one in this dark corner of her mind. It was blank, empty, void.

And then she heard it. The slightest flutter. A rhythmic flow. A give and take.

In, Out, In, Out

Her eyes snapped open, staring, straining, spying into the last of the dusty gloom. And there, bloodied and battered and covered in gore, shrouded in dust, two blue eyes popped into focus. The most beautiful she'd ever seen. And trailing farther down the planes of his face were white teeth. Bared in a wolfish grin.

A sob escaped her lips and she rose, pounding across the sands and jumping into Denavar's arms. He swayed beneath her weight and they rolled in a heap on the ground. Him laughing, her shaking.

"Be still, my love," he said, stroking her silver hair, planting a kiss on her forehead. "Not just a pretty face, remember?"

She laughed at that, her breath hitching before sighing in release. She reached up, tilted his head and kissed him, softly, gently, lingering on its meaning, drowning in its promise, her teeth nipping at his bottom lip before the release.

He wrapped her in his arms, sheltering her from the world, burying his face into her hair, the silver strands glinting white gold in the sunlight. Ashalea peered up at her friends, relief etched into the wizard's face, a smirk on Shara's.

Denavar pulled away from her, assessing her at length, cupping her face in his hands.

"Ashalea, I—"

A shrill noise filled the air and Denavar released Ashalea, placing two hands on his ears, white teeth clenched now in pain. Ashalea mimicked the movement, her face screwed up in agony, the scream so loud, so abrasive, she could feel the blood thinning in her ears, scrambling in her elvish tips.

She curled into a ball, exposed, helpless. Her friends fell to the ground like stones, Shara sprawled out on the sands, Wezlan on his back, writhing in pain. The sound increased to an inhuman pitch, its ferocity making her head feel like it would explode.

And as she twisted on the ground, Ashalea realised the noise wasn't coming from without, it was coming from within. Inside. Buried in her mind like a shard of glass, *grinding, stabbing, slicing*. The torment so unbearable that if she were able, she'd open her throat and enter blissful silence.

Stars exploded behind her eyes, the world spinning, the light darkening, and as her vision blurred, she saw orange and red and golden-brown flash before her. Something shaped similarly to a dog. Or a lion. Or something in between.

Her thoughts grew muddy, her mind a puddle of nothing.

Woof, she thought nonsensically.

And then she thought nothing at all.

A Den of Diodonians

ASHALEA

THROBBING, SCREECHING, PIERCING. Blinding pain and stars exploding. That's all she could remember from before. And the aftermath wasn't much better. Groggily, Ashalea opened her eyes, reaching a hand to her head as the blood pulsed too loud, too intrusive through her skull. Her head still thumped like an over-enthusiastic drummer.

She took in her surroundings. A large cave, smooth walls of yellow and white rock streaked with dashes of purple and pinks. Soft red sand, the occasional hollow in a wall where fire crackled and burned from no visible source, instead hanging suspended in mid-air.

Various pits dotted the ground, which were strewn with plush cushions and rugs, and it was oddly cool in here. Her fingers curled into the sand, soft and relieving to her heated skin.

Her eyes found her friends crumpled in a heap to the side of her. Panic flooded her stomach, heart thrilling in protest, but upon closer inspection she found no visible injuries, their chests rising and falling gently. They were unbound just as she was.

And then she saw it. Shuffling in the gloom, multiple pairs of silver eyes peering from the depths, the fires' reflection glinting with a freaky sheen as it is wont to do with animals in the dark. She counted one, two, five, nine ... orange and red and golden-brown. She swallowed. Hard. There was no question what these beasts were.

"Diodonians," she breathed.

With unparalleled speed one of the beasts pounced from the shadows, an impossible leap sending her crashing back into the ground as it held a giant paw to her chest and loomed above. It snarled, fangs bared, those intelligent, worldly silver eyes piercing into her own. Its claws extracted ever so slightly—not enough to pierce her skin—but to warn her. Move, and she'd be sorry.

Ashalea gaped at the creature with wide eyes, silver braid dishevelled, mouth in an 'o' as she leaned back on scraped elbows. One wrong move and she'd be Diodonian dinner. But this wasn't how it was supposed to be. An alliance was to be made, a Guardian to be found.

The beast before her was a picture of glory; its coat shiny, blindingly bright like the sun itself. It stood double the size of the largest dog she'd seen, and it peered down its muzzle at her with a nobility fit for a king. And there was something else ... an aura that seemed to radiate from it, that called to her. Some form of old Magicka oozing from its body like salt spray from the ocean.

She steeled her resolve, took a deep breath, and surprised herself when the words came out steady and firm.

"We seek your chief. We seek the son of Razgeir."

The beast pulled its head back and snapped its maw shut, silver eyes narrowed in uncanny similarity to a human. Cautiously, it retreated a few steps, allowing Ashalea to sit up. The other Diodonians prowled in the shadows, and the beast before her stared for a time. Contemplating. Considering. Then finally ...

"And who does the seeking?"

Ashalea blinked. The creature's mouth did not move, and her friends still lay unconscious beside her. She saw no human hiding in the dark. The Diodonian swished its tail back and forth in the air, the furry tip exploding into a fireball on its own accord, the flames rippling up its back to rest at the rear of its head, forming a living, breathing mane. To her credit she remained still even as the warmth flooded her skin.

Her mind drifted back to ancient texts she'd once pored over, soaking up information on these beasts with enthusiasm. *Bearing a strong resemblance to hounds, though these magnificent creatures were much larger, golden, red and brown, with a fiery mane and fangs ... highly intelligent ... psychic powers.*

"Holy mother," she whispered in awe. Ashalea gazed at the beast with newfound interest, temporarily forgetting it could club her with its giant paw without a second thought. "You're speaking to me in my ... in my mind?"

Its tail swished in annoyance, and it only stared. Watching. Waiting.

She gulped down a breath. "My name is Ashalea Kindaris, my companions, Wezlan Shadowbreaker, Denavar Andaro, Shara Silvaren. We've come for the next Guardian of the Grove. We've come to find our own."

Its tail ceased moving at the last, and the flames died to a gentle simmer. The beast cocked its head, and from the movement of the

pack she guessed some psychic conversation she wasn't privy to had passed. They advanced from the shadows, seating themselves around the room, some curling up amid the concaves piled with upholstery. Though lazy and aloof in appearance now, she knew they would have her throat in an instant if she tried something foolish.

She blinked again, fully comprehending where she was, and who she was speaking to. It was one of the most bizarre things Ashalea had ever seen and possibly ever would. But there was no mistaking the intelligence in this race, no denying the power that radiated from their massive, glorious bodies that fit somewhere between a dog and what she had heard of the exotic golden cats that resided far east of this land.

"We have been watching from the moment you stepped into Hallow's Pass. Quite a display, what you did to the Uulakh, though there will be no returning through that passage now. Not without our help."

Nonchalantly, it licked a paw with a pink tongue before its silver eyes pierced her own. Every time it gazed at her, Ashalea felt naked. Like all her truths were laid bare, all her secrets come to light.

"We are grateful for your assistance with those vile creatures. They have been a thorn in our sides since arriving in our lands." It paused for a moment. *"You are lucky to be alive."*

"Arrived?" Ashalea didn't like the sound of that. She raised a brow.

The creature snarled, a vicious sound that raised the hairs on her neck. *"They come in droves through a portal in the Ruins. Their master searches the sands. We dispatch his monsters, but he only sends more."*

"Wait," Ashalea shook her head, trying to grasp what she was hearing. "The Uulakh enter from a different dimension? Have you seen their master? Is he here?"

If the creature had brows, she was most certain they'd be raised.

135

"We have not seen his like step foot here, but we sense a presence beyond. Dark, hateful ... wrong." It growled from deep in its throat. "Something wicked awaits. Something foul it plots."

A soft groan stole Ashalea's attention and she found Denavar stirring beside her. Like Ashalea, he moved slow, placing a palm to his forehead and wincing. After scanning the room his brain seemed to register what his eyes were conveying, and upon seeing the Diodonian sitting not two feet away from Ashalea he uttered a strange, unbecoming squeak.

At her raised eyebrow he cleared his throat, seemed to sense she was in no immediate danger and allowed his body to slacken. The others woke from their slumber shortly after and went through much the same steps. Shara immediately reached for weapons that weren't there and then stilled quickly at the growls of warning surrounding her.

Wezlan's mouth split into a broad grin. "In all my years, I never tire of seeing the great Diodonians." He appraised the beast before him, nodded in satisfaction. "Your father would be proud of you, Chieftain Razakh."

The hound-like creature turned its giant head towards Wezlan. "You ... know me?"

Ashalea heard its words spill forth in her mind and again stared in awe. Such power of the psyche, to break mental barriers, to enter more than one mind at once. Apparently, she wasn't the only one surprised.

Shara blinked. Several times. "The dog is speaking," she said bluntly.

A fierce growl rumbled deep from within Razakh's throat. "We bite too, girl. We are not common hounds. We are Diodonians."

At his retort Shara scowled. "Cranky."

136

Razakh only swished his tail in annoyance, the flames on his back stoking to life with renewed vigour. Ashalea bit her lip to hold back bubbling laughter.

Denavar merely shrugged. "Don't mind the viper," he said. "She's less poisonous than she seems."

He was answered with an exaggerated hiss.

Wezlan chuckled, ignoring their jibes. "I know your father well," he said to Razakh. "A strong and noble Diodonian. A good friend and a proud Guardian."

The muscles in Razakh's bunched shoulders seemed to ease at that. *"You are the great wizard who started the order,"* he said. It wasn't a question.

Wezlan grinned. "In the flesh."

The Diodonian seemed to hesitate before asking. *"How–how is he doing?"*

Wezlan's smile faltered and he sighed. "I haven't seen Razgeir for some years." He looked at Ashalea sidelong before gazing into the beast's silver eyes once more. "It's ... complicated ... but last I saw the old boy he was not faring so well."

Razakh lowered his head onto two front paws, giving the appearance of a scolded pet. *"Last I saw my father I was but a pup. But I have done my duty and ruled in his stead. The tribe has stood strong in his absence. The lands are ever patrolled. Work is never finished but ... we prosper."*

The wizard inclined his head. "I am sure your father will be most pleased to hear that. He spoke fondly of you. And often."

Wezlan looked around the cave at the Diodonian faces peering back at him, smiling softly at the young balls of fluff peeking out from between their parents' forelegs.

"I see Kalanor's Klan has some new faces in its midst. I knew

Diodonian numbers had dwindled since the hunting all those years ago. Your father would be proud and joyful to know younglings will carry on the line."

Ashalea recalled Wezlan informing the crew about the capture and cruel experiments of Diodonians in olden times. She gazed at the pups around the cave, golden and brown, vivid red or flaming orange, their fur all fuzzy and dishevelled from sleep, their eyes wide and full of wonder.

A few broke free from their parents and ambled towards her and the others, stumbling along the way as they nipped playfully at each other's ears. There were no flames present on their backs yet, and their eyes were a deep, sky blue. Ashalea laughed as a pack descended upon Shara, tugging on her clothes and gnawing at her hands.

"Ow! Like little needles!" A scowl crossed the girl's features as she tried to free her fingers, but even she couldn't stop the creeping smile or the hands that reached to stroke their fur. Her eyes widened in surprise and she glanced at Ashalea with an unabashed grin. "So soft!"

Ashalea rolled her eyes, an amused smile curling her lips. One of the youngest stumbled over to Ashalea, and with a yawn and a gentle lick, it climbed aboard her lap, turned thrice, then curled in, nuzzling its wee muzzle into her britches. She smoothed a hand along its golden back, delighting in its fur.

Ohhh, like sunlight woven into velvet.

A question popped into her head and she looked up at Razakh. "Why are their eyes blue instead of silver? And where are the flames? And how—"

A strange grumble erupted from the Diodonian and, dumbfounded, she stared at him curiously until she realised. *He's laughing.*

Indeed, his maw was stretched into what she assumed was the

nearest expression to a smile, fangs jutting out in between loose folds of skin. "*The younglings don't receive their flames until they reach maturity. It would be ... somewhat problematic if they carried them from birth. They aren't the most cautious of babes.*" The Diodonian uttered a grumbling laugh again. "*As for their eyes, they shift to silver at their own pace. Most pups will have them within a hundred years, some not for hundreds.*"

Ashalea gaped at him, Denavar mimicking her sentiment.

"How long *do* you live for?" he asked incredulously.

Razakh shrugged. "*A couple hundred centuries at worst, a millennium at best.*"

Incredulous, Denavar's jaw dropped. "So, had it not been for the human campaigns ..."

Ashalea saw the slightest hint of remorse cloud Razakh's eyes before the silver reassumed steely resolve. The beast dipped his head.

"*Aye,*" Razakh said, a mental sigh burrowing into her mind. "*The tribe would be countless, not countable. Our flames would be searing, our pack as mighty as the sun itself. But we were foolish back then. Trusting. Tame. We will not make the same mistake twice.*"

Wezlan pursed his lips. "The world is changed. The tyrants who once ruled over the human cities are diminished. There is some semblance of peace in Everosia."

Shara scoffed and was rewarded with a withering glare from the wizard.

The Diodonian narrowed his eyes. "*I'm inclined to agree with the girl. You let the fruit ripen too long, rot will take place. You do your best to cleanse the earth of taint, but it takes root in new form. Power is a disease, and humans wield it as their mightiest weapon.*"

"Hold on a sec, dog," Shara retorted.

Oh shit. Here we go. Ashalea hunkered down, cradling her ball of fluff and stroking the cub, her gaze flicking to the Diodonian.

Razakh growled, baring wicked fangs.

Shara ignored him. "If you mean to say the entire race is a blight than you're stupider than you look. Whether you like it or not, one of you," she said, eyes raking over every Diodonian adult present, "is to be a Guardian. Which means protecting the species you are *so very fond of*, not to mention Everosia in its entirety. I suggest you come to terms with that."

Denavar chuckled, and Ashalea buried her face in the warm fur of the cub to avoid revealing her smile. Even Wezlan's eyes glittered with amusement.

The duo stared off at each other for a time, silver and gold eyes unwavering. Both as stubborn as each other, yet remarkably alike. Both were fire, unyielding, scorching, relentless. Both were cunning, sly, strong. Their party was about to get a whole lot more interesting.

And there it was again, the strange aura radiating from Razakh. It rippled from him like a wave of Magicka, and yet wholly different. Harrietti had said that Guardians would display great power—each one in their own unique way.

Razakh was not only the chieftain of this race, but the blood of his father—the current Diodonian Guardian—ran through his veins. This was not a coincidence. He was the one.

She glanced at Wezlan who, given the squinting eyes, wayward beard-stroking-hand, and the slight angle of his head, she guessed was thinking much the same thing. He turned to her with brows downturned.

He is the one. He is the next Guardian, she tried to convey, and he offered her the smallest nod. Ever so gently, she lifted the fuzzball from her lap and laid the youngling down in a small hollow near her feet. It curled up, yawning with tiny teeth before dozing once more.

Ashalea's long limbs creaked as she rose, wincing at the pain still

thrumming in her mind and up her spine after that crushing pounce from Razakh. Stars threatened to overwhelm her as she moved too fast, a dizziness washing down her throat in a nauseating wave. She felt a strong hand grip her leg, as if the touch alone would ground her. And as always, it did.

She smiled at Denavar, cupping one hand gently, lovingly, to his jaw. She planted a soft kiss on his temple; assurance that she was in control, that she knew what she was doing.

Ashalea strode purposefully into the gap between her friend and her—hopefully—new companion. She stopped inches from his maw, bearing down on her as he was. She gazed into the quicksilver and fancied the slight shimmer as she studied the lazy flow of swirls. He had no irises, no pupils, just a silver ocean of metallic awareness, like a stream of consciousness that saw and knew all.

"Razakh," she breathed, "I'm just going to speak plainly. You are the next Guardian."

She swore the silver flared to life when she said that, but then it slowed to a cooling calm, shuttering slightly before returning to normal—as if he were weighing up those words, analysing them to every possible end.

After a minute, he sat on his haunches and inclined his head respectfully, almost reverently. "*A part of me always knew this day would come. That I was destined to walk in the pawprints of my father. I want to help you, but I cannot ignore the plight of my tribe. The Uulakh raid the desert and, if left unchecked, their numbers will grow substantially. I will not risk the wellbeing of my Klan. As chieftain, it is my duty to protect them.*"

A deep thrumming came from his chest as he rose to his full height, flames bursting to life with renewed vigour on his back. Not with intention to harm, but with pride. With passion. He shook his head.

141

"I am sorry. I cannot join you on this quest. You may stay here as long as you wish, but my priority is the Diodonians and I will not leave until I know they are safe."

Ashalea's heart sank. Razakh was the next Guardian, she was sure of it. But if he refused to join them, short of kidnapping him, there was little they could do. And she didn't think that would go down well with the Diodonians. She sighed.

They had come all this way for nothing. Unless she could convince him to join them. Unless she could give Razakh a reason worth leaving for. She screwed her nose up in thought, studying his face as she considered.

What could sway a chieftain to leave his people? What could she offer him to change his mind?

And then it hit her. Razakh was a proud and noble beast who believed in destiny. If she could show him how honourable the Guardians could be, how trustworthy, he might be inclined to join them. Who could refuse destiny, after all? And with his father being a Guardian of old, it could be Razakh's last chance to say goodbye to his sire—to say everything he may never have had the chance to before.

A balance between duty and care, and a whole lot of hope it would be enough.

The sun was waning, and the temperature plummeted as the shadows deepened across the desert. Ashalea was amazed at the sudden change in the environment. Where the day had been sweltering, the night pressing in brought a cool breeze that raised the hairs on her arms.

She clutched the rug around her shoulders tighter and trudged

up the dune towards the lone figure atop the rise. Razakh sat still as a statue, gazing out across the sea of sand, his fiery mane rippling gently. He didn't acknowledge her as she approached, and he had the look of someone deep in thought.

Ashalea gestured at the space beside him. "May I?"

He nodded in assent and they sat quietly for a time, enjoying companionable silence. The colours of the sky shifted from orange to pink to red; a myriad of shades that burst from behind fluffy clouds.

"It's beautiful," she whispered. "I can see why you're loath to leave this place."

His silver eyes regarded her, and an odd expression shifted his face. *"I shall never tire of this view, though a part of me longs to see other sights. Green pastures, snowy mountains ... But we Diodonians are lucky to see the sun set in our quiet corner of the world. There is a wildness to the desert that I would see untamed—untouched by mankind."*

"You worry a time will come when humans invade this territory," she hedged.

"The Diodonians have experienced much pain at the hands of humans. Better to stay out of their affairs altogether."

Ashalea grabbed a fistful of sand and watched the grains trickle through her fingers. "In my experience, it is folly to ignore destiny. Events will run their course whether you want them to or not. The question is, will you be ready for them when they do?"

"We are prepared to defend ourselves by any means necessary should that time come."

"And what if the world were at risk? What if Everosia were to burn and fall into shadow? Would you be prepared to stand up for the greater good then?"

Razakh bared his teeth. *"I know what you're doing, and my answer still stands. I will not leave the Diodonians whilst the Uulakh raid our land. I*

143

must protect my own. That, above all else, is the duty of a chieftain. It is what my father would want."

They lapsed into silence, and Ashalea cursed herself silently. Razakh would not change his mind so easily. Not without cause or motivation. But perhaps there was another way she could play this. She gazed at the darkening sky, suppressing a shiver as the air grew colder.

"Wezlan told me about your father," she uttered softly. "Said he is loyal to the last, honourable, a good friend. He also told me Razgeir saved his life once."

Razakh cocked his head at that, his silver eyes piercing Ashalea's own with newfound curiosity. *"Would you tell me the story?"*

Ashalea smiled. "Wezlan and Razgeir had gone to the Marshes of Deyvall to investigate reports on a particularly nasty creature that had a fondness for mutton. Apparently, it was determined to eat every last sheep in the town of Nenth, and as you can imagine, the villagers were none too pleased about that."

Razakh's mouth pulled back into a clumsy grin, and he settled his great head on his paws. *"What happened?"*

"They caught it mid-meal at a farm on the outskirts of the village. A horrid thing. All sharp teeth and claws, and it was fast—too fast for Wezlan's old legs to move out of harm's way. The creature had him pinned and paralysed within seconds." She chuckled. "He was on his arse and about to be dessert when Razgeir leaped to his rescue."

"He couldn't use Magicka against it?"

"The monster's skin secreted a toxin that rendered its victim immobile. Once it touched him, Wezlan couldn't move or speak. I suppose that's why no one ever heard the sheep fussing when it hunted late at night. In any case, it was Razgeir's quick thinking that saved him. With a whip of fire, he burned the monster's flesh—only then was he able to dispatch it with fang and claw."

Razakh stared at Ashalea in wonder. *"It is fortunate then, that your wizard had my father at his side."*

Ashalea laughed. "A fact he was quick to remind Wezlan of for many days after, much to Wezlan's dismay. But I'm grateful for your father, otherwise I wouldn't be alive to this day, and I certainly wouldn't have one wily wizard to guide me."

Razakh rumbled in amusement, but his eyes soon turned thoughtful and he cocked his head to the side. *"You care deeply for him, don't you?"*

"Aye. Wezlan is like a father to me." She sighed; her fondness overcome with a deeper sadness. "I never knew my birth parents, and I lost my adoptive ones, too. Wezlan is the only reason I still walk this earth."

She lifted her shirt to reveal the puckered scar on her belly, now stark on her skin under the moonlit sky. "This wound would have caused my death if he had not healed me."

Razakh's eyes followed her movement. *"It is a worthy battle scar. A reminder of what it is you fight for, and what you have lost."*

Ashalea's lips thinned. "I will never stop fighting until the darkness pays for what he has done, but this is beyond me—beyond any of us. The vengeance that fires through my veins is but a small sliver of a greater picture. If the Guardians don't unite, if we can't close the portal once and for all, everything will be lost, and there won't *be* anything left to fight for."

"And if fighting for the greater good means you might die in the process, would you? Would you die for the people you love, Ashalea?"

Her jaw set as she gazed at him fiercely. "Without hesitation."

Slowly, Razakh rose to his full height and he turned to face her, the flames on his back flaring brighter—like lava flowing down his

145

back—coursing with renewed purpose. Ashalea looked into his eyes, the silver eddies swirling and unfathomably deep, and she was struck once more by the wisdom that lay within.

"I understand now, what drives you on this quest. You fight for the ones you love. You fight for a future where all in Everosia might dwell in peace. I would see this dream come true for my tribe. I would see this quest fulfilled so the Diodonian cubs will live to see a tomorrow."

Ashalea gaped at him, daring to hope with every fibre of her being. "Are you saying—" she swallowed. "Are you saying you will you join the Guardians?"

Razakh gazed at her with a hardness that bore into her soul. *"I will do whatever it takes to save the Diodonians, but before I go anywhere, there's something I need from you first."*

It took a moment to register his words, and she shook her head, feeling equal parts flabbergasted and overjoyed. "Anything, Razakh. Ask and it is yours."

A low growl ripped through the silence of the sands, and the hackles on his neck rose. *"Tomorrow you and I shall hunt. We've some Uulakh to kill."*

The Guardians were sprawled out lazily in one of the many chambers within the Diodonian Den. Wezlan, Shara, Denavar—and the newest addition to their pack—each nestled amongst pillows and rugs that littered the wide hollow in the ground. Ashalea had just informed them of Razakh's decision to join them, and all had readily accepted.

All but one.

Shara's eyes narrowed. *"He's the one who'll be joining us on our*

expedition? Tell me you're joking."

Razakh stiffened and his words were dangerously slow, edged with warning as they sliced coolly through Ashalea's mind—in all their minds.

"Your opinion of me is neither warranted nor asked for, girl. And whether you like me or not I will be accompanying you on this journey. In return for your help in ridding the desert of those foul reptilian creatures, I will join the Guardians. You might be human, and I might not like this arrangement, but you're a part of this world and I will do my duty to protect it."

Shara growled. "You miserable—"

"Enough!" Ashalea barked. She rose, crossing the floor to stand between Shara and Razakh. "We don't have time for petty jabs. Put your differences aside and let's focus on the task at hand."

Shara recoiled, a flash of hurt creasing her features before it was just as quickly smoothed away.

Ashalea threw her an apologetic smile, but where her heart wilted for snapping, her resolve was steel. They didn't have time for games, for how-do-you-do's or 'who's the better wordsmith'. Duty was demanding, and the darkness would wait for no one.

"Ashalea ..." Shara started.

Denavar gave her a warning look before joining Ashalea in between woman and beast. "She's right, Shara. We need to be united. Now is not the time."

The assassin sealed her lips in a tight line, retreating with rigid steps to sit beside Wezlan. Razakh watched her with wary eyes before reclining lazily, an idle tongue cleaning his fur. Ashalea almost smiled in amusement as she gazed upon him. A mix between a hound and a cat, giant though he may be. He was ferocious and passionate one second, feline and aloof the next. And despite Shara's reservations, she already liked him.

Razakh paused his grooming to blink at her—as if reading her thoughts. Hell, maybe he could. She breathed in relief now that her comrades had backed down, and Denavar intertwined his fingers between hers, his thumb brushing lazy circles on the back of her hand.

But they had pressing matters to address, plans to forge. She turned to face the others. "Earlier this evening, Razakh informed me the Uulakh have been entering through portals in Madoc Ruins." She took a deep breath. "*He* hasn't been sighted, but it's all part of some new scheme, no doubt."

"Naturally," Wezlan said. He rose from his perch and began pacing back and forth, hands clasped behind his back. "The desert is, well, for want of a better word, deserted. It's a good place to hide an army in secret, though severely lacking in resources. No one would guess at the darkness building a new base here, and certainly no one would come looking for it."

Denavar dragged a hand through his hair. "Which begs the question, how does he plan on sustaining his armies? No food, no water ... it is illogical and improbable."

"*I believe I can answer that,*" Razakh said. "*If one knows where to look, there are small watering holes dotted around the desert. Despite the arid heat and the lack of rain, they do not drain or dry up. I believe they were Magicked from your ilk in times past,*" he nodded to Wezlan.

"The mages?" Wezlan scratched his beard. "It is possible they did this to assist travellers on their way to the city. But even these caches of water are surely not sustainable for an army so vast?"

"*We thought so, too,*" Razakh agreed. "*There are ... other sources of water.*" The great beast grinned, or as near to as possible. "*Come with me.*"

He rose and padded towards one of the cave passageways. Curious, the rest of them followed on silent feet. The cave was more complex than she'd originally gleaned. Multiple pathways curved into the rock, offering different dens, open hollows and escape routes that burrowed underground and perhaps even led to the other end of the desert.

Clever.

Yet the most fascinating of all had Ashalea short of breath. She stepped into a vast cavern overrun with sprawling green; curling branches, spiked leaves, twisted roots, all fighting for floor space. Palm trees towered high above, reaching for the heavens as the cavern opened into its own natural sunroof. Sunset hibiscuses bloomed and yellow angels' trumpets waved from a makeshift archway.

Cotton pink and dusky red bromeliads swept around the vast clearing, lemon gingers flared proudly, and vines of ivory jasmine curled in clever patterns. Their sweet fragrance perfumed the air and she inhaled deeply, taking in every aspect of this tropical garden.

But the sight that loomed as a behemoth before her eyes was the waterfall cascading from several grooves inset into the rock above, plunging to form a pool of aquamarine in the centre of the cavern. It was tranquil. Untouched. A place of natural beauty that burst forth with life in a place otherwise devoid of it.

She peered over the smooth rock into the water's depths. Giant fish swam in lazy circles, their iridescent scales gleaming in shades of yellow, orange and pink, like the plant life surrounding them.

Her gaze wandered to Razakh who was proudly standing opposite her, even more breath-taking with true sunlight reflected off his shiny coat. She stared pointedly at the waterfall above, a small smile on her lips.

"Just a small water source, no big thing," she teased.

He barked with amusement before appraising the group. *"It is our most precious commodity, the treasure of our tribe. For even gold does not glitter so brightly. This water source has sustained our tribe for many years. It* never dries, never ceases to flow. A gift from the earth itself." He glanced at Ashalea and the others. Slowly, carefully. "*This secret is not given lightly. Consider this a token of my trust—my acceptance to join the Guardians.*"

Ashalea noticed the silver eyes glare at Shara at the last. But the girl, to her credit, kept her mouth shut, though her eyes burned, no small number of retorts at the tip of her tongue.

"This is truly a sight, Razakh," Denavar said with a small bow. "Thank you."

Razakh inclined his head. "*It has been many years since a human or elf last walked among us. To see this—it is one of the highest honours we can give. But now you know how we survive day to day without the threat of death hanging over us. Now you know why someone else might be eager to seek out such a prize.*"

Shara's eyes narrowed. "Crinos," she spat. "You think he knows about this oasis?"

"*I think it's wise for us to assume the worst, though I cannot fathom how he'd have knowledge of this place. It is why we've been picking off the Uulakh scouting parties. Why we were watching Hallow's Pass when you entered.*"

"Why you clubbed us in the head after we rid you of them?" Denavar asked with a smirk.

Razakh bared his teeth in a lazy grin. "*Ah. Sorry about that. One can't be too careful.*"

"No matter," Ashalea flapped her hand, "it proved advantageous in the end." She winced. "Though this ringing in my head is currently saying otherwise."

"*The pain will pass within the hour, as will any dizziness or nausea. Your minds will try to protect themselves from the invasion, but this too will lessen in time. Though, it is likely worse for you humans, than the elves.*"

"My head is on fire," Shara growled. "The next time you feel like blowing a trumpet in my head I'll—"

"Shara." The reprimand came from Denavar, surprisingly, and even more so was the fact she obeyed it, lips tightening into a scowl, eyes blackening.

She crossed her arms with a huff. "Dirty mongrel," she muttered. "*Foulmouthed wench.*"

Ashalea placed a hand to her head. Sighed. "This alliance is going to go swimmingly."

Denavar grinned. "Would you really have it any other way?"

A Touch of Peppermint

ASHALEA

RAZAKH WAS TRUE TO HIS WORD. The thrumming in her head had died down to a gentle simmer, a soft nudge at her brain's mental barriers. She was reclined on a rather decadent assortment of pillows and rugs, wound up in a tangle of arms and legs as she lay with Denavar. They'd been given their own 'den' as bed chambers without doors could hardly be called such at all.

Still, she'd marvelled at the rich silks and velvets that adorned the hollow in the ground and sighed with bliss when she'd settled onto the array of cushioning fabrics. There were even curtains of purple and pink taffeta draping over the makeshift bed, hiding them from view.

Ashalea stroked Denavar's golden arm with one fingertip, swirling shapeless lines along his warm skin, revelling in some alone time with her lover.

"Do you think they'll ever get along?" she asked vaguely.

He snorted whilst shifting onto his back, stretching muscled arms behind his head. She nuzzled into his chest, feeling the rise and fall of his ribs, the soft beat of his heart as it pumped underneath her ear.

"Both stubborn, both fiery, somewhat literally in our houndish friend," he grinned. "Aye, I think they'll warm to each other in the end. Might earn themselves a few burns in the process but, like calls to like, as they say."

"Enough with the fire puns, please."

He only chuckled in amusement, and Ashalea shifted her cheek, savouring that sweet minty fragrance that seemed to ooze from his pores. She sat up straight. "Why do you always smell like peppermint? Even beneath the blood, sweat and gore that we seem so fond of being drenched in, you ALWAYS smell like it."

"Is it not to your taste?" he purred, leaning in and expelling cool breaths upon her neck, leaving gentle kisses down the nape, curving around to her ear with a gentle nip. She shivered, feeling a rush run down her spine.

"The contrary, actually," she crooned.

He chuckled. "Like humans, elves generally have a unique scent about them. There's no reasoning for what it is, no genetic makeup or chemical imbalance. It just ... is."

"What do I smell like?"

Denavar nibbled on her earlobe, made his way to her nose where he planted a soft kiss upon her freckles. "You smell like the trees after a spring rain." A kiss on the forehead. "Like crushed lavender and honey." A kiss to the cheek. "Like moonlight and stars and pure, heady desire."

It wasn't the words, but the way he said them that had her curling

153

her toes in anticipation. "The latter doesn't actually smell like—"

Her words were crushed beneath his lips, his tongue searching, exploring, meeting her own as they collapsed into each other, her arms around his neck, his hands sliding up the slip of material covering her back.

She rolled over so she was straddling his powerful legs, squeezing with her own, caressing his tongue and letting desire drive her body with delicious fervour. His hands shifted to her midriff, teasing with soft strokes along her hipline, carving tantalising lines in low arcs, tickling the soft skin below her navel.

A soft moan escaped her lips, and he shuddered, the girth beneath her turning hard. His hands trailed up, sliding over her hardened stomach, cupping her full, heavy breasts as they heaved with desire.

She needed this man as surely as vengeance fired through her veins and the promise of justice surged in her soul, swelling, blindingly bright. He was hers and she his. Two lovers set upon a path of death and destruction, if only to reach greener pastures when all was said and done.

He tweaked her nipple with a thumb and forefinger, and she arched her back, leaning into his touch, his promise. He shredded the thin cotton shirt on her body like a wolf, the victor before the victim. His piercing blue eyes raked over her upper body, and his own body responded with a nod of approval.

He unravelled her britches, watching with hungry eyes as she shimmied them down her thighs, and as she leaned forwards to lengthen her legs, he flicked a tongue across her breast, sending her quaking with need. He clenched her arse with one hand, guiding her close to his length.

She could feel the heat rising with his desire. Primal. Passionate. And looking her right in the eyes he sent her lower still, nudging against him, a soft caress, a gentle hello. A gasp escaped her lips, "Denavar."

The name on her lips was almost enough to undo him, but ever the gentleman—or perhaps the sly fox—he set her down just shy of his girth, and slipped a casual finger into her wetness, moving with expertise, circling with keen awareness of her roiling desire. His touch was fire to her core, setting her alight and shaking her from the inside-out.

And just when she thought she would unravel he lifted her body with ease, placing her gently within the hollow. And went to work with his mouth. Easing down her legs, his tongue drawing lines, his teeth grazing over the sensitive skin until she fisted a hand in his dark hair, pulling him closer to that sweet spot, twisting with desire.

"Tsk, tsk," he purred. "Too impatient. Too quick to reach the close."

And with that he dove, tongue flicking, sweeping, circling until she was moaning in utter bliss, arching her bottom into the air, wanting more. More of him. All of him.

The want was gone. Replaced only with an unshakeable need for him to take every part of her. And as his storm-blue eyes raked over the quivering of her body, he at last shifted, and slowly, torturously, pulled his pants down, down below his waist until he sprang forth eagerly.

He cast his eyes over her naked body once again, and beneath the primal desire etched into every line, limb, and what lay between, she saw the oceans-deep affection, the softness, the love. The love he would bear until he grew old and grey or took the sword's blow meant for her. Because there was nothing that he would not do for her. Just as she would do anything for him.

The kiss was gentle as his lips found hers again. A whisper of his devotion, a sigh of his bliss. Their tongues connected and swirled in the eddies of it, their bodies drowning in it, their hearts the lifeline that tied them together.

And as he pulled away, he winked before thrusting, and when his girth filled her deep, she gasped, eyes shuttering in pleasure. He pulled out painstakingly slow, and then thrusted with renewed vigour, teasing her again and again so the bliss stretched for so long she almost hurt with the need for release, until finally he quickened, and her name haunted his lips.

"Ashalea ..."

"I am yours," she breathed, and together, they were undone. His body shuddered, his tight abdomen flinching in staggered bursts. She threw her head back and moaned her delight to the stillness, and when their hearts ceased their drumming and breaths resumed a steady flow, they collapsed into each other.

She stared at his blue eyes, and he gazed into her emerald ones. And no words were needed. Just the gentle sigh of the world as it cradled them in its arms and sent them rocking into dreamless sleep.

She hadn't known just how much that release was needed. Her worries felt less significant, her stress somehow deflated as she lay in Denavar's arms. His grin suggested the feeling was mutual.

"I could really go a wine right now," he sighed as he sank into a particularly spongey cushion.

Ashalea groaned. "A spicy red accompanied by some cheeses and bread." She licked her lips, and her tummy growled in response. "If only."

"Well," he said, rifling through their packs the Diodonians had

so thoughtfully brought along after they'd knocked them out with screeching mind powers, "there's no wine or cheese stashed in here, but I do have pickled vegetables and a hunk of bread."

She smiled. "Good enough." He tore off a chunk of the crusty loaf and pried open the jar containing the vegetables. When the lid came off, she was just about salivating at the smell.

Denavar laughed before popping a pickle into her mouth. She sagged with contentment, her taste buds drinking in the juices with glee. He raised a brow at the vegetable half hanging between her lips.

"If you're hungry I have something else you can eat," he crooned suggestively.

"Scoundrel," she teased, just as the thrill jolted through her core. But she raised a brow of her own before biting down with a resounding crunch.

He winced and clutched at his manhood. "Perhaps another time," he said with roguish charm.

She was too ravenous to reply, grunting as she stuffed all sorts of plant matter into her mouth, chewing with bulging cheeks. Denavar laughed. "My lady, deliverer of vengeance and devourer of fermented goods."

Ashalea swallowed. "It's the crunch that really does the trick on both accounts."

His mouth curled in amusement. "Well then, by all means, bite *hard*."

They ate their fill in silence after that, and once more leaned back into a pillow of clouds, sighing their content. It was after a time spent kneading the muscles screaming in her back that Denavar said, carefully and quietly, "Has it happened again?"

She didn't need to ask specifics. He was talking, of course, about the visions and lucid dreams that plagued her back in Shadowvale.

Some small nag from her conscience told her that perhaps he had seen or heard it happen when camping, too. The question was what to do about it. Or rather, what *could* she do about it?

Ashalea closed her eyes, wishing they could just forget everything and burrow into this den forever. But try as she might, she knew these visions were just the beginning. And she couldn't keep lying about it. Things always had a way of announcing themselves rather loudly and at inopportune moments when ignored for too long.

When she opened her lids, she found him staring at her, concern etched into his brow, mouth pursed. There would be no denying him now. The charmless, witless, uncharacteristically serious face was a mark of worry that rarely showed itself.

She sighed. "When we were camping after Shadowvale, I dreamed. I—I saw him. His memories."

Denavar swore before running a hand through his hair. "How is this even possible?"

"I don't know. But what I saw, they weren't lies or my mind making up narratives of its own. I believe these were honest memories. True memories. I can't explain it."

He took a breath and reached for her hands—the strength, the sincerity in those calloused palms enough to ground her. "What did you see?"

She gulped down the nerves fluttering in her belly. "I saw him as a child. Innocent, curious. He was running through a field, playing chasey with a woman. I think ... I think she was my mother."

Denavar's eyes widened but he said nothing, the silence urging her to continue.

"The vision changed to him as a youth. He was with other boys his age. They ..." she swallowed again, "they were beating on him. Savage. Cruel."

 158

Denavar cocked his head thoughtfully. "Go on."

"The visions kept changing, but each time he was older." Her nose puckered as she frowned. "He was misunderstood. Treated unkindly, abused because of his status and his power. People were afraid. I think ... I think even my parents were afraid."

"Did you see them? In the vision?" His hands squeezed her own in reassurance.

"No. Their faces were always clouded, covered in a sort of fog."

He nodded in understanding and she continued. "The last vision was at Renlock on the day of his examination. Wezlan was there with the other wizards. I saw them fail Crinos on the spot."

"Because of the imbalance," Denavar breathed. "Because darkness overshadowed the light inside."

She nodded, suddenly overcome with emotion, a twang of sympathy firing in her heart. "His face when they denied him, it was heart-breaking. It was—"

"Necessary," Denavar cut in sharply. He noticed her flinch slightly at his words, and she observed his immediate regret at the tone. "I don't need to remind you of what he's done, Ashalea. What destruction he reaped upon Renlock back then, upon the Moonglade Meadows. Upon ..." he trailed off, not wanting to say the words.

"Upon my parents," she said with a heavy heart. "Both my birth parents and adoptive mother and father. I know. But a part of me can't help but feel sorry for the innocent child, for the hopeful young man."

Denavar's eyes hardened, not at her, but at the thought of the dark creature Crinos had become. "You can feel sorry for him when his body is rotting in the ground, Ashalea. Because if he ever hurts you, if he ever hurts anyone else that I care about, I'll rip his throat out myself."

13

A Lovely Liar

DENAVAR

IT TAKES COURAGE, to reveal one's innermost feelings, to unveil the fears and doubts and misgivings inside. To lay bare all that makes you vulnerable. Once said, the words cannot be withdrawn, only acted upon.

Ashalea had kept her secret a few days longer, not wanting to worry the others, instead keeping it to herself as the Guardians became acquainted with Razakh. The chieftain had affairs to attend to before upping and leaving, and truthfully, Denavar was in no real rush to keep moving. As much as he loved travelling and exploring, the road had been long, their party constantly moving.

And he had made exceptionally good use of his time with Ashalea. As he rolled his muscles and stretched, he couldn't remember feeling so light. If only his partner could say the same.

As Ashalea approached the group, Denavar sensed her anxiety radiating in small waves. Saw her body shift uncomfortably, the bob of her throat, the nails clicking against each other. Was it harder to admit one's faults to friends? Did she suspect they'd think less of her for what she was facing alone?

Ashalea cleared her throat, and they gazed at her expectantly. Wezlan stared at her knowingly, as if he were privy to all the secrets in her head. He might be getting on in age, but the old boy didn't miss a thing with those stormy, calculating eyes.

"I need to tell you something," she said slowly, looking to him uncertainly. From his casual position leaning against the cave wall, he nodded his consent. His support.

"I've been having visions of the darkness. At first it was like a phantom in my mind, trying to reel me in, trying to convince me to forgive him, to let go of my humanity and give in to the ... bloodthirst."

Wezlan cocked a head and asked with measured calm, "When did they start occurring?"

Abashed, Ashalea picked at an invisible thread on her britches. "Back in Shadowvale," she admitted.

"And have they impacted you physically in any way?" her mentor asked.

"Well ..." Ashalea gazed at Denavar, swallowed. "When the first one occurred, I lost control of my body ... or at least I wasn't aware of my actions at the time."

Wezlan's eyes darted to Denavar for explanation.

"She had a blade to my throat," he said casually.

Ashalea glared at him and he offered her an apologetic smile. *Honesty is the best course,* he tried to tell her with his eyes. A small nod in return seemed to be her reluctant answer.

"What?" Shara's eyes narrowed, her voice high. "And you only

thought to tell us now?"

Ashalea winced. "I ... I wanted to know more about what was happening to me. I wanted to understand it. And Denavar wasn't hurt—just a scratch, really."

"You drew blood?" a shriek now, and Ashalea shrank in on herself. A rare sight indeed for his courageous warrior woman.

There was a low rumble and the assassin realised Razakh was sniggering. "Oh, don't even start," she snapped.

This is going to get ugly real soon, Denavar thought with a grimace. And as if reading his thoughts, Wezlan stepped forward, hands raised placatingly. His stern gaze silenced Razakh, and a glare at Shara managed to restrain her ever so slightly.

"Let's all just take a minute. No one has been hurt, Ashalea is okay. We're all fine." He paused. "Have you learnt anything from these visions? Foresight into the future?"

Ashalea shook her head. "The opposite, actually. The last revealed snippets of his past. Who he used to be ... what changed him into what he has become."

"The examination at Renlock," Denavar confirmed.

Sorrow glazed over Wezlan's eyes, pulled at the lines of his mouth, and Denavar wondered if that was guilt or remorse causing his shoulders to sag a little lower. He had been the judge and jury at Crinos's trial, after all. But one of several, and mage law had always been unflinching, irrefutable. Whether it was his choice or not, the outcome would have always been the same.

Ironic, given their attempt to prevent an individual from abusing his power was in fact the very reason it caused it to erupt so catastrophically. The rejection being the final blow to Crinos's pride, the proverbial straw that didn't break the beast, but the one that created it.

"A small part of me will always wonder if things could have gone differently. If we had been gentler, kinder, if we had given him another purpose to use his skills for good." Wezlan sighed. "But that was then, this is now, and it is best we leave the past well alone and focus on our current situation."

Razakh peered at Ashalea with those wise eyes. *"Perhaps it would be prudent if we discover whether these visions are harmful or not."*

Shara snorted. "Apparently that's of little consequence here. If anyone makes a wrong move, they'll hear about it but oh no, Wezlan's precious ward gets off with barely a warning. Your lies put us in danger, Ashalea!"

"I wasn't talking about them being harmful to the rest of you. I was talking about their effect on her," Razakh drawled.

Denavar saw the guilt deepen on his partner's face before it morphed into rage, her fingers clenching, teeth bared. He had never seen her look so angry, and over such a small quarrel, no less. Were the visions affecting her psyche, too?

"Drive the knife a little deeper, why don't you," Ashalea spat at Shara. "I would never do anything to hurt Denavar, to hurt any of you. I should have told you straight away, but I thought there was a chance we could use them to our advantage."

There was silence for a beat, and Wezlan and Razakh padded quietly from the den, sensing the argument was one between friends, rather than Guardians. Denavar watched on, still leaning casually against the wall, his cool demeanour betraying nothing of his thoughts. And for good reason, too.

He loved this woman like he'd loved nothing and no one before. She was his silver-haired queen, his pride, his purpose in every step and every swing of the sword. He would fight for her, with her, against the darkness, and yet she would only make his role harder if she wasn't honest and open. If her secrets were a shield to block him out ... block them all out.

And then those two words puffed out on an icy breath, more cutting and colder than yelling or walking away ever could be.

"You *lied*," Shara said.

He'd never really seen shock fill Ashalea's face. Not like this. Those beautiful features contorted into furrowed brows, a pinched nose ... but it was the eyes that betrayed her. Green, soulful eyes that lost the anger and widened with sadness. That learnt for perhaps the first time what it was to have a friend ... and to hurt them.

"Shara, I ..." Ashalea stumbled, at a loss for words. A lump in her throat rose and fell. "I didn't mean to keep this from you, to hurt you. I just ... I didn't want to be a burden on everyone. To have eyes glued to my every movement, to have pity shine in my friends' eyes."

Shara's face softened a little. The hard lines easing, the amber eyes dimming to embers instead of wildfire. "Do you think me so heartless?" she said gently.

Ashalea approached her friend, placed a hand on her shoulder. "Never. But I know you care for me. For our strange little family. And I know you've never really ... never really had that before. Not like this anyway. To care is to be vulnerable. Friendship, love, it's a distraction that could be costly."

Shara shook her head, black hair tumbling around her face. "If the last few months have taught me anything, it's that we are stronger together. United. We've got each other's backs; we trust in each other—are honest with each other. Do you think I'd still be standing here, alive and mostly whole had I not had a reason to push through the pain? Had I not had a reason to hold onto life, rather than let the darkness consume me? Let the darkness break me?"

Ashalea opened her mouth to speak but the assassin simply raised

a hand, commanding the room to be silent. "I never really told you how thankful I am. For what you did. Death is always a breath away in my line of work, but I never feared it. Never worried when it would take me. And it wasn't until I was close to dying in that cell beneath the earth that I really wondered how much I cared if I left this world."

Her eyes glazed, turning contemplative as the girl dredged up memories of her time in that cell. Tortured by her brother. Abused by the darkness and his plaything, Vera. Left to rot amongst the deranged, the murderous, and even the innocent, whose screams Denavar had no doubt would haunt Shara until the end of her days.

His hands balled into fists at the thought of it. How the darkness had starved her, had his lackeys taunt her and carve cruel reminders into her flesh. He remembered seeing the jagged lines etched into her skin the day her frail body was laid onto a cot in Shadowvale, the filthy scrap of clothes she wore hanging like a sack upon her bony, hollow frame.

The fissures that quaked upon her back, red, raw, and oozing with infection. He remembered combining his Magicka with Ashalea and Wezlan, the three of them working in unison to clean her body of the rot that had taken hold, of the tainted blood, the ruptured cells and flesh beneath the outside shell. He remembered the pinch of Wezlan's brows, the horror that swam on his beloved's face right before she emptied her stomach at the sight of it all. The guilt, the sorrow, the pain of what had occurred emptying out of her in waves.

But they had worked relentlessly to repair the damage that had been done. As much as they could at least. Some hurts ran too deep, some scars could not be mended. And what they could save on the outside was little comfort to the pain she carried inside. To the damage that could heal only with time.

He saw that hurt reflecting in her eyes now, glistening as she

recalled those dark days. But he noticed, too, the shoulders squaring in defiance, the hands curling into fists and the steely glint that crept into her eyes. A deep inhale followed by a release of tension and trauma.

"I thought about the promises that would go unfulfilled, the wrongs never righted, the duties I held. Most of all I thought of you," she said with a glance between them. "I thought of the people I'd leave behind, and my heart ached. Truly *ached* with a different kind of pain at that thought.

"I remembered your kindness, Ashalea, and your ridiculous humour and ill-mannered jokes, Denavar." She smiled, and he grinned in reply. "I remembered Wezlan's stormy eyes and his ability to find wisdom in everything, damn him."

They all laughed softly at that.

"So, thank you, Ashalea. From one crooked assassin to another. For giving me a reason to stick around and keep you on course, for showing me the meaning of friendship, for giving me life again." Her eyes burned and she swallowed a lump in her throat. "You lot are the family I should have had when I grew up. So now you know, this second time around, why I want us to always be straightforward, to be honest, to not build walls around us. No more lies."

Her glare was icy enough to wither everything in its path, and yet, still conveyed warmth. Denavar had to laugh. "I'd listen to her, Ashalea, the mistress of hounds knows her stuff."

Shara's wrath turned on Denavar. "One Diodonian I am slow to place my trust in, and you've already got new material?" She rolled her eyes. "Unbelievable. Perhaps it's you who needs a short leash."

He flashed her his most dashing smile, noticing Ashalea biting her lip to stop from howling. But the mood quickly shifted before settling into neutrality.

Ashalea offered Shara a hand in supplication. "No more lies."

They shook hands, and the cave seemed to breathe a sigh of relief as both women smiled at each other, all discord forgotten.

"Crisis averted then, I'd say," Denavar said cheerfully.

Both women gifted him with their most furious glares and his insides fluttered with amusement.

Yep. The world had resumed its normal rhythm once again.

The central chamber was full of Diodonians, their golden, red, and brown bodies looming in the dimly lit cave, the fires on their backs swaying gently, soft blue flames sighing in the near still air. And in the middle stood two humans and two elves, small specks amid the hulking beasts surrounding them.

Denavar eyed off the creatures with a casual but critical eye. His elven senses on high alert, his stance lazy but his muscles ready to spring into action if need be. Their weapons had not yet been returned, but his hands were mightier than the sword. His Magicka rippled beneath the surface, veins surging with its power. And despite the formidable jaws and the giant paws etched with dagger-sharp claws, it was the Diodonians' telepathic powers that would be the breaking point. One repeat of that mind-blowing screech would have him on all fours, utterly helpless and vulnerable.

His instincts told him Razakh had honest intentions, that this noble beast was true to his word. And even though their meeting had proved conveniently easy, almost sudden, some logical part of Denavar's senses told him the Guardians would play a bigger role in this desert before they'd see the other side, which of course meant alliances would need strengthening and all species would need to work together.

Ashalea and Wezlan had agreed Razakh was the next Guardian. If Denavar was being honest with himself, he'd felt that pull as well. The aura that seemed to radiate from the chieftain; a soothing, golden shroud that spoke of strength, purity, honour. He'd always trusted his instincts—they'd not failed him yet, so he wasn't about to ignore them now.

Only, it wasn't the chieftain that concerned him, but the beasts that obeyed their leader. Denavar sensed the uneasiness in the air, the mistrust—even hatred—for a species not their own. The past was still too painful. He had no doubt that some in this room—the elderly and the children of long-gone souls—had lost mates, sons and daughters, fathers and mothers, to the campaign of humans long dead and rotting in the ground.

He could understand why they'd be so hesitant to trust, to accept their presence. Especially where Wezlan and Shara were concerned. Perhaps the wizard was granted some leniency, some semblance of respect for his station and the general do-good history associated with wizards, but for Shara ... An assassin who'd already shown contempt to their leader? Not a marriage for the ages.

Denavar could sense their readiness to clamp mighty jaws around her neck and snap it in two. An outcome that was simply not possible. He wouldn't allow it, and so the uncomfortable tension in the air lingered. He gathered his Magicka to the fore, his own casual aura of power emanating from him that he was sure had not gone unnoticed.

Razakh stalked around the circle, eying off his kin and the group before him—the group he was now to be a part of. He wore nobility well; the proud shoulders rippling with power as one giant paw after the other advanced, head held high, silver eyes scanning his family, his friends, his soldiers.

The other Diodonians bowed slightly when he looked at them, not out of fear or an unspoken command, but out of respect for their leader. The chieftain who was to walk in his father's pawprints. Denavar wondered who his replacement would be, though he didn't have to wait long.

"*The people—humans and elves alike—that stand before you are tasked with protecting Everosia,*" Razakh began. "*As you have all heard the stories, the Grove stands as the last barrier of protection in Everosia. The gate being the portal that locked away the very darkness that now sends creatures to roam freely in our lands.*" Razakh cocked a head to Wezlan, who cleared his throat and continued the story.

"Over time this blight grew in power, pooling its Magicka until it could escape the other dimension. The gate—the lock we placed to prevent this—remains closed, meaning the darkness is still partially bound to the other realm. It cannot walk Everosia for long, and whilst the gate still stands, it has limited power to send its armies here. But if that gate is broken ... if the portal is undone ..."

"A storm will unleash on our world," Denavar clarified. "The darkness will be free to stay here and wreak havoc, his armies will flow through the portal and destroy everything in their path."

Razakh stopped his pacing and sat on his haunches. "*Which is why I must leave. To become a Guardian, to stand in my sire's place and continue his work.*"

Bells pealed in Denavar's head as the Diodonians' voices flooded through his mind, their alarm and dismay clanging like chimes upon the hour, each growing more frantic than the last, their emotions ringing through the words in nauseating waves. He could feel their pain, their hate, their dread.

"*You're leaving us?*"

"*The Diodonians can fend for themselves.*"

"The humans don't deserve your help."

He raised his hands to his ears, gritting his teeth, and found his friends doing much the same. All but Wezlan, who with a few muttered words, sent a Magickal shroud to fall upon their shoulders, numbing the invasion of their minds, dulling the pain to a whisper.

He nodded at Wezlan in thanks, earning a smile that didn't meet the wizard's eyes. The wizard was all business now and careful courtesies. They weren't in familiar territory anymore.

A low rumble from Razakh silenced the chamber and immediately the bells ceased their symphony. Denavar straightened, resuming his relaxed stance just as he heard the audible sighs of relief from Shara and Ashalea.

"I understand your anger towards the humans. I feel it in my bones ... for it is also in my heart. The visions of that horrible time gifted to me by my father—a warning, and a lesson. But we cannot hold an entire race accountable for the actions of their ancestors. We cannot ignore the world in its time of need. I will do my duty as the next Guardian of the Grove, just as I expect you all to do what is right."

Deathly silence settled in the cave, more deafening than any choir. He was asking them to fight, Denavar realised. To reveal themselves once again, to take a stand against the darkness. And to do that meant joining with the other races. To forge new allegiances. Tension roiled in his stomach as he considered the possible consequences of this.

Would old hurts shed new blood? The Diodonians certainly wouldn't forget, but could they forgive?

He glanced at Ashalea and found a slight frown on her pouted lips, brows and eyes downturned as she, too, considered what this meant. Shara, to her credit, remained silent throughout this show. Not a glimmer of emotion on her face, her pose that of on an Onyxonite, a soldier. And soldiers knew when to fall in line, when to keep their opinions behind closed lips.

A beast approached from the ranks, taking his place at Razak's left. He was magnificent, and, if Denavar was being honest, a little fear inducing. He towered over his chieftain, his coat a vibrant red, not the glimmer of an ember or the ray of a rising sun, but fire incarnate. Battle scars lined his fur, and an eye was missing from its socket, the other a swirl of metallic steel.

Denavar knew immediately he was Razakh's second. And one look told him this beast would die for his Klan. For his chieftain. He would follow orders—no questions asked—whether he thought it wise or not. But he wouldn't be carrying out orders anymore, he'd be giving them.

And sure enough, as Razakh shared a careful glance with his second, the beast responded with a swish of his tail. Answer enough for the chieftain.

"It pains me to leave you all in a time of need and disarray. Many things will change. Many obstacles will block your path, and many of you may die. I say this with a heavy heart, but it is time. Time for us to rise up, to step from the shadows and reclaim our rightful place in this world as equals."

Razakh's flames flared to life, his form resplendent in the half-dark. He rose, addressing the Klan with fire in his belly, his eyes, his very core. *"We are a proud race. One worthy of the pages of history. One worthy of mention in days to come. And when this war is done, should anyone be left standing, I want us to enter the new world as masters of the sand. Masters of our own future. And should any man seek to claim our power then wicked will his ending be."*

The Diodonians roared their answer, their own flames spurting to life one by one, their collective heat a blazing whirlwind of fire as bright as the sun high in the sky. Its force caused beads of sweat to form on Denavar's brow, the sweltering cave nearly impossible to bear.

But he stood his ground, as did his comrades, braving their might and standing united. When the Diodonians finally quieted, Wezlan approached Razakh, head dipped in earnest.

"It is time we work together once again. Man, Diodonian, elf, and dwarf. We must work towards peace, starting with you, Razakh, to join the Guardians and lend us your might."

Denavar walked to the chieftain, stretched out a palm, "Together."

Wezlan mimicked his movements, determination bright in his eyes.

Ashalea crept to Denavar's side, squeezed his free hand with her own while extending the other.

And then there was Shara. Hesitant but proud, a warrior unwavering, unyielding. Hard as metal, cunning, mighty as a dragon. For a moment Denavar feared she would not comply, not set aside her reservations. But metal can be adaptable, reformed, strengthened. With squared shoulders and a hard gleam in her eye, she approached, eyeing off the circle.

"Together."

Razakh moved his muzzle to their hands, and as they connected it was as though a bond rippled through them, his aura merging with their own, the shroud somehow growing brighter, larger. And thus, a new Guardian was born.

Shara gasped, feeling Magicka ripple through her human body, and Denavar smirked.

"Kind of hard to deny he's one of us now, eh?"

She glared at him and tossed her hair back. "Not another word."

"*Ready to apologise, wrath?*"

She rolled her eyes. "Oh, quit your growling, dog."

But her mouth betrayed the smallest crinkle of a smile, and Denavar noticed Razakh's eyes flare in amusement. Perhaps there was

hope for them yet. Despite Shara's bark being as sharp as her bite.

Razakh glanced at his second, and a nod prompted the beast to move front and centre. Razakh appraised him with a nod of approval. *"I present your new chieftain, Linar. There is no one I trust more to lead you into battle and protect our most vulnerable. May he bring honour to Kalanor's Klan. May he lead you well."*

As one, the Diodonians bowed deeply, but Denavar looked not to the Klan but to their new chieftain who stood staunch, still as a stone statue upon the Isle of Dread. Which reminded Denavar, there *had* been Diodonian statues on that nightmare island.

He recalled seeing Diodonians amid the numerous creatures trapped in stone not so long ago, when the Guardians and a crew of seafaring fools had sailed across the Onyx Ocean to find an old tome. One that contained the spell to drain the darkness of his ability to conjure portals. The spell that Denavar, Wezlan, and Ashalea had been too late to use.

It had all been for nothing. The loss of the Violet Star and most of its crew—the remains of the ship having long since settled at the bottom of the Onyx Ocean. Some had died on the Isle of Dread, lost to the leering faces and bared fangs of those creatures come to life on a phantom wind: on that chessboard of death, a massacre of men laid at their feet.

The moment they had been released from their tombs of stone was one he'd never forget. He still didn't know how or why they'd come to life, but he knew there was an ancient Magicka over that island that sought death and destruction. He hoped he never had reason to step foot on that place again.

He hoped he never found a reason as to why there had been Diodonian statues on that Isle. He hoped he'd never see them on the *wrong* side of war again. Because they certainly hadn't been statues on the losing team. Perhaps he'd ask Razakh about it, or perhaps he'd leave the past alone.

Denavar's icy blue eyes pierced into Linar now, studying him, weighing his measure. So much intelligence in those eyes, but the intention beneath them was unknown. Denavar couldn't grasp it, and he usually had a knack for judging one's character. His instincts raised no immediate alarms, but he'd been wrong before, when that worm, Avari Ventiri, had betrayed the mages at Renlock, and supplied information that led to the deaths of many.

His Magicka uncoiled with icy intent at that thought. It begged to be released, to be let loose upon the darkness with all his might. His most powerful weapon, his greatest chance at bringing justice to those whose ashes had been scattered on the winds. To his friends. To Farah. That fiery mane as bright as the Diodonians around him. Long gone from this world.

Reminders of her everywhere he looked ate away at his insides. Every time he saw a flame, felt its warmth and heard that crackle and spit of fire, he was reminded of her brilliance and passion. But when he remembered her, his thoughts inevitably turned to the image burned into his mind of her broken body crumpled in the mud, flaming hair seemingly dulled as it fanned around her petite frame.

She had loved him for so long, and Denavar had loved her too, in his own way. But it stoked the guilt inside when he thought of her feelings for him, unreturned. He had always loved Farah as a friend. Never more. Never like she wanted. He'd never loved anyone until Ashalea, and he felt there had been a reason for that.

He couldn't keep his promise to Finnicus—his childhood friend, skilled mage, and troublemaker to boot—who with his last words beseeched Denavar to protect his twin sister. But Denavar had failed, and that broken promise was just another kernel of guilt that festered inside.

Denavar felt a gentle squeeze of his hand and started out of his memories and back into the present. Ashalea was gazing at him with concern, her lovely face lined with worry. Such a beautiful elf. So full of love and kindness and yet so twisted from the deeds of her dark and demented brother. He wished he could wipe the slate clean and start fresh with her, start a life together without the burdens that awaited them, and carried with them wherever they went. Instead, he squeezed back, his palm brushing the callouses on her hand. A warrior's hand.

Are you okay? her questioning stare said. All he could do was smile broadly and offer a wink. She knew better of course; her sad smile suggested as much. But they were together, and they would tackle this beast of a battle side-by-side.

And if it came to it, they'd die that way, too.

Tooth and Claw

SHARA

SHARA MADE HER WAY UP THE SILKEN SLOPE, hoping to gain a good vantage point to spy on the activity ahead. She wriggled her way up to the rise, grunting as she did. *Sand.* She hated the stuff. Course, grainy, irritating, it got everywhere: in her hair, in her boots, in the corset she wore and somehow beneath it, scratching her skin.

She shook her ebony hair in annoyance. Once again, she'd been tasked with scouting duty, this time overlooking the actions not of men, but the darkness's creatures. An easy enough job, sure, but the sun was scorching, the heat as stifling as the smell from Fari's Dungeon. She snorted. At least she hadn't had to do the honours for that one. Poor Denavar had copped that job back on the Isle of Dread.

Taking a swig from a canteen at her hip, her amber eyes squinted against the glare. She made sure to stay low as she observed, not wishing to give away her position. Shadows and stealth were her forte, night was an ally for her line of work, not glaring suns and giant dogs. She peered at the companion she had been lumped with.

"*I can feel you staring,*" Razakh said with a soft growl.

"I can barely see," she complained. "One of the elves would have been better suited to this. Unless *your* vision is better?"

He turned to her with a snarl, "*As a matter of fact, Diodonians can see far better than you humans. We've a knack for hunting and scouting. Our packs are born for it.*"

She waved a hand in dismissal before rolling onto her back, uttering an exaggerated yawn and stretching her arms behind her. "Well, don't let me stop you then. Report once you're done."

Razakh snapped his mighty jaws a few inches from her face and she smirked. Baiting him was going to be a whole lot of fun. But what he said next surprised her. Blunt, unfeeling, straight to the point.

"*I see through you, girl. The bravery, the façade. So quick to anger, to mask what hides beneath.*"

His voice was soft, gentle, but her stomach clenched, and she swallowed her surprise with distaste; dry and crunchy as the sand around her.

"What would you know of who I am?" she spat.

He ignored the sting. "*I know what it is to feel empty. To feel incomplete. I have known pain, loss ... helplessness.*"

Shara's heart wilted at the last. Just the very word was enough to dredge up memories and phantom pains that danced along her skin. The pain she could take, the hunger, the thirst, but feeling helpless was what almost broke her. Feeling powerless and vulnerable, all the tools she had: her mind, her weapons training, sweet talking of people,

traps, and locks, all useless.

She turned on her side and studied the silver eyes that bore into her own, as if they were digging into her foundation, the fabric of her being, uncovering all her secrets. They swirled slowly, lazily, and Shara could only wonder if the power hidden within was not of this world.

"You—" She looked at him curiously, her interest piqued at the change of dynamic. She hunkered into the sand, forgetting their mission entirely. "You experienced ... you were ..." The words wouldn't come. Giving voice to it just seemed wrong, cruel.

The Diodonian shook his head. *"My mother and I were captured, trapped by bandits from the merchant city of Madoc and sold to slavers from Maynesgate."*

Shara's face tightened, the colour draining from her skin. "Slavers? I thought slavery was abolished hundreds of years ago."

Razgeir growled. *"By law, yes. But there will always be those who trade in misery and misfortune when the price is right. And slavery did indeed fetch a high price back then. Especially when the slaves in question were a Diodonian mother and her pup. Ripe for experimentation."*

Bile rose in her throat, threatening to overcome her as she looked at Razakh in a new light. He spoke so calmly, his voice a whisper in her mind. But she *felt* the bitterness laced in those words, the anger that charged beneath them.

Shara swallowed her contempt, biting her lip uncertainly before asking, "And did they ... did she?"

A sigh echoed through her mind. A strange notion given that such acts are physical in nature. But the air huffed with malcontent in her brain, the heat of it tingling her nerves.

"They never laid a hand on me. Didn't have the chance to. They began with my mother. Wanted to ensure they 'didn't damage the goods' I heard them say. They operated on her even as she breathed, even as life coursed

178

through her. And they did the same when she was dead."

There was silence for a beat. Horror coursed through Shara's core as she imagined him then. Barely more than a pup, terrified, alone, *helpless*, while humans experimented on his mother, rifled through her mind, scrambling it like eggs upon a skillet. How frightened he must have been. How small he must have felt. But how did he escape?

"A slave boy saved me," Razakh whispered, and Shara started, realising he could *read* her mind as well as speak in it.

His silver eyes swirled, caught in a memory as he continued, *"He crept in late at night, the clever little cub had snatched himself the jailor's keys. He tried to save as many as he could, I think. But he freed me from my cage first. Perhaps it was a kinship of age, an understanding of what it was to lose a parent. I never asked. Never spoke a word to him. But when I made towards my mother, the boy simply shook his head. It was answer enough but ... but I'll always wonder if I should have tried. Should have looked ... made sure there was nothing that could be done."*

Shara's voice was hoarse, laden with sorrow. "You were just a youngling. There was nothing—"

But Razakh was utterly lost now. He either chose not to or simply didn't hear her. *"I never saw that boy again. Never learned if he made it out. He told me to run and run I did. I never looked back. But I'll always remember. Always be grateful for that one human, who against all odds decided to be someone better."*

Silence. Then, "I'm sorry."

He snapped out of his memories and looked her straight in the eye. Razakh was strength and resilience and toughness. Hardness limned his features as she gazed upon him now. *"Why ever would you be?"*

She stared straight back, unflinching. "I'm not sorry for circumstance or history. I'm not sorry for events that made you stronger. Harder." A cruel grin swept across her face. "I'm sorry I couldn't be there to end those cowards myself."

Razakh cocked a head at her, less the noble Diodonian and more a hound with a penchant for mischief. An understanding flickered between them. A mutual agreement. They were one and the same, Shara and he; both victims of abuse, cruelty and misfortune, yet both survivors ... warriors.

It was a bold move to reveal his secrets to her. It took courage, trust, even after he had said the Diodonians would not so easily trust in the virtue of men. But everything he carried inside, all the emotions he buried deep, so too did Shara. Finally, someone who understood.

She would shed no tears over his story, and he would not ask of her own. But deep down they would both know they made it out, and woe is the fate of those who got in their way. Shara shuffled back up the sand, peering at the activity—or lack thereof—from the Uulakh in the distance.

"You know, I really can't see what's happening yonder." All she saw were dark shapes splodging about, little more than specks on the horizon. The glare was too bright, and the sands seemed to blend into a great stretch of blotchy red.

A chuckle rumbled through her mind as Razakh turned his attention to the encampment ahead. "*I know.*" He edged forward, stance like that of a predator hunting its prey. "*The Uulakh gather supplies from the portal. Crates of food, water, containers of weapons. Nothing much has changed since our last raid, though their numbers have grown whilst we've been occupied for the last few days.*"

She sighed. "They'll continue to swarm through that portal until they've found what they want or until they're dead. I'm sure the darkness will kill them himself should they fail to do his bidding."

And he would, too. He'd probably slice their throats or snap their

necks should they disappoint him. Her own neck itched suddenly, and it took every effort not to raise a hand to that place. The supple flesh that had once been bruised and wrung out like a wet towel until—

She felt Razakh's eyes rake over her, widen ever so slightly in surprise, and she shook her head. Thinking of such matters wasn't healthy *or* helpful.

"*So use it then.*"

She frowned. "What?"

"*The pain. The anger. Use it against him. To spite him.*"

The frown deepened to a scowl. "I don't remember inviting you to read my thoughts. Your voice clanging in my head is annoying enough," she huffed.

A knowing look followed by rippling amusement. "*Cranky. Fine.*" He puffed. "*I shall allow you that privacy, at least.*"

She couldn't stop the smile that edged onto her lips. *Clever little beast.*

"*Big beast,*" he corrected before she felt his presence exit her mind.

Shara rolled her eyes, focusing again on the task at hand. And then an idea popped into her head. The clarity of it bright and searing as the sun bearing down on her. One immaculate brow lifted. "The darkness will kill them if they fail ... unless we beat him to it."

The Diodonian grinned clumsily, loose skin stretching along his fangs. She wasn't sure if she should laugh or grimace at the odd display.

"*What are you thinking?*" he asked, those wise, silver eyes swirling with curiosity.

Shara smiled devilishly. "I've a notion," she said.

Razakh groaned. Yes, groaned, like a human. "*Don't think too hard or you'll tear a muscle.*"

Her answering grin was villainous. "I've a notion ... involving two

elves and a wizard ... and a spell for sealing portals." She flicked her hair, "And the talents of yours truly, of course."

A grumble. "*You should be so lucky.*"

<hr />

Her plan was a sound one. And provided the darkness offered no surprises, they would be in and out and home for dinner. Though, not a very tempting notion, really. They had rationed non-perishable supplies for their journey, and Goddess knows what food source the Diodonians lived off. Apparently, all but the younglings, the mothers, and the elderly, went hunting every night. "*Easier to find prey,*" Razakh had said, though looking at the barren lands surrounding her, she couldn't imagine what animals actually lived in this place.

She sighed. A hot meal after battle would be unlikely; maybe she'd just skewer one of the fish in the waterfall's pond later. Shara cackled. Razakh would certainly have something to say about that.

She was halfway down the sand dune, making her way towards the Ruins ahead. Her eyes widened as she gazed upon the remains of ancient buildings that once stood proudly within a golden city. Towers of smooth sandstone, now crumbled and decrepit, reached half-heartedly to the sky above. Rogue walls staggered here and there, all that was left of houses and markets and barracks—a city swallowed by the sands.

Some archways curved triumphantly, the elegant swirls and whorls of intricate design half ravaged by time and the unchecked power of mages long turned to dust. Try as she might, Shara couldn't picture the city in days past.

It would have been a sight to behold. Not the shining city of crystals in Windarion, or the great autumnal village of Woodrandia

that Ashalea had spoken so fondly of, but a behemoth stone city: a fortress of might, a maze of wonder, a marketplace of the world. She imagined it would have been teeming with life and colour and Magicka of a different kind, a simple kind. A glorious blend of laughter and simplicity and peace.

No such city remained. Madoc was no more, nothing left but the Ruins of its namesake. But the wreckage that stood yonder told a different story of the city. One where greed and politics and power combined ended in slaughter and savagery and the poisoning of a king and his people. She frowned. That combined with the tale she had heard from Razakh just before ... No wonder the Diodonians were loath to trust in mankind.

Mentally, she swept aside these thoughts from her mind. Her task was a simple one: distract and destroy. She sprinted across the sand dunes and, at the last slope, slid down it with steady feet, her boots skimming the sandy red loam with ease.

A horde of Uulakh gathered at the old entrance to the Ruins, their scaled heads lifting to see a single figure skating across the desert with fleetfooted purpose. Their reptilian eyes would have distinguished her features now and ascertained a human woman was running towards her death. They grinned with ugly faces, salivating at the prospect of a carcass worth ravaging, worth making a meal over.

With a bloodcurdling cry they descended on Shara, a great mass of fangs and forked tongues and scaly, long-tailed hides. Hundreds of yellow eyes gazed upon their victim, and still she sprinted towards the throng, raising two silver swords high above her head, their keen edges glinting in the sun.

The signal had been sent; the trap sprung.

With roars that shook the earth, the Diodonians attacked, lunging from behind fallen walls and chunks of rock to the Uulakhs'

right, another flank incoming from the left, preparing to box in their unwanted guests. The golden beasts' muscles rippled like the sand beneath her feet, their paws thundering on the ground, glints of red and brown reflecting off their coats like a desert storm. They knew the land better than any, could blend into the environment with ease, and how they fought? Well, Shara was *very* interested to watch.

With a clash, the first Diodonian reached its quarry, great fangs sinking into a reptile's neck as it dove gracefully with deadly intent. The battle of beasts had begun. The Diodonians reached the Uulakh before Shara did, their trap catching the enemy off guard and creating waves of panic that crashed down upon them, drowning them in blood.

Roars and hisses filled the air, and the occasional whoosh of a spear as it was hurled towards a target, but even those that found their mark in shoulders and haunches did not fell the mighty Diodonians. They attacked relentlessly, great paws batting away crude weapons, fangs gnashing, biting, gnawing. Their claws as long and as vicious as daggers when unleashed from in between furry pads.

The Uulakh, initially scattered and panicked, tried their best to form ranks, the tallest and broadest of the bunch hissing orders in a guttural tongue. The reptiles closed the gaps where they could, bunching together to decrease weak points in their horde. Though most of them were unarmed due to the surprise ambush, some had gathered shields and swords, aiming to create a blockade of steel to detain the Diodonians.

And finally, Shara reached the fray. With a battle cry equal to that of her allies, she swept her swords in arcs, gutting the first reptile with ease, its innards spilling in uncoiling piles to its clawed feet. She ducked under the arm of another, slashed its back with one sword and then stabbed a stomach with her other.

If battle was a sonnet, she was the poet, her footwork the whispered words of a lover, her swords dancing with haunting beauty, their slash the kiss of death. This was her art, her creation, her muse.

When she fought, time seemed to slow, her breath the only sound, her swords an extension of her arms, eyes moving from one target to the next, her body relying on instinct and her feet responding in turn. As the creatures spat and bit and clawed and writhed, she only danced, pirouetting with grace and agility.

And then she saw them, Wezlan, Denavar and Ashalea, creeping towards the portal that crackled and hummed with bright blue light. If they succeeded this time, if they closed the portal, it was unlikely the darkness would attempt to set a base in the desert again. A wicked grin split her lips as she considered how frustrated he would be. How angry that once again, their group had thwarted his efforts to some degree, ever the thorn in his side.

Good, she thought, spitting for good measure, viciously sending her blade home through another scaly side. It slid out, covered in sticky, tarlike blood, and she silenced its owner with one final blow, cutting its hiss short.

He would find another place to operate, but at least the Diodonians could focus their attention elsewhere. They would look to the other races in the hope of forming an allegiance, in the hope of growing an army for Everosia so vast that the darkness would be forced to flee and forfeit attempts at burning the damn world to bits.

She knew that would never happen. That he would never stoop so low, that he'd never surrender. If he were the victor, mercy would certainly not be considered. His armies were probably more endless than she could imagine. Still, one could dream.

Her blades whipped in a flurry around her, breath coming out in ragged pants as her energy waned. The Uulakh numbers were

thinning, the fight would soon be done, but until every reptile was dead, she was taking no chances at them interrupting her friends. They would need every minute, every second to complete the spell.

"*To your left!*" A warning peeled in her mind, and she lifted a blade just in time to block the thrust of an Uulakh who had slipped through her guard. She cursed. Such was the price if one was distracted.

Shara turned to finish him when a mighty beast pounced over her head and pinned the reptile, its body twisting and tail flailing as it struggled beneath the weight of the creature. She recognised fear in its eyes, the slit of its pupil dilated, drunk with it. Then the yellow eyes shuttered as its jugular was ripped from its throat in a bloody chunk and spat upon the sands, now stained black from the blood.

And as the Diodonian turned, its maw bloodied with gore and fangs dripping with blood, she recognised it to be Razakh. She offered a curt nod by way of thanks, and soundlessly they both engaged in battle, her attention half on her friends, half on the next victim to her swords.

When the last few Uulakh were being felled by fang or claw—a triumphant grin on her face—she focused wholly on the trio who were stood in a triangle around the portal. Their lips moved with fervour, sweat dripping down their foreheads and beading on their lips. And, in Wezlan's case, drenching his beard.

Their hands were outstretched to one another, no doubt in some Magickal bond to connect their minds and enhance their power. Even she, a human without a scrap of the gift running through her veins, could sense a shift in the air. She could sense a force radiating from them. A wind unfelt on Shara's skin seemed to blast with fury as it whipped Ashalea's silver braid about her face and ruffled Denavar's dark hair.

It rose to a crescendo, so violent that the breeze became a storm,

a hurricane circling her friends as their lips moved ever faster, their faces straining with the effort, muscles bunching in shoulders as they tried to hold their ground. The aura changed, a sense of foreboding thick in the air.

Shara started towards the hurricane, uncaring of the danger, seeking only to protect her friends. Her family. Razakh leaped to her side, blocking most of the force as it smacked against them. The sand lifted, swirling around the clearing, grating against her cheeks and narrowed eyes.

And still the trio stood fast, muttering, chanting. Closer now, just a little closer and Shara would be there, ready to rip them from the spell if need be. And then Ashalea's eyes snapped open, and Shara recognised the look all too well.

Not relief, not triumph, not even exhaustion or pain. It was pure terror. Shara's own widened in fear, and she felt the cold slice of panic jolt through her belly. Something had gone terribly wrong.

She tried with all her might to wade through the sandstorm, Razakh doing his best to shield her and form a path towards the portal. Then, suddenly, as quick as it came, the storm ceased to stillness.

And there, where her friends had been chanting, where the portal had been sizzling, where the world had threatened to break into chaos was ... nothing.

Dread clawed at Shara's heart as she realised with a tangible clarity, so bright and searing as the sun bearing down on her ...

Ashalea, Denavar, and Wezlan, were gone.

15

Far from Home

ASHALEA

THE PORTAL WAS UNLIKE THE LAST ONE and indeed the one before that. As she crept towards the crackle and spit of its crystalline blue surface, the power emanating from it was different. Changed. Gone was the glasslike interior through which one could normally see the destination. Instead, it rippled with mystery, almost beckoning them to approach, to *try* to close it.

And try they did.

They had formed a triangle around it, gathering their power, summoning the Magicka and awakening the energy within. So strong did it feel, so electric was the current that ran between them, sparking her nerves with a hum of delight. As it travelled through her system, it seemed to bounce into Denavar, then to Wezlan, and back, swelling in size, drinking in the energy that gave Magicka life.

Ashalea had uttered the words—the spell needed to close the rift—and at first it seemed to be working. The portal had sputtered, shrinking in on itself as if in fear, but then it bounced back, grew indignant, angry at their intrusion.

The wind began, a gentle breeze before it whirled into a raging hurricane, shifting the world around them, lifting the sand on hateful wings and blotting out the sun. She felt it then; his power calling to her, laughing at her.

A metallic tang had filled the air, and try as she might to break the spell, to stop her lips from moving, she couldn't. Her body rebelled as if someone else controlled it, as though even her will had been swept from her reach.

She'd caught Shara's eyes. Amber eyes swimming with victory and glee that soon turned puzzled, fearful. For the look in her eyes reflected what she knew was in her own. The sand lashed out with fury, the hurricane howled, and in a blink, she was falling.

Tumbling. Drowning. Swimming in an ocean of black broken by transcendent swirls of all the colours of the world. Colours even she had never seen in paint or picture or the paradise of nature. Her eyes could barely register the motion, the dizzying heights as she fell, down, down, into a vortex that went beyond all reason and recognition.

And then, just as her stomach threatened to spill its contents into the void, she was dumped onto white sand. A smooth sand as white as snow that stretched as far as her elf eyes could see. No plants dotted the ground, no water, no life. And it was dark, so dark it was almost blinding. She lifted her gaze to the sky above and found only black. A void—no sun or moon or stars to fill its depths—only an emptiness that spoke of misery. Only an eerie light that came from nothing and nowhere.

She was still gazing, wondering how it was she could see anything

189

at all in this dark when Denavar was spat out of the air, landing with a thump on top of her, almost breaking her back in the process. She groaned, and he mimicked the sentiment.

He frowned, confusion knitting his brows. "What happened?"

It hit her all at once. The realisation. The despair of reality. "It was a trap," she whispered in disbelief. "The bastard rigged the portal. He wanted us to close it. To come to ... to ..."

She looked around her before cocking her head at Denavar. He merely shrugged his shoulders, eyes widening as he too gazed at the band of black above, then farther out to the emptiness surrounding them.

His frown deepened; eyes suddenly alert as they scanned the land around them. "Where is Wezlan?"

She hadn't even noticed he was missing. She had been too focused on her anger and confusion, too anxious and afraid. But she was sure he'd been sucked into that portal just as they were, sure he would be here somewhere. Anywhere but ...

Ashalea jumped to her feet, the pieces of the puzzle coming together. It was a trap the darkness had set, not just for her, but all three of them. And if Wezlan wasn't here ... Her mind could only come to one logical conclusion. The darkness had planned this too, he had separated them for a reason. Perhaps Wezlan had arrived first and reset the landing place for her and Denavar. Perhaps this torture was all part of some sick game her brother had concocted.

Her green eyes widened, and somehow, Denavar seemed to glean her way of thinking, his own stark blue eyes glinting with understanding. He had Wezlan. The darkness had her friend.

Wezlan was the bait. All Ashalea and Denavar had to do was fall for it.

Terror gripped Ashalea, her chest ceasing to fill with much needed

air, panic gripping at her heart, squeezing with glee until it raced so hard and fast, she thought it might pounce out of its cage. Her knees buckled, and she came crashing down.

Alarmed, Denavar caught her, easing her gently onto the ground, careful to give her space but let her know he was there. He smoothed the hair away from her face, silky strands having stuck to the sweat now beading on her brow.

"Breathe, Ashalea. Slow your heart, empty your mind. Just breathe."

She felt weak, dizzy, stars threatening to overwhelm her, but she closed her eyes, tried to listen, tried to do as he bid. She didn't know how long she sat there, didn't know how long it was that her lungs warned to shut down, her airways attempted to block, her heart and soul just wanted to scream and rage within.

But she forced the thoughts to quieten, forced her elvish senses to kick in, to slow her heart, to will air into her lungs. And after a few sucks of air, she collapsed, defeated. Tears streamed down her face as all the ugly thoughts came to the fore.

You're weak. You'll never win.

He's too smart. You're too slow.

You are nothing. No one.

And then Denavar was there. Cradling her, whispering soft words of encouragement, of peace, of whispering woods sighing in the breeze and of gentle waterfalls, of meadows and of all that is green and good. He spoke of the stars and a moon so bright and beautiful, so in awe of an elven child it kissed her brow and turned her hair to silver. And he spoke of love. His love. Unfaltering. Ever present.

It could have been an age that she lay there in his arms, sobbing, shaking, her body crumpled under the pressure of a duty she had no idea how to fulfil. Her mind boggling at a task that seemed too much.

Denavar sat there patiently, stroking her hair, planting a light kiss to her heated body.

The air was chilly. It seeped through the thin cotton shirt upon her back and burrowed underneath her britches. There was no light or warmth to cling to except the familiarity, the soothing heat that radiated from Denavar's body. When her body stilled its shivers, and her eyes ceased the soft spill of tears, she gazed up at his face. So patient, so understanding. The quiet, collected, gentle self he showed only to her.

She took a deep breath and pushed herself up to sit, Denavar's fingers trailing down her spine as she moved, making her shiver in a different way altogether. He allowed her a moment to compose before rising, stalking around to come kneel before her. He cocked his head, blue eyes questioning, and she nodded.

And then she was lifted to her feet, the pair of them staring out at the expanse.

"Well, we're very obviously not in Everosia anymore," she managed with a weak grin.

Denavar barked a laugh. "I think we're very, very far from home. A few dimensions over, in fact."

Ashalea's heart dropped into her stomach before a tendril of fear crept in its place. "What about Shara and Razakh?"

"I don't believe they were invited. They didn't interact with the portal, weren't close enough when we were sucked into its void."

Ashalea breathed a sigh of relief. "So how do you suppose we get home?"

Denavar closed his eyes, appearing to listen, to attune his senses to this strange place. "The Magicka here is not like home. It seems to ... resist. It's not a matter of jumping into a portal knowing where to come out of. I have no idea what dimension this is. No idea if I can

travel through time and space itself to get us home. Or if we would be alive after the attempt."

Ashalea gritted her teeth and mashed a palm into her forehead. "We need to find Wezlan."

Denavar prowled a few steps away, his shoulders bunched and head down as he considered. "You know it's another trap ..."

"Naturally. But what else can we do but play his game? I'm not leaving without him."

Denavar loosed a sigh. "We have no weapons."

Indeed, they'd been well equipped back in Madoc Ruins in case things went awry and the Uulakh slipped through Shara's fingers and the Diodonians' paws. But now, Ashalea's scimitar, her bow and arrows, her collection of daggers and shurikens and switchblades ... They were all gone. As were Denavar's twin swords.

Denavar growled in frustration, and she couldn't help but agree with the sentiment. But they weren't entirely defenceless.

"We have Magicka still," she offered meekly.

His face was grim as he turned to face her. "Let's hope it's enough. We're in his territory now, and"—he looked around warily—"who knows what else resides here."

She didn't wait to consider. Striding purposefully across the white stretch of sand, she approached Denavar and gifted him a cunning smile. "Ready, my love?"

His answering grin was devious. "Always."

A Reminder of Consequence

WEZLAN

H E WOULD NEVER FORGET THE FACE OF THAT YOUNG MAN. Ambitious, proud, hopeful. Barely more than a boy. He'd been so sure of his triumph, so ready to shout it to the world and prove he was worthy of them. His parents. His people. He still remembered the confusion on those handsome features, skin like ivory, hair silver, a crescent scar branded on his face.

And those eyes ... the eyes of a wizened man who had known a long life, staring innocently back from a young man's body. Wezlan remembered those eyes as the man was told his dreams would never come true, his chance at becoming a wizard forfeit.

He remembered seeing the confusion shift to anger, to pain, to a promise of consequence. And he had done nothing. None of them had. Not until the moment Crinos wreaked havoc upon Renlock.

Until the moment he killed his first victims. A taste, it seemed, his palette grew hungrier for when he returned to Moonglade Meadows and continued that work.

Even when Wezlan's friends had died fighting the monster he became, even when Wezlan thought he'd smote him into ruin, locked him away into a dimension he'd never look upon again, that promise had remained. A reminder of consequence.

And as Wezlan peered into those eyes now, no glimmer of that innocent boy remained. Only the echo of a promise. One he had come to exact.

The darkness sneered at him, those handsome features contorted, lips curled into a cruel smile. He sat upon a throne of shadows that shimmered like obsidian glass, undulating beneath Crinos in glee.

Wezlan merely stared back, trying his best to school his features into blankness, trying to still the quickening heart within his chest. To ignore the aching in his bones. He stifled a groan as he attempted to stretch the muscles in his back, but found his arms pinned to his sides, his feet unable to move.

"How does it feel to be trapped, Wezlan Shadowbreaker? Taken from your world? Imprisoned?"

Wezlan mustered all his courage, painted a bored expression on his face, and to his surprise, his voice did not quaver as he said, "You always did like the sound of your own voice, Crinos. Did you enjoy talking to none but yourself in isolation?"

The darkness's eyes flashed. "Perhaps I'll let you find out for yourself."

Wezlan snorted. "We both know I'm not alone, you're too clever for that. Where are they?"

He need not specify who. Wezlan knew Ashalea and Denavar had been thrown into this void with him. The portal had been rigged, and

Wezlan had walked right into it and dragged the others with him. He cursed himself for being so careless. If he had taken the pains to study it closely, carefully, he might have heard the off-key crackle, might have noticed the way the crystalline blue had flecks of black within its core. Evidence of tampering. A tainting of natural Magicka.

Crinos sniggered, his shadows twisting lazily around him. "I imagine they're on their way as we speak."

Wezlan considered his words. Considered why it was that he was here, trapped, and the others were not. It held the promise of hope. But it also set his stomach wriggling with uncertainty.

"Why is it my companions weren't sent here with me? What is the point of having them land somewhere else?"

Wezlan noted a flash of annoyance cross the darkness's face before the furrows and lines smoothed out again, replaced by a too-confident smile. *Interesting. Not intentional at all. A mistake.* The thought gave Wezlan comfort, kept the small flames of hope burning within.

"A small problem with rigging the portal is all, though it's of little consequence. I am, perhaps, not the worst thing they could face in this land. It is full of horrors both unforgiving and untamed. Creatures born from misery and malice, feeding on desolation, and, when the chance comes around, the flesh of the living."

The calm and collected smile deepened into something cruel. Joyful. Crinos was a being that thrived off power and flattery. Shrugging off recognition was not in his nature. And if something else truly did dwell in the wasteland surrounding them, Crinos seemed confident it would put up a good fight. He was trying to unnerve Wezlan, and for all the wizard was worth, it was working. The burning fire in Wezlan's pit had all but sputtered out.

"They won't come for me. They will find a way back to Everosia," Wezlan insisted. But even as he spoke, he knew it wasn't true. His

ward was many things, loyal being one of her highest qualities. Even knowing it was a trap, that it was suicide, she would come.

The darkness knew that too, his shadows forming a jagged split down Crinos's frame, striking a line between elf and monster. His personality, his very being, was fragmented into two parts: one being all that was left of his humanity—his conscience—the other a metamorphosis of power, hate, and destruction.

A smile that was one half sparkling white molars, incisors and canines, the other half all jagged points, sharp as blades and stained as if from one too many wines. Or something else entirely ...

"She will come, ever the faithful, the daughter you never had. And by her side will be her loyal pet, ready to die for the one he loves. Rather poetic, don't you think?"

Wezlan ignored him, sizing up his surroundings, looking for all possible exits or chances of diversion. He was in the middle of an encampment, crude tents in chaotic lines and cages full of yipping, howling, hissing creatures that seemed too intent on killing to be trusted to roam loose.

All manner of beasts filled the place, and Wezlan surveyed them with hidden horror, trying to keep his disdain in check. Bones scattered the ground in great heaps, picked clean, not a scrap of meat to them. They were a perfect ivory, as if the white soil of this place seeped into anything it touched.

Then his gaze found those whose fate would soon be the same, and his eyes burned. Burned with the wrongness of it all, with sickness, with rage. Humans and beasts alike were strung up on racks, the creatures mightier than them torturing them, *eating* them, some while they were still alive.

Screams rang out through the camp, some shrill, some guttural, some low moans. Nausea swirled in Wezlan's stomach and he made every effort to not be sick. He wouldn't give the darkness the satisfaction of seeing his fear. He twisted in his bonds—tendrils of shadow that kept him firmly in place—and stared hatefully at the darkness.

Crinos smiled as their eyes met. "Do you like what I've done with the place?"

"Mark my words, Crinos, you will not win this war," Wezlan spat. "The four races of Everosia will triumph, the Guardians will seal the gate for good, and you ... you will meet your end at her hands. And when she is finished, I will smile, knowing that your presence is wiped from the world. All worlds, as if you never existed."

Crinos's eyes only narrowed, the silver shifting into red, the elven form twisting into a phantasmal nightmare. And for all his bravery, the next words struck foreboding into Wezlan's heart as they dripped with malice.

"We will see."

Bravery and Strength

ASHALEA

ASHALEA TRUDGED ALONG THE WHITE EXPANSE OF SAND, panting as she went. "How long do you suppose it's been?"

Denavar shrugged as he matched her pace, followed by a pointed look at the sky. "No way to tell but I'd say we've been walking for around half a day."

A frown, deepening into a scowl. "Every second spent away from him is another chance for the darkness to interrogate him, torture him, to—"

"Ashalea." His voice was gentle but firm. "You can't think like that. Not for one second. I need you here, focused, with me." Denavar loosed a breath. "Besides, we still don't know if Wezlan is in his grasp, anyway."

She snorted. "Oh, he's got him all right. I have no doubt about

that. It's just a matter of where."

Denavar shook his head uncertainly. "Wherever he is, it will be near impossible to free him. We need to come up with some sort of plan."

"A little hard to do considering we know nothing of this place. We have no idea how many grunts there will be, where he is trapped, if there are spells ..." She started listing her worries on her fingers but Denavar halted suddenly, his hand in the air, calling for silence.

She sucked in a breath, forcing her body to still, straining her ears against the deafening silence ... and heard nothing. But she *sensed* a presence nearby. A multitude of bodies, actually. She cursed herself for not paying attention. But she could hear neither pulse nor breath nor footsteps upon the ground.

Only a rumbling of sorts. A vibration that snaked its way towards them rather than pounded. Her eyes hastily took in their environment. Nothing around bar a copse of spindly trees and a pile of rocks stacked precariously on top of each other.

But then it hit her. A stench so putrid it spoke of rot and decay and blood. It had the smell of bodies unburied, of gore left to bake under the sun for insects to feast on. It accosted her elvish nose, seeping into her airways so she felt the very breaths she took were poison. Even on the battlefield, she had never smelt something so vile.

And with the smell brought fear. An unseen wave that undulated dread, hopelessness, and despair. Her stomach set to roiling and nausea washed over her, bile rising in her throat. She stifled a gag. So terrible was the feeling that she crumbled to her knees, wanting nothing more than to scream and curl up in a ball. A panicked glance at Denavar showed the feeling was mutual.

Both elves were doubled over, trying not to vomit, trying to breathe in hitched gasps, mostly trying not to give in to the fear and

leave themselves vulnerable.

And then they saw it. A writhing mass of pinks and reds and whites. A looming spectacle made up of not just one body but hundreds. Faces with leering mouths and lips open wide as if in a scream before they died. They were young and old and rotten and whole. Humans, elves, dwarves, and beasts of all shapes and sizes, some she had never seen before. All of them forever trapped, now a part of this hulking abomination.

The faces screamed silently, almost accusingly, as the creature lurched its way towards her, leaving a trail of slime in its wake. And in between the faces of the dead were organs of all varieties, glistening red and pink, oozing bodily fluids and blood. And finally, smooth white plates that were inset to the patches of skin. After closer inspection, she realised they were bones, skulls—sucked into this monstrosity which wore them like armour.

The mass writhed slowly, hideously, and every time it moved new faces would regard her, rolling over one another, disappearing back into folds of red and pink and resurfacing at some other midsection. She couldn't decide if they were screaming at her to run or insisting that she join them.

Ashalea's stomach rebelled, and she spewed its contents onto the white sand. She felt Denavar's palm on her back tracing small comforting circles even as the being drew nearer, even as it, too, spewed a misty cloud of Goddess knew what.

But then Denavar's palm came to a halt, fingers merely twitching. She glanced at his face to find a new kind of panic taking hold, eyes stricken, jaw wobbling as though he couldn't speak.

She stretched a free hand out ever so slowly, painfully, to Denavar, squeezing his own for comfort, for encouragement, for strength. Then *she* couldn't move. Couldn't scream, couldn't force her legs to rise and hold her steady. And even as they gasped, even as Denavar's mouth twitched, his fingers fumbling for purchase, when her eyes met his she saw defiance; a refusal to give in.

She closed her eyes, stilled her mind and listened to the Magicka flowing through her veins, willing it to take root and fill her body with purpose. It tingled through her, slipping between Denavar's consciousness and her own until both elves felt its presence rising to the surface. Her partner echoed the movement, and between them a connection was forged, burning bright like wildfire.

It surged through their forms, burning the dread, the hopelessness, the despair, until the heaviness in their bones lifted, the fear fizzled out and a sense of renewed bravery took place. Her eyes snapped open, and she gazed at the horror before her with only one thing in mind: kill or be killed.

She could feel warmth seep back into her limbs and control of her own body returned. She sucked in a deep breath of air just as she felt Denavar's body slacken beside her, air returning to his lungs again, too. They cast each other a sidelong glance as the creature drew just a few feet away.

"Be brave, my love," he whispered.

"Strength, my darling," she replied.

And then they rose to their feet, half crouching, palms out, battle stance engaged. They had no weapons of their own. They *were* the weapons. The creature saw their movement, sensed their Magicka gathering and, enraged from its paralysis being rendered ineffective, it charged, rolling sickeningly towards them.

"Fire," Ashalea yelled before uttering a yelp as she dived out of the way just in time. She did not wish to be caught underneath its bulk and join the myriad of faces within its grotesque, spineless body.

Denavar only grunted in response, sidestepping and sending a

cascade of blistering fire down its back. The flesh sizzled—the stench of decay even more prominent in the air. The smell of burning, rotting skin made Ashalea want to vomit again, but she pressed on, sending her own volley of flames towards it.

The faces broke their silence, and as the fires burned, they moaned; a chorus of voices, shrieking, groaning, hissing in response. It sent shivers down Ashalea's spine; her arms now covered in small bumps. She doubled her efforts, and between them, Ashalea and Denavar ran circles around the lump, singeing every possible surface.

The screams heightened to deafening proportions, and Ashalea gritted her teeth, ignoring the drumming in her elvish ears. She caught a glimpse of Denavar as he swept past her, blood trickling from his own. They kept their tactic simple, advancing to attack, retreating when the monster came too close. But every time the flames flared in triumph the monster just kept rolling, regurgitating new flesh from its insides.

"It's no use," Denavar roared. "The skin keeps regenerating."

Ashalea hissed her displeasure, but he was right. No matter how much they burned its skin or ruptured its organs, the creature pressed on as if nothing were amiss. Seeking only to devour them whole and add two more faces to its bulk.

She dashed in for another volley, yelling over her shoulder, "Lightning?"

He did not need to be asked twice. In a desperate bid he threw out a palm, the Magicka building bright under the pink of his skin, and let loose with a boom, "Thindarōs!"

The bolt struck with a resounding crack, lighting up the dark with a flash of white and a force so strong even Ashalea felt the air hum with his power. She looked at him in amazement, the sheer power of his Magicka beyond what she knew him to be capable of.

Indeed, when she peered at the creature, it had been cleaved in two, its slimy gore melting into two halves, dribbling over the ground in a mess of red and pink and all sorts of insides she could never un-see. She gazed at it a moment longer, waiting, watching ... but the oozing creature appeared to have met its end.

With a shout of victory, she sped towards Denavar, planted his face in her hands and smacked a big kiss to his lips. He returned the gesture enthusiastically before a crooked grin sprawled across his features.

She cocked a head at him, eyes tilted upwards. "Remind me not to get on your bad side."

He jabbed her playfully in the ribs, "I hardly think you'll—"

The sentence died on his lips, awe-filled eyes landing on something beside her. His posture stiffened, and she felt his pulse stir, readied for action.

She sighed. "Don't tell me ... the creature isn't dead."

A shake of his head.

"It's stirring behind me."

A nod.

She sighed again. Deeply. Dramatically.

"This day just gets better and better."

A Binding Prophecy

SHARA

"YOU'RE TELLING ME THEY'RE NOT EVEN IN THIS WORLD ANYMORE?" Shara said incredulously, her tone dripping with poison.

After her friends had vanished miraculously into thin air, she and Razakh had returned to the Diodonian den, leaving the fallen to rot on the sands. *"They won't last long,"* Razakh had said of the dead Uulakh. *"Sand dwellers are always eager for a meal. The only sign of battle will be fallen blades and black blood."*

She hadn't pressed him for explanation. Whatever lay on or underneath the sand could eat to their heart's delight for all she cared. No Diodonians had fallen, so that only left the mystery of her friends' disappearance.

A rumble sounded in Razakh's throat, snapping her attention back to the present, and she supposed it was the human version of a sigh. He followed it up with an answering stare that held true wisdom—an authority that would rival kings and queens—and confirmed what her heart dared not believe to be true.

"*They are no longer in Everosia,*" Razakh said, driving the point home.

She glared at him, and still she pressed. "How do you know?"

His silver eyes narrowed as he considered her question. "*Once a Diodonian touches the mind of a human or an elf or any other species for that matter, we remain connected to that thread of consciousness for the rest of our lives.*"

Shara couldn't help but gape. "Is that not an invasion of privacy? To enter their minds from anywhere in the world you please?"

Razakh shook his head, the great flaming mane rippling in protest. "*You misunderstand. We are unable to communicate with individuals from afar. For our telepathy to work, the speaker must be in range and accepting of our advances.*"

She snorted. "Sounds like you're trying to woo the subject in question."

Razakh stared at her blankly. "*I do not know this term, 'woo'. What do you mean?*"

"When you're trying to impress someone? When you're seeking comfort and you want them to like you enough to have a pants-off party and—you know what? Never mind."

Razakh yawned and gave her a sidelong glance. "*You humans are strange creatures.*"

"You have no idea." She grinned before tossing her raven hair. "But I digress. What you were really getting at was your power is of no help to us unless the subject has accepted your … *request* to enter their mind from great distances?"

"*To a degree. For us to do that a ceremony of power is conducted. Magicka*

206

that only we can wield is woven within the heart and mind and a bond is formed. It is ... personal to both Diodonian and the individual in question."

Shara sighed. "If only we had done this before, perhaps you could have sensed where they had gone."

"I'm afraid it's not that simple."

And she nodded, for simple was a word that held neither place nor meaning in her world. Simple was a word that rich wives would use to describe a too-plain gown; a word used for weddings that came without pomp and glamour; a meal cooked without spice or sweetness.

Simple meant nothing to her because *nothing* was simple.

"It never is," she sighed.

Shara felt a tiredness deep in her bones. Her muscles threatened to spasm with overuse and too much swordplay. Her duty—her old duty as an Onyxonite—was a game of shadows. Her work was quick, quiet, and over with one slash of a blade. She could kill her marks with whispers, mix poisons with perfection, jimmy traps, sweet talk locks, and turn men and women against each other with a few carefully placed plots.

But that seemed a lifetime ago. Now she was a Guardian, and with strength came responsibility, or some other such nonsense some scholar shat out of a privy and onto a page. Shara didn't have time for such heroism. All she cared about was ridding herself of the darkness, stopping the world from being ripped apart inside-out and doing whatever duty required to seal the damned Gate of the Grove.

What that actually entailed, she still wasn't sure. But this quest, as Wezlan would so proudly dub this mess, was getting harder and harder with each passing day. Especially when she seemed to be the only Guardian present who had no Magicka. *Not even a kernel*, she thought miserably. If she had, perhaps she would have a chance at saving them. Perhaps she could glean some information that could—

"*You need to get out of your head,*" Razakh offered.

"And you need to get out of mine," Shara said crossly. "Unless you have something useful to say, I'll remind you we made a pact you wouldn't spy anymore."

"*Apologies,*" Razakh said, and at his politeness she raised a brow. "*Cranky,*" he added, and Shara couldn't help but chuckle.

"Okay," she breathed. "So, what do we do then?"

Razakh was silent for a beat. "*The darkness must have had something to do with the portal, which means they're exactly where he wants them to be.*"

"Not exactly a comforting thought," Shara drawled. Indeed, fear crept into her belly as she considered this prospect. If the darkness had them, who knew what chaos was occurring in this distant realm? Perhaps he'd even … She swallowed. "Do you think they're still …"

Razakh didn't need to listen to her thoughts to know what she was thinking. "*What does your heart tell you?*" he said gently.

Her eyes widened. "M—My heart?"

He dipped his head slightly. "*Humans are known to trust in their heart more than their brains. Perhaps too much, some might say. But we Diodonians know that the heart speaks to more truth than most other things in this life. Trust in it. What does it say?*"

Shara considered the wisdom in his words. She wasn't sure she'd ever really consulted with that beating, thrumming organ in her chest; wasn't sure she'd ever really sat down and had a good chat with the *feelings* inside. It was easier to lock them away. But she indulged him in this small gesture. She searched her heart, and it told her that yes, her friends were alive. Far, far away, but alive.

Her lingering smile must have told Razakh as much because he nodded in admission. "*I think so, too. Perhaps not out of danger, perhaps in the grasp of horrible, horrible things, but alive nonetheless.*"

Her glare was smouldering. "Thanks, Razakh, for that drop of

wisdom," she drawled sarcastically. "Very helpful."

"I expect not, but if we can find out just where they may be, it could prove useful. Do they have any Magicka—an item in their possession which could draw them to us or vice versa?"

Her fingers were fumbling for the necklace before her brain followed course. "You mean like a talisman?"

Razakh's eyes flared. *"Precisely."*

Shara pulled the ornament from her neck—a plain silver piece with an onyx gem at its centre—and held it out for Razakh to see. "This is an Onyxonite talisman. It recognises one of our order, much like your bonding ritual, though less creepy."

He cut in with a warning growl, but she ignored him. "It acts as a sort of beacon with fellow Onyxonites whom you have a personal connection to. Ashalea is such a person."

Razakh sat up straighter, tail swishing in thought. *"I saw the bands of this necklace around Ashalea's own throat just yesterday."* He studied the gem inset into the plain silver core. *"This is the Magicka that binds you?"*

A nod. "This will tell me where she is. But I need maps. All of them."

Razakh looked at the walls surrounding them. The red rock streaked with yellow, the flames floating ethereally on the walls, the pillows and cushions and the meagre belongings that hinted at comfort and luxury. The obvious lack of books and scrolls and items crafted by man. Then he lay down, crossed his paws like a polite, elderly gentleman, and drawled:

"Do I look like I read maps to you?"

———————————— ◆◆●◆◆ ————————————

The new Diodonian chieftain sat before them, as radiant as a ruby, his red coat glimmering as it caught the shine from the flames. He was a wonder to look at—not because he was beautiful or magnificent or awe inspiring in the way of heroes—he was none of that. But when Shara's eyes roved the many scars that scrabbled over his muzzle, the brooding stare, the scowling pull of his teeth, she felt unnerved. Almost afraid ... almost.

That one eye of his could command the attention of all, send his foes fleeing, demand obedience. The other was a wreckage. There was no sign of an eye at all, just a hollow bereft of its former glory. That was probably more unnerving than anything else, and it took every effort for Shara not to let her gaze wander to it.

"Are you going to stare at me all day or shall we continue with our plans?"

Even his voice was gruff as it banged through her skull. It certainly wasn't the lilting, hypnotic notes of Razakh. Even so, his piercing stare had her cheeks reddening, an abashed smile on her face, and she felt a small tremble from Razakh beside her, realising he was trying not to chuckle. A quick elbow to his ribs stilled the tremor.

"Bastard," she mouthed at her companion, before muttering to Linar, eyes downcast, "sorry."

"Perhaps we should focus on the task at hand," Razakh said with amusement.

"If Magicka and maps are what you seek, it seems prudent to me that you visit the mages at Renlock," Linar stated. *"You are unable to perform Magicka yourself, correct?"*

"No need to remind me," Shara said with a scowl. "But yes, I cannot perform the spell needed to find our companions, and the only map I have on me is one of Everosia, which is useless in this case."

"Do the mages have an understanding of other dimensions?"

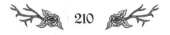

210

Shara grimaced. "That's what I'm afraid of. Renlock Academy is something of a shamble now. Those left in charge, well, they need some guidance. Have needed it for some time. After the recent battle … I'm not sure there's anyone left with the knowledge to help me. The one person I need is the one person we seek."

"What about the Grove?" Linar asked.

"I would be able to see my father again," Razakh said, boyish excitement ringing through Shara's head.

She wasn't sure how old he was, but she supposed even if he had lived for a hundred moons now, that was still young by Diodonian standards. She raised a brow and he rumbled, as if clearing his throat in embarrassment.

"His counsel has always proved beneficial."

"The Grove is protected by the keepers. More than that, I have no doubt there are many Magickal wards in place to prevent intruders or curious onlookers. I wouldn't even know *how* to get into the forest."

"But surely the forest would recognise one of its own? You are a Guardian after all."

Shara gifted the Diodonians with a pointed stare. "Would you want to risk being obliterated or spiked by some ancient, angry tree?"

"I don't think the protectors of the forest would skewer anyone just for getting too close. Much less a Guardian," Razakh said with a not-eyebrow raised.

"I don't want to go to the Grove without the others. It would feel like an infringement of our trust. Incomplete. Like I'm breaking some unspoken rule. No," she said with a shake of her head. "There must be another course."

There was silence as the three of them considered options. And then, ever so softly in her mind, *"There is one more option."*

Shara swivelled to face Razakh in earnest, waiting, and it wouldn't

be the first time that she wished she too had the power to listen in to thoughts. To explore someone else's mind. When the answer wasn't forthcoming, she tapped her foot impatiently, finally bursting out, "Well?"

But it was Linar who replied. *"There was a prophecy made long ago ... a promise that tied two races together. A child would be born of each, destined to forge a new future for our kinds. One that walked the balance of the world."*

"She who is born of moons and meadows, drowned in the blood of memory, shall wade in sorrowful waters. Blind shall he stay, he who is born of the midday sun, a whisper of a warrior to be.

But fated together, a new reign will rule. Lifted shall the veil be and drained the seas of sorrow, until tree and flower become one, and the sands of time shall bloom.

By blade and bow and staff combined, Magicka shall out. Destiny shalt come."

When Razakh finished the prophecy, Shara just stared between the Diodonians. "Pretty words, but can someone please decipher the riddle?"

Linar harrumphed like an old man, stretching much like one too. But the new chieftain settled back on his haunches, as if readying himself for story time with the children. Shara didn't miss his huff that seeped into her mind.

"It is said the prophecy speaks of Diodonians and elves. It has been passed on for generations, dating back hundreds of years, though for how long, I do not know."

This piqued Shara's interest, and the more she chewed over the words, the more it made sense. She gave Razakh an appraising once-over before clucking her tongue.

"And you think this warrior the prophecy speaks of is already in our midst?"

It made sense of course, though she dared not be so presumptuous as to assume it revolved around her suspicions. But a warrior of the sun ... sands ... Could it just be a coincidence that they had just found someone of this description?

She glanced again at Razakh's shiny coat, golden and glorious. He had proven himself admirable in battle, a worthy ally to have by her side. He may have even saved her life. Maybe ... She was still convinced she'd have handled that Uulakh. But still ...

Razakh's silver eyes widened in that too-human way as he studied her face. "*You think I am one of the children it speaks of?*"

"Stop reading my mind," Shara said with a scowl, crossing her arms in defiance.

A sliver of amusement laced Linar's words as he said, "*He didn't need to, young one. It's written all over your face.*" He turned to Razakh, a slight dip of his head. "*I am inclined to agree with the human. The prophecy is befitting of you. The time, the need for war. And the woman you seek is an elf ...*"

Silence once again filled the air as time ticked by, and she was sure the Diodonians held their own private council. "Of course," she grumbled, "invade my head and then keep secrets from me."

"*My guidance is for my chieftain alone,*" Linar growled.

Shara put her hands up in mock defeat, rolling her eyes with exaggerated gusto.

"*You are the new leader,*" Razakh said with an awkward, painful-to-look-at smile.

Linar shook his head. "*You will always be my chieftain.*"

"Okay, enough of the puppy love. Let's say that Razakh is this golden boy, and Ashalea is the elf child. What purpose does this serve? How does it help our current situation?"

"*It is not to the child we look, but her kin. Fabled stargazers, moon seers,*"

213

and elves with Magicka born not of this world but many over. They will have knowledge of the other dimensions. It is they who will have the answers you seek."

"Of course," Shara breathed, excitement bubbling in her chest. "Why didn't you just say so?"

Razakh's eyes narrowed in confusion. "*I believe he just did.*"

Shara waved him off, her enthusiasm bouncing around the room, but it died when a sudden thought grinded her joy to a halt. "I don't think the Moonglade elves are even aware Ashalea is alive. Her parents ... they were murdered by the darkness when she was just a babe. They may not be so willing to aid us without proof of her existence. They may see us as a threat if we can even find them."

"*We will find them. Then we will make them believe. We prove that we are the next Guardians. We urge them to honour the prophecy.*"

"No small feat ..."

"*A minor task really.*"

"Nothing we can't handle."

"*A walk in green pastures.*"

"Razakh, you live in a desert. Have you even seen one of those?"

His indignance clanged in her head. "*Of course I—*"

"IF YOU'RE QUITE DONE?" Linar bellowed. As loud as one can bellow in another's mind.

Shara and Razakh looked at each other, amber eyes meeting silver ones, and she felt a wave of uncalled for hysteria roll over her. She bit her lip to keep from laughing, but she couldn't help but release a strange yip of amusement. Old man indeed, Linar even lectured her like one, too.

Razakh sensed her amusement and shook his great head, blue flames gently flowing down his back. "*You humans* really *are strange creatures.*"

She tossed her hair back, a smirk on her full lips. "And like I said before, Razakh, you have no idea."

<hr />

As it turns out, the oasis that sprawled in a tropical tangle within the Diodonian den wasn't the only secret they had kept. Hidden in the mountain was a tunnel that cleaved deep, slicing through the caverns with purposeful strokes.

The tunnel, Razakh said, was manmade, dating back thousands of moons, to a time when man and Diodonian were on good terms. Its purpose was simple: an emergency exit, a quick retreat should any dangers breach the caves in which the mighty beasts dwelled.

It hadn't been used in an age considering the Diodonians had no real need of it. Of the many beasts that had been captured and experimented on in times past, they had been caught in traps and snares of cruel design or hunted down in the desert.

Of all the Diodonians captured, not one had given away their secrets. Not one had revealed the den's whereabouts, uttered a word of the oasis or a hint of the tunnel. And it seemed that the alliance of old must have had a gag-order preventing any human from spilling the secret of its making, too.

Proud, noble, and loyal to the last; that's what these beasts were, and Shara respected them more for it after hearing this story. She glanced at Razakh through downturned lashes and realised how wrong she had been about the Diodonians. And how poorly she had judged him.

She hefted her pack on one shoulder, which was significantly heavier now. A canteen freshly filled with water from the oasis, meagre rations of stale bread and dried meats, a spare shirt, blades belonging to her friends, and a scratchy, tired-looking bedroll. Her weapons were strapped in their many hidden compartments, Ashalea's bow and quiver were slung over her shoulder, and in one hand she carried Wezlan's staff.

It felt like a sin to hold it. The wizard was rarely without it, and an uneasiness settled in her stomach that he could be alone somewhere without his fondest possession. What the staff did, she had no idea. Didn't Magicka come from within? What power did it hold anyway? Her questions just made her sadder that he couldn't answer them with a chuckle or a stroke of his beard.

"Do not look so glum," Razakh said as he padded beside her. *"We will find a way to bring them home."*

"Home," she repeated. The word was salty to her tongue. A bitterness to the bite. Had Shadowvale ever really felt like a home? And with her being a Guardian, did she have one anymore?

"Tell me about yours," Razakh purred.

She took a breath. What was there to say? *My mother died of sickness. My father had me tortured and starved when I was a child. My kinsmen taught me how to murder people?*

Her silence was answer enough, but Razakh said in his gentle lilt, *"We are not bound by the blood in our veins, nor the rooves that watched over our youth."*

Shara's amber eyes narrowed. From the darkness they descended into or the burning reminder of her past, she did not know. And whether Razakh had crept silently into her mind to rifle through those thoughts, whether her silence spoke volumes, she could only guess.

"Can you see in this dark?" she changed the subject, stumbling over a pebble at an appropriate time, catching herself with a hand on Razakh's back. She would never admit it, but the fur was gloriously soft, and it gave her happy little endorphins just to touch it.

"Our eyes adjust to the light, yes."

"Are you colour blind?"

A snarl rippled through the tunnel, echoing down the shaft just as it echoed in her mind. *"For the last time, Shara, we are not dogs."* A huff. *"Besides, dogs aren't colour blind. They merely see in a limited spectrum."*

"How would you know that if you're not a dog?" she teased.

This time she practically felt his growl rumble the tunnel they walked. *"We might not be able to read or write but information is a precious tool for us Diodonians. The knowledge we're gifted we keep forever, and pass that down to future generations."*

Shara grinned, imagining a classroom of Diodonians learning how to spell, to read, to identify etiquette between races, something she was surely breaking by calling this mighty beast a hound. "So ... someone sits down with your younglings and teaches them the importance of a dog's vision."

"For the life of me, you're insufferable." He ruffled his fur, throwing her hand off his back.

But even as she chuckled, a light flared in the darkness, and she saw the flames on Razakh's spine spark to life. The warmth seeped into her bones, staving off the chill air of the dank tunnel, and illuminating the black, tearing the blindfold off.

It reminded her of the prophecy. Of *lifting the veil.* But was the veil blinding him ... or someone else? She sighed, kicking a rock and sending it tumbling down the corridor. It was surprisingly loud as the sound reverberated off the rock walls.

"I wouldn't do that if I were you."

She cast a sidelong glance at Razakh, frowning. "Afraid I'll wake monsters in the dark?"

"That's exactly what I'm afraid of."

This was a new tone she had not yet heard. Grim, laced with—

"You fear ..." she said in surprise, scrutinising his face. "Something is down here—which you rudely forgot to mention by the way—and even you are quavering in those big paws of yours."

He bared his teeth. *"Would it have mattered had I told you? You're stubborn as a mule and I doubt you would have accepted any other path. Besides, you hate sand."*

He said the latter as if that was the be all, end all to this journey, and she scowled. "True and true—nice colloquialism by the way, very human of you—and the fact that I *dislike* sand is not enough to stop me doing my duty." She huffed. "I just prefer the easier route."

They travelled in silence for a time, making their way at a quick but comfortable pace down the tunnel. It curved downwards ever so slightly, their descent into the belly of the mountain making the air thicker, more stagnant. Even for one so used to the dark, Shara felt stifled by it, claustrophobic with only one way forward or back.

"If we keep up this pace, we'll be out of the tunnel come nightfall," Razakh said.

"Nightfall?" Shara groaned. "We're spending the better part of a day in here?"

"It's not so bad. The quiet is calming. It gives one time to think."

That's exactly what Shara was afraid of, but she shrugged off his comment with a snort.

"Oh great, extra time to consider what manner of beast awaits us down here. Can't you just ... let me hop on your back?"

Razakh pulled up short and gave her a hard look. *"I am NOT a steed for you to ride on."*

"But it would be so much quicker," she pouted. "We'd be out of here in a matter of hours and no one has to know."

His snarl ripped through the tunnel, silencing further protests before they came. She only chuckled in amusement, the jingling mirth

so out of place under the earth. Razakh's flames began to waver by air filtering through crevices in the walls, and she fancied at their dance on his back, focusing on it to keep her fear at bay.

The flames grew tame, dwindling to blue, sputtering as they walked deeper into the mountain. A dread filled her as she gazed at their brilliance having all but disappeared. And then she felt a chill, penetrating her skin, sinking into her bones until it settled in a ball of fear in her gut.

"Razakh ... you can control the flames on your back, right? It's a little chilly down here, they're almost out."

The Diodonian paused, sniffing the air. *"They answer to my call, yes. There's only a few instances when I have no control over–"* He stiffened. *"Be still."*

In the near black, Shara struggled to keep her body from shivering, her hands from shaking. The cold had taken root, her core was as ice; unforgiving and unmoving inside. She stared at Razakh's flames, the only thing keeping her heart from pounding out of her chest.

Then, with a last sigh, the flames went out and she was blind. She threw a hand to his side, fumbling for the comforting fur, and when she felt it, she latched on, panic rising in her throat.

"Razakh," she croaked.

"Silence," he demanded.

And they both listened. The stillness was deafening at first, lending further to her panic and claustrophobia. She clutched at his fur, digging fingernails into fistfuls of the silken coat. Until finally, there ... A far away crunch, crunch, crunch. Like the sound of dirt being shovelled, followed by a slithering, how Shara would imagine a snake curving its body along the ground would sound.

The noise quietened momentarily, and she breathed a sigh of relief, straining her ears for any further sign of this uninvited guest.

Silence for a beat. Then ... click, click, click. Shara just about shed her skin in fright. It was much closer this time, and its greeting was anything but friendly.

"Razakh," she insisted.

"*I agree*," he said, turning his attention to the way forward. "*RUN!*

Family Reunions

ASHALEA

SHE RAN, BOOTS POUNDING THE EARTH, one hand clasping Denavar's, the other hurling fireballs in her wake. The creature was gaining on them, hungry for their blood, their bodies and their skin. Eager to feed its bulk and add to the many anguished faces of the dead.

It was angry, rolling sloppily, quickly, in its haste to reach them. It had certainly not taken kindly to Denavar's lightning, and when its oozing organs and melted flesh had recombined, a single purpose drove the creature, only aggravating the monster with renewed vigour.

"I think you made it mad, dear," Ashalea panted.

Denavar shrugged even as he pounded across the soil. "An unfortunate habit of mine."

She grunted in reply. If they didn't find haven soon, they were

going to be in serious trouble. They had been running for hours, and she suspected the better part of a day had gone by. They could run for a while—they were elves after all—but to what end? They'd be running to nothing and no one. And yet, there, a black dot marred the white sands ahead.

"Do you see it?" she managed in between pants. "Something in the distance. A village? Or camp of some sort?"

He turned on his feet, running backwards as he tossed a lightning bolt in the monster's path. It crackled with glee, sending blue veins of electricity swirling delicately in and around the creature's body ... or bodies.

The answering moans and screams almost buckled Ashalea's knees, her throat bobbing as she kept her focus pinned straight ahead. That sound took the warmth from her very soul and made her want to weep with the ache of their hurts. Their voices lost forever and made one with this creature.

She wondered then, what became of *their* souls, considering their bodies were consumed, neither buried nor burned but some sickening in between of life and death. Elf, dwarf, man, beast, all trapped in that cage of flesh. Sneering and screaming, mouths and eyes open wide with horror. She knew she would never forget the sight of it if she lived to tell the tale.

What made her even more uncomfortable was how it held the faces of species common to Everosia. Had the creature resided there once upon a time? Or had this land once been prosperous, rich with life and the living?

She shook her head. Useless questions she would never have an answer to.

"That should buy us more time," Denavar said as he turned, sprinting to catch up.

"For what?" Ashalea gasped, eyeballing him incredulously.

His reply was interrupted with a whoosh of air as something spiralled past their noses, just shy of both of their skulls. Eyes widening, they turned to see yet another creature of new making popping into view from the midnight sky. This one less nightmarish but still posing a significant threat. It raced towards them on bat wings, eyes red as blood, teeth jutting in crooked fangs from its maw.

The thing was a mess of patchy hair and scabbed skin, sinuous wings stretching and pushing out spikes of ... bone? She had little time to study them before it heaved inwards, and she realised what was coming.

A creature of different design had done something similar back on their voyage to the Isle of Dread. The Violet Star—the beautiful ship which bore them hence, now shredded and lying at the bottom of Onyx Ocean—and its crew had paid the price of an attack such as this. Ashalea was not about to make that same mistake.

"Dive!" And dive she did, tackling Denavar to the ground just before a vicious spurt of shards flew over their heads and straight towards their other dinner guest.

The bat-thing screeched, decided to follow suit, and, tucking its leathery wings in, glided straight towards Denavar's throat.

"Denavar!"

It crashed into him, trying to open its wings at the last minute to slow its flight, but it miscalculated and Denavar swiped at the wing's membranes, grappling as they flapped against him. Beast and elf rolled in a flurry on the ground, Ashalea utterly helpless to step in, afraid she would hurt Denavar with her Magicka.

He roared at the creature, muscles in his arms bunching as he pushed and pulled with all his might. The bat snapped with drooling jaws, narrowly missing Denavar's neck and sinking into his shoulder instead. He barked in pain, and as the creature pulled too close, he let go of both wing tips and punched the bat square in the nose.

He found purchase on the sinewy cords of one wing while it howled in pain, and Ashalea seized the moment to grab the spare. It fluttered against them, now helpless with the two elves gripping on for dear life. And as one, they dug fingernails into the membranes in each wing, pulled, and shattered the bone with a resounding *snap*.

Gasping, they stepped back as it floundered in pain, attempting in vain to take to the skies in defeat. One look over their shoulders told Ashalea and Denavar they had no time to waste. The *other one* was coming.

They ran ahead, boots sinking purposefully into the sand, and they only turned once they were a safe distance from both creatures, watching, waiting with bated breath to see what would happen.

The writhing mass of body parts slunk ever closer to its prey, seemingly satisfied to have a small measure of victory. Slowly, achingly, it dribbled to the bat, the creature now screeching in fear as it realised it had no chance of escape. Scrabbling uselessly, Ashalea saw its eyes, the blood red orbs, wide, full of defeat, and she realised even monsters are no match for fear.

Finally, she swallowed with revulsion as it disappeared—was consumed—by the pink and red mass and, before she turned away, she saw a new face in its hide. A bat-like thing with big round eyes and jutting fangs open wide. And she swore the monster that happily chased them like a dog with a bone grew just a little bigger than it was moments before.

Ashalea's lips thinned in disgust, and she turned to look at that dark mass on the horizon. After much squinting, her elvish eyes made out a sprawl of tents—a campground—and not just any, but a war camp for the darkness, judging by the various creatures that milled around within it.

Her eyes widened, and the beginnings of a plan took root in her mind. She faced Denavar with a sly smile. "I have an idea."

———◆•◆———

"You're either insane or an absolute genius," he said with a face the definition of flabbergasted.

She shrugged as they walked towards the dark speck in the distance. Walked now, because the biological anomaly had grown rather lazy since its meal, sluggishly rolling towards them in pursuit. Its new face stared accusingly at Ashalea.

"It's not my finest idea, but if it does what I think it will, we'll have ourselves the perfect diversion."

He glanced back at the creature, uncertainty crippling his features. "I don't know ... what if it's some minion of the darkness and his guards are immune to it?"

She raised a brow. "You saw what Pinky did to Batty. It slobbered that thing up like an afternoon snack."

He answered with two raised brows. "Pinky? Batty?"

Ashalea shrugged. "There's probably an abundance of 'its' in this place. Seems easier to identify them."

A snort. "Okay, we head straight and true, we *hope* there's just a few guards there. We *assume* there's an army. Then what? You want to just run in, Magicka blazing, and hope that"—he cast a discerning look at the blob—"that Pinky cleans up for us?"

"Precisely. The darkness won't be expecting us to come with backup. And if we set this thing loose there will be utter chaos."

Denavar frowned. "Need I remind you that it will just as happily 'slobber us up' as you say?"

She scowled, but her fingernails clicked together, her nose puckered in worry. The plan was a stretch, she knew, and it could make their situation even worse, but what other option did they have? Sneaking in would be problematic without having any idea of the layout and without having help. If the army were distracted, if the darkness were busy dealing with other things, it would give them time to slip past the commotion and free Wezlan. She hoped.

Denavar must have noticed her agitation, for he pulled her closer and kissed her gently on the nose. "I don't like our odds ... but it's the best plan we've got."

He frowned, and the stubble on his chin scratched her face as she nestled into his chest.

"The only plan," she said with a muffled voice.

"Unless ..."

At that she perked her head up. "Oh, I like unless. Tell me you have another idea."

He raked a hand through his hair. "Welllll ... it may not work because of the environment we're in but ... it could also be an advantage. You know about moulding light and darkness to oneself, yes?"

She nodded. "I've heard of it. I know it's a part of the factions at Renlock Academy." She shrugged. "Why?"

Denavar raised fingers to his chin, stroking the stubble in contemplation. It reminded her of Wezlan, and a pang of worry fired through her. If the roles were reversed, Wezlan would know what to do. He would trust in his instincts, in his Magicka. He would trust in his friends.

"If we could mould the shadows to ourselves, we'd have the power to sneak through undetected. Use the darkness's own tools against him so we could be, essentially, invisible to the naked eye."

Ashalea frowned. "The beasts in his army might not know better, but won't the darkness detect the Magicka? Be able to sense it?"

"Perhaps. If one looks closely enough, they might notice a shimmer that doesn't belong or a hum of power, but if we also unleash our new friend here, the distraction may be enough that he won't notice the illusion. It would give us enough time to search the camp and find where Wezlan is hiding."

She nodded excitedly. "It's our best chance. Once we free Wezlan, between the three of us we may just be able to navigate our way home somehow ... there's just one problem."

"Naturally. Go on?"

"Wezlan never taught me this Magicka. I—I have no clue how to work the spell."

Denavar's roguish smile melted her doubts. He waved her off with one hand, took hold of her shoulders and kissed her lips. The reassurance pressed firmly against her mouth and the peppermint tingled, sighing down her throat like a breath of fresh air. Her shoulders positively melted under his touch and he massaged them gently with the balls of his thumbs.

"A minor inconvenience," he said, and his tone was so confident she believed him.

"I can teach you," he continued. "You need only believe in yourself, Ashalea. Believe, as I do. You're a survivor. The light that you conjured atop Renlock Academy? The blast of moonlight you Magicked? That is more powerful than anything I've ever seen. You can do this."

"You're forgetting I've since lost that ability. Not to mention my healing powers." She stared at her trembling hands before he took them gently in his own.

"The only one holding you back is yourself. Never bend to

the weight of insecurity." He placed a hand over her heart, his eyes burning fiercely, passionately. "Never let fear mute the strength of what's inside."

"I—"

Her response died as pain seared in her head, the sheer surge of it forcing her to collapse, knees grinding into the ground. She slammed both palms to her temple, trying to block it out, teeth bared as her mouth split wide in agony.

Denavar was kneeling beside her, shouting, gripping at her skin, but she heard nothing, saw nothing but the curve of his lips as they moved, saying something indecipherable. And then the pain just stopped. And she was not with her partner in a world of white and black, but in a grey land, with neither earth nor sky. She was just ... floating.

"Hello, Ashalea."

The words were as sharp as the pain she felt prior and there was no doubt in her mind as to who was speaking. "Crinos," she gritted out.

"How lovely of you to join me," he purred, appearing before her eyes, floating on his cloud of darkness. He was in his elven form, steely eyes regarding her. Assessing her.

She spat, "Like I had a choice."

He chuckled at that. "All the same. I thought it was time we had a little one-on-one. You know so much about me now, after your rifling through my memories. I thought it was only fair I have the chance to know you, too."

Her eyes widened. "How do you—"

"Oh, come now. You think I didn't know?" He tutted as a finger waggled near her face and she squirmed away, causing a slight frown to flutter across Crinos's face before just as quickly vanishing.

 228

"I wanted you to see them, Ashalea. I wanted you to know why I am," he paused before gesturing at himself, "this."

"A monster. That's what you are, and all you'll ever amount to."

She assumed he was expecting a different answer because a flash of red burned in his eyes before they returned to steely grey. His next words were a complete change of tactic.

"It was good of you to let me in on your plans. The attempt to close the portal, seal off my armies, protect the Diodonians." He sneered. "Very noble."

Ashalea stared at him in dismay as the realisation hit her. "You knew. All along you knew everything we were doing," she breathed.

Crinos shrugged. "Not entirely. I can only catch small glimpses into your mind. How else do you think I knew to rig the portal?"

Her heart sank. A heavy stone that plummeted to the depths of her soul, dragging her spirit down, down, down. The portal, their travel to this world, Wezlan's capture ... it was all her fault.

Shara's words swam accusingly in her head. *Your lies put us in danger, Ashalea.*

She had lied. And it had cost them. A heavy price to pay for her curiosity. For her foolishness. But she couldn't let Crinos see he'd won. He could keep that small victory, and she would offer him no satisfaction.

"The memories you showed me. Were they even real?"

He scoffed. "I might not be proud or noble, but I have always been honest with you, Ashalea."

She eyed him off with mistrust, but she could not quell the wonder, and before she could stop herself, she blurted, "What were they like? Our parents?"

Crinos blinked. The only surprise likely to show on his face. "Mother was ... kind. She had a gentle nature, quick to laugh, was firm but fair." He looked at Ashalea with an expression she could not place. "She had hair like yours. Dipped in moonlight."

Ashalea contained the smile threatening to unleash, but her insides fluttered with a small joy. This, at least, was a pain she could bear, and she noted this tiny titbit of information was a kindness he was under no obligation to give. That his words were laced with sorrow, perhaps even ... regret. *Interesting.*

"And Father?" she said softly.

Crinos's face hardened. "Ill-tempered. Blind to the truth. Mistrusting."

"Blind to *your* truth, you mean?"

He whirled on her, but remained tight-lipped, and they both stared defiantly at the other. Siblings. So alike yet so different. Ashalea gazed at him and studied—really studied—him. The silver hair near identical to her own, once long and flowing as a boy, now cropped, practical.

His eyes bore into her own and she noted the tiniest flecks of green amid the silver. So faint one wouldn't notice unless peering as she was now. And then the crescent scar upon a high cheekbone. Its ivory brand was stark even against his pale skin, which might have held the tanned, sun-kissed glow of her own had he chosen not to dwell in shadows.

"Where did you get your scar from?" she asked warily, afraid to blow the lid on his temper. Perhaps something he acquired from their father.

His lips curved ever so slightly. "I called you here, and you wish to discuss old wounds?"

She cocked a head. "Some wounds heal." She peeled up her shirt to reveal her own scar, vivid against her stomach, gifted to her by Crinos himself back on the night her adoptive parents died. When

he killed them. "Others run too deep. Leave reminders too painful."

His eyes roved to the white pucker on her stomach, and to her surprise, he smiled with fondness of all things. To the memory of hurting her or to Ashalea herself, she had no idea.

"I had expected nothing but a slip of a girl when I met you that night. A defenceless, meek maiden who would go screaming to her death. I was half right. How surprised I was to find the defiance in you. You put up quite a fight."

"I'll never stop fighting," she said, her voice low. "Tell me, what became of the blade that stabbed me? It was your passage into Everosia, right? The talisman that allowed you to enter our world once more."

His grin was deadly, but he merely shook his head. "Clever girl, but you shan't have my secrets. Besides, we came here to talk about you, not I."

"And what would you know of your long-lost sister? I thought it was your nature to kill first and forget the questions," she hissed.

He ignored the sting, his smile growing ever wider. "I think you've told me much already. We are so alike, Ashalea," he crooned, "born of the same blood, the same ambition. Your heart hungers for purpose. I can see it in you. Feel it in you, ever since the full might of your power unleashed that night atop the tower. A power birthed from the moon and stars themselves. Do you deny the power flooding through your veins? The eagerness to release it on the world?"

The power I no longer have, Ashalea thought bitterly, donning a blank expression to hide such information.

His eyes glinted knowingly. "Ahh but you're keeping secrets from me. I thought we were going to be honest with each other, sister." He pouted—an ugly mockery of emotion that made Ashalea want to drive her fist through his teeth.

"I know that power abandoned you because the moment it hit

me, I felt it inside of *me*."

Her emerald eyes widened and her brows downturned in alarm. If Crinos had that power at his disposal as well as the dark? No, it felt like a betrayal. She had thought it a gift, a sign to show she was special. But now ... She shuddered to think of what new monster would be made from its power.

"That beam of light bonded us, Ashalea. Bridged the connection of our minds. It is how I speak to you now, whilst your true body dwells back in Kiletch. It is how I foresaw all your plans, all your despair. It is why you are here, now, a guest in my dimension."

It made sense. The visions, the memories ... The darkness that swelled within her own mind.

"Why do you waste my time with this nonsense?" Ashalea snarled. "I tire of this charade. Get to the point or let us have it out when I find you. And I *will* find you, Crinos. Wezlan, Denavar and I, we will escape this damned place." Her eyes narrowed in warning. A promise she intended to keep.

"I look forward to seeing you soon," he said, words dripping with poison. "You see, I have troubles of my own, dear sister. The power you gifted me doesn't want to play nice. So, here's *my* promise. I will have answers before I have blood. And if that still doesn't please me, I will wring every ounce of your power from your bones until there is nought but flesh and meat and hollowness inside."

Gone was the silver-haired, handsome elf, replaced with shadow and death and dark. Red eyes gleaming with thirst and teeth bared in suspense. And all hopes she had of there being some morsel of humanity left, all sorrow and despair she held for that little boy long ago, vanished as quickly as the smile from his face.

There would be no reuniting of brother and sister, no forgiveness, no truce. There would be only death, and she planned on landing the killing blow.

"Be seeing you soon, *brother*," she spat venomously.

"I can't wait," he hissed in reply.

And she was floating no more as the grey of this in-between swirled into nothing. Instead, she fell.

Dashing Through the Dark

SHARA

E LURCHED AHEAD and she almost stumbled as she lost her grip on his fur, almost stumbled in her haste to be anywhere but stuck near the approaching creature, but as her legs pinwheeled after Razakh, a new dread overwhelmed her. The tunnel was near straight as an arrow, but in the darkness, she was blind as they come.

"I can't see," she cried out. "Razakh, I—"

The beast snarled as he turned back, and with a reluctant growl his voice boomed in her mind, "*Get on my back.*"

"What? I thought you said—"

"*Never mind what I said. If you don't get on my back, you will die.*"

Shara didn't need telling twice. She reached out in the dark, finding purchase on his back, and in one movement she leaped up, the Diodonian nudging her arse up with his snout so she could swing a leg over, almost dropping Wezlan's staff in the process.

"Thanks," she breathed.

"Don't mention it. Ever."

Then he was off, bounding down the corridor on huge paws, the corded muscles in his legs rippling with each stride. He was fast—real fast. Shara felt a weightlessness as she gripped his mane with a clenched fist, the flame that would have burnt her nowhere to be seen or felt, sputtered out from the unworldly chill the creature produced.

Her hair whipped behind her and she felt a dizzying sense of unreality as she clung to this moving beast in the pitch black. And still she heard it, that *thing* approaching. Digging towards them, writhing through rock like butter churned in a baker's bowl.

Click, click, click. Closer still. Shara squeezed her eyes shut as the cold deepened. Her fingers grew numb and she tried to imagine herself knee deep in snow, icicles hanging from branches in the early morning, a frigid air ticking her nose and reddening her cheeks. It was a pleasant scene that gave reasoning for the sudden temperature drop. She tried to immerse herself in it, melt her mind in it.

A loud bang ruptured it entirely. Out of the rock sprawled ... something. A huge, skittering, clicking, *something*. She felt the spray of dirt as it pelted them in small granules, and Shara offered a small prayer of thanks to any God or Goddess listening that the entire cave roof had not tumbled down upon them.

The creature was behind them, so close she could feel hot air upon the nape of her neck, smell a damp, earthy, off stench that wafted and stifled her further still.

"Run, Razakh, run!" she urged, and the Diodonian picked up a burst of speed, sending them thundering through the tunnel.

She cursed her inability to see, and then remembered Wezlan's

staff. The emerald glow she had seen it radiate, had seen light up the darkness for them. She gripped it tighter in her palm and wished with all her might for it to light up. But what can a girl with no Magicka do?

Another curse. Another round of wishful thinking. And then, miraculously, the staff hummed with power. The emerald atop its smooth jade surface sputtered to life, the elvish runes within the staff glowed azure in the pitch black, and she let go a roar of triumph.

Turning carefully on Razakh's back, she raised the staff above her head and immediately regretted it. The creature hot on Razakh's tail was repulsive. It trundled towards them on its hundreds of legs, its bulk beetle-black, the green light shining off its carapace. Its mouth wriggled open and closed, four fang-like pincers chattering and clicking away.

"Oh, shit." Shara shivered involuntarily, stifling a gag. If there was one thing she couldn't stand, it was bugs. Why, oh why, did it have to be a bug?

She looked about her, but there was nothing to use against it save the weapons strapped at her waist and slipped in every possible hidden sleeve or crevice on her body. "Shuriken it is."

Squeezing her thighs to Razakh's sides with all her strength, her quick fingers, now dull with pain from the cold, unclipped a shuriken at her waist, and, leaning backwards, her vision upside down, she aimed and sent the silver star flying.

It sailed past the creature's head, embedding itself uselessly in the cavern wall. With a hiss of frustration, she raised a middle finger at the weapon and righted herself on Razakh's back.

"*You better do something quick,*" Razakh huffed into her head, "*or we'll be mincemeat for the Wyrmear.*"

"I'm trying," she snapped back, and reclining with somewhat

236

nauseating dizziness in her stomach, she focused, the steel points of her weapon almost grating her nose. Leaning back, she let it loose in quick procession, watching its path until it hit the mark with satisfying force.

"How do you like them apples, you overgrown centipede!"

The creature hissed, blood spurting in great bouts down its face, one beady black eye punctured and oozing over the ground. Clickclickclickclick. The chatter increased in rage, and instead of retreating to see to its wounds, it angled to the wall and climbed above, gripping the cave roof so it was skittering above them.

The queasiness in Shara's stomach rebelled and she hunkered down on Razakh in fear. "It's on the roof," she screamed. "Hurry up!"

"I'm going as fast as I can," Razakh yelled back, and Shara could *feel* the usually clear bells of his voice ringing with alarm. *"You must find a way to stop its path. I can't outrun it forever."*

"With what?" Shara screeched. She had a handful of projectile weapons left and the angle of the beast made it impossible to aim for the other eye. She drew a dagger from her calf strap and squared it off towards the creature above, scrutinising its body in the staff's green light. Her amber eyes squinted as she tried to focus on small areas as the rest of the world went flying past.

The belly was covered in a hard shell and the legs were like metal needles piercing the cave above. But there, just between the steely plates of its black shell, she found vulnerable slivers of juicy, bulbous skin. Each segment of its body had its own weak spot, unarmoured and just asking for her blade.

She raised her staff hand upward, her right hand clenched on the hilt of a needle of her own, the point sharp and glistening in the emerald light. And just as she was about to send it carving through the air, the Wyrmear sent a volley of its own design.

Shards of frosty blue spewed from its mouth in waves, the pincers clicking eagerly as it eyed its quarry. She felt the temperature plummet as the chilly winds blew towards them, and she screamed, "Bank left," and Razakh did as she bid, nearly chucking her off in the process. "Right," she yelled again.

He obeyed her commands silently, trying for all his strength to gain ground ahead of the creature, but his energy was waning, the powerful stroke of his legs against the ground beginning to slow, unused to the burden on his back.

"Throw your ... weapon ... Shara," he panted, both in her mind and with steamy breaths that swished back over her face.

A plume of ice froze the ground before him, leaving tiny stalagmites glittering with wicked intent. Too late he noticed the danger, and one giant paw slammed onto the trap, the icy daggers embedding themselves deep into the skin.

Razakh howled in pain, stumbling as he came crashing down, skidding across the earth to land heavily on one shoulder. Just in time, Shara bucked off his back with all her strength and for one wild moment as she hung suspended in mid-air, time seemed to slow, and she took aim at one of the many mid-sections of the beast, and swung her blade.

She watched it arc through the air, hoping, praying, until the steel found its mark with a satisfying squelch. The beast roared, shivered, and Shara had seconds to sprint out of the way before it dropped from the ceiling with an earth-shaking boom.

Now was her chance. She looked at Razakh, fangs bared in pain, and he nodded. Limping as he was, the Diodonian would never shy from a fight. They both descended on the creature, Shara slashing its weak spots with her blade, rending the skin in neat slices from top to bottom until its insides were as jelly pouring from the wounds.

 238

Razakh dashed in and out, careful to keep his injured paw lifted, but tearing at the creature's soft spots with no mercy. His fangs sank deep into the skin, blue blood bursting like fresh drops of rain.

Shara watched him even as she sank her blade into her foe over and over. One could almost forget how intelligent he was, how ... human ... as his animalistic nature took over and he maimed with tooth and claw.

And at last, when the creature sank onto its belly, the strength of its hundreds, thousands of legs giving way, she stalked to its gigantic head, pincers snapping lazily, the chittering long since quieted, and withdrew her sword from its sheath. She took one last look at the depths of its beady black eyes and thrusted her blade up into its mouth and out of the back of its head.

It shuddered at last, the tremor reverberating down its body until it released one last sigh and departed the world.

Shara stumbled over to Razakh, her energy all but spent on felling the beast. She took the Diodonian's measure. His maw was covered in blue slime, blood still dripping in globs from his fangs, and he was limping badly. She pointed to his leg cautiously.

"May I?"

He was silent as she gently took his paw—so large it was almost the size of her head—and studied the damage. His paw was badly hurt, full of icy splinters, and cold ... Practically frozen to the touch. Shara frowned as she prodded it.

"Do you feel this?"

He winced, though admitting, *"Not as much as I should."*

"That's what I'm afraid of. I need to remove these shards immediately and get the blood pumping again. Your paw is numb, and I'm worried the frost damage will be irreparable."

A sigh echoed in her mind and she offered an apologetic glance.

"This may hurt, but I promise I'll have it fixed in no time at all."

She supported his weight as much as a slender human could a mass of muscle and fur while they retreated a respectful distance from the carapace of their foe. The smell was overpowering, the stench of death lingering in the damp air of the tunnel.

Shara appraised the corridor and blew a soft whistle. "We were lucky the whole mountain didn't come crashing down on us." She propped the staff against the wall, then slid onto her arse, crossing her legs and patting a knee.

Razakh hopped towards her, settling down and placing his giant paw where she gestured. He huffed in pain, rolled over, and nestled his great head to the ground, silver eyes watching her. *"The mountain has stood many an age. It would take more than a few knocks to send the topside caving under."*

Shara nodded whilst working, her concentration wholly on the shards that protruded from in between the pads of his paw, sticking out of the sensitive skin. She sucked in a breath and plucked one with deft fingers, lending to a growl from Razakh.

"Sorry," she said with a wince of her own. "What was that thing anyway?"

"Wymears," Razakh said matter-of-factly. *"Earth worms that tunnel through mountains and caves. They're dangerous creatures. Can survive on little sustenance but are awfully hard to shake when it has your scent. Its specialty—as you noticed from before—is ice. The cold slows its prey, and the shards work as a trapping device. The unlucky victims are preserved for a time in the frost so the beast can slowly devour the victim while they're still alive."*

Shara's stomach rebelled. "Okay, that took away any appetite I had. So ... how long do you suppose that one's been around for?"

"Their average lifespan is not known to us, but most of them were cleared out by hunting parties in moons past. The odd one still lingers in the mountain,

but they shy away from the sun, so they are left to their own devices." He shrugged. *"No Diodonian or human has come this deep into the mountain for many moons. It was probably curious."*

"And hungry," Shara muttered.

Razakh offered a clumsy smile. *"Aye. That too."*

She scowled. "Why didn't you warn me of this ahead of time?"

"I truly did not expect we'd have the pleasure of meeting one. Or perhaps I just foolishly hoped we wouldn't. As you noticed, the creatures have an adverse effect on Diodonians. The frost ... the cold, it somehow inhibits the flames on our backs. It is ... unnerving."

Her brows raised in amusement. "As opposed to fumbling blind in the dark, you mean?"

Razakh lowered his head, gave her the puppy dog eyes, and even though they were silver quicksand, it still had a winning effect.

A harrumph. "Not a dog, huh?"

The answering purr in her mind was filled with humour.

Shara pulled the next shard viciously from his paw and he snarled. She ignored the fangs leering in her face and then, surprisingly, they *both* laughed, the sound of his amusement a joyous melody in her mind, even as the rumble that came out his mouth was strange and gravelly.

She pulled another one and his laughter turned into a yelp.

"Oh, stop your whining, you big baby. The shards are all out now, but I need to get the blood pumping and warm your paw."

She set to work massaging the pads and gently kneading the skin in between, surprised to find how soft they were. She supposed smooth sands had something to do with that. After a time, his painful wincing turned into groans of pleasure, the silver eyes shuttering as the Diodonian enjoyed the massage.

She even risked a few pats on his back and head, revelling in the

soft golden fur, and even as one eye opened in surprise, she received no complaints or refusal. After a time, she deemed her work was done, nodding in satisfaction at the warmth restored to his paw.

As if in answer to her treatment, the flames of his back roared to life and she withdrew her hand with a cry, nearly being burnt in the process. Her amber eyes stared accusingly into his silver gaze, and she huffed. "At least we know it worked."

Tearing a strip off her cotton shirt, Shara wrapped his paw, gently tying the cloth with a neat bow. It wasn't to a medic's standard, sure, but it would do the job. After stepping back with a nod of approval, the Diodonian uttered a strange howl, in between a whine and a yip.

"*It's how we say thanks,*" he drawled, as if it should have been obvious.

She smiled. "You Diodonians are a strange lot."

He returned a lopsided grin, all toothy and stretched skin. "*You have no idea.*"

And she wondered, then, if they might very well become good friends.

◆◆●◆◆

The taste of fresh air was a blessing on her tongue, the sun smiling on her face a tender kiss upon her brow. She took a deep breath of warm, clean air and inhaled the smell of earthy soil and tree sap. Looking around, she saw the familiar shapes of swollen trees, looking as if they had overindulged on too much water.

They had finally broken free of the underground passage, its opening hidden behind a stack of rocks and nearly covered in overgrown grass, keeping it well hidden from prying eyes. It reminded her of the hidden exit below Maynesgate, and she thought fondly of the street rats who'd guided them through the bowels of that city what seemed like forever ago, when she'd first met Wezlan and Ashalea.

How things have changed since then.

She fully took in her surroundings and realised with surprise, "We're near Hallow's Pass?"

Razakh hummed in response. "Not just for emergencies, the tunnel doubled as a secondary measure in the event of battle. Its corridor is narrow, but just wide enough to allow small troops of either men or Diodonians to pass through."

"Smart," Shara said. "Was it ever used for this purpose?"

"Not to my knowledge. The only war ever fought in the Diodon Mountains was the one fought by humans ... in their own city no less." He shook his head, his teeth bared in anger. "Mankind never learns."

Shara couldn't argue with that so instead she withdrew her crumpled map of Everosia, now looking sorry for itself after the wear and tear of this trip. Placing it on the ground and slapping some pebbles on for placeholders, she trailed their position with a finger.

"Moonglade Meadows is south-west of us," she explained to Razakh, who peered over her shoulder. "Without mounts it will take too long to reach it, and with your paw ..."

She eyed off the injury with pursed lips. He was able to walk, gingerly, but there was no way he'd be running anytime soon. Not unless he was seen to by a medical professional, which posed its own problems. Diodonians had not been sighted in Everosia for Goddess knows how long. Many humans would never have heard of the species at all, it had been so long since they'd integrated with the other races.

For them to see one now ...

"You know, it would be much easier if you allowed me into your thoughts," Razakh drawled.

"You, my friend, are safer on the outside. There are some things,

personal things, you wouldn't know what to do with."

He grumbled in response. *"What's your plan, then?"*

She sighed. "There are horses waiting for us at Galanor. A contact of Wezlan's is caring for them, along with the rest of our supplies. We'll need to stop by. The journey will take too long on foot and your injury needs someone with some actual medical experience to assess you."

"I'm fine," Razakh growled, and Shara shrank a little at the tone of his words. He huffed again, and his flames simmered to a rippling blue. *"It's just ... you and Wezlan are the first humans I've met since ..."*

He didn't need to finish for Shara to follow his thought trail. It was a long and winding path that travelled back to his childhood. When he was small and helpless and unable to stop the monstrosities of men—the cruel capabilities of mankind. She could understand why he was hesitant to meet humans.

"We aren't all bad," she said softly. "We get along, right? And if you knew what I did before I became a Guardian you might not judge me so lightly."

His silver eyes regarded her. "You are an Onyxonite. I know what deeds are done in the dark. But you have a code. You do not murder and exploit without cause or good reason. You do not experiment on your quarry."

She swallowed hard at that and prepared herself for the rejection she'd face once the words were out of her mouth. "I've done horrible things, Razakh. I dream of it sometimes ... of their faces. I am skilled with a blade. Perhaps too much. And I have honed that skill until I am nothing but a monster when I wield it. I—"

"Stop."

Her lips opened and closed like a fish out of water. "But—"

"I do not need to hear you belittle yourself. You are an Onyxonite, proud

244

and honourable, and whatever you did in the past you did for your tribe. For your family. I can understand that more than most. But more than an assassin, you are human. And while I do not understand many of the things your kind do, I know there are some with big and honest hearts. Like you."

His words were an injection of empathy and strength, a kernel of wisdom she needed more than she'd ever admit. She clung to them, to his kindness. Tears burned at the edge of her vision and she turned from Razakh, her pride bristling. And it occurred to her that of all the humans or even elves in the world, including those dearest to her, this strange creature–this Diodonian–understood her better than any.

The one she'd scorned, mistrusted, been so eager to turn away. She turned to him then, unashamed of the tear that slipped down her face. Unbothered by the display of emotion, the vulnerability she was showing–that she'd always been taught to hide by her father. And she cried. Prideful, gloating, smirking Shara, washed away in this moment in time. Instead revealing a girl. Emotional, healing, and anything but simple.

She padded to his side, ran a hand through his coat, and in response he snuffed out the flames so she could bury her face in his fur. Nothing but velvet reassurance against a tear-stained face. She cried and cried; over her childhood, over the anguished faces of those she tortured, at the pain and mutilation of her own torture, over the fear and panic that Wezlan and Ashalea and Denavar–her only friends–were missing from this world.

Then, a soft and gentle voice, imploring, curious. "Am I not your friend, too?"

She gripped his fur tighter. "Of course you are, you silly dog," she whispered somewhere in between hysterical sobs and a murmur of laughter.

And she hadn't the heart to tell him to get out of her head. For all she cared, he was welcome there forever.

We Make Our Own Fate

ASHALEA

ER EYES FLUTTERED OPEN to find the ocean blue of Denavar's swirling in a choppy storm of worry and discontent. As she inhaled a deep breath, he sent his own whooshing out, the peppermint tang on the air grounding her, familiarising her with where she was again.

"Thank Prianara for bringing you back to me," he sighed, the lines in his face softening, his knitted brows loosening.

Ashalea grinned. "I don't think the Moon Goddess played any part in that, my love." She looked around and realised Denavar was carrying her in his arms like a prize worthy of a war. Her eyes trailed back to the blob still following them.

"How long was I out for?"

He frowned, concern drawing new lines on his gilded face. "Long

enough to make me want to pull my hair out. I was afraid ..." A sharp intake of breath. "I don't know what I thought. Just don't do it again."

She raised a hand to cup his face, smoothing her fingers along his jawline. "If I could have stopped it, I would. But I was with *him*."

Denavar pulled up short. "You what?"

Ashalea sighed. "It was like a dream, only we were in some in-between place. We discussed some things. He—the dreams, Denavar. The visions. He knew everything. Allowed me to see his past. And through me he was able to see our present. Everything that's happened ... it's all my fault."

Her voice broke at the last and he cradled her ever tighter. No judgement on his face, only a look of pure love and longing; a need to comfort her, console her. Was there anything he wouldn't do to keep her safe? The thought was more frightening than ever, for Ashalea knew Denavar would die if it meant she could live. But what would an elvish life be without him in it? What would immortality be worth?

"You are responsible for nothing," his voice cut through her thoughts. "The darkness is the only one at fault here. The only one who deserves pain and suffering from his actions. Remember that, Ashalea. Remember why we're here."

She resolved to get it together and nodded firmly. "Right. But there's one more thing."

Denavar cocked a head, eyes on her, though she knew his ears were pricked for any danger, mindful of the creature behind them, sensing any other presence, his vision widened in order to spot approaching foes in his peripheral.

"When I used the moon Magicka that day at Renlock, my power transferred to the darkness."

She felt Denavar stiffen, his hands tighten, but he kept quiet as she continued.

"Lucky for us, he doesn't know how to summon the Magicka to use it. The unlucky part is—"

"He wants you to tell him," Denavar finished with a grim frown. "Here. In this realm where we have no hope of escaping without Wezlan ... whom he'll be closely guarding."

She nodded. "Even if I knew how I managed to call forth that Magicka, I would never tell him, of course, but ... it's troubling to consider he'll go to any lengths for this."

Denavar smiled, no amount of joy reaching his eyes. "I know you wouldn't. But he won't stop. He will torture you until he has what he seeks. And if you didn't break, he would move on to Wezlan and myself. He knows how loyal you are, Ashalea. The cocky bastard is assured of his plan because he knows you'd never leave Wezlan. Never leave me."

He was right. Gods, but he was right. If the darkness so much as laid a hand on Denavar she would bend to his will. And Wezlan ... her heart ached for him. The wizard had probably already suffered some form of physical abuse since being here. She just hoped he could hold out until she arrived.

"I'm coming, Wezlan," she whispered, both to herself and as a promise to her old mentor.

Her throat bobbed as her mind raced through all the different ways in which this could end, but she shook her head and considered their chances. The darkness didn't seem to know about the creature they had on their heels. He was too fixated on the power he'd received unknowingly from her. So that left surprise on their side.

She peered up at Denavar's face. Carved to perfection, the planes of his face smooth and angular, the square jaw and high cheek bones, the blue piercing eyes she'd be ever so happy to drown in and never resurface from. He would do whatever she asked without question.

And right now, she needed him more than ever to help stop the darkness and to save Wezlan.

He looked down at her, sensing her focus, and gifted her a smile. One reserved only for her. One that said everything, and nothing at all.

"We need to get my power back, Denavar," she whispered. "We need to steal it back and find a way to use it against him. He's tainted everything good in his life ... twisted it all into something dark and horrible. He will not have this. Not my parent's power. Not my birth right."

His eyes hardened, resolve edging into his gritted teeth, a muscle pulsing beneath the skin. Ashalea could sense his anger. His pain. He wanted the darkness ended as much as she, had reasons of his own to see this through. Personal reasons. Not just for Everosia and all who dwelled within it, but for Farah. For Renlock. For his people.

Her people.

For it was not just her parents that had died in Crinos's raid on the Moonglade Meadows. Many families had perished. Sons, daughters, husbands, wives, fathers, mothers. Many of Denavar's childhood friends—fellow students, his parent's friends, neighbours—thankfully, his own mother and father had been visiting brethren in Windarion that day, else they would not have been so lucky.

Though, Ashalea supposed luck was a matter of perception. She didn't feel lucky that her adoptive parents died years ago, and she survived. She did not think it lucky that Wezlan arrived after their murder, not before. Luck had nothing to do with it.

"We make our own fate," she murmured, determined eyes scanning their surroundings. She spied a tall tree standing on its lonesome just ahead, and she jerked her chin at it. "We need to rest. Who knows how much time has passed here, and we'll need our strength."

He threw a wary glance over his shoulder at the blob still ambling after them. "What about our new friend?"

Ashalea frowned. "Let's hope it can't climb. We'll take shifts to get some sleep. Carry on once we've had some rest."

He nodded. "I'll take first watch."

She looked up to find Denavar staring at her in concern, but she offered a reassuring smile. "You can put me down now."

He settled her down carefully, as if the slightest bump would cause her to shatter like glass on stone floors. Ashalea smiled. "I am stronger than I look, you know."

Denavar gave her an appraising glance before looking ahead to the encampment not so far away now.

"Aye, inside and out, and it's a good thing, too. We'll need it."

A Collection of Curses

WEZLAN

IS MUSCLES, NAY, HIS VERY BONES screamed with exhaustion and pain. To an unknowing eye, one would think him a broken man. And that he was, to some extent. His body was bruised, bleeding, the structural integrity of his human form now compromised after several of his ribs had been cracked, a couple fingers broken, and one leg shattered.

But a mage doesn't sign up to be a wizard without knowing the consequences. If the world isn't in some way marginally at risk during the extensive years of a wizard's life, either he or she did their duty exceptionally well or the villains of the world were doing a poor job of it.

Wezlan wasn't sure of either of those things, when it came down to a bottom line. "Every action has a reaction," his dearest friend

Barlok used to say. In fact, they were the very last words out of the wizard's mouth before he gave all his power to Wezlan. Right before the darkness shuttered the life from his eyes and cast his body from a cliff into the nothingness below.

That action had cost Barlok his life, and spared Wezlan's. He would always remember that moment, just as he'd always remember plunging his sword into the darkness's body. It had been a moment of triumph. Of victory. But it had all been in vain because the darkness hadn't died, hadn't been vanquished or been rendered powerless. He had simply ceased to be a problem for a time, then popped up in another.

But the past was neither here nor there. No, there was simply just now. Him. The darkness. And two elves he was most fond of, likely headed his way now. And here he was, tied to a rack, a fool thinking of foolish things when all the seconds in the world counted for something greater.

Wezlan cursed for the tenth time in so many minutes. He missed his staff. Not that it was needed to perform Magicka, of course, but it was something he'd come to rely on. A crux of his power—of Barlok's power. A shard of history nestled in emerald brilliance at its top, and he wondered now where on Everosia it could be. If it was buried beneath sands or in the hands of a friend.

At least Shara and Razakh were safe. He hoped. Knowing the stubborn assassin, she'd be doing everything in her power to find them, and with Razakh at her side, perhaps they'd do just that. He smiled—a half grimace as the action pulled at the cut in his lips—but it soon died as he focused on the task at hand.

The darkness may have snared him, but there was still hope for the Guardians. There was still hope for—

His thoughts quieted as a tornado of black erupted before his

eyes, and within it, the familiar flash of the darkness as he reappeared. And as the shadows parted before him, he cursed not for the last time in so many minutes.

23

An Unexpected Tumble

SHARA

THE TWO ASSES WAS A DIVE. Shara should have guessed as much by the name, but in a small ramshackle town such as this, choices were in short supply. At least she understood the title. Upon entering the pub, she noticed two donkeys watching her from a hangar across the pathway. One brayed at her before she entered, and she curtseyed in amusement.

The mascots of the town, perhaps. And admittedly, she did find the name *was* rather entertaining. She suspected the inn would do quite well in a large city like Maynesgate; it would provide a few laughs for drunken patrons, and would certainly not be confused with other pubs.

After a little investigating upon their arrival to this town—and prior to entering the pub—Shara had discovered their horses had been well fed, washed, groomed, and housed in a nearby stable. Their saddlebags were noticeably absent, but only a fool would have left them with the nags. Shara shrugged. She would come back for them later tonight. The moon was freshly risen, and the woman who was housing them could wait.

So, she'd taken her 'investigations' to the inn, plonked some coin on the bar and demanded the best meal this fine establishment could offer. She'd slapped an extra couple of coins on the table to keep the ale coming.

The hostess, a scrawny woman who was all angles and hard lines in the face, had stared at her beneath unkempt brows for a long minute. She'd then shrugged before taking the money. Patrons such as Shara were rare, true, and perhaps not welcomed with open arms—just one look at Shara's assortment of weapons and most of the populace had given her a wide berth—but beggars can't be choosers, and by the looks of the tavern, the town of Galanor had seen better days.

Still, she'd scraped the bowl clean of all dregs and wolfed down the hot stew with gusto. The ale was sub-par, but it was ale and that was a reward in itself. Hell, after the last few days, Shara figured it was well earned.

"*What's taking so long?*" the whine of Razakh had echoed in her brain.

"A girl's gotta eat," she had thought back, wondering whether he'd hear.

The answering huff was confirmation enough. Razakh, of course, had neglected to join her, and was off in the wild somewhere doing whatever dogs did.

"*For the last time,*" he said gruffly. "*I'm not a dog. And for your information, I'm hunting. Some of us have to earn our keep.*"

She smiled before slurping down a mouthful of froth. "Well,

don't let me distract you. Have fun with that."

A rumble of unintelligible grumbles sounded through her mind before all went quiet. And then she listened with her ears, for scraps of information were always to be found in a thoroughfare such as this. She didn't know much of the southern villages of Everosia, but she did know of the Dreadlands and the marshes of Deyvall. The former lay south-east from here, but Deyvall lay directly south. Both were not places she cared to visit, for even before the darkness had loosed his foul beings across this land, stories had always spread of the creatures that resided in those locales. Rumours of monsters that dwelled within the marshes. No one was stupid enough to venture there, and if they did, none ever returned.

It was to these rumours that Shara listened now, one ear cocked for information as she scoured the pub's interior. Most chatter was mere speculation and drunken babble, so she focused on her surroundings instead. Whoever decorated the place did a horrid job. Antlers poked out from walls on crooked angles, and the fireplace was buried beneath a mountain of cinders. The tables had been stained and gouged by all manner of pointy objects, and she didn't want to know what was stuck to their undersides.

A filthy rug with muted shades of green and blue lay sloppily over the floor, giving the appearance of cracked eggshells. She pursed her lips with distaste. She may be an assassin, but at least she had class.

Then her ear pricked on a musical sound ringing from the far corner. A voice, lilting and hauntingly beautiful, so pretty it made her stomach ache. She strained her neck to get a glimpse of the owner, but the mystery woman was blocked from view by balding scalps and greasy heads.

A lyre started up, the notes in perfect harmony with the songstress ensnaring the attention of all in the room. Unable to ignore her curiosity any longer, Shara snatched up her ale and made for the corner. She garnered the attention of several sets of eyes around the room, one half of them ogling at her curves and the plunge of her neckline, the other half—mostly women, though some did offer appreciative glances—rolling their eyes and slapping at their counterparts in rage.

None attempted to flatter or lay a move, and she hip-and-shouldered the rest in her way so she could squeeze to the front of the crowd. The woman she found was one of the most beautiful she'd ever laid eyes on. Long brown hair fell in soft waves to her waist, half of it pinned in braids and tied with small beads and charms.

Soft brown eyes like that of a doe peered out from full lashes that fluttered as she sang, silky pouting lips that were wicked curves and gentle innocence all at once. Her clothes were bright and somewhat garish, though formfitting in all the right places. Shara gazed at her with hard eyes and tight lips, but the minstrel's answering wink had her cheeks reddening.

She stayed there for a long while. Right up until the singer had finished her songs, and the minstrel had packed away his instrument. She'd then turned around and headed straight back to the bar, sat herself down and ordered another ale, ready to chaste herself for wasted time when—

"A coin for your thoughts?"

The soft voice was so startling and so close to her ear that Shara almost dropped her drink, looking up in surprise. It was a rare thing for someone to sneak up on her, and her fingers twitched in annoyance.

A soft chuckle sounded from the woman's lips, and she sidled into the chair besides Shara. "Sorry. I command my audience's attention with song, but I can be quiet as a mouse off the stage."

Shara's lips curved in amusement. "You don't say."

"Oh, but I do," the lady responded. She shrugged. "Or I can be

loud. Depends what mood I'm in."

Shara raised an eyebrow before ordering another two drinks from the barkeep and offering one of the tankards to her guest. She nodded in thanks and took the cup with long, slender fingers.

"That was a fine show," Shara said. "You have a gifted voice." And she meant it.

The minstrel gave a pretty smile. "Most of the patrons are drunk out of their minds or half asleep, so it's not usually hard to please. But you ..." she looked Shara up and down, a blunt appraisal which was *very* thorough. Apparently Shara passed the test, for the woman nodded.

Shara cleared her throat. Was this woman checking her out? She was no meek maiden, and she'd had her fair share of men *and* women of all shapes, sizes and skillsets, but this one was brazen, confident ... and Shara liked it.

"What brings you to Galanor?" the woman asked.

"That business is my own," she responded, and the words sounded tart even to her own ears.

The minstrel merely laughed. "You're equipped up to your ears with blades, you're wearing all black and you're alone. I can imagine there's only one reason an Onyxonite would be in this backwater, though why someone in a town full of farmers and small merchants would warrant your attention ... now *that* is a mystery."

Shara turned to the woman, her knees brushing against the stranger, and she leaned in, so close she could smell the woman's perfume on her collarbone: jasmine and sandalwood. It was intoxicating and dangerous all at once.

"Perhaps the target I seek is here, in this very room. Perhaps she's sitting right in front of me. What would you say then?" Shara's voice was low. It might be a threat, or an invitation; she hadn't decided which.

After all, it never ended well for people poking their noses in her business. But this woman ... Shara was intrigued. There was something about her, and it made Shara curious. Perhaps the woman's answer would decide her fate.

The minstrel took a large unladylike sip from the tankard, then pursed her lips thoughtfully. "I'd say that's too bad. I'd say ... at least I went out to the sound of applause and coins thrown at my feet. Though I wouldn't have minded one more run for my money." She placed a hand suggestively on Shara's knee.

Shara's amber eyes sparkled. "Are you flirting with me, minstrel? I could end your life with a flick of my wrist and without a second thought. You're ballsy, I'll give you that."

The woman laughed, a musical bell of a sound. "Oh, no, my dear assassin, I'm so much more than that."

Then she took Shara's hand and led her upstairs into darker places, and for once in her life, Shara was at a loss for words or wit.

"*Are you sure about this?*"

Shara rolled her eyes in exasperation. "Honestly, beneath that ridiculously soft fur of yours, your gut is even softer. Harden up. I'm sure you've faced worse."

She stood before a doorway, hand raised to rap on the wood, even as her amber eyes pierced the darkness of the narrow alley to find a Diodonian shrinking in cowardice. An amusing sight, truth be told, to see the giant beast crouched uncertainly over the mere thought of saying a 'howdy-do' to a human.

Before he could further object she knocked thrice, a little harder

than she had meant to. The moon was high in the sky and it was late, given how inebriated the patrons of the local pub had been when she had left. Given how busy—and how long—Shara had been attending to something else just prior to this moment.

The minstrel had treated her to a show of her own. A very entertaining—and pleasurable—show. There was something about that woman. She was a people person, but more than that she seemed to capture the attention of everyone in the room—Shara included. Her body language, her words, the power of her music, it demanded attention. Demanded worshipping.

Of course, after the ruffle of covers had ceased and Shara had drifted off to sleep feeling much lighter and less stressed for the first time in a while, she'd woken to find most of her money missing, as well as several small blades that would fetch a pretty price. She'd cursed herself then. She never let her guard down. Ever.

She hadn't even got the woman's name. And yet, perhaps it was better that way. The sheer cheek of her was flabbergasting. Shara was impressed enough by her cunning, and in a good enough mood to consider letting the minstrel steal away with her goods. Maybe.

"Blasted woman," she mumbled now with a chuckle. "Fingers as good for thieving as they are for—"

The door opened a crack, and Shara plastered a smile on her face. The woman on the other side glared at her with one visible eye, lips pressed in a thin line. There was silence for a few beats.

"Well, are you just plain daft or did you wake me up at this hour for a reason?"

Razakh's laughter tinkled in Shara's mind and she scowled, both at the woman and in indignation.

"I'm a friend of Wezlan Shadowbreaker's. It would appear you have been charged with our horses and equipment."

The woman's eye narrowed before she opened the door fully, and not without protection, Shara noted. A butcher knife glinted from her free hand, and she ushered Shara in with little more than a lazy wave.

"If I may ..." Shara started.

The old woman raised a thin eyebrow, and Shara marvelled at the paper-thin skin holding it in place. The lady was ancient. Beyond ancient. It was a wonder she didn't die on the spot and turn to ash where she stood.

She placed quavering hands on her jutting hips. "Well? I'm sure you've noticed, girl, but I don't have all day."

Or perhaps even the night, Shara thought meanly. But she breathed through her nose and forced her body to relax. "I'm with a friend," she said lamely.

"Well invite him in then," the woman snapped. "Where are your manners?"

"I–" Shara sputtered over what to say. This woman was a real piece of work.

"*Reminds me of someone else I know,*" Razakh's amusement jingled in her head.

"He's not human," Shara blurted finally.

The old lady snorted. "Oh aye, lass. I gathered as much when I caught his silver eyes a-starin' from the shadows." She glared at Shara before calling out the door, "Come in, Diodonian. You don't scare me."

Shara's jaw dropped. A rare thing for the assassin. "How did you know?"

The old lady tottered to a small kitchen area and chuckled as she lit some candles around the room with Magicka. She set to work on a pot of tea and ignored Shara's question. Her pink nightgown swirled around as she moved, practically swimming on her frail body.

Razakh stalked into the house, nudging the door shut with his muzzle after entering. He glanced at Shara, amusement and curiosity swirling in those silver eyes. Shara merely raised her shoulders and lifted her hands in a 'don't ask me' motion.

They both stood awkwardly, studying the room as they waited. The kitchen was small but tidy with a very homely feel to it. Garlands of herbs, garlic, and flowers draped from the far wall, and burnished pots and pans hung in a neat row above the stove top. A modest fireplace watched on from the corner, and two red, wing-backed chairs guarded the hearth.

Small, neat, and cosy. Just how Shara liked it.

"Well, sit down then," the old lady muttered, and Shara frowned. Perhaps not *quite* how she liked it.

But Shara did as she was asked, and Razakh curled up by the hearth, watching the woman intently. She tottered back on over with a cup of tea in her hand for Shara, offering nothing to Razakh.

Her eyes roved over the jade staff Shara had propped against the wall, the runes flickering softly in the dim light. "Where is Wezlan?"

Shara swallowed. "He's not with us."

"I can see that," the old lady snapped. "Where?"

Shara's cheeks burned, her temper rising. "If I knew that, we wouldn't be here," she huffed. "He's gone, along with Ashalea and Denavar, and I don't know where or how to get them back."

The woman pursed her lips wryly. "He told me about you. The fiery Onyxonite."

Shara opened her mouth to spew venom but Razakh interrupted: "*Shara.*"

The old lady's gaze flashed to Razakh and she grinned. "He didn't tell me about *you* though. A Diodonian of old. Hmph. 'Tis rare indeed to see one of your kind. I should count my lucky stars."

"And do you?" Shara drawled.

A frown. "That's for me to know and you to mind your business. Now, when you say Wezlan is gone, do you mean—"

"I mean gone. Not in this world. Not on Everosia."

"Well ... that is problematic."

Shara wanted to wring the elder woman's leathery neck. "Do you have anything useful to add or are you just here for the one-liners? You haven't even told me your name."

That earned a chortle, which ended in a fit of coughing, something sinister bubbling in the old lady's chest. "My name is Leanna," she managed to say in between gasps.

"I'm—"

Leanna put up a hand. "I know who you are, girl. You're Shara Silvaren, next Guardian in line for the Grove. As are you." Her eyes shifted to Razakh, who had remained silent thus far. "I was a mage at Renlock once upon a time. Under the guidance of Wezlan himself."

Shara eyed her off sceptically. "But you're so—"

"Old?" Leanna barked a bitter laugh, another fit of coughs racking her frail chest. She noticed Shara's stare and shot a withering glare back. "Oh no, don't you pity me."

"I don't," Shara remarked simply, and the old woman nodded.

Leanna's lips curled in amusement, puckering as if she'd tasted something sour. "Wezlan has lived many, many years. The gift of becoming a wizard, I suppose. Some might say it's a curse. But either way, he has done many a great deed in his time. Sickness does not ail him, nor has time been unkind. But me ..." She snorted then. "I am dying. My Magicka wears thin, like the veil of its power has worn with time, rotted with age and idleness."

"We all die eventually," Shara said. "You should be grateful to be blessed with Magicka at all."

Leanna stared into the crackling fire. "Aye. There is truth in that. A cruel truth, but no less arguable."

Shara sighed. "Leanna, I did not come here for stories and regret—I have enough of my own. Wezlan trusted you for a reason, and that is good enough for me. You have supplies that we need. And the horses."

Leanna looked up then, an odd expression on her face. "If you're not careful, girl, you'll end up alone and equally regretful, with nothing but those stories to keep you company. Don't harden your heart too much, else you'll find it breaks alone with no one around to mourn you."

Shara didn't know why, but the words stung like a slap to the face. She glanced at the woman with disdain. Who was she to judge? What did she know of love and longing? And then she realised: nothing ... and everything.

This bitter woman was a hard shell—any creamy, splendid warmth one might find on the inside had long since dried up. She sensed a strength to her, something that suggested she was more—so much more—than what she'd become. Had she pushed everyone away? Had she hardened her heart like she accused Shara of doing?

The door burst open then, and a flash of garish colour blocked the entrance. Shara's eyes narrowed in annoyance as she recognised the long brown hair curling to the woman's waist, and the hideous outfit the minstrel was wearing.

"Grandma?" the woman asked groggily, blearily. Shara could smell the alcohol oozing from her pores and the bottle hanging precariously in one hand. She also noticed the bulging coin purse strapped to her hip.

Then the minstrel noticed Shara standing there and she giggled in between hiccups, raising her hands in merriment as if to say, 'oops, you got me'. Her eyes widened when she spied Razakh sitting by the hearth, tail streaked with fire swishing lazily above his head. She squinted, as if not trusting her vision in that drunken state.

And just like that she dove involuntarily to the ground and Shara caught her in strong arms, frowning at the buxom beauty who was now passed out and snoring. Shara glanced at Leanna before staring pointedly at the woman now cradled in her grasp. "Is this yours?"

"Aye," Leanna said after a heavy sigh. "If you don't mind, can you place her on a cot in the back room?"

Shara rolled her eyes but she lifted the unconscious woman with ease. She was heavier than she looked, but she was on the curvier side after all. Shara remembered the sweep of her hips, of her breasts, the silkiness of her navel and—she cleared her throat, colour deepening on her cheeks.

She settled the woman gently on the bed, smoothing the now unruly curls back from her heart-shaped face. Hesitantly, she trailed a finger down the smooth cheek before making to turn away.

The woman grabbed her wrist, long lashes fluttering open ever so slowly. She gifted Shara the most saintly, gorgeous smile, before uttering, "Back for another round?"

She tried to wink but in her drunken state her eyes wouldn't comply.

"My name is Telilah," she said with a goofy grin.

And then she blacked out.

A Way Forward

SHARA

SHARA SLEPT SOUNDLY THAT NIGHT. She dreamed, but instead of claws and blades and dark and dreadful things, she dreamed of colour and life and the sound of a tinkling laugh ringing like a bell. When she woke, she felt more refreshed than she had been in some time—lighter, almost.

Leanna only had two beds—one for the *thief* and for herself—so Shara had slept near the hearth, a bed of blankets and cushions and the glorious velvet of Razakh's fur to keep her cosy. Her companion hadn't objected, and Shara had noted the flames of his tail flickered out so as to not burn her.

He still lay there now, chest rising and falling, giant body curled up in a ball that looked very uncomfortable. Shara sat up with a yawn, stretching her arms in the air, noting the rosy glow of morning. Her

eyes fell on a shard of light that peeked into the room and followed its path to a window and the sunrise beyond. Tea rose pink and peach fuzz filtered through the glass panes. Beautiful.

She left the sleeping Diodonian and moseyed over to Telilah's room, carefully twisting the doorknob so as not to make a sound. She peered around the frame, noting the mound of blankets and the snoring minstrel buried within them.

Shara grinned wickedly before storming to the bed and prodding the sleeping girl, who mumbled her protests with a croaky voice.

"Grandma, stop. I had a late night," she grumbled.

"Oh yes, a very late night. Spent doing sinful things with dangerous women, stealing, and drinking your way to death's door."

Telilah slowly peeled the covers back to squint at Shara's face. She blinked several times. "You're not Grandma."

Shara raised an immaculate brow and shook her hair. "I should hope not. Now get up. You took my things and I want them back."

The woman glared at her before attempting to pull the blankets back over her head, but Shara was having none of it. She swooped in and ripped the lot from the girl, only to realise that her quarry was naked underneath.

Telilah smirked as she noted Shara's wandering stare. "Like what you see?"

Shara's amber eyes smouldered. "I already had it once, and once was enough," she bit back. "You're even worse than I am. Wezlan would all but rip out his beard if he met you."

At the mention of the wizard's name, the girl's eyes glimmered, and she sat up quickly, groaning in the process. She didn't attempt to cover herself, and it took every effort for Shara not to stare.

But the girl simply yawned, put a hand to her head as if the touch alone would halt a hangover. Her brown eyes peered at Shara

with interest. "Wezlan Shadowbreaker? The wizard who trained my Grandma?"

"The very one."

"How do you know him? No one has seen him in these parts for an age. I doubt many people would know him if they did. I was just a child when last I saw him."

"Not that it's any of your business," Shara huffed, "but he's a good friend and ... he's missing, along with two others."

The brown eyes dimmed, a small pout forming on those luscious lips. "Missing? But how can that be? He's more powerful than anything or anyone. He—"

"I didn't say he was dead," Shara barked, and the tone ceased Telilah's chattering. "My companion and I are trying to find him and bring him back. That's all you need to know."

Telilah rubbed her eyes. "Your companion being the giant dog-thing?"

Shara frowned. "Only *I* get to call him names." With that, she picked up a blanket and threw it at the woman's flabbergasted face. "Get dressed, and I'll give you the dignity of returning my items yourself, rather than taking them. Which, by the way, I would normally do in a much less forgiving manner."

She stalked from the room, leaving Telilah speechless, and returned to the living area to find Razakh basking in the morning rays, silver eyes swirling calmly. Upon her entrance, he grinned clumsily.

"I take it that went well?"

Shara frowned. "I can't believe how stupid someone can be to try and steal from an Onyxonite."

"Only she didn't try, she succeeded," he quipped. *"A parting gift after your little romp together last night."*

"Okay, first of all, you must have been rifling through my thoughts

269

to know that, and second ... well ... no one asked for your opinion," she snapped.

"Actually, I can tell because of two things: the first being that your scent changed significantly once you were in that room, and the second; how else would a human being with no skills manage to steal from you?"

Shara cringed. "That's disgusting. Please don't speak of my scent *ever* again."

"Whose scent are we talking about?" Telilah wafted in like a spring breeze, her hair sleep-mussed, and she was wearing loose cotton pyjamas that showed her midriff. She stopped in the sunlight, the rays forming a halo around her head and gilding the creamy skin of her arms and legs. She held a wrapped bundle in her arms.

"You're doing that thing again," Razakh said.

Shara threw him a withering glare, cheeks reddening slightly, before sniffing the air and turning to Telilah. "You smell like ale. It's oozing out of your pores."

Telilah pouted again before smelling an underarm. Her nose puckered in distaste. "You're not wrong." She sighed and crossed the floor to Shara. "Your things, my lady." She bowed with mock reverence.

Shara snorted, but she grabbed the bundle and checked that all lost blades were there. When she spied no coins, she held one hand out expectantly.

Telilah rolled her eyes before relinquishing a purse. "Everything is there. You needn't count it."

"And I should trust the word of a thief?" Shara said pointedly. But she didn't open the pouch to check.

The front door banged open then, and all eyes turned to Leanna, who had a basket full of eggs and fresh produce tucked under her arm. Her gaze fell on Telilah, a scathing look in her eyes.

 270

Shara wondered if the woman ever smiled or laughed. She wondered more so how it was an old crone such as she was so spritely and strong at her age, and at the crack of dawn no less. Perhaps a result of the Magicka still lingering in her blood.

Finally, Leanna set down her goods and sniffed the air.

"It smells like a brothel in here."

And Shara could have punched Razakh for his thunderous laughter in her head.

"If your friends have left this world, there is nothing I can do," Leanna said grimly as they all crowded around her tiny kitchen table.

Razakh nodded. *"We're hoping the elves can help us. Their Magicka is old, their lore extensive—of this world and others."*

Shara dug into her breakfast ruthlessly, hacking at the eggs and bacon. The subject made her tense, eager to be back on the road again, no matter how tasty the bacon was that crunched between her teeth. No matter how *distracting* her night had been here. She had to remain focused and get her friends back no matter what.

Still, as she chewed thoughtfully—and loudly judging by Leanna's disapproving glance—she couldn't help but smirk at Telilah's face upon hearing Razakh's words telepathically. She shoved more bacon in her mouth to stifle the laughter bubbling up.

"To which elves do you seek answers from?" Leanna asked cautiously.

"The Moonglade elves. That is where two members of our party are from."

Shara noted he failed to mention Ashalea was their rightful queen. But perhaps it was best left unsaid. Who knows if they could really trust this woman? After all, Telilah said it had been many years since she'd seen Wezlan.

Leanna's eyes narrowed. "The Moonglade elves do not trust easily. You will find it hard to gain answers from them if you can even find them."

Shara swallowed a lump of food. "What do you mean?"

"Since the darkness destroyed much of the village, the remaining elves placed wards over it, protecting the city and its inhabitants from outsiders and unfriendly eyes. Wezlan helped make it so."

"He was there when the wards were erected?"

"Aye. A few centuries ago. Not long after the darkness made his move. The wards were strengthened every so often by mages from all three Elven cities. I was fortunate enough to venture there once on a diplomatic mission with Wezlan. I know where the fallen city lies."

Shara considered Leanna's words. If what she said was true, it would be impossible to breach the wards without Magicka or permission from the elves to enter, and she didn't see that happening anytime soon—even if they stood at the doorstep and yelled themselves hoarse. Leanna herself was too old to be riding horseback and venturing into the wilds, so where did that leave them?

She shoved her plate aside and spread out her trusty map of Everosia. The location of the Moonglade Meadows lay beyond the Purple Plains and over a small mountain range—mild compared to the far stretches of the Diodon Mountains, meagre in size compared to the hulking snow peaks of Kingsgareth.

"Has the city been rebuilt in another location?"

Leanna shook her head. "No, the map remains true."

Shara was baffled. It seemed obvious then, how one might find the Meadows. She opened her mouth to argue this point, but Telilah beat her to it with a wink.

"The wards shroud the Meadows in a fog so dense that not even

the sun can pierce its mist. With no way to tell time or direction, and no landmarks to guide you, if you stepped in, you would likely not come out unless you knew what signs to look for."

"*And what hints might one find in such a place?*"

Telilah tapped her nose, a playful grin on her face, but she turned to her grandma, waiting expectantly.

Leanna's brow furrowed. "If I told you the way through, there is no guarantee the elves will treat with you. They might just as equally kill you on the spot ... or never let you leave."

"*Nothing you say will deter us from our course. We need to do this. Not just for our sakes or that of our friends, but for the Grove. We cannot win this war without the Guardians. The Gates must be sealed before the darkness can unleash the full force of his armies into this world.*"

Shara looked at her friend—truly looked into the swirling silver of his eyes. He meant every word, and even though he hardly knew the others, his loyalty was unwavering. His determination, steadfast. It really hit her then, the importance of her task and the consequences if she failed.

The darkness may have the power to open his portals wherever and whenever he pleased, but the cost was high; the result being that he could only allow a small troop of beasts through at a time. But with each passing day the darkness mustered his strength and assembled his army. If he was left unchecked—if he waged war on the four races of Everosia and won—there would be only the Guardians to stand against an army. The Grove would fall to ruin, and the Gates would be opened once again, allowing him to access any dimension and let evil purge the world of good.

That could never happen. Would never happen. Shara vowed it to herself, and once she committed to something, she always followed through. To whatever end.

She gave Leanna a once-over and shrugged. "What he said."

The old woman sighed, her face a canvas of wriggling lines and hollowed cheeks. Her shoulders slumped as if she carried all the burdens of the world, the weight heavier than her frail form could hold. "Do not mistake me, child. I know how important your task is. I have seen first-hand the damage the darkness has wrought. It is no easy thing to watch the world pass you by and simply blink the days away. Once I would have joined you, shown you the way, but now ..."

"Grandma," Telilah said softly.

For the first time, Shara saw a hint of fondness reach Leanna's eyes, and the woman reached across the table to her granddaughter, taking soft, youthful hands in her old leathery ones. "I've lived a long life, full of adventure and action. Full of sadness and despair, too. But I am not long for this world." Upon seeing Telilah's eyes glisten, she shook her head. "Don't cry. If it wasn't for you, I'd already be long gone. You cannot stay here, wasting the days away taking care of an ailing woman. You are meant for a happy life full of love and laughter and misbegotten adventures."

A single tear slid down Telilah's beautiful face. "What are you saying, Grandma? You want me to leave?"

"My dear, I want many things, but your leaving here isn't one of them. I need you to leave for *you*. I'll not have you live out your life in a simple town, in this simple house, wasting away the nights singing to drunkards and stealing from unsuspecting victims."

She lowered her brows then, gave Shara a knowing stare, and both women had the decency to look abashed.

"Grandma ... I was going to tell you," Telilah said softly. "It was just the once—"

Leanna silenced her with a loud harrumph. "Don't lie, girl, it's unbecoming. I don't care who you take to the sheets or how often.

They can be male, female, elf or dwarf, pink or blue for all I care, but I'll not have a thief under my roof."

Technically, if she left, she wouldn't be under your roof, Shara wanted to say, but she kept her lips sealed. Now was not the moment for an ill-timed joke.

Leanna turned back to Shara and Razakh, lips pursed thoughtfully. "There is still a way I may help you *and* soothe my own worries."

The old woman rose from her seat, stalked to the window and peered out for a long minute. By now the sun had well and truly risen, but it was hidden, shrouded in dark and stormy clouds. It lent a mystery to the air, the current in the room as charged and electric as the sky above.

Shara waited patiently, as did Razakh, though the Diodonian perked up eagerly, his flames blaring to life. Telilah uttered a small squeak of surprise as she was nearly singed. All three looked at Leanna, Shara's chest hammering, hoping whatever morsel of knowledge Leanna had could be the answer they needed to gain passage to the Meadows.

She risked a glance at Telilah, whose skin had shifted to a sickly green. The girl looked as if she'd barf any moment. It was no wonder with how many drinks she'd downed last night. She had managed quite a few during their time together. Shara had been rather impressed at how much ale the woman could hold. But she quickly realised the woman's pallor had nothing to do with drink.

Leanna finally turned from her post by the window, her face as grey and cloudy as the storm threatening outside.

"You are to leave for the Meadows today … and my granddaughter is coming with you."

"What?" the reply was echoed by the two women, and though Shara was shocked by this announcement, she could see it hadn't come as a surprise to Telilah. Perhaps not music to her ears, given the nervous sweat now on her brow and the panicked eyes, but certainly not a surprise.

Shara turned to Leanna. "And why on Everosia would we want to drag her arse with us? She's a minstrel, a songstress. She will be of no use for this journey."

Even as she said the words, they sounded harsh, and Shara noticed the pang of hurt flit across Telilah's face. She wished she could take them back. Then she wondered at why she cared. But all her concerns washed away with one final proclamation.

Leanna smiled with knowing eyes. "Because Telilah knows the way to the Meadows—can interpret the danger you will face ... Because she's your only option at getting in."

The Valiant Knight

ASHALEA

THE PLAN UNFOLDED EXACTLY AS SHE'D HOPED. Better, even, for the chaos Ashalea and Denavar had brought with them had been an unwelcome surprise for the darkness's armies. The creatures had been told to look for two elves, no doubt, but their quarry's companion had certainly not been mentioned in the memo.

Ashalea and Denavar had sprinted through the gates and dispatched the guards before so much as a horn or a shout could be sounded. And then there were flames. Curling, licking, biting at the flesh of creature and camp materials alike.

The crude wooden structures and tents of the camp were burning within seconds, unleashing a panic not so easily quelled by the soldiers in charge. Ashalea ripped through the outer wall, tossing fireballs in front and behind, sending bolts of vicious electricity surging through the sands and frying all within its path. Denavar sent a whirlwind tearing torches from the ground and campfires from their hollows, creating a firestorm of blazing heat.

Soldiers of all shapes and sizes screeched from within, some being woken from their slumber, others never to awaken again, and yet more were scrambling for sword or spear or acting on pure animalistic instinct, lunging with tooth and claw instead.

For two elves with no weapons, victory was never on the cards, and they were loath to spend too much energy on lesser foes, but they needed time. Just a little more time.

Ashalea had her back to Denavar, defending each other even as they attacked aggressively. Their Magicka seemed stronger here. Like the very air they breathed had a tangible static coursing through it.

Like the dark itself longed to eat up their energy, consume the bright light and warmth of their spells. And perhaps it did, even as lives were cut short, perhaps the dark fed on the death and destruction with greedy lips.

Ashalea didn't care what it did so long as they survived, and she watched in awe of Denavar, her green eyes holding the reflection of the flames and electricity he threw at his foes, sparking like fireworks in the air; Magickal bursts of energy in blues and whites and reds. He was resplendent, and she was sure her elf eyes proved accurate when his flames seemed to burn a little brighter than hers, his electricity more charged, his wind more forceful as it tossed creatures sky high.

He was every bit the Guardian one could hope for. And for Ashalea, so much more.

They danced around each other, one step, two step, one step, crouching and twirling, and as a creature came too close to her loved one, she vaulted over his back and sent flames of fury down its maw. When that movement left her side exposed, Denavar's hands found a

278

reptile's neck and wrung the life from its lungs.

A formidable team. A warrior duo worthy of the pages of history. But their love would be testament to no ink or scroll should they die this day. Sweat poured down Ashalea's face, the heat of their fireballs like a smithy's forge in the days before battle, the charge of electricity as it left her fingers causing her heart to race in anticipation.

Her silver braid whipped across her back like an angry viper, her breath coming harsher and more ragged as she expelled energy. The creatures snarled and hissed; Uulakh, birds and bats, snakelike beasts, attacking from every which way. And for every creature that was felled, another took its place.

But then ... then she saw it. The writhing mass of tissue and organ and bone that rolled into the fray, its movement now fast, furious. She could feel its eagerness. The anticipation of new meat, new souls to consume. Its form moaned with the voices of many, and Ashalea shivered, the small bumps rising on her arms, her hackles raised in self-defence.

All eyes swivelled to the creature, all stopped what they were doing to assess this new presence, to deem it friend or foe. Ashalea and Denavar had time to do neither. They glanced at each other, a quick nod confirming their next course: run. Flee the scene, disappear into the shadows, find their way to Wezlan.

The gleaming mess of pink and red and bone-white assessed the scene with the eyes of its many victims before bowling into the fight. It consumed all in its path, their screams falling short as it rolled over them with a sticky wet sound that made Ashalea gag and her stomach flip thrice over.

The assembled soldiers threw spears from afar, the winged beasts diving to shred with talons before taking to the skies again, but all did nothing to deter the monster from its meal. It tumbled sloppily over the gathered, drinking in their innards, feeding on their fear, and for every fallen soldier it sucked in, the creature grew in both size and greed.

Ashalea and Denavar seized their chance and slipped into the dark, trailing the outskirts of tents, keeping low and crouched as they hurried away from the chaos. And all the while, Ashalea flinched with fear and untethered dread. One look at Denavar's pale face told her he could still feel the creature's effects, too.

She cast a final glance over her shoulder at the monster slurping up new faces, at the new organs gleaming in its bulk, at the ever-open eyes of the dead within its form. But it wasn't so much the sight of the creature that clawed at her stomach and caused fear to burrow down into her bones.

It was the screams. The moans that echoed through the camp in a ghostly choir. The moans full of sorrow and hate and fear and regret. Souls trapped and tormented until time itself was undone. It was a fate she'd wish on no one. Not even her worst enemy. Not even the darkness.

Denavar grabbed her face then, firm but gentle hands urging her chin towards him. His eyes burned with blue fire, commanding her attention.

"Don't look back, Ashalea. Don't look back."

So she looked forward instead. To what lay ahead. To Wezlan and the darkness. Enough time spent scrawling through books and battle tactics informed her that kings and queens, generals and commanding officers, and whoever else oversaw an army were usually somewhat separated from the grunts.

The camp was a large one, sprawled in lazy disarray, tents and all manner of clutter that made for lodgings dribbling along in rows and rows. For an army made up of beasts, Ashalea supposed that routine and regularity were in short supply here. The air was putrid; a sweaty, oily, rank stench that hovered like a smog above the camp.

Given that the terrain was fairly flat, undulating only in soft rises and falls, there was no clear distance between any given area of the camp—no tents or the like that appeared grander or were perched on an overlying cliff or knoll like a beacon of command. It likely meant one thing: the darkness was smack bang in the centre.

A clever locale on his part but a frustrating mark for Ashalea and Denavar. Sneaking there would be easy enough while Pinky played its part and stole the attention of the camp. But getting out? That would be difficult, especially if Wezlan was injured ... or worse.

Ashalea shook her head, loose strands of silver hair curling defiantly about her face, which she fed back into her braid vigorously. *Focus, Ashalea. Focus on your task.*

Denavar took the lead, guiding her with every careful step, ears pricked for trouble, eyes dashing back and forth, assessing the best path. He had more experience with missions such as these, he had said, though why a mage from Renlock would be required to sneak around was anyone's guess.

When she'd asked him about it, Denavar said he had spent some summers with the elves of Windarion. Practicing swordsmanship, treating with the elven mages, learning the lore and layout of the land. But more than that he had learned to hone his elven senses, to sharpen them to a fine blade so he may strain them to see across even longer distances, concentrate in order to focus his hearing selectively, move so he may be silent as a mouse and quick as a whip.

It made sense she supposed—it was probably why he was in Windarion at King Tiderion's beck and call when she had first arrived in the Aquafarian Province. When she had first laid eyes on Denavar.

Such lessons had placed him in many a different situation, with

nothing but his wits and training to keep him alive. And she had no doubt the mages of Renlock would have used them from time to time. Even diplomatic parties had their resources. Yes. If anyone would cleave a path through this place undetected, it was Denavar.

The camp was a cacophony of noise. Creatures ran or slithered through the rows, headed towards the commotion at Ashalea and Denavar's backs, and yet others headed in a different direction. Perhaps towards the darkness. Perhaps towards a new portal that would take them back to Everosia. One could only hope.

As they crept on silent feet towards the central encampment, Ashalea heard muffled sounds growing louder. But they were unmistakably human. And they were in pain ... dying. She tugged on Denavar's shirt and he crouched beside her.

"We have to help them," she insisted.

"There's no time, Ashalea," he shot back. "Every second we waste is precious time lost. Wezlan needs us."

She hunched in the dark, torn between rescuing her mentor or doing right by those suffering and risk jeopardising the whole mission in the process. But the people in trouble were so close, little more than a few tents away. She lifted her eyes skyward and snarled in frustration.

"Would you hesitate if it were me? If it were Shara or someone else that we cared about?" she whispered.

A sigh. He bent his head, back slumping ever so slightly, and Ashalea knew his answer before the words came out.

"I'd already be on my way." And seeing Ashalea at war with herself, Denavar placed a hand on her shoulder. "I will go."

Ashalea opened her lips to argue but he was gone in a blink, and she rushed to the edge of the shadows, careful to avoid the light of torches dotting the walkway. She peered around the corner of a tent and spotted him darting under cover. Then her eyes caught the source of the sound.

Bound to wooden posts were three humans, naked and shivering, wounds littering their bodies from head to toe. Bite marks and scratches and the cruel curving streaks of blades upon their flesh. She gasped as she saw the red welts puckering the young woman's back, raw and oozing with infection, and then her gaze travelled to the young man, ribs caved in from hunger and abuse, his breath coming in ragged gasps. The last, an old man skinny as a rake, had already spent his last breath, his head sagging to the ground.

Ashalea circled round in the dark to further study the darkness's captives. The two youths were around Ashalea's age in human years. In their mid-twenties, perhaps. Underneath the bruises on the woman's face, she recognised a simple beauty. Plain enough, but with comely lips that would offer an attractive smile, and soft, rounded cheeks. Her hair was long and, though limp and dirty, the colour of burnished gold.

The young man had ashen hair tied in a strip of cloth, golden skin, dull eyes that showed the promise of blue-burned skies in good health. Underneath a gag tied over his lips was a chiselled jawline, and Ashalea could see how attractive he was even in his current state.

But age and beauty aside, one thing drew her attention the most. Despite the torture, they gazed at each other with longing. With defiance. Bound and stripped of dignity as they were, their eyes held no sorrow as they looked upon each other, and Ashalea knew without a doubt, they were lovers.

Her heart broke further still as she saw the look in their eyes. Adoration. Passion. A need to defend the other—die for the other. The same words conveyed in that glance that Ashalea would say to Denavar a thousand times over. A lover's promise.

He had to save them. Denavar had to make this right. They both did.

She saw the shroud of Magicka fall away from his form; the cloak that helped them blend into their environment dissipate entirely so he was clearly visible in the strange glow of this world. Under the sky with no sun or stars or moon, just an eerie light of a different kind.

Denavar slipped to the woman first, one finger placed upon his lips, the other raised in a gesture of peace. "I'm here to help," he whispered, and with wide eyes, she nodded understanding. But even his deft fingers were taking too long with the rope snaring her wrists and feet.

Ashalea grinded her teeth from the shadows, eyes darting nervously to all possible entrances to the clearing. This was taking too long. She crept to a stack of crates nearby, quietly rummaging through the contents and discovering a rusty blade buried in the bottom.

Sucking in a breath, she mustered her courage and made for the posts. Denavar frowned, threw her a look that said *you were meant to wait,* and she raised the small blade pointedly before making to remove the gag on the male, but something stayed her hand.

Her gut swam with anxiety, nerves rising in her throat. Her palms tingled with cold sweat. Something wasn't right. She looked at Denavar, now speaking quietly to the woman as he checked her wounds and tried to help her stand.

"Something's wrong," she hissed.

Denavar frowned. "That's putting it mildly."

"No. I mean ... it's too easy. Where are the guards? And there just happens to be a blade stowed nearby? Convenient."

"Regardless, we need to move," Denavar said in hushed tones. "Let's think about that later."

He was right. There was no point second-guessing their luck. Her time was better spent freeing this poor soul. She glanced at the man's

face, pity welling in her eyes as she saw the hollows and gaunt skin, the haunted, emptiness in his eyes. It reminded her of Shara in the days after her rescue. She never wished to see her friend that way again.

With steely determination she removed the gag from the man's cracked lips. "We're going to get you out of here," she said soothingly, noticing his alarm at the blade in her hand. Then a look of pure terror crossed his eyes as he registered her face.

"No ... no please," he said with rising panic. "Please don't hurt me."

Her brows knitted together in confusion. "What? No, I—"

The man's voice rose hysterically. "Stay away from me!"

"I'm here to help you," she insisted, but the man was having none of it. He pulled at his binds, trying frantically to lean as far away as possible from her touch. Flabbergasted, she glanced at Denavar, who firmly told the woman to "stay there" before rushing to Ashalea's side.

"You *must* be quiet," he demanded of the man. "Please, we're here to help set you free, not to hurt you."

"RUN!" the male screamed at the top of his lungs. "Get out of—"

Denavar clapped a hand to the man's mouth, stifling his shouts before stuffing the gag back in. The woman he had freed made a bolt for it, and Ashalea lunged for her, elven speed far outmatching the weak human.

Ashalea pulled her back to Denavar as gently as possible. If the female escaped, it would be the end for all of them.

Denavar swore before taking the woman by the shoulders and giving her a rough shake. "If you don't shut up now those creatures will discover us and we're all going to die. Do you want to live?"

The woman nodded slowly; fearful gaze plastered on Ashalea's face as she sat rigidly beneath Denavar's palms.

"And you want him to live too, right?"

Another nod, more fervent this time. Then, little more than a croak, "You look just like him." Her voice was a mixture of fear, awe, and confusion as she stared at Ashalea.

Then it all clicked, and Ashalea realised what she meant. They were terrified because her face was unmistakably alike to another. Because her face bore resemblance to—

A soft clapping broke her thoughts and Ashalea whirled to face the source. A dark cloud of wispy tendrils, and within it, phasing violently between elf and monster, was the darkness. His eyes flashed from red to silver, hands shifting from slender, pale flesh to blackened claws, that ever-familiar smell of rot floating towards her. And in his eyes, in both forms, Ashalea saw nothing but a bottomless well. No light to pierce the depths, no ripple of humanity. Nothing but greed. A malicious greed that could be sated only from cruelty and destruction.

She bared her teeth and crouched into a defensive stance, feeling Denavar shift protectively at her side, a warning snarl rumbling from his throat.

Crinos only smiled in glee. "So predictable, dear sister. So easy to manipulate. The pawns were placed, and you, the valiant knight, so eager to rescue them, walked right into my trap."

Denavar sent a fireball hurtling at the darkness, but it fizzled harmlessly against the wisps of smoke. The darkness ignored it, his eyes firmly on Ashalea.

She glanced at Denavar instead and drawled, "I told you it was too easy." Then she shifted her focus to Crinos, choosing her words carefully. "There's no denying it. We played right into your game. The blade, the unguarded captives. We should have guessed."

"Only you did," he hissed in amusement. "You should have trusted your instincts and ran when you had the chance."

"Except that would make me a coward, Crinos, and I see only one

286

of those here."

His eyes narrowed. "Careful now. You'll make me lose my temper before the fun begins."

The humans whimpered at that, knowing full well what Crinos classed as fun in this place. Ashalea hoped it wouldn't come to that. Several different scenarios raced through her mind as she played for time. She could create a distraction, give the humans a chance to break for it. But what would that achieve? They had nowhere to go. None of them did. Still ...

Ashalea raised a hand placatingly, concealing the small blade in the palm of the other, its curve pressed firmly against her wrist, her fingers curled around the hilt. "You've got me, brother. Cornered, unarmed, outwitted." His eyes flashed at the last, his pride greedily drinking in the praise. "So, now what?"

The darkness sneered with tooth and fang. "You're going to tell me how to use this new Magicka of mine. If you don't, I'll kill your pet wizard and your lover."

Ashalea swallowed the lump in her throat. "You're going to kill us all anyway. Why should I bother helping you?"

Crinos sighed before clucking his lips in boredom. "Because if you don't, sister mine, I'll kill them slowly, agonisingly, and then I'll find the lovely Shara Silvaren, and make you watch as I peel the skin from her face strip by strip."

At Ashalea's shocked expression, his eyes narrowed. "Oh yes, I know you brought her back to life. But there will be no second chances this time, and once I'm done with her, I will keep you in a cage, with nothing but a mirror to keep you company—so you may reflect on the cause of so much despair."

His eyes glinted, red as rubies and rivers of blood, and he smiled, cold and fleeting. "If you cooperate, I will spare them the pain. It will

be quick. Clean. An honourable death."

His words stole the fire from her belly. The purpose in her heart, the strength in her legs. But still she stood there, rooted in place, in awe of a being so careless, so cruel, so utterly unfeeling.

And her words rang clear as a bell, the toll of defeat a heavy burden on her tongue. "I will help you with this power. *If* you take me to Wezlan. And only if we come to better terms of an agreement."

The darkness cackled. "You're hardly in any position to bargain, but I would expect nothing less." He cocked his head as if considering. "Very well. We will talk terms back at my quarters. There's someone who's *dying* to see you."

Fresh Meat

RAZAKH

RAZAKH STALKED BESIDE THE HORSES AND THEIR RIDERS, trying his hardest to suppress the amusement bubbling to the surface. They were an odd troupe: an assassin, a minstrel, and a Diodonian. The former was grumbling to herself whilst the minstrel chirped nonsense about Galanor, her grandma and various run of the mill topics.

He was beginning to suspect the woman had been hoping for an adventure like this, though he doubted she knew how dangerous it could be. Indeed, it seemed that Grandma Dearest had told Telilah next to nothing about the oncoming war. The darkness was out for blood. He would stop at nothing to see the Guardians dead and Everosia overthrown—and at the root of that was his sister.

Fortunately, Razakh had not been graced with the displeasure

of the darkness's company, but he knew there would be a reckoning at the end. There always was when it came to good versus evil. All the stories his ancestors had passed down through the generations suggested it was so.

His mind drifted to his father, Razgeir, whom he had not seen for an age. By Diodonian standards he was old, lucky to still be alive. But perhaps the Magicka of the Grove had something to do with that. There was still so much Razakh did not know about Magicka, the Grove, his fate—still so much he had to learn. And at the heart of it all, there was doubt. Was he worthy of such a position? Was merging with the rest of the world the right thing to do?

Only time would tell, and he knew there would be teething problems at first. The Diodonians held a deep-seated grudge against the humans for the crimes of the past. Hell, he had issues of his own. But it was necessary, he believed, to band together. To unite against the darkness as one army.

He regarded the world around him. Plants and trees and rolling green hills. They cut through fields now, the grass long and lush, various plant species scattered around, the odd flower scrambling their way up past weed and root. This was a world full of life. A world he wanted to be a part of. No red sands and barren landscapes, no dry, scorching heat, and swathes of orange.

He loved the rugged landscape of the Diodon Mountains. The peaks and troughs of the mountains, the winding curves of the earth. But there was more—so much more to see and do. He wanted to see the ocean, feel snow under his paws, feel the wrath of a storm.

And the latter, it seemed, he would get sooner than he'd hoped.

Rain began to fall in gentle droplets, and he peered at the skies. They were dark, angry. A storm had brewed, ready to release its might upon the cauldron of this world. As if in answer to his thoughts, the

290

skies fully opened, and the rain hammered down in a sudden burst. Thunder roiled above, and lightning flashed its warning beyond the clouds.

"That's just great," Shara grumbled. "What else could possibly go wrong?"

Telilah sniffed. "I don't see why you're in such a bad mood. A little bit of rain won't hurt anyone. I rather like it."

A loud clap rang out, and she squealed, hunkering down in the saddle.

Shara snorted. "You were saying?"

Razakh rumbled with glee. His mirth rang out in waves and he cared not whose mind could hear it. The women looked at him in awe. Shara rolled her eyes, but Telilah cocked a head curiously.

"Is this normal behaviour for them?" she yelled above the roar of the storm.

Shara looked at her pointedly. "Why don't you ask him yourself? He can hear you, ya know, and speak."

Razakh grinned at the sky, tilting his head back to feel the full blast of the wet upon his fur. It sank beneath the topcoat, clinging to his skin. He felt alive. Invigorated. He wanted to run with the storm and roar at the heavens. He glanced at the females and noted their shivering, hair plastered to their skin, teeth chattering, and his elation fizzled like the flames upon his back.

Humans. What useless protection and warmth their skin provided. But even the horses were loath to tromp through the muddy fields. He sensed their trepidation at the thunder, and they walked on with heads hung, trying to shield their eyes from the pinpricks of the rain.

"We need to find shelter."

Shara frowned, but at the sight of a bedraggled Telilah—looking like a rainbow in her kaleidoscope of clothes—and the miserable horses, she nodded. "Lead on. I trust your nose or eyes can help us? I can't see anything in this rain."

In truth, Razakh wasn't sure where to look. Everything smelt different when wet, and he hadn't caught a whiff of these scents for many years—before his sense of smell had really developed, even. But his eyes were trustworthy, and in the distance, he could see a copse of trees atop a hill that would provide some relief. It wasn't much, and it left them exposed to any threats, but it would do.

He took point, eyes scanning the fields, nose keenly sensitive to any smells that might spell danger. One could never be too careful. In the desert, foresight and pure instinct were the tools to survival. When to travel, what areas to avoid, how to navigate the sands. All basic skills that Diodonians learnt as a pup. Here, the same could be applied, but Razakh didn't know these lands, nor what manner of bird and beast dwelled within them.

They hiked up the gradual incline, the horses making short work of the climb, careful not to slip on the mud. Razakh prowled ahead, making sure the copse was suitable for camp. The trees were clustered together, making for a surprisingly dry nest inside. There was even room for a campfire to be made in its centre once the rain had let up a little.

Shara hopped off her mount and helped Telilah down. *Unusually chivalrous of her*, Razakh noted. He hadn't known Shara long, but there were three things that were distinctly clear from the moment he met her: she was *not* someone to cross, she was loyal to no end, and she carried a weight with her. A sadness that she buried beneath witty retorts and sly smiles.

Their pasts were different, but similar, too. They had both experienced pain, loss, torment. And both had come out all the stronger for it. There was nothing sweet about her—she was fire and spice and perhaps a bit poisonous to some palettes, but that's why he liked her. A murderer. A thief. And yet here she was, the smallest hint of red gracing her cheeks as she placed hands around the hips of this woman they'd been saddled with.

There was a current between these two. Time would tell if it would spark or sizzle out.

After the girls had unsaddled the horses and supplies—they were once again stocked on provisions and everyone's favoured weapons were bundled—Shara and Telilah settled beneath the canopy. The horses were left to wander at will, but all four stood huddled together for warmth.

Razakh circled the copse once more, surveying the rolling hills in all directions. No movement skittered in any direction, save the swaying of plants and grass from the storm's force. Satisfied, he made to join the group when some peculiar markings caught his eye.

Scratch marks on the tree bark, like someone was marking their territory or sharpening their claws. They were big—bigger than a common animal ought to have in these parts. He studied them closely, from the top, which was as high as Razakh's reach, to the bottom. A gash in the tree's skin.

Something uneasy gnawed at his stomach. He had seen similar markings before. Only ... it couldn't be. He shook his head and considered whether it was wise to inform the others about his find or if the information would cause more trouble than it was worth. He scanned the fields once more, a new wariness in his movements, his instincts demanding alertness and care.

He returned to Shara and Telilah, who, it seemed, were making every effort not to look at each other but sneaking peeks all the same. He almost rolled his eyes. Humans were so strange.

A crack startled Razakh awake—like a twig snapping—and immediately he was on full alert, hackles raised, and teeth bared. Shara sat on the opposite side of the campfire, back rigid, still as stone as she listened. Just as well he'd opted for honesty, for he had insisted on lookout duty throughout the night. Shara, surprisingly, had agreed instantly. Once the rain had passed, she had built a campfire to dry off, and Telilah had fallen fast asleep, snoring with her mouth open and saliva dribbling out.

That was some hours ago when the sun was dipping beneath the horizon. Now, the stars were splattered across a midnight sky, all clouds long since moved on. It was a clear night, which meant the humans would be better able to see.

He looked to the assassin. She put a finger to her lips and lifted two digits with her other hand before gesturing in a circle.

Razakh understood. Two enemies, both circling the perimeter of the trees. Ever so slowly, he rose to his paws and regarded the hillock beyond their camp. She was right. Dark shapes loomed beyond the treeline. They quietly stalked, and yellow eyes flashed from the gloom. He caught a glimpse of a huge paw, another of bared teeth, and finally, flames, blue flames simmering down the back of one predator. And he suddenly realised what was hunting them. But that would mean ...

"*Look out!*" he cried, and Shara dove to the side, flattening her body against the ground. Telilah woke then, the commotion in and outside of her mind causing her to gasp awake. When she saw the beast she screamed, and Razakh grimaced at the sound. She certainly had a pair of lungs on her.

His attention returned to their foe. A hulking beast pounced on the empty space, snarling, drooling in hunger. Razakh stared in horror, momentarily confounded at the creature upon which he gazed.

For standing before him was a Diodonian, only it was no Diodonian he'd ever seen the likes of before. It was different ... it was *wrong*. The muscled body was jet black, like the shadows had been weaved into a living, breathing thing. Even its fangs were as stone, and it rippled with a strange Magicka. Nothing Razakh had ever seen or felt before. It was an abomination of his kind, and it was on the hunt for fresh meat. *Their* fresh meat.

He paused only for a second before launching towards the creature, but he was knocked off course by a second non-Diodonian, all its weight behind the paws that pinned him down. It leered at him with yellow eyes, opened its giant maw to sink stone teeth into him, and Razakh struggled beneath its weight, bracing himself for the blow that would—

A silver object sang through the air and embedded itself in the creature's ribs. It howled in pain and Razakh took his chance. Kicking with all his strength, he pushed his assailant off and leapt into the fray, standing protectively in front of Shara and Telilah, who was still screaming her head off.

He regarded the two monsters pacing back and forth opposite him, sizing up their prey, recalculating the risks. Razakh looked at Shara—the determined gleam in her amber eyes. Two against two ... with some baggage to protect. They each nodded.

Game on.

Shadow and Smoke

SHARA

HARA SHOVED TELILAH BEHIND HER before drawing her blades. Their curved edges glinted in the firelight, the cold steel menacing and hungry for blood. She took her place at Razakh's side, studying the movements of the beasts. One bat of their big paws, one bite from those sharp fangs and she'd be a fresh carcass for the picking.

Razakh crouched, his hindlegs bunched, ready to dive into action. Shara couldn't decide if the fighting ground was for better or worse. The copse of trees made it difficult for the large creatures to run and leap, but the small clearing meant combat was close, leaving no room for mistakes.

There would be no outrunning these foes. Not with Telilah in tow. It was fight or die, and she had no plans for the latter. She eyed off her opponent on the left. Its stance was like Razakh's—coiled muscles, legs depressing as it made ready to spring. She waited patiently, and as it pounced towards her, she vaulted to the left, swivelling on the spot. It growled at Telilah, stalking towards her, licking its maw. She was unarmed. Fearful. Easy prey.

"Oh no you don't," Shara yelled. The creature turned and she slashed a cross on its chest with a sweep of both swords. It yelped in pain before snapping its fangs in fury. Shara retreated, circling the beast, drawing it away from Telilah, who looked ready to swoon from fright.

Her breaths were measured, fingers firmly wrapped around the hilts of the blades. This was a game of patience—like pieces on a chessboard. Make a wrong move, the prize is open for the kill. Amber eyes pierced yellow ones. Two monsters of a different making. Two killers with a different purpose.

The creature lunged, but she was too slow to react. Fangs sank into her left shoulder; needles injecting a spasm of pain into her flesh. Her muscles barked in protest, the cuff on the joint crying out in dismay, as she too, grunted her distress. She dropped the sword in that arm, and it thumped onto the grass.

They fell in a heap, Shara crashing to the ground as the Diodonian pinned her down, its jaw locked on to her body, sneering even as it clamped onto her shoulder. It released its hold and blood seeped from jagged holes, weeping down her arm, running down her fingers until her hand was slick and sticky with warmth.

Sensing its victory, the beast glanced quickly at its ally, and Shara followed its line of sight. Razakh was fire incarnate. His flames flared with ferocity, the gilded-red of his coat rippling like molten gold. He was a forge that mastered all weapons. No, he *was* the weapon.

The duo roared, batting with great paws at each other, both

Diodonians—real and otherwise—on hind legs, snapping and clawing. Blood crept down Razakh's hide; swirls of scarlet that stained his fur. The other Diodonian's coat was shadow and smoke. It shifted with every movement, like a cloak made of Magicka upon its body.

It reared up and smashed a paw upon Razakh's head, bludgeoning the Diodonian near senseless. Her friend wobbled, lost his footing, and crashed upon a pillow of grass.

"Get up. Get up and fight!" she roared, and her voice was a call to arms, for he rose, staggering, blood dripping in one eye.

He lunged for the shadow one's neck with a wildness she had not yet seen from him, and he bit into the tenderness of its jugular and tore, ripping his teeth into the black, shaking his head back and forth like a pet with a new toy.

Its neck spewed shadows, like a candle emits smoke when blown out, and just like a wax stick, the Diodonian melted, dripping into nothing, its life snuffed out. One moment the black whorls were there, the next they were gone.

Her own assailant roared, and when it looked at her then, she saw hatred, evil ... death. Its maw opened wide as it leaned in for the kill, and Shara braced herself for the end. The beast looked at her hungrily, and right before its teeth found her jugular, a steel tip was thrust through its neck. Shara's eyes widened as it made a strangled sound, its throat ruined from the blade, eyes dimming as they lost focus.

The Diodonian uttered a last sigh, and it too gave way to shadow and dust, disappearing before her as if it were all just a dream. Shara's eyes widened, heart pummelling her chest as it demanded to know what on Everosia just happened. And as the last of the creature faded from existence, she saw Telilah standing before her, arms shaking, brown eyes cloaked in terror and disbelief, fingers barely holding on to the blade that saved her.

Shara gaped at her in awe. "You ... you saved me."

Telilah let the blade clang to the ground, raising quivering hands to her face, staring as if searching for the root of her courage. "Yes ..." she whispered.

"You risked your life for me," Shara breathed.

Telilah nodded, her eyes haunted, lacking the usual mirth and spryness they held just hours earlier. Shara didn't like it. Those eyes were meant to laugh, her voice meant to sing, not scream.

"Yes," Telilah repeated.

Shara glanced at Razakh, who was sprawled on the grass, licking his wounds. He must have felt her attention for he raised his great head, assessing Telilah.

"I think she may be in shock."

Shara swivelled back to Telilah. The woman had settled on a tree root, arms wrapped around her. The shivering had ceased, but the faraway look was still planted in her eyes. Shara made to stand but a dizziness washed over her, and she clutched her shoulder in pain with a small groan.

The sound earned both Razakh and Telilah's attention.

"Your wound needs cleaning," he observed. *"Shall I help?"*

Shara stared at him incredulously. "What are you going to do, lick it clean with your *tongue*? That's been who knows where? No thank you, I'd sooner get an infection," she scoffed.

Razakh grunted his indignation. *"A likely possibility if you leave it like so."*

"There will be no licking required, nor will there be an infection," Telilah said firmly, and both Razakh and Shara stared at her in surprise. "I will see to it. The fire will need rebuilding, and I need freshly cut bandages."

Shara assessed their little nook amongst the trees and sighed. The campfire had been well and truly snuffed; the wood they'd collected now strewn about the clearing, their belongings scattered here and there. She checked their gear and breathed in relief. All weapons were present and still wrapped in their bindings; Ashalea's scimitar, her bow and quiver, Wezlan's staff and sword, Denavar's twin blades. Weapons could be replaced but she knew some of these items held sentimental value for her friends. Especially those gifted by the elves of Woodrandia—from the Lady Nirandia herself—ruler of the province.

She gathered a bundle of twigs in one arm, brow furrowed in thought. Perhaps she'd meet this queen someday. The chances were staggering considering the threat of war. A war for Everosia. Not for cities or provinces, but the entire land and all within it. A treaty would need to be made between the races if they stood any chance of beating the darkness.

So, she supposed, she would likely meet all the rulers of the races. The king of Maynesgate, the dwarven king of Kingsgareth Mountains, and the Lady Nirandia of Woodrandia. The others—King Tiderion and Queen Rivarnar of the Aquafarian Province—she'd met. Which left two others. The new chieftain of the Diodonians, Linar, and ... Ashalea.

A queen by blood if not in name. The Moonglade elves had no knowledge of her existence, if Wezlan's words were true, and Shara had no idea how receptive they'd be to her crowning. She was a Guardian, after all, so her duties lay foremost in protecting the land, else there would be no Moonglade Meadows to rule over.

She dumped her kindling back into the recess and set about stripping fresh branches and bark to add to the nest. When finished, she dusted her hands off, causing the tendons in her shoulder to groan in protest, and Razakh ambled over to sit beside her.

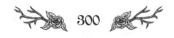

"Are you okay?"

Shara gave Telilah the side eye and Razakh shook his head. *"This conversation is ours alone."*

She raised her good arm, ran her nails through the soft—if a little matted—fur along his back. The heat of his flames warmed the fingertips, and she exhaled, letting the tension flow from her muscles, still tense from the fight.

"I'm worried about Telilah," she whispered. "She's not cut out for this stuff. For battle."

"Says the woman who *owes* me for saving her life."

Shara started at the voice so close to her ear. "Would you stop doing that?" she frowned. "I'm grateful, Telilah, I really am, but you have to agree, this isn't ideal. You're a damned minstrel for goodness sake. Better with honeyed words and hands than a steel blade."

Hurt flashed across the woman's face and Shara immediately regretted her words. A sigh. "I just mean I'd feel better knowing you could protect yourself if my back is turned, you know?"

Telilah huffed. "I can look after myself. I handled that ... that thing, didn't I?" She sat down next to Shara and poked the pile of sticks. "What were they anyway?"

Shara tossed the hair out of her face and chewed her lip thoughtfully. Razakh's tail swished near her head and she grabbed it in annoyance. Then she smirked and pulled it around to light the kindling with its flame. The sticks crackled to life merrily, hissing and snapping as they ate away at the wood.

Razakh growled but she ignored him and made to lean into his side, quickly thinking better of it after noting the still oozing wounds. His grooming had certainly failed to do the trick. Telilah caught Shara's gaze too, and she clucked at the gashes striping across his body.

She set to work putting a pot and fresh water over the fire and started tearing colourful strips from her skirts. Shara watched in amusement, trying to focus on anything but the throbbing pain in her shoulder. Quick-fingered indeed. She could see how the girl found it so easy to steal. Her charming personality, sultry nature, the glow of her skin, the brown eyes with long, fluttering lashes, the soft, kissable lips ...

Shara shook her head. Thoughts like those led her into dangerous territory. She could not allow herself to feel something for this woman. Telilah was a liability, a distraction. And distractions were costly affairs when mere seconds could change the course of one's life—or end it.

Plus, she talked too much. Incessant rambling about things that did not concern Shara—had never concerned her. Things that spoke of a normal life and trivial affairs. And yet, a small part of her questioned what that would be like. A simple life without death and destruction and pain. One where she could curl up in a chair, read a damned book for the first time in years, tend to a garden ... help life grow instead of taking it away.

Was that something she wanted one day? When all this was over?

"Ahem?"

Telilah's sarcastic tone drew Shara from her thoughts and she raised a brow. The girl sighed dramatically.

"You didn't answer my question. If I'm going to risk my arse—and it's an exceptionally good one by the way, as you know"—she looked at Shara with a sly smile—"then I ought to know what we're up against."

"I don't know what they were," Shara admitted. But that wasn't entirely true. They were Diodonians in all the wrong ways. And she'd seen the likes of them before. Not beings of shadow like the ones they'd just killed, but everything about them reminded her of the beasts seen on the Isle of Dread. The ones locked in stone, leering in eternity at those who dared cross that island. She wondered, should she return, if she'd find those stone statues broken. If their prisoners had been released.

But if that were true then there would be more of them around Everosia. Much more. She wriggled uncomfortably. The thought did not bode well.

She relayed her suspicions to the others and Razakh nodded his agreement.

"*There is no possible way they could be Diodonians from my home. They were ...*" he paused, at a loss for words. A rare occasion for the beast who always seemed to have answers.

"Creepy beyond all reason?" she supplied, and her friend rumbled in amusement, but his mirth quickly soured.

"*If the darkness is creating life from shadows, there could be no end to his army. Not to mention it is ill-timed considering the real Diodonians will be resurfacing soon to join the fight. The humans, elves, dwarves ... they might not understand the perversion of my race. They might think we are all evil.*"

"Just add it to our list of troubles," Shara said, slapping a palm over her eyes.

She felt a hot cloth glide over her wound and she hissed. Telilah shrugged. "Sorry, but I need to sterilise your injuries as best I can before I bind them."

The assassin glared at her, bracing for the sharp pangs skittering down her arm, but her resolve melted at the careful consideration the minstrel was applying. She bit her lip as she worked, and her tousled hair tumbled around her face. Gods she was pretty.

Shara closed her eyes, ignoring the excitement that rushed through her veins at the woman's touch. Painful and pleasurable all at once. Instead, she considered their plight. "We'll have to inform the Moonglade elves when we arrive. They might not listen, but who knows what other forms the darkness has raised with these new shadows of his."

Razakh yawned before settling down on his front paws to watch with wise, silver eyes. *"It seems no matter what we do, the darkness is always one step ahead."*

He was right. Everywhere they went, every step they took, the darkness seemed to know. Shara questioned why. How. Her mind drifted to Ashalea and the visions she was having. It had to be connected. There had to be a reason for how spectacularly messy things had gotten of late. She opened her eyes and peeked at Razakh. At least she had him.

Once she wouldn't have given a second thought about working alone. In the dark. But she liked the shadows less now. They no longer meant the same things to her anymore. They no longer shielded her from prying eyes and predators, no longer cradled her with loving arms and soft whispers of encouragement. All they meant was death. All they meant was *him*.

And so she took comfort in the presence of others—in people, in friends. They gave her a different kind of power, made her realise there was strength in trusting others, fighting with others—for others. She smiled at Razakh and he cocked his head curiously.

She shook her own as she placed a hand back on his fur, and even risked a scratch behind his ear. A small rumble confirmed he liked it. Then she looked to Telilah, who was finishing her work on Shara, readying to move on to Razakh.

"Telilah ..."

At Shara's tone the woman looked up sharply, concern in her big brown eyes. A carefulness that was not there earlier today. A hardness. Shara smiled regretfully. Such a shame to dull one's light.

"Telilah, it's time we had a long talk."

And she explained everything that had happened on her

journey, from the moment she first saw Ashalea in the marketplace of Maynesgate right up until she walked into The Two Asses—the bar with the most unfortunate name.

Razakh supplied snippets of information in the short time he featured in the story, and together they talked long into the night.

Her shoulder was throbbing, she had a headache, and the lack of sleep had her irritable and snappy. She raked dirty fingernails through her hair, the strands so matted they got stuck halfway through. Ugh. What she would not give for a bath. A little luxury, even. She damn well deserved it.

She had planned to rent a room at the Two Asses back in Galanor and maybe order supplies for a bath, but that night had gone very differently. She glanced at Telilah, who was whistling a gawdy tune, and the woman gave her a wink when she caught Shara's stare. She rolled her eyes. Very differently indeed, which wasn't a bad thing, but one night of fun was all she had wanted, not a minstrel tagalong.

Harrumph. Shara didn't know what to make of the woman. She would be lying if she didn't admit there was something intriguing about the girl. Telilah was irritatingly chirpy all the time, never shut up, and she was another liability to add to their baggage, but she did bring a certain cheer to their party, and she *was* nice to look at. Better than nice.

Razakh must have sensed her mood for he hadn't dared venture into her mind to listen or to chat. Even Telilah was quieter than usual this morning, which wasn't surprising given last night's events. The girl had been fed a lot of information, none of which was comforting or promising news.

Their trek across the fields had been a gloomy one this morning. They'd been travelling for several hours already, having set off before daybreak, and a biting wind snapped at their clothes, hair, fur, sinking into their bones. It was miserably cold today. Was the darkness's power holding sway over the elements, too? Even the plants looked sad, branches sagging towards the grass which shot towards the sky, tall and lush and so very green.

It was a pretty place. Aside from creepy shadow dogs, Shara imagined it was rarely travelled, and the rolling expanse had a wildness to it. The trees that dotted the fields stood large and proud, as if they had stood guard for years and years. The air was fresh from the recent rain, with an earthy, almost musky scent.

Shara took a deep breath, mentally sweeping aside the pain and exhaustion, quieting her mind until there was nothing but the gentle sway of the horse she rode and the steady clop, clop, clop of his hooves. They'd soon be approaching Telridge, though everyone agreed it was best they skirt the town.

The darkness's spies could be anywhere, and after their introduction to the shadow beings last night, everyone was on edge. Cautious. Wary. Then there was the matter of Razakh. He would receive too much attention if met by the townsfolk—and being in the spotlight was the last thing they needed now.

Best to push on and avoid it altogether. Beyond Telridge was the lake, and opposite that was Deyvall. The marshes that were rumoured to have all manner of monsters surfacing from the depths, daring to advance towards the populace, no doubt eager to make a meal of the villagers there. The rumours that may yet prove factual if the darkness had any say in them.

She leaned down the side of her horse, plucking a lone flower from the roiling green. Its pale blue petals surrounded a violet centre, soft and feathery to the touch. She smiled sadly. No one had ever given her a flower. Not family or friends or lovers. And she didn't know why but she turned in her saddle and offered the stalk to Telilah.

"For you," Shara said simply, feeling lame and embarrassed.

Telilah's answering beam was better than a hundred flowers. All white teeth, soft lips and crinkling eyes. She even had dimples in her cheeks. Dimples for goodness' sake. Shara looked away, feeling abashed. Making Telilah smile made her feel good. Which was new, strange. Perhaps worth exploring when she didn't feel like hiding and her cheeks weren't warm.

But the minstrel only dipped her head gracefully and raised the flower to her nose. The first real ladylike action Shara had seen from the so far drunken, gawdy nuisance of a woman. Shara smiled back, glad one small deed had lifted someone's spirits. But, as usual, their smiles were lost upon the wind, forgotten.

Razakh stopped in his tracks, causing Shara to rein in Fallar. The horse was skittish around the Diodonian, not to mention any creature other than a human or elf, which had proven most annoying on their trip. She glared at the top of the nag's head, reining it in sharply. Kaylin—who was Ashalea's horse—and now Telilah's mount, stopped on his own accord, as did Lerian and the final horse in tow.

"*Smoke rises in the distance,*" Razakh said. "*I smell it on the winds.*"

Shara frowned. "Smoke?" She squinted at the horizon, and there, spiralling into the already grey skies, was a column of smoke, black and ominous. Her eyes widened. "But that would mean ..."

"Telridge!" Telilah exclaimed. "We need to help them. We have to go, now." The woman spurred her horse to fall in line beside Shara. Telilah waited, and Shara caught the anxious movement of her fingers, fiddling with the reins. "Please, Shara," she begged. "I have friends there. I need to ... need to know if they're okay."

Shara warred with her conscience. It could be an accidental fire—nothing sinister about it—or it could be something worse. She looked to her left, towards the marshes in the distance. Then she jerked her head towards Razakh, her eyes voicing the question. He merely shook his head.

"*It is your choice.*"

She gritted her teeth. It could be a trap, it could be—

"Shara!" Telilah stared at her imploringly.

A sigh. "Okay, we'll go. But everyone be on their guard." She unsheathed one of her blades and handed it hilt first to Telilah. "You may need this. Keep it close and *don't* lose it."

"B-but ... I don't know how to use this," Telilah stammered.

Shara grinned. "Stab them with the business end."

Monsters of the Marsh

SHARA

THE HORSES' HOOVES THUNDERED ACROSS THE GROUND, every beat, every stride, taking them closer to chaos. The fires were visible now, consuming the soft flesh of thatched rooves and the bones of the buildings themselves. Screams could be heard from behind the gated walls of Telridge. And they weren't the kind of call for help one might expect with your average accidental fire—maybe even that of an arsonist's doing—no, these screams were terror, hopelessness, death.

Shara spurred Fallar on even harder, thighs squeezed tightly against the horse's sides, shoulder howling in protest with every jar of hooves on compact earth. A bell rang several chimes, and through the smog Shara could just make out its bronze body, banging ferociously from side to side. A call to arms, or an order to flee. It was silenced soon after; what happened to the person who tolled it was anyone's guess.

Closer now. Closer towards the wooden walls of Telridge, whose gates had been rent open, one half hanging precariously on its hinge, the other splattered upon the muddy walkway. Then she saw it: a scene of carnage and destruction.

Monsters of all shapes and sizes, and, running from them in all directions, the villagers. The town of Telridge was larger than Galanor, and the folk ran in droves like sheep herded by hounds. It is said humans have a basic instinct when survival is at stake: fight or flight, and Shara cursed with frustration as the villagers worked against each other in their terror.

Some men were armed with pitchforks and axes and various other garden variety tools, others shoved their way through the crowds, no greater goal than saving their own skin. And yet others who were pushed to the ground were trampled underfoot. They did not rise again.

"Where is the guard?" Shara demanded to no one in particular.

"There isn't one," Telilah responded in between puffs of breath. "Not really. A small handful of fighters, that's it."

Razakh bounded ahead, his paw having quickly healed, and Shara appreciated for the first time how fast he could run. It was one thing to be riding him whilst he sprinted, another to see it in front of her eyes. He'd reach the village ahead of them. She growled in frustration.

"Be careful, Razakh," and whether her words were lost on the wind, she didn't know. Her eyes met Telilah's, the soft brown tinged with fear, her lips trembling ever so slightly. Shara gave her a winning smile; a mask of bravery and triumph, for she was not afraid for herself, but *terrified* for the woman opposite her.

"I want you to focus on helping the townspeople escape. Lead them as far as you can to the west. Don't wait for me. Don't stop.

And if you see a monster approach, run. If you can't ..." she looked pointedly at the blade strapped to Telilah's waist. "You know what to do."

The woman stared back with wide eyes, but she nodded, focused on the small stretch before them. Shara unsheathed her blade, held it high in her good arm, and charged right into the fray.

Smoke assailed her nostrils, burning down her throat as she breathed the tainted air. It was mayhem. Men rallied against monsters in every direction. Women stumbled towards the exits—behind her and ahead—clutching at babes and screeching the names of their young. Animals brayed in barns and stables, their owners forgetting to free them from their stalls in the panic.

And all around her, everything burned. She saw Razakh taking on a slimy, dripping mass of mud-brown, its face perpetually locked in a sad smile, black eyes peeping out from under the sludge. It smelt like ... marshland. She almost gagged and forced the bile down, coming to his aid. But then she saw men on the ramparts above, crossbows locked not on the gooey thing before her but Razakh.

"No," she screamed, and their eyes darted to hers. "He's an ally. He's on our side."

They looked at each other in confusion before noting the black outfit she donned, the blade in her hand, and that seemed to be enough for one—who she assumed was the commander of this small troop—barked orders and they lined up their bolts with a large beast lined with wicked spikes on its back.

She charged towards the slimeball and was surprised to find how easy its head lopped off. Perhaps there wasn't much to its liquid form. She looked to Razakh and raised a brow. "Together?"

He nodded, the flames on his back blaring to life, barely contained to his spine as they roared, threatening to incinerate any

who approached. "*Together.*"

She grinned wickedly and they raced onwards. Her blade cleaving, flashing in violent arcs, his teeth and claws ripping, tearing in merciless bouts. Together they fought, side by side, assassin and Diodonian, and Guardians both. There were scores of beasts, all smelling like rotten marshes, all hungry for blood.

They were up against a thin rake of a creature now, its arms ending in sickle-like claws, wings fluttering in a blur upon its brown back. It darted from the skies, easily picking off people as they crowded against each other. Shara saw its bug eyes land on a woman with two children in tow, and she gasped in dismay.

There was no way she could get through the crowd without crushing them on her horse, and she dismounted, rushing towards the small family.

"Move," she demanded, but the townsfolk didn't listen, barging past her, shoving into her sides and bashing her hurt shoulder so forcefully she almost blacked out with pain. "Get out the way," she hissed, but it was no use. The woman was mere seconds away from certain death. "Razakh," she cried, pointing towards the bug's next victim.

He nodded, and turning to the crowd, his body tensed momentarily before unleashing a mighty roar. A deep rumble that echoed through the village. The women screamed, the men yelped, and they all ran in the opposite direction. The bug took its chance and dove, stretching out a scythe, swiping in one quick motion until—

"Duck!" Shara screamed, and the woman had enough sense about her to fall flat to the ground, shoving her children beneath her to shield them. Shara blocked the creature's blade with her own, head tilted back just in time for the scythe to slide along her sword, mere inches from her face.

Razakh lunged at the bug, his claws latching on and pinning its blade-like arms. Teeth gnashed at the wings on its back, stripping them like silk until they were nothing but ruined ribbons. They twisted through the air in a flurry of red and brown and came crashing down in the mud.

Shara stayed long enough to watch her friend maul the creature in flashes of white teeth, green blood spewing in streams from the bug. Razakh looked up with his silver eyes and for a moment there was no emotion in the swirling depths of liquid steel, just pure animal instinct. She nodded once and turned her attention to the chaos.

Most of the townspeople were out now; the last few stragglers filing out of the western gates, the men still alive on the walls picking off their foes with crossbow bolts. A voice rang out clear and true above the din of wails and the thud of steel finding flesh. Telilah. Her gaudy skirts whirled in flashes of colour as she hailed the crowd towards her, helping carry children out the gate and lending a hand to the frail and elderly.

The fires had consumed much of the village now. The smell of burning flesh was suffocating, writhing down her throat and coiling around her lungs. She coughed into a sleeve, eyes squinting against the smoke. If she stayed much longer, she would risk the effects of severe smoke inhalation, but people were still trapped in the town, and monsters still roamed the streets.

A muffled screech came from one of the houses near her, and she strained her ears to find the source. There it was again. Crying. A child. She peered at the home; she had minutes, if that, before the fires would devour the walls and support beams. She raised her eyes skywards and cursed. "Nothing is ever bleeding easy."

She stormed into the abode, shoving the thick material of her top up over her nose, careful not to touch anything as she looked around

frantically. The thin sheet of sweat already coating her skin turned into a blanket, dripping from her neck and creeping down her spine, drenching her clothes.

"Where are you?" she cried, anxious to find the child and be gone.

Sobs answered her and she delved deeper into the house. Its contents were strewn about the room; a table, chairs, cabinets and various trinkets having toppled over or smashed in a trail of breadcrumbs around the room.

"Where—" she choked, coughing on smoke. "Where are you?"

"Here," a small voice called, and Shara followed the sound. There, leg trapped under a wooden beam, was a boy no more than five summers old. His face was a mask of soot and sweat, tears trickling down his cheeks as he sobbed. She crouched down and put a hand on his face gently.

"I'm going to get you out of here, okay? I need you to be brave now."

The boy nodded, wiping a snotty nose with his shirt sleeve. Shara gave him an encouraging smile, ripped her tunic off and bundled her hands in the material. She mustered all her strength, set her hands on the beam and heaved with all her might.

It groaned as she lifted it an inch or two before resting back over the boy's boot. She glanced at him—his eyes wide in panic. "Again," she said, both for his benefit and hers. She heaved, her muscles balking at the weight, her shoulder screaming in pain. She felt a different kind of wet ooze down her arm and realised her wound had started bleeding again.

This time the beam fell with force and the boy yelped from the searing hot plank. Shara whimpered with frustration, her head becoming foggy with lack of oxygen, her throat constricting. The beam was so heavy. It was so hot. She felt herself failing, and every instinct

demanded she escape this house, to not look back.

But she searched the boy's face and saw the hopefulness of escape. The dread of perishing. And she could not—would not—leave him. So, she braced her hands on the beam, summoned the last kernel of strength inside and pulled, pulled, pulled. Just as she thought she might let go again she felt the weight shift. And there, beside her, his shoulder bunched under the searing wood, was Razakh, straining against the beam until, together, they lifted it high enough for the boy to wriggle free.

Razakh grabbed the boy's shirt with his teeth and flung him over his back—now free from flames—and charged towards the exit. Shara followed suit, stumbling, coughing, knees buckling under threat of giving way, until finally she burst free from the house, gulped in marginally fresher air, and collapsed in the mud.

Stars flared in her vision, and the smoke seemed to start swirling in a mesmerising wave. She felt dizzy, nauseous, her body weak and empty. She tried to sit up and immediately regretted it, overwhelmed by pinpricks of black and white in her eyes. One glance at her bad arm confirmed the black sleeve was slathered in blood. She groaned. Everything hurt. Everything burned. And still monsters stalked the town of Telridge. The town of fire and foe.

She felt a humming in her mind, an insistent nagging that seemed to grow more frantic. Perhaps Razakh, trying to speak to her. But she couldn't make out words. Couldn't make sense of anything. She saw red appear above her, a flash of silver eyes, and then she let her head fall flat to the mud, a satisfying squelch as her cheekbones nestled into the pillow of dirt.

Dizzy. So dizzy. So hard to breathe. Her eyes threatened to close, and the swirling of the world grew even fainter, but before her eyes shut, she saw copper. Burnished copper and golds in waves of steel brilliance, bright as the sun and even more dazzling. There were flashes of reds and browns, long blonde hair and angular faces as beautiful as Gods and Goddesses.

They were elves. The elves of Woodrandia had come.

Tricks and Torment

ASHALEA

RAGE SEARED HER INSIDES AT THE SIGHT OF HIM. Bruised, bloody, bent. His fingers at odd angles, leg pulverised, a look of horror on the wizard's face as he saw the two people he least wanted to see. Wezlan Shadowbreaker had broken no shadow this day; it had broken him.

But not inside. Never that. Ashalea knew her mentor was all powerful—even as the strength waned from his body—it would take more than physical pain to stop him. Yet there he was, tied to a rack, his arms stretched wide as if in a silent plea to be released. It hurt to see him this way, and her stomach knotted in fear and anguish.

She didn't miss his curse as they swept into view from a black tornado and dropped like flies to the sand—all except the darkness of course, who floated on his clouds, red eyes regarding them with glee.

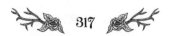

He'd even deigned to bring the humans with them, which did not bode well. Ashalea looked at their faces in pity, all wide eyes and whimpers as their bodies shook and shivered. They were naked still, and they huddled together on the ground, preserving what dignity they could. It mattered little. She doubted they'd last much longer—if any of them would.

The darkness swept down, clawed fingers steepled in front of him like a saint; the red of his eyes and the rotten stench that lingered in this monstrous form a clear indication he was anything but. He floated towards Wezlan, trailing one claw over the wizard's face. Ashalea rose sharply to her feet.

"Don't you touch him," she spat, the hackles rising on her neck. "Don't you lay another finger on him, or I won't give you what you so desperately seek."

He sniggered. "We both know you will, Ashalea. If it means he will live, if he will suffer less the insult, you will."

She felt Denavar stiffen at her side, the muscles coiled to release, one arm raised protectively in front of her. "Let him go, and then we can talk."

The darkness grinned with a mouthful of daggers. "But the party is just getting started. It would be inhospitable of me not to treat our guests to our finest service."

He morphed into his elven form and waved a hand lazily, his gaze resting somewhere past Ashalea. She and Denavar turned to see a group of five reptiles approaching, their forked tongues flicking in anticipation. The biggest of the group—a tall Uulakh with a yellow stripe down his body and a missing eye—sneered at Ashalea, as if gloating. His one eye roved the clearing before he uttered a grunt of frustration, and Ashalea had to wonder what he was looking for. Or perhaps who ...

Crinos approached Ashalea from behind whilst she was distracted, placing a hand on each shoulder. She writhed under his grip, straining to free herself from his grasp with the instincts of a cornered animal. With a snarl, Denavar lunged, and Ashalea saw his face: feral, full of hate, teeth gritted and anger roiling in his eyes.

Crinos batted him aside with one hand, sending Denavar hurtling, flicked aside like he weighed no more than paper. And still Ashalea struggled, but he was strong. Too strong. With a squeeze of his palms she was near whimpering under his touch, the tendons in her biceps screeching in pain. It was a command to stay still, and still she stayed.

He turned her to face the Uulakh, who were now circling the male and female. They clutched at each other in fear, and it was the woman who threw herself protectively over the man. Her eyes burned with defiance, and even as she shivered with terror, she held her head high.

Crinos leaned in to Ashalea's ear, his breath grating on her skin, the iciness a frosty mist on her cheek. "This is the price you pay for heroism, Ashalea. This is what happens when you test my patience."

And with a flourish of his wrist the creatures pounced. Ashalea watched on in horror as her eyes met the female's just before the reptiles closed, and to Ashalea's surprise, the woman offered a small nod. A thank you for trying to save them. For doing what was right. She smiled softly then. The curve of her lips reminiscent of a life full of love, and remorse that it should end this way.

Tears prickled Ashalea's eyes, stinging like nettle meeting flesh, burning with sorrow and anger. She curled her fists, tried to stifle the sob climbing her throat.

And even as the first reptile sunk its fangs into the woman's flesh, those brown eyes flared, and she screamed, long and guttural. She swung fists and kicked feet and fought to the last. The Uulakh tore her flesh asunder, fangs ripping the supple skin, claws slicing through her navel and gouging into her neck. Blood ran as rivers, and the sands drank for all their worth until the ground was stained with regret.

For a moment Ashalea was back in her old home. Not the great oak tree where she dwelled with Wezlan, but the house above the sea, nestled atop a cliff like a shining beacon. A home where her parents were still alive. The place where her mother sang and laughed and made merry; the place her father taught her how to shoot arrows, told stories and counted clouds with her.

For a moment she was standing at the end of her parent's bed on the morning of her sixteenth birthday, eyes wide and mouth open, staring at their cold, dead bodies drenched in a sheet of ruby silk. Not so long ago, and yet it felt like a lifetime.

And she remembered that primal need to avenge them, to seek retribution for their deaths. A need to end the creature that had taken everything from her. Her fists clenched so tightly she drew blood with her nails. The pain grounded her—reminded Ashalea that she was alive. That she would do everything in her power to have her revenge.

But nothing had changed. The darkness still murdered the innocent. Good people were still dying. And always, it seemed, Ashalea was powerless to stop it. Her chest constricted, her breaths came in short gasps, and a cold sweat broke out on her brow.

"Stop this, please," she whimpered to the darkness, but he merely watched in silence, keeping her caged beneath his grasp.

The red was everywhere now. She was drowning in it, unable to blink it away or run from the sight of it. An Uulakh disembowelled the woman and the contents of her stomach fell out in a steaming mess of pink. And it wasn't the sight of death that made her vomit; it was the smell. The cruelty of it lingered in the air, hot and wet and sticky.

Ashalea retched at her feet, spitting acid from her stomach, gasping for air. She wriggled beneath Crinos's grip again before settling on turning her head away, but he grabbed her cheeks, the claws of his other hand halfway extended from his fingers.

"You will look," he hissed, and still she squirmed. "LOOK AT THEM!"

Ashalea cried out in anguish, and at the sound of her pain Denavar was on his feet, sending volley after volley of fireballs. All sputtered out mid-air, and he roared, charging towards them both with agile feet. The darkness didn't even look at him—*didn't even flinch.* He threw one hand out and in a matter of seconds Denavar was bound by writhing black ropes of shadow. He fell to the ground in a tumble.

She met his gaze and her heart fluttered at the panic in his eyes. The flash of understanding that flitted across his face and settled into tired, defeated features. The darkness was too strong. Denavar was powerless. They all were.

Seconds passed with agonising slowness. The Uulakh ate their fill, leaving nothing but bloody carcasses in their wake. Tears trickled in silent streams down her face until, at last, the darkness shoved her away. She stumbled to Denavar, hands cupping his face too tightly, in grief and shock and fear of what was to come. She checked him over for wounds, and he nodded that he was okay.

Her anger pulsed beneath her skin like a leashed dog, snapping and clawing its way to the surface. There was nothing else in that moment. The sadness fizzled, replaced by something greater: rage. She looked at him, and her words were barbed and dripping with poison. "I am going to kill you, Crinos. I swear it by all the Gods. My face will be the last thing you see before I carve your blackened heart from your chest."

He assessed her with silver eyes, scrutinising the worth of her

words. Then he sneered. "I do believe you'll try. But not today, dear sister. Today you will teach me how to unlock that moon Magicka. The gift of our bloodline which conveniently happened to skip the first born."

Ashalea laughed bitterly. "Perhaps even the Moon Goddess knew what a failure you'd be. What a *disappointment* you would be to our parents. To our city."

He lashed out and morphed into his other form, shooting in a cloud of smoke and shadow to Wezlan. He appeared again behind the rack, both hands placed on Wezlan's shoulders, squeezing the muscles. The clawed tips pierced the skin beneath the wizard's collar bone, sinking into the flesh, sending blood trickling down his chest.

The threat gave rise to panic in Ashalea's chest, but she remained steadfast, biding her time, waiting for an opening. "We're not here to discuss the opinions of the dead," she said quickly. "We have a deal to make."

She caught Wezlan's eyes, the exhaustion dulling their glow, the pain flickering beneath. The storms had ceased, nothing but flat emptiness in the irises. He gave the slightest shake of his head. A small plea to not do anything foolish. She smiled back, and he hung his head, for Wezlan knew better than most how stubborn she could be. How loyal.

The darkness released Wezlan and the old man sagged against his bonds, a soft moan escaping his lips. She mustered all her strength, willed herself to stand still despite how much her hands itched to untie her mentor—how much they itched to drive a blade through the darkness.

His cruel smile was a crooked line she wished to scratch from his face. His eyes a sight she longed to poke out and never look upon again. But this was his domain. He was the master here.

Crinos began circling Wezlan, hands clasped behind his back. "And what terms would you make?"

"I will teach you how to use the Magicka. With my help you'll be able to harness the power of the moon."

A cruel line cut the darkness's face. "I have a better idea."

In a blink he was at Denavar's back this time, one hand pulling his head back by the hair, the other wrapped around a sword. The point was firmly against her beloved's throat, and a trickle of blood danced down his skin.

Fear crept down Ashalea's spine, and a small whimper betrayed her as she caught his face. His handsome, lovely, beautiful face. She raised her hands slowly. "Crinos, you don't have to do this, you don't—"

Her eyes caught sight of the sword. It was the most beautiful weapon she'd ever seen. A white hilt carved to perfection; a crest of moons in their different stages lining the hilt, finishing in the waxing cycle that curved above the fingers. The steel itself glittered like starlight and engraved in the blade were symbols of ancient elvish.

Something about it was familiar ... Yes. She knew this sword—knew it from the moment when ... when ... Her breath caught in her throat as she recognised it. The same blade that almost ended her life, that allowed the darkness to traverse between realms when he was in a weaker state.

The scar on her stomach burned with the memory and she clutched at it, keenly aware of the pain she had once felt.

Crinos sneered. "I thought you might appreciate the irony. It was our father's sword, you know. Carved by our ancestors, passed down through the generations. He never gave it to me, of course, but I took it all the same. Right before I plunged it into his chest."

Ashalea snarled. "You won't make that mistake again. Touch one

hair on Denavar's head and I'll make sure the power you seek is lost to you."

Crinos looked at her with an expression almost akin to pity, if not for the hunger burning in his eyes and the unmistakable spark of joy. "Oh, Ashalea, we both know that's not true."

He brought his blade down and thrust it through Denavar's shoulder. And his scream—it ripped through the silence, and Ashalea could only stare in horror. At her brother, the male who shared the same blood running through his veins. At her partner, the one she loved more than anything.

She remembered what the darkness said about being connected. About the poison that had taken root in her mind, festering and swelling the more visions she had, the more she let him in.

No. More.

And then she howled, fingers splaying, toes curling, her body shrinking in on itself as she buried deeper and deeper into the fabric of her being, clawing into her mind's core and summoning every drop of strength she had. She followed the Magicka's path, slipping through every nerve, every strand of silken thread the darkness had linked to her brain.

Ashalea followed them, speeding towards the source, sifting through every memory until there, in a dark corner in her mind, a spider's web pulsed. At the heart of it, an orb of black throbbed, leaking its toxin—its evil spreading through her mind like a disease.

She imagined herself as a blade, sharp and true and searing hot as she sliced through the web, its membrane exploding, shrinking, dying ...

The darkness screamed, and even as she severed the bonds, one by one, in her mind her eyes were wide open, and she watched him crumple to the ground in agony. The same agony she felt every time the connection weakened, every time the mental bond was snapped.

Denavar lurched away from Crinos, hands outstretched to her, but she shook her head even as tears streamed down her face and her body burned with a feverish fire. "Save Wezlan," she gasped. "Set him free."

With a bewildered nod he scrambled to the fallen blade and swept it up in one motion, groaning in pain, one hand pressed against his shoulder to staunch the bleeding. It dribbled from the wound, and he stumbled as he ran, the loss of blood likely impeding his body's ability to move ... to think.

Denavar set to work on Wezlan's bonds, and before she disappeared into her mind entirely, she saw Wezlan sag to the ground. Free. Safe. At least for now. She exhaled a shaky breath, stars threatening to overwhelm her vision, sweat drenching her body, and still her skin burned with pain, her brain felt close to exploding, but she pushed. She fought, even as the darkness clung to her mind with clawed fingers.

But her Magicka was strong. Eager. It didn't want the foreign presence in its bloodstream—for the darkness to spread and infect. It wanted light. It wanted suns and stars and moons, light and colour and warmth. Everything the darkness wasn't. Everything he could never be.

She sped along the nerves, and there, just out of reach, was the last connection to the darkness. The last bond that, once severed, would mean no more visions, no more being spied on, no lack of control over her actions.

Something glittered inside the black. Something shiny, something good. And she fed on it, discarding the rot and the dark, consuming only the light. *Her* power. *Her* Magicka. She drank it in; an elixir that eased her suffering, eased the pain racking through her body.

The world was clear again. The burning ceased and the hurt stopped. And with one satisfied smile, she cleaved through that last bond with a savage stroke, breaking the connection. A shriek snapped her back to the present, and before her, the darkness clutched at his head, screaming in anguish, in pain. *In fury.*

She leaned down to whisper in his ear. "I'm always true to my word, Crinos. The power you so desperately wanted is gone. Lost ... because I took it back."

He raised his eyes and looked at her with hatred, seeing the restored power swirling beneath her skin whilst his own breath rattled in his chest. "You will regret the day you were born, Ashalea. Everything you know, everyone you love, will burn."

Ashalea spat, "Your words are as empty as your soul."

She conjured a ball of white light—perfectly round, pristine, pure—and marvelled at the coolness that radiated from its core. Its power had been hers all along. Its allegiance never wavering, if only she had trusted in it. If she had only smashed the glass walls of her own limitations and realised her potential was endless.

"Death is too easy for you, *Brother*, but life is a luxury you don't deserve." Ashalea lifted the ball higher, and just as she was about to hurl it into his chest the darkness hissed, tendrils of shadow stretching out with renewed vigour, the shadows binding her legs, crushing her, stealing the breath from her lungs.

He laughed wickedly and without humour, and Ashalea suppressed a shudder at its cruelty. It echoed through the realm as if amplified, and she shrank in horror, gasping for air. The black thickened to a tornado, whirling around her, consuming her.

"Do you really think me so weak? You may have our family's power, but in breaking the connection, you restored the power *I* lost. My shadows. My dark."

A voice boomed from somewhere far away, and light pierced the deepening black. And there, Magicka beaming from his palm, was Wezlan, his beard whipping in the wind, eyes the colour of tempestuous seas, determination raging like a storm in their windows.

"You will not have her," he vowed, and the power deepened to a surge of white. Ashalea's bonds released and she sucked in oxygen, her fingers curling around her throat.

Denavar stumbled through the black, one hand wrapped firmly around the sword's hilt, the other reaching for Ashalea. Their hands met, and as she clasped his calloused palm, he lifted her up and cradled her in one arm. Denavar braced his body against the howling wind, shielding her from the dark, pressing her cheek to his chest.

They scrabbled over to Wezlan, seeking cover behind the might of his power. And above the biting wind they heard the darkness, grunting just as Wezlan moaned, their powers clashing in a blaze, each exerting their strength. One dark. One light.

He looked at her, one hand blasting a spiral of light, the other outstretched, already at work forming a new spell. Ashalea gasped as a portal flared to life, the mirrored surface shining on an unfamiliar place. Somewhere she'd never been before, and yet ... it called to her. Beckoned her.

She swung her head back to Wezlan, eyes widening as she realised his intentions.

"Go," he yelled. "Return to the Guardians, seal the Gates of the Grove!" He groaned anew, his already bent form slumping further, his mangled leg propped up against all odds.

"No," she screamed. "You're coming with me. You're coming home."

She glanced imploringly at Denavar, expecting to find the same fire in his eyes, the same defiance. But his eyes were sad. Apologetic.

Defeated. Wezlan didn't answer, and his silence spoke volumes.

"No ... It can't end like this." Tears streamed down her face, unbidden and unwanted. "I won't go without you." Her voice broke as she choked on the fear of losing him. She couldn't leave him. Not after everything, not after—

"Ashalea." The name was a gentle whisper on his lips, but when her eyes met the grey of Wezlan Shadowbreaker, there was no fear. No regret. Only love. Only acceptance.

And she knew he was not asking. This would be the final task from her dear mentor. The man she'd come to think of as a father. The man who knew her like no other in this world—in all worlds.

"Please ..." The plea in his voice all but shattered her heart.

"I can't do this without you Wezlan, I can't—I can't beat him." She was sobbing now, hysterical, pain lancing through her body sharper than any blade she'd ever known.

Wezlan grunted with the effort of keeping not one but two spells ongoing. "My power is waning. Please, Ashalea. I need to do this. Let me do this for you." His eyes shifted focus. "Take her home, Denavar. Keep her safe."

She felt him stiffen at her side, saw the nod from the corner of her eyes. A gentle hand snaked around her waist. "It's time, Ashalea. Let's go home."

She looked into the eyes of the man she loved, felt the caress of his fingers on her chin as they traced a line down her jaw. And as she nodded her acceptance, her soul dimmed. Her resolve shattered, and she knew a piece of her would die here that she would never get back.

But Ashalea allowed Denavar to guide her to the portal. Forced her feet to take one step, then another, and another, until she was planted before their means of freedom, looking through a doorway she could never come back from.

She cast one more glance over her shoulder, tried to convey all her love in a final look, and Wezlan smiled; the lines of his weathered face smoothed even as the crinkles around his eyes deepened. She burned the image into her mind, savouring it—that smile, that cheek, that kindness—and she vowed to remember it, always.

He winked at her at last. "What's a wizard without his tricks?"

And Denavar pulled her through the portal, right before the darkness consumed Wezlan, and he was lost forever.

Help from Higher Powers

SHARA

THE SWEET SMELL OF JASMINE AND SANDALWOOD regaled her, brought her back to the living. The last thing Shara remembered was the blistering heat of the fire and searing pain in her shoulder. Her hand strayed to the wound, and yet, there was nothing there. Not a crack or bump beneath her fingertips. She opened her eyes and examined her injury—or lack thereof—in disbelief, hands circling the unmarred olive skin.

"The elves healed it for you," said a soft voice, and the source of it was smiling gently, brows knitted in concern, the same old ugly clothes swathing over every glorious curve of the woman's body.

"Telilah? But ... how?"

The minstrel grinned wider. "After you so recklessly decided to risk your life for the boy, you passed out in the middle of the street.

Monsters still running amok, mind. Lucky for you the elves arrived in the nick of time."

"The elves of Woodrandia," Shara breathed. "Of course. I remember hearing Wezlan say they would be patrolling these areas due to the rumoured monsters of the marshes."

Telilah snorted. "Rather more real than rumour, I'm afraid."

Shara smiled at that. "It would seem so."

She sat up, taking in her surroundings. They were in an ivory tent, swathes of rust-coloured silk draped from the apex. A small bowl was set on a stack of crates to her right, and a looking mirror, hairbrush, and a few bottles of who knows what were scattered around it.

Shara rubbed her forehead, trying to ignore the steady pound. Telilah noticed the movement, and procured a wooden cup from across the room, filling it with water from a carafe. She offered it to Shara, who accepted gratefully.

She chugged the liquid, smacking her dried lips together when done. "Where is Razakh?"

"He's consulting with the elven commander. I think he hopes to secure their aid in getting to the Meadows faster."

Shara nodded. "We're running out of time. If they could conjure a portal, speak with the Moonglade elves—anything—we'll be in their debt." She rolled her shoulder joint, sighing in relief at the freedom of movement, the only sign of her injury a dull pang in the muscle. "What about the people? The town?"

"There were many casualties, but thanks to you, many got out. The elves have set up a camp here for temporary refuge and boarding for the villagers. The town is ... well, it's seen better days."

Shara cocked a brow. "In other words, it's nothing but rubble."

Telilah chuckled. "You sure know how to soften the blow, huh."

Shara flicked her hair, which was now clean and ... smelt of roses?

Florals weren't her thing, but she was certainly thankful to be clean again. She had also been redressed in flowing white pants and a loose shirt. She wondered if Telilah had been the one to change her, and her cheeks glowed. "If there's one thing you can count on, it's that there's *nothing* soft about me."

"I think you're more bark than bite," Telilah teased. "As for the softness, well, I can think of a few things ..."

She let her suggestion fill the emptiness of the tent, and Shara shuffled uncomfortably. Telilah just laughed and reached for the empty cup. Their fingers met as Shara handed it back, and she felt one slender digit graze along her own; an electric charge that travelled down through her body. Telilah smirked before placing the cup on the crates and heading for a screen in the corner of the tent.

A moment later the hideousness that was her rainbow skirts came flying over to land on Shara's head. She grumbled as she slipped the still warm fabric from her face and tried not to stare at the corner. The light was seeping through, showing a shadowy outline of Telilah through the screen. She sneaked a peek at the silhouette; long cascading hair fell in soft curls, and the soft curve of her breasts hitched as she shimmied pants over her full hips.

Shara breathed. Even the sight of Telilah's shadow did things to her core. But she glared in irritation. Telilah was doing this on purpose. A game. And Shara didn't have the time nor patience to play. Why should she? Shara Silvaren, Onyxonite and Guardian, a mere plaything for a songstress? She snorted. Unlikely.

But when the woman stepped out from behind the screen Shara had to force her jaw from dropping. She had donned a white shirt with a low neckline, showing off her assets rather blatantly, with a brown leather corset with gilded clasps down the front. Daring yet somewhat practical. Leather pants for bottoms, and brown boots.

She'd even strapped a belt to her hip to sheathe a weapon or two, not that she knew how to use them.

"What do you think?" Telilah asked, and she turned on the spot, gifting Shara a full view of her rear as well.

Shara raised a brow. "Beautiful, obviously. But you already knew that."

Telilah grinned devilishly. "Obviously. But it doesn't hurt to hear it from someone else's lips."

"There's a little something called modesty, you know, you should try it."

The minstrel rolled her eyes. "Because we both know you excel in that."

"It's part of my charm." Shara yawned. "Ravishing outfits and immodest minstrels aside, how long have I been out for?"

Telilah shrugged.

Shara narrowed her eyes. A little too casual for her liking. "How. Long."

Telilah found her long brown hair suddenly very interesting, curling strands around her finger, refusing to meet Shara's gaze. "Welllll ..."

"Songstress, I swear on all the—"

"All right, all right," Telilah huffed. "It's been a day."

"What!?" Shara's voice rose a few octaves, and Telilah winced. "You let me sleep this long? We need to get going."

"Shara ... your lungs were burned from the fire and your shoulder was badly hurt from overuse. You needed to rest. The elves healed you while you slept. That, at least, is a mercy."

She was right, of course, but Shara couldn't help feeling aggravated at the lost time. Her friends needed her, and it seemed every step of the way something had hindered their progress. She sighed. If they didn't hurry soon, there might not be anyone left to save.

As if sensing her worry, Telilah said, "Your friends will be okay, Shara. I know they will. I promise we'll get to the Meadows and we'll find a way to bring them home."

Unreasonable rage swelled in Shara's chest. "What do you care? You know nothing of responsibility. Of loss. You're only with us because your grandma forced you to come."

Telilah's eyes lost the mischievous spark. Her expression turned solemn, a deep-rooted sadness filled her eyes, and Shara knew she'd hit a nerve. She immediately regretted her words, silently cursing herself for her temper. Why did she always have to go and say the wrong thing? Why did her emotions always get the better of her?

She put her head in her hands, letting the coolness of her palms and the shade over her eyelids ground her. Because she bottled up her feelings, she realised. Shoved them into a glass, buried them with sand and sealed it with a stopper. It was why she had never allowed herself to get too close to anyone. To even try to know someone—know their touch, their truths, their mistakes ... their love.

And it smacked her in the face, the unreasonable weight of that. It reminded her of Ashalea—holding back her secrets about her visions of the darkness. She hadn't wanted the others to worry, to fear for her. And it had cost them. What had Leanna said back in Galanor? *"Don't harden your heart too much, else you'll find it breaks alone with no one around to mourn you."*

Perhaps the old crone was right. Maybe she would end up alone, withering away to dust just as Leanna was; paper thin and wearing a pink nightgown. That thought scared Shara more than any monster ever would. *No,* she resolved. *I will not live a life of regret. I will not push people away.*

"I know of loss, Shara," Telilah said quietly. "It will shadow me

every step of this journey."

"Telilah," she began, but when she lifted her head the woman was already gone.

Shara liked the Captain of the Woodrandian patrol immediately. He was tall—naturally, given he was elvish—with cropped blonde hair, hazel eyes, and a smile worth swooning over. And contrary to popular elf stereotypes, he swore like a sailor and had a flask in hand she suspected did not hold water.

Caelor, he was called, and he had led the charge through the burning husk of Telridge, effectively slaying all monsters in the vicinity and freeing the trapped citizens. It wasn't hard to pick him as the leader. Both males and females flocked around him, taking orders, sharing a laugh, and his armour was a shade darker than that of his brethren, making him stand out in a crowd.

She couldn't decide if that was stupid or smart, so she settled on daring. A bold move if war came knocking, which it would very soon. She studied him for a moment. He was young and quite handsome. Early thirties perhaps, but who could know how old he really was? He might be old enough to be her grandfather and then some. It just wasn't fair, really.

Shara strode to him purposefully, the soft, loose cottons she wore so out of place in a field of metal. She was also human, which made her the minority here. The villagers of Telridge had been boarded in a separate campground a block over, the fields now dotted with multiple cream tents. A bigger, grander one the colour of red autumn leaves perched just behind the captain.

Their eyes met, and he grinned rakishly, saluting her with his flask before taking a hearty sip. "Shara Silvaren," he said as she planted her slippered feet before him. Slippers, because apparently that was practical in a campground of soldiers. She didn't bother to ask what he knew of her, and didn't have to, for he said, "Slayed most of the marsh monsters, rescued forgotten children, risked the wrath of scorching fires ... you're quite a hero to the people of Telridge."

His voice was smooth, enticing—like the first sip of whiskey as it sailed down one's throat, encouraging the next gulp. He genuinely looked impressed, but she knew it would take more than idle chatter from overexcited peasants to stir true cause to admire.

Shara shrugged. "It was more of a right place, wrong time scenario."

He dipped his head knowingly. "That's not what your friend Telilah said. But let's not argue your reasons. Come." He turned on his heel and headed inside the red tent.

Shara followed his lead, stepping into an autumnal paradise. Red, brown and gold leaves lined the mossy floor, trickling down from a canopy of branches that made for the ceiling. A fireball floated in the tent's centre, crackling away merrily despite the lack of kindling to ignite it. Shara gawked at it in awe. It was a cloudy day, and yet the interior of this tent defied the natural seasons of the world. She shook her head. Magicka. She would never tire of the mystical.

On one side of the room was an artfully crafted wooden table and set of chairs, paperwork and maps strewn across the carved surface. On the other was a simple setup of washing materials, and in the corner was a lavish bed, adorned with beautiful velvet blankets, chiffon and taffeta pillows in mustards and oranges and golds.

And standing behind the fireball was a lady garbed in white, her long, flowing locks of blonde falling to her waist, lips painted red, hazel eyes twinkling. She smiled in greeting, and Shara needed no introduction.

"The Lady Nirandia," she said in awe, standing awkwardly, unsure whether to curtsy or nod. Razakh slipped through the tent entrance and offered Shara his lopsided grin. She ran a hand through his fur by way of hello, thankful for the timely interruption.

Caelor took his respective place by the lady's side and Shara ogled at the pair of them. They were almost identical. Twins, she realised. Like her and Flynn. She wondered how her brother was going with his new duties as chieftain-to-be.

Nirandia's attention was on Razakh and she grinned even wider. "Razakh, dear one, just in time." Her eyes shifted back to Shara, and she felt the weight of that penetrating gaze driving into her. A power that lay beneath the grace and beauty on the outside. A whisper of elegance that demanded attention and commanded obedience.

"It is good to meet you, Shara Silvaren," Nirandia said, dipping her head slightly. "I understand you played a vital role in saving the people of this town. It is saddening to see so many fell during the raid." She ushered a slender arm towards the table and chairs, and they all sat.

Shara frowned. "How did this happen? I thought—and I mean no disrespect, My Lady—but I thought the elves were scouting the area for this purpose?"

Nirandia pursed her lips. "As this raid hit Telridge, another marched on Galanor. We did not have enough forces amassed to be in both places at once. We were able to save the village, but the lives lost—"

"Galanor, you say?" Shara cut in with alarm. "But that's ..." she looked at Razakh, who shook his head slowly, confirming her fears. She sighed, exhaling the name on regretful lips. "Leanna."

Guilt. She felt heavy, toxic, ugly guilt as she thought of her

conversation with Telilah this morning. How she had snapped without cause. The sadness on Telilah's soft, heart-shaped face, in her gentle brown eyes. The last words the songstress had said before walking out. *"I know of loss, Shara. It will shadow me every step of this journey."*

She hadn't had the chance to ask what Telilah meant, but now it was clear. And Shara had hit her while she was down. Even after the woman had watched over her. Cared for her. *Perhaps I'm more of a monster than the ones out there*, she thought miserably. She eyed off the vacant chair at the table, which somehow seemed lonelier after realising why Telilah's delightful rump wasn't seated in it.

"Monsters don't give meaning to life, they end it," Razakh said in her mind, and she knew it was only for her. *"They don't regret or feel remorse."* Her heart climbed her throat, and she felt undeserving of his kindness, but she petted him gently before looking back at the twins.

"Telilah's grandma lived in Galanor. It was their hometown."

Nirandia smiled sadly. "I am sorry for your loss. War is a nasty affair on all accounts. Without the full support of all races, we are outnumbered and unable to be in all places at once. I understand the Aquafarian elves have been working with you?"

Shara nodded. "They aided the mages in the battle for Renlock. The king and queen will join our forces when the time comes."

"That will be a sight," Caelor grinned, and Nirandia gave him a look.

But Shara's interest was piqued. She waited expectantly; hands folded neatly on the table; one brow cocked. Nirandia sighed, and her brother smirked.

"Tiderion is not the easiest ally to deal with. He can be ..." she searched for the words, trying to tread carefully.

"Pig-headed, quick to anger, and kind of a brute?" Shara supplied.

Nirandia's eyes sparkled. "Exactly. He is wise, and when he

speaks you listen, but I just wish he would be more forthcoming with decisions during council meetings. It is his way or none, and it has been so for as long as I can remember."

"Some inconsequential number of years in a long lifespan, then," Razakh said bluntly.

The she-elf smiled. "A lady never tells, but yes, something like that."

"He's as bad as a dwarf to reason with, but you won't find a more loyal ally and we'll need as many as we can get when the time comes," Caelor said. "Given the aggressive attacks of late, and the number of monsters coming from the marshes—and from what I've heard, other corners of the land too," he looked at Razakh before continuing, "we can afford to waste no more time aligning the races to one purpose."

"To destroy the darkness."

"And seal the Gate of the Grove for good," Shara added.

Caelor nodded. "Now that the Diodonians have pledged an alliance, we are left with the king of Maynesgate to convince, and the dwarves. Nirandia has made some progress in coming to terms with the latter but the human king ..."

Nirandia waved a hand in agitation. "King Grayden will be difficult to persuade. He is surrounded by the politics of court and the conflicts of power within his own grand city. He cares little for his people beyond the walls of Maynesgate. He is foolish. Easily manipulated. A child on puppet's strings."

"With two—maybe three—of the four races allied, surely his court will have no choice but to accept diplomacy in otherwise tenuous times. If we could arrange a council where leaders of all races are present, it would hold more sway with the humans."

Shara chewed on her lip. "If what you say is true, that still might not be enough. What if we arranged for the chieftain of Shadowvale to attend? We may not be able to speak on behalf of the human populace, but with an army of considerable soldiers, I think our voice would hold sway with the people. Perhaps give hope to the towns throughout Everosia. Show them that we're willing to fight for them."

Nirandia looked at her brother, who stroked his chin thoughtfully. "It would show a united front," he agreed. "And after what you did for Telridge ... word will spread quick of the 'Onyxonite and Diodonian that saved the people'." He moved his hands through the air as if an invisible banner declared the message for all to see.

The she-elf was nodding eagerly. "I think this may work. Even better, if the Guardians themselves were present to make known their intentions ..." she trailed off, sensing the mood shift in the room.

"Our comrades are missing," Shara said softly. "The darkness has taken them to another world."

"Razakh has already updated us on what happened," Caelor said. "We want to help."

"Wezlan is a dear friend of mine," Nirandia agreed, "and we will do anything we can to help you get them back. The Guardians are the key to ending all of this. Our fates are entwined in your destinies."

"So, you have the Magicka needed to bring them home?" Shara asked eagerly, hopefully, so anxious she gripped Razakh's fur tightly with one hand, to which he glared at her with silver eyes. She released her hold slightly, needing something comfortable and familiar to keep from swallowing the heart now thudding in her throat.

Caelor grimaced and Nirandia's face fell. "I'm sorry, but we don't have the power to forge a portal through time and space, nor do we have knowledge or written word on this phenomenon. Our Magicka is of the earth. It is all around us in nature itself. But the power you seek ... it is fragile, fickle. It is the moon and stars and the very shape of everything beyond our world. There is only one people who can help you now."

"The Moonglade elves," Shara said. "We are headed there but keep getting waylaid. I don't suppose you could help us reason with them. Show us the way?"

Caelor snorted. "We've not laid eyes on the Meadows for an age. They zealously guard their city under spells of old. Even we cannot enter if they do not wish an audience."

"They will not treat with their own brethren?"

Nirandia drummed delicate fingers on the table. "Since the darkness wrought so much destruction that day, they meet with no one. I could try to use my Magicka to help you but I'm afraid that show of force would not bode well. We have to be careful how we tread or risk losing their alliance altogether."

Silence fell over the group and a heavy lump settled in Shara's stomach. If even the Lady Nirandia herself could not help them, what hope did they have? An assassin, a Diodonian, and a singer knocking on their gate asking for entry? They'd just as soon be skewered than asked for tea and cake while discussing the perils their queen-in-waiting faced.

Nirandia reached across the table to grasp Shara's hands with her own milky, soft ones. Her grip was surprisingly strong, but as Shara met her eyes, they held nothing but sincerity. "This task is yours. You and Razakh, you were meant to travel this path together, just as Ashalea, Wezlan and Denavar were meant to divert from the course."

Shara stared at Nirandia blankly. "You expect me to believe everything happens for a reason? Our friends' deaths, my torture, every damned thing the darkness has done?"

Nirandia sighed, and for the first time Shara saw her age. Not in the flawless complexion of her face, the creamy canvas of her skin or the fullness to her lips, but the sadness in her eyes, the weariness, the strained tug of her smile. She had seen it before in Wezlan, and she wondered how old this woman really was. How many lifetimes of wisdom she might have lived.

"We elves live long lives. Rarely does it seem happenstance and fate walk hand in hand. The Magicka in this world—the fabric of our Goddess given lives—it is beyond comprehension. Elves are gifted longevity of life, beauty long lasting, and in return we nurture the soil beneath our feet. And it speaks to us ... if one listens hard enough. It whispers secrets of what is to come. Perhaps not so comprehensive a conversation as you and I are having right now, but it knows when dark things are abounding."

"There is a great oak in our home. Its roots spiral deep into the ground, into the very core of Magicka itself," Caelor said. "It is through this tree that we have learned much over the passage of time. It does not speak to all ... but it did to Ashalea, didn't it, Sister?"

Nirandia nodded absentmindedly, her gaze in some far-off place. "It did not speak to her, rather it *chose* her. It has been whispering of her ever since she set foot in our home."

Shara looked from sister to brother and back again. "What does that even mean?"

Caelor shrugged and took a sip from his flask. "Every so often the tree selects an individual destined for a greater purpose and follows their path. Guides them. And Nirandia, for that matter, for our Lady is the caretaker of Woodrandia."

"So, you're telling me a tree knows better than we do what's to happen in the future?" Shara scoffed. "Well, it's done a piss poor job at guiding us so far."

"*Shara,*" Razakh growled. "*You shouldn't mock things you don't understand.*"

She glared at him before raising her head regally. "Oh, I understand

just perfectly. But I make my own damn path, I forge my own destiny. Ancient talking trees, Magicka, and fate?" She snorted. "They're just words in a foreign language, as unreliable as a sinner in a sanctum. So here's what's going to happen: I'm going to the Meadows. I'm going to bring the others home. And you're going to help me."

Nirandia blinked at Shara before side-eying her brother, who just chuckled in response and planted his boots on the table. "About damn time. I'd been told of your fiery nature, but until now I'd seen only mildness and misery." He cocked a brow and pulled an apple from his pocket, rubbing the waxy red fruit on his breaches before opening his mouth for a bite.

In seconds Shara had unsheathed the dagger strapped under her pants and hurled it towards Caelor. The small dagger sailed tip to hilt in rotating arcs to pierce the apple's flesh and *riiip* into the far tent wall.

"Misery can be arranged," she said coldly.

Caelor laughed heartily, and Nirandia just stared, her usually serene face now a mask of horror and disapproval.

"Okay, assassin," Caelor said as he went to retrieve his apple. "You want my help? You'll get it. We're on the same team here. We want the same things. So, what do you require?"

Shara glanced at Razakh and the flames on his back flared to life. She grinned. "We will need a portal."

"To the entrance of the Moonglade Meadows."

"At the very doorway to the fog."

Caelor plucked the knife from the tent wall and strode before the pair of them, who were now standing side by side. "And when do your majesties require said portal?"

Shara and Razakh looked at each other and nodded. She plucked the apple from Caelor's hand, his mouth once again open to take

a bite. His eyes fluttered with disappointment as she sunk her own teeth into the flesh, the sweet, supple fruit immediately flushing her taste buds. She let him stew whilst she chewed and swallowed with tantalising slowness.

Then her and Razakh strode from the tent without so much as a glance in his direction, and she threw the apple over her shoulder with a smirk.

"We leave now."

Riddles and Wraiths

Razakh

RAZAKH WAS THANKFUL TO BE LEAVING. After the monsters had been put down and the village had been doused of all flames, only then did the hard part come. After Shara had blacked out he had propped her limp form on his back and guided both the child and her to safety. Children are trusting, and the boy was too awed to shy away from what he had later referred to Razakh as 'the strange dog that saved me', but men and women, for all their years of maturity, were much, much worse to deal with.

Some crowded him with thanks, petting his fur like he was a prized pony, and others shivered at the sight of him, flinching at his telepathy or spitting in his direction. There was even the odd 'hero' who shouted a string of curses at him, hissing all kinds of inventive threats his way.

All because he was different. All because he wasn't human. An oddity. An abomination gifted with Magicka undeserved. This was why he had not been eager to return to humanity. This was why there would always be a small part of him that would loathe this species; the ones among the good who would hurt him, abuse him, kill him. Everyone had a dark side; humans just tended to give it more space in their hearts.

At least that's what he'd come to believe. And until he'd met Shara—an assassin of all things—he wouldn't have believed in the integrity of mankind. In compassion, loyalty, friendship among races. But that is what she shared with the others—with Wezlan, Ashalea, and Denavar. An odd ensemble of companions, but a strong one. A united one.

He did not share the same fondness for the others as Shara did. Not yet. But time would make or break them, and they still had one more Guardian to find. A dwarf from Kingsgareth Mountains. Now that would be interesting. They already had one hothead in the group and even Razakh—having been isolated in the deserts for so long—knew how fiery they could be. Tempers that burned like the forges in their mountains, and the stubbornness of stone.

But he was getting ahead of himself. There would be no search for the dwarf if they failed in finding the others—in bringing them home. He watched Shara now, talking animatedly with Caelor, the pair of them discussing the logistics of this mission. What supplies they would need, if the horses should join them, what was required to set up a council meeting.

They were all stately affairs Razakh would not be much help with. He couldn't read, after all, and his knowledge of the world was somewhat lacking. Well, truth be told, not lacking—non-existent. The price to pay for dominion over the desert had been ignorance to life beyond the tall walls of the Diodon Mountains. Solitude and stories being his only friends during childhood and the years that followed since his mother was killed and his father left to become a Guardian.

He observed the hustle and bustle of the camp. Elves still garbed in copper plates, greaves and spaulders fulfilled their tasks, cleaning armour, fletching new arrows, forging new blades, gathering food and water for the villagers. What the people would do for lodgings on a more permanent basis, he did not know. The town was little more than a decrepit husk. The only reason the fires had been quenched was in thanks to the few elves proficient with water Magicka.

But Razakh couldn't think about that now. He had done his part to help these people. Now he needed to do his part to save *all* peoples of *all* races.

Shara stalked over to him. "Are you ready?"

He flicked his tail at her. *"Always."*

Her amber eyes scanned the campground, and he knew what—or rather who—she was looking for.

"Telilah is with the humans, helping to pass around food."

"I never thought I'd say it but damn her for being so good," Shara grumbled. "We need to leave, now. Could you go fetch her please?" She plastered a saintly smile on her face.

He growled, bared his fangs. *"Stop that."*

"What?"

"You're avoiding her and this play-pretend at being sweet doesn't suit you. Now toughen up and go get the girl."

She crossed her arms and harrumphed like an unimpressed horse. "It's too much effort to be nice. I'm much better at hurting people to get what I want." She pouted for added measure.

"Shara, if you had it your way there'd be no one left to save by the end of all this."

She scowled. "Fine. Flea-riddled mutt."

"You wound me, oh maiden with the raging hormones."

The assassin opened her mouth to speak but promptly chomped it shut, a nerve pulsing in her jawline, eyes like rivers of gold. Then she turned on her feet and stormed towards the neighbouring camp, muttering as she went.

Razakh chuckled. At least some things he could rely on. He continued watching the hustle and bustle of the camp. If there was to be an alliance, there would soon be all manner of races working together, camping with each other. Equals.

The elves would pose no threats—as caretakers of the land and its denizens, Razakh knew they would make strong allies. The dwarves too, despite their stubbornness and fiery tempers. Which just left the humans. He shook his head. He could only hope that once the Diodonians joined the Everosians, they would work as a single unit.

He felt a presence saunter up beside him. Caelor.

"She's a whirlwind, that Shara. The kind of woman soldiers fight battles for, or poets write ballads about. Just as likely to kill you in your sleep as make you the happiest man alive."

"Perhaps both. The happiest man alive until he is dead in his bed."

Caelor chuckled. "Aye, but after sharing a bed with her I can't imagine he'd be sorry for it."

"Can't say I share the same sentiment."

"No. But she might. I see the way she looks at Shara." He jerked his chin towards Telilah as the women re-entered the camp. Both were making every effort to avoid each other, Shara all scowling and broody, Telilah pouting, her face tear-streaked. Razakh felt weary just looking at them.

"Happiness doesn't seem to be an ongoing theme in our company," Razakh stated bluntly. *"They don't have the luxury or the time to—what*

was it Shara called it? Ah ... 'woo' each other."

"My dear Diodonian," Caelor said with a grin. "Love is a two-sided coin. It's either shiny and new or faded with the stain of time. But no matter who holds it, no matter which side faces up, the value is always the same."

"How can you place a price on love?"

But Caelor just tapped a finger to his nose, a grin sweeping across his face. "Let me know, will you? If the lovebirds sing ... or squawk."

And the elf walked away, leaving Razakh more perplexed than ever.

<hr/>

Razakh had never seen fog before. It was fascinating, the way it shrouded all within it, shifting, undulating with every sigh of the wind. It held mystery and intrigue. A desire to see what lay on the other side. But it also held danger, for if they entered the mist and lost their way, they might never come out.

The three of them stood before the entrance now, gaping at the grey and white cloud that stretched endlessly before them. At their backs stood the small mountains that divided the Meadows from the Purple Plains to the north, and Woodrandia to the west. A small corner of Everosia, nestled in the valley straight ahead.

The mountains themselves would pose no problem to climb should they find the need to turn back, but Razakh knew that wasn't an option. The elves were their last resort. The fog was their only way forward, and they couldn't exactly portal back to the elves. Neither Shara, Telilah nor he possessed the Magicka for that.

"Well?" Shara demanded, chin raised haughtily. "Do you know the way to go?"

"Give me a minute," Telilah snapped. She was leaning over the plaque Leanna promised would be waiting at the entrance, reading the scripture carved on its obsidian surface. It had taken them almost an hour to find it after stepping out from the portal Nirandia had created. Portal travel had not sat well with Razakh. His stomach gurgled in displeasure—either that or the fowl he'd eaten this morning had been in poor health.

He sniffed the air. Nothing but damp wetness and the familiar scents of his companions filled his nostrils. That was a positive, at least. No shadow beings or much of anything else around here save the odd rabbit or fox nearby.

It was deathly still. No sound, and not even the sun was shining, hidden behind clouds on a dark and gloomy day. He wondered if whatever Gods and Goddesses existed held their breaths in anticipation.

Shara started tapping her feet impatiently, which he noticed set Telilah's teeth on edge. He glared at the assassin until she noticed his pointed stare.

"Give her some room," he urged. *"Be patient."*

Her answering huff was confirmation she wasn't about to play nice. "Can you at least tell us what it says?"

He should have known that asking Shara to do one thing meant she'd do the exact opposite.

"Can you stop being such a brat?" Telilah answered. "I'm trying to help you and nagging me isn't in your favour."

Shara puffed her chest up like an absurd bird of prey. "Look, I'm sorry about what I said before but—"

"Enough," Razakh barked, and his words pierced their minds with enough bite they both winced in pain. *"We need to work together if we're going to survive this. So please, if you could both cooperate, we'll find our*

friends much faster." He turned to Telilah, sparking the flames on his back for good measure. "*Would you be so kind as to read the scripture aloud?*"

She nodded, looking sheepish as she glanced sideways at Shara. "The passage reads:

> *Through hallowed grounds you must tread*
> *Stray from the path and death you'll wed*
> *For flowers grow, sweet and weeping,*
> *smell or touch them, you'll be sleeping.*
> *Twenty paces 'til fire you meet*
> *The deepening fog you'll need to beat*
> *Follow the lights through winding wreath*
> *Carved in hollows of wooden teeth*
> *Play my game, alive you'll stay,*
> *you may yet live to stay the day.*

Shara frowned. "I'm beginning to wonder if Ashalea's ilk aren't entirely insane. Do we really have to do this again? What *is* it with elves and riddles?"

"Again?"

"*Yes, do tell,*" Razakh said, and he sat on his haunches.

Shara sighed. "When we were on the Isle of Dread—you've both heard of that right?"

Razakh and Telilah nodded, and Shara took a deep breath.

"Okay so, we were looking for an ancient artefact that would help us to remove the darkness's portal powers. We weren't successful, obviously, but that's another story. But anyway, on this isle Denavar had to go down some dungeon, fight a really big monster, steal this stupid book, and, well, then I got kidnapped by the darkness and that

really isn't a fun topic but—"

She stopped talking, registering the bewilderment on Razakh's face and Telilah's. Shara never talked this much. But at the mention of her kidnapping, Razakh didn't need to wonder why. He shook his head. *"Carry on."*

Shara crossed her arms, shifted on her feet. "Well, basically we had to figure out a bizarre riddle and use a contraption with all this ancient Magicka on it to open the dungeon door."

"You have experience with these riddles then?" Razakh said.

Telilah nodded. "Should be a piece of cake for you, right?"

Shara frowned. "First of all, one doesn't get a figure like this from eating cake." She gestured to her body, and Razakh noted Telilah's agreeing—and appraising—nod. "Secondly, you're supposed to know the way to go! We shouldn't need to unpack any mysteries here."

Telilah's throat bobbed and she smoothed down her tunic. "Well, I did know the way. I mean, I do, but it's just … it's been a while since Grandma talked me through this. I think she hoped I'd never need to know it. It was more of a precaution really."

"Talked you through it? You've never been here before?"

Telilah blinked. "When Grandma was last here, I wasn't even born yet. But for whatever reason, she thought it necessary I know the way through. She explained the meaning behind the riddles. I guess we'll soon find out why."

Shara grumbled. "If we even make it out alive."

The minstrel shot her a filthy glare. "I'll get you through the fog, Shara. Grandma believed I could do this, why can't you? Have a little faith."

Razakh uttered a warning growl. *"Please, for the love of all that is good, can we skip the angsty back and forth and move on? I've had enough of raging female hormones for one day."*

 352

Both women turned on him and Razakh thought he might rather risk the elves' wrath than theirs. How he'd been tasked with babysitting two females who didn't know how to behave around each other was quite an impossible task. *Just kiss already ... or whatever humans do when they want one thing but act the opposite. Humans ... such strange creatures.*

He left them glaring at his haunches as he stalked into the fog. *"I'm going in. Kindly leave your drama at the entrance and help me figure out how to not fall into eternal slumber. Thanks ever so much."*

———————◆•●•◆———————

Razakh decided his previous excitement over the fog had been severely overrated. Now it felt like he was drowning in it, floundering, blind. No scent carried on its silky plumes; and he could see no farther than the tip of his snout.

He led the way, cutting a straight line ahead, their footprints immediately swallowed by the fog as they walked. The flames on his back stayed the chill from his fur as a perpetual dampness hung in the air, biting into the flesh beneath his coat. And all the while he counted. *Twenty paces.*

The girls huddled behind him, careful to stay close so they didn't lose each other in the dense grey. There was a small clicking noise and Razakh realised it was Telilah's teeth chattering as she shivered. He moved slowly, wary of predators, conscious of every breath his comrades took.

But there, just a few strides away, light blared suddenly to life, as if ushering them over with a cheery wave. A closer inspection revealed three fire sprites floating in a clearing. Their tiny bodies flitted through the fog playfully, their flames dancing as they chased each other in glee. Telilah lurched forward eagerly, and Shara grabbed her wrist.

"Be careful." Her eyes narrowed. "We don't know if they can be trusted."

Telilah nodded, but she turned and approached the sprites cautiously, propping a finger on her chin. "From what Grandma told me, the fire sprites will help us travel through the fog. But we must be careful—sprites are known to frighten easily and will abandon us if danger approaches.

"*There are spells within spells guarding this place,*" Razakh said. "*I expect we'll find more than sprites in this mist.*"

Telilah giggled as one of them dashed around her face, and she flapped her hands to send it sailing on a makeshift wind. "If I remember correctly, the true path to travel shall leave a breeze of flames in their wake. A sort of Magickal dust from their wings, I suppose."

Shara scoffed. "What breeze? I could break wind and we'd still be standing in the stench."

Razakh looked at her sideways. "*Charming.*"

She smirked in return before blowing him a kiss. But her gesture was quickly swept away in a sudden gust that stole the flames from the sprites and sent them scurrying for cover. Shara and Telilah shrieked in unison, clutching each other's arms in fright. Phantom voices whispered in an old, unknown dialect and—if it was even possible—the fog deepened into an even darker haze and an eerie silence descended.

Telilah's eyes boggled at their surroundings. "Okay ... that was creepy."

Razakh noticed an unmistakable shiver rack Shara's skin, and he cocked a head. "*The brave Onyxonite, scared?*"

"Monsters and men, I can deal with ... Ghosts? Can't sink my blade into those."

Razakh leered at her. "*Ghosts don't exist. They're just entertaining pastimes for parents with rebellious children.*"

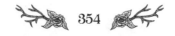

Telilah shook her head. "What if they're not ghosts but ... spirits? What remains of those who died because of the darkness?"

"Then they must be angry. Very angry." Shara's eyes darted warily as she coaxed the sprites out from their hiding place in the mossy grass. Their tiny bodies shook with fear, but after some words of encouragement, their flames seemed to rekindle. Nothing came for them out of the fog, and the women sighed in relief. But they weren't alone. Every movement felt monitored. Every word, measured.

Razakh's hackles raised and he had the distinct feeling he was being watched. *"Whatever the case, I think we should keep moving."*

Telilah eyed off one of the sprites before glancing at Razakh. He waved his tail, the flame burning brightly on its tip, and she nodded. "Let's go."

With the sprites hovering just out of arm's reach, Telilah took point. Razakh could sense her fear; not in her smell, which was a pleasant enough aroma, but in the way she carried herself. Tense muscles, small, tentative steps, a slight tremble to her hands. Shara intertwined slender fingers in her free hand and squeezed, and Razakh noticed Telilah melt into Shara's touch, her shoulders relaxing.

Good. The humans were behaving. Razakh studied the tiny creatures leading them, watching their flames flicker, reaching towards him. Embers fluttered through the air like crimson butterflies in their wake. If what Telilah said was correct, they just had to trust in the sprites.

It was a slow trek into the heart of the fog. What could have only been a few minutes felt like hours; a slow wane of time that eroded Razakh's confidence and muddled his mind. He padded onwards, searching for the so-called lights to guide them, until in the distance he saw a flicker of blue flash like lightning in his vision. Again.

It beckoned like a beacon, and he answered, trotting ahead to an

orb of blue clenched in the jaws of a tree. It was monstrous, leering with jagged teeth and unseeing eyes, taunting him to reach for the light. The phantoms shrieked, no longer whispering but shouting in anger, in pain—their accusatory tones melding together until his mind all but broke under the pressure.

He shrank down, quavering from the onslaught, wanting nothing more than to curl in a ball and bury into the darkest corner of himself. He squeezed his eyes shut, but a giddy sensation of rolling black curled beneath, and he opened them, regretfully so. They circled him. Wraithlike creatures that were neither man nor elf but a whisper of something long forgotten. And something mad.

They dashed around him like a gale, clawing at his fur, knocking his body even as he dug his own claws into the ground. A small whimper escaped his maw, and a feeling unlike anything he'd ever experienced clutched at his heart. At his soul.

Fear. Cold as steel, it spiralled through his blood until he was so icy, so feverish with it, he wondered if winter was so cruel. If snowflakes and snowstorms would be so wicked. And then he stopped wondering anything at all and sank into the roiling black and nothingness.

◆◆●◆▶

He felt hands pawing at his fur, clutching at the skin beneath. A voice called, over and over, and it sounded alarmed. Frantic. Groggily, Razakh lifted his head, which felt impossibly heavy, almost unattached. His vision swam, but he could make out amber eyes and moving lips.

"Wake up," she seemed to be saying, but how could he wake up when he'd never fallen asleep? Was this a dream?

He felt a sharp flick to his snout, and he growled in irritation. Certainly not a dream he cared for. He pulled himself up with effort,

staggering to his full height so he could peer into the gold of Shara's eyes.

"*Kindly stop prodding me, heathen.*"

She smirked. "That's more like it. What happened to you? One moment you were looking into the light, the next you were cowering like a whipped dog."

He snapped his jaws inches from her face and Shara threw her hands up placatingly. Telilah looked down her nose disapprovingly at the assassin, but the woman only smiled innocently, that damned haughty grin on her face suggesting she was anything but sorry.

Telilah placed a gentle hand on his back. "Tell us what you saw, Razakh."

He blinked. "*What I saw? The wraiths, obviously. They were everywhere, hundreds of them, whipping around like a whirlwind. And they were angry. So much hate, so much pain.*"

Shara and Telilah stared at him blankly before sharing an uneasy glance.

"It has to be an illusion," Telilah stated. "Some kind of Magicka meant to ward off would-be visitors."

"*But I saw them. The wind, the—the fear. I've never ...*" He shook his head and shivered, noting the odd expression in Shara's eyes. Something like pity. Something he never wished to see again. Not from her.

"There was nothing there, Razakh," she said. "Let's just keep moving, okay?"

Telilah nodded her agreement, and they turned their backs to walk away. Razakh stared at them, flabbergasted. How could an illusion inflict so much emotion? How could something that wasn't real make him paralysed with fear? He had passed out. Not only was that embarrassing—he was sure Shara would never let him hear the end of it—it was ridiculous.

He huffed, irritation seeping from his body in thick waves. Or maybe that was his temperature. He felt feverish, cold and clammy, yet hot and humid. He shook his head. This damnable fog was playing tricks—addling his mind.

"*How do the sprites know where to go?*"

Shara glanced over her shoulder and shrugged. "They're Magickal creatures. Who knows? Besides, the line in the riddle: 'Carved in hollow teeth'? It's the blue orbs in the tree mouths. I think they're breadcrumbs for us to follow in case we get lost." She glanced at the sprites, which were now playing chasey around Telilah, and drawled, "or if our guides abandon us."

He huffed, padding behind them. "*Let us hope they lead us away from the fog then.*"

Telilah smiled at him, small and grim. "They will. But first we find the belly of the beast before we can rip our way out of it."

A Quick Nap

SHARA

"**D**OES THIS WRETCHED PLACE EVER END?**"

Shara glanced at Telilah, who was shuffling through the mist dejectedly. Razakh seemed to share her unease, for he had remained silent since his supposed encounter with the wraiths. Even the sprites were now quiet, as if they too dreaded what awaited them in the dark.

She sighed, casting a sidelong glance at her Diodonian friend. It wasn't that she didn't believe him about the phantoms, but she didn't care to find out if what he said was true. Better they skip the drama altogether and head straight for the exit, wherever that may be.

The trees, with their crooked teeth and gaping smiles, continued to mark the way through the mist, and time felt like it had ground to a halt. The farther they travelled, the more she felt a weight settling on her shoulders. Several times she'd seen glimpses of white flashing past her vision. Whether it was real or not, she'd rather not guess.

More than once they had almost lost their bearings. The sprites were skittish, and the flaming paths they left in their wake were quickly swallowed by the fog. Shara could hardly blame them. Every noise filled her with existential dread and thoughts of wraiths sucking the life from her. And, as if on cue, another shriek ruptured the silence and she jumped. The sprites followed suit, squeaking as they flew into the mist.

"No, wait!" Shara yelled. But it was no use. Their guides had abandoned them again, and not for the first time they now stood in a copse of trees, trying to discern where the tiny creatures had flown.

Minutes ticked by, and after what felt like an eternity, the sprites had not returned.

"This is ridiculous," Telilah whined, stamping her foot with a stubbornness commonly found in rich men's prudish daughters.

Shara raised a brow. "I don't like this any more than you but whinging about it won't help. Just shut up and wait for the sprites to come back."

Telilah pouted, and Shara caught the annoyance in the swish of Razakh's tail. Everyone was irritable, snappy. As though the fog itself was made to muddle with their moods. The tree closest to her grinned broadly, and she scowled. "Oh, rack off."

"I didn't say anything," Telilah snapped, and Shara raised a palm to her face, grinding her eye socket to relieve the pressure building there.

"*Enough. Everyone form a triangle and keep an eye out for the sprites. If they circle back for us, we should be able to see the light from their flames. Shara, you look at my back.*"

She grunted her agreement, and she and Razakh took their

post at the base whilst Telilah formed the apex. Shara narrowed her eyes, willing the fog to disperse and praying that the sprites hadn't abandoned them for good.

"Little beastly creatures," she muttered grumpily.

But the damp smog lingered, oblivious to Shara's prayers and uncaring of her misery. She thought she saw a glimmer of fire once, but when she rubbed her eyes, there was nothing there. Just the fog playing tricks on her mind. With a resounding sigh, she glanced at Razakh and shook her head.

"And my flames?"

A slight ripple fanned down the blue fire on his back, but nothing unnatural. It seemed the sprites were their only hope out of this mess. Shara shook her head and he rumbled with displeasure. She bristled at his grumbling. Someone was in a mood today.

"Okay, Telilah," she said, turning on the spot, "looks like we'll have to—"

She stopped abruptly. Telilah was nowhere to be found. Panic raked down her spine like cat claws in curtains. She swivelled back to Razakh to find even his swirling silver orbs boggled with fear. The same fear that spoke of wraiths and whirlwinds.

"Telilah?" her voice sounded shrill even to her own ears. "Telilah? Where are you?"

Frantically, she searched the surrounding trees, keenly aware of their sneering faces, gleefully laughing at this prank. Shara considered grabbing Razakh's tail and setting them all on fire before dismissing the idea. She was sure the elves wouldn't appreciate that.

"We'll find her, Shara, we'll—" He stopped midsentence, and Shara ceased her pacing, eyes narrowing at his stance. Razakh stood stiffly, ears perked, nose sniffing the air. *"What is that smell?"*

She thrust her head skyward and took a whiff. Sure enough, there

was the faintest odour. A cloying sweetness in the air wafting like the smell from baked pies on grandmas' windowsills. Shara smacked her lips together. "It's delicious."

Her stomach gurgled and she clutched it with a grimace, suddenly realising how hungry she was. So ... hungry. Her mind clouded, and everything but the need to find the source of the smell blurred. Surely, Telilah could wait a few moments. She shook her head, eyes snapping open. Telilah!

Razakh was already ambling towards the smell, and she hurried after. "Stick to the path," she hissed, but it was no use, she pulled at his haunches and tugged his head, but he was transfixed on something. And then she saw them. Roses. Creamy petals of silk speckled with vibrant purple that sparkled like starlight, so bright and happy and utterly out of place.

And there, sprawled in the centre of the meadow, was Telilah, eyes glazed and face slack as she lay on her side, laughing. She twirled a flower in her finger and beckoned Shara forward. "Come lie with me. Let me tend to your needs," she giggled.

She started humming and began to strip, peeling her top away with deft fingers, a dangerous smile on her face. She tossed it at Shara provocatively and Shara's breath hitched in her throat. She was so beautiful. Like the flowers at her feet. And if she were a rose, Shara was the thorns. A role she could play quite happily.

Razakh darted forwards, heedless of Telilah's bizarre behaviour. *"I think I'll take a quick nap,"* he said lazily, the words sluggish as they drifted through her mind. She had to admit, it was an agreeable prospect, and her legs were already propelling her to Telilah's open arms.

The smell was so delightful. She was so sleepy. And Telilah was so deliciously, gorgeously naked. Her eyelids began to droop, and

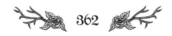

it took every effort to make the last few steps towards her friends. But something niggled at her brain. Like a gnat she tried to swat the thought away, but it buzzed incessantly, trying to warn her. Trying to make her see reason.

Reason.

Why was she here again? Why were they in this never-ending mist in the first place? *Something about elves,* she thought tiredly. She snapped her eyes open. Elves. Moonglade Elves. Who she needed in order to find her friends. Ashalea. Wezlan. Denavar.

"Oh shit," she muttered. "Razakh, don't close your eyes! It's the flowers, they're playing tricks on our minds, forcing us to sleep, just like the riddle said."

He looked at her blearily, the silver eddies swirling idly. His eyes began to shutter and Shara crossed the floor to give him a big wallop over the head. "Remember the reason we're here," Shara screeched. "Remember the Guardians!"

Comprehension snapped back into focus and she saw him blink away the sleep. He was on his paws immediately, shaking the cloud of poison from his mind. Razakh glanced at Telilah, but it was too late, the girl was asleep, snoring away like she hadn't a care in the world. She was also fully clothed, and Shara had to rub her eyes to make sure.

"But ..."

"*It's an illusion,*" Razakh said.

"You saw her naked and singing?" Shara said, incredulous.

"*What?*"

"What?" Shara shifted her feet, cheeks burning. An uncomfortable silence settled, accompanied by the sweet stench of the flowers—only now it was tinged with decay, of corruption. She could sense a tingling in the air, a sigh of Magicka.

"*We need to move. Now. Put her on my back.*" He extinguished the

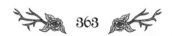

363

flames and huddled down beside her, careful not to stick his muzzle into the roses.

"Just great," Shara fumed, and she shoved Telilah none too gently onto Razakh's back. "Our solver of riddles is out cold. You'll be the death of me, woman."

She gazed at the fog enveloping them, desperately hoping to see three tiny sprites appear to guide them. But the mist remained unbroken, and Shara set her mouth in a hard line, her eyes focused on the way forward. No sprites were coming to save them.

"Let's move."

A shriek broke the silence, and her heart threatened to abandon her. She cast her eyes around, searching for the source, hands trembling despite her best efforts at composure. It was joined by more moans, unearthly wails forming a chorus of dissent, and she, the cause.

Wraiths sped in droves, forming a wall of white as they raced around her—through her—cold as a corpse, angry as a hive of bees protecting their queen. Only there was no queen now. Just the remains of a tribe wronged and ruined.

But Shara would not suffer the dead, she was too invested in the living. Setting her jaw and looking at Razakh resolutely, she clasped her torches like weapons and brandished them at the phantoms. They scattered as the fire passed through their ethereal bodies.

"We run ... or we die. Now!"

They broke out of the spectral mass and bolted through the fog, Shara leading the way with her sword drawn and fist raised, Razakh and a sleeping Telilah right behind her. She brushed aside her foes with the blade, bellowing her anger, thrusting aside all fear.

Fog clawed at her and she ran blindly, eyes searching frantically for the crooked smiles and ghostly lights in the trees.

"*This is madness,*" Razakh roared in her mind. "*We'll never find our*

way through."

"Then call me a mad woman but I'm not stopping," she yelled over her shoulder, and whether it was sheer determination or blind, dumb luck, she noticed the fog diminished up ahead, curling tendrils sputtering out and pluming up an unseen wall.

She exerted all her energy, pummelling one boot after another into the ground, driving off the wraiths with fire and fury. They scratched at her with clawed fingers, pulled at her hair, bit into her flesh, but she ran onwards, stumbling to freedom.

They shrieked with renewed anger, determined to pull her into the void, eager to turn her supple skin into rot and bone so she may join them, feel their pain, know their suffering. They dragged her down, pawing at her legs, and behind her, she saw the same happening to Razakh. But she would crawl if she had to.

"Let me go," she implored them. "I seek retribution. I am a Guardian, born to exact justice and protect the innocent. I will seek your vengeance. I will restore your memory."

There was silence for a moment, as if time itself stood still. And then, by some miracle or unspoken agreement, they were just ... gone.

Shara pushed to her feet, checked Telilah and Razakh. Both were lined with cuts and bloody stripes, but both were breathing. Alive. She sighed in relief and turned to the edge of the fog.

"*We made it,*" Razakh said in disbelief.

"Yup," Shara said tiredly. "And now the great mystery of how to enter."

They walked out of the mist and Shara gulped in fresh air, greedily lapping up the sight of greenery, a starlit sky gleaming up above. She took another step and ... banged into an invisible wall. She staggered back in surprise, rubbing her nose which was smarting from the impact.

"*The entrance to the Meadows?*" Razakh said hopefully, and Shara nodded.

"The one and only. Now if I can just get them to open the door ..." She began pounding the wall with both fists, screaming all manner of expletives, wondering if the elves on the other side could hear her.

She felt Razakh's eyes boring into the back of her head and sighed. "I didn't come all this way to be left begging like a street rat for scraps." She sniffed.

"*Perhaps another tactic?*"

Despite everything, his words were dripping with amusement and she scowled. "Very well then." She cleared her throat with an exaggerated snort. "My name is Shara Silvaren, daughter of Lord Harvar Silvaren of the Onyxonites, and a Guardian of the Grove. I come on behalf of my friends—Ashalea Kindaris, Denavar Andaro, and Wezlan Shadowbreaker. Please, let us enter."

When nothing happened, she turned around to give Razakh her best 'I told you so' stare, but in the silver depths his amusement soon turned to awe, and she cocked a head in puzzlement.

"Well now, why didn't you say so sooner?"

Shara whirled on her feet, and her own eyes boggled in amazement, for there, where nothing but grass had just before stood, was a city of wonder. A city that was, for the most part, very much still thriving.

"Oh, shit," she breathed.

The figure before her chuckled; a pleasant, warm sound. The sound of a woman. "We've been expecting you," the silky voice said.

Shara narrowed her eyes, trying to see behind the veil covering the face. Something about her was oddly familiar. Sensing Shara's scrutiny, the woman lifted a pale hand to her face and peeled the mask from her features like ripping a bandage from a wound.

And for the first time in Shara's life she was at a loss for words,

uttering the only comprehensible thing that came to mind.

"Oh shiiiieeeettttt."

Gone

ASHALEA

THEY TUMBLED THROUGH TIME AND SPACE; the same sickening feeling of falling as their bodies were sucked through a tunnel at dizzying speeds until finally the portal spat them out and Ashalea landed on a bed of green, Denavar thumping down beside her.

She curled into a ball and cried. Ugly tears of anger and hatred and regret and sorrow, all streaming down in a torrent of pain. He was gone. And she had walked away. Willingly, and yet not.

Ashalea gasped, cursing herself for being here, alive and breathing, when he would never do so again. The hairs on her arms raised, and her skin prickled as her body registered the shock and trauma. Her head was heavy, her skin cold like slate. She was too miserable, too tired to take in her surroundings. She didn't care where they had landed nor what happened to Everosia.

But she cared about Denavar. He was real, and he was hurt.

Exhausted, Ashalea lifted her head, and immediately she was assaulted with a new problem. Denavar was sprawled on the ground, body spasming, limbs jerking, the wound in his shoulder dripping, blood pooling on the grass.

She crawled to him, cradling his head in her lap, watching helplessly as his eyes rolled back into his head and he shook, over and over, on and on.

"Denavar, what's happening? What do I do?" She reached inside for the healing power, for the light, for anything that might help, and calling forth the Magicka, Ashalea placed a palm on his forehead.

The Magicka glowed, but nothing happened. She hissed in frustration and retreated into her mind, calling on the power and willing it to the surface. The nerves sparked to life, and a charge of electricity jolted through her veins. The power was reacting, the Magicka was there, but still he spasmed. She shifted her palm to his shoulder and tried again, concentrating, expelling her energy. The wound began to knit together, and she sighed in relief as the white light crept into the flesh and cleaned him from the inside out, healing him entirely.

He stopped spasming and she stared at him hopefully, waiting. "Please, Denavar, please."

His eyes snapped open and he lurched forward, gasping for air, his chest heaving and his pulse hammering in this throat. He stared at Ashalea incredulously for the longest minute until she couldn't stand it anymore.

"What?"

He shook his head, seemingly at a loss for words. "It's Wezlan ... he ... his power ..."

She held her breath, waiting, nails digging into his leg. When he only shook his head she snapped, "What, Denavar?"

"His power is inside me, Ashalea. He sacrificed himself to pass it all to me."

***

They lay there, mentally and physically exhausted, bruised, battered and—for Ashalea's part—broken. She didn't know how many more blows she could take, how much more she could lose.

Wezlan was dead. He had sacrificed himself for them, given every kernel of his power to Denavar before the darkness could snuff out his life. Just like Barlok had done so many years ago. And despite Wezlan's valiant deeds, it still didn't change anything.

The darkness was alive, and Wezlan was gone.

He.

Was.

Gone.

She couldn't even cry anymore. Her tears had dried, the well had emptied. Now she just felt hollow. Incomplete. Wezlan had been her knight, and a queen was nothing without her army. She sighed, a raspy croak that rattled out her chest.

Denavar brushed a hand along her face, and she took his fist in her own, clutching it for all she was worth. The warmth seeped into her fingers, and he brought her hand to his lips. The affection washed over her, through her. A warm summer's breeze to stave off the chill of a coming winter.

His eyes glittered with sorrow, periwinkle blue shuttering as he pressed her hand to his heart. "I know how much he meant to you, Ashalea. I know he was like a father."

There's that word. *Was*. Her eyes prickled after all.

Denavar's throat bobbed. "He wouldn't want you to lose your way. To become lost in the memory of him. I—I'm here for you. To lean on, to talk to. Anything you need while you mourn."

Rage flared in her blood and she saw him wince, immediately regretting his choice of words.

"I don't want to mourn him," she snapped. "I want to avenge him. Wezlan, my parents, the mages, Shara, the crew from the Violet Star, the Windarion elves, Kinna and Ondori ... my friends, Denavar. Everyone we've ever cared about. Everyone we've lost."

"And we will, Ashalea. I promise you. I have a stake in this, too. He will die for everything he's done." His face softened a little, and he stroked a strand of silver behind her ear. "I love you, Ashalea."

The anger dissipated, and she sighed. "I love you too."

He leaned in close, kissing her deeply, passionately on the lips. She sank into his warmth, melting into his familiarity, relishing the taste of peppermint and the curl of his tongue around hers. She crushed his lips in return, wanting nothing more than to forget the pain and sorrow—to thrust the hurt aside and focus on something, anything else.

They held each other for a time with nothing but the moon and the stars to see their sadness. Ashalea could have stayed there forever in that moment, but with a disgruntled sigh she leaned up on her elbows and cast her eyes around the place. They were in a field of green—a meadow—wildflowers of purple and white surrounding them. Fireflies danced, shimmering speckles of gold, and the sky above was so clear, dusted with stars. Utterly beautiful.

There was something so familiar about this place, and she had the distinct feeling she'd been here before. In a dream or ... or maybe a vision.

371

"Where are we Denavar?"

He groaned as he pulled himself up to sit and glanced at the stretch of grass alongside them, then up to the small mountains to their right. More like overgrown hills, really. But his eyes widened with tell-tale satisfaction as he realised where they were. As his eyes fully took in their surroundings.

"We're home."

She stared at him blankly.

"Ashalea. We're *home*."

Her eyes boggled as it dawned on her. There was only one place other than Renlock he'd call home. "Wait, you can't mean ... THE Meadows?"

"That's precisely what he means."

Ashalea shrieked, the silky voice causing her to jump to her feet. She whirled on the intruder, indignant and puzzled at their sudden appearance and how on Everosia she hadn't heard them. The voice belonged to a hooded figure, cloaked in midnight blue, the face fully hidden by shadow.

Ashalea narrowed her eyes, slipping into a crouch, fireball burning in hand. Denavar stiffened at her side and moved into a defensive position, shoving her behind him. She peeked out from behind his shoulder.

The stranger laughed—soft peals ringing through the air. Endearing, happy laughter. Pretty as a nightingale. Oddly charming. Oddly ... familiar. "There's no need to fear. I won't hurt you."

"Then why do you hide your identity?" Ashalea snarled.

A small smile shadowed the face and two slender hands reached up towards the hood, grasping the velvet material and sweeping it back in one motion.

Long wavy hair cascaded down her shoulders, framing an angular jaw, high cheekbones and full lips. Her skin was milky, smooth, a perfect canvas for a beautiful smile and a narrow nose. Hazel eyes twinkled from beneath immaculate brows. But beyond all that, Ashalea could only stare in bewilderment at the person who stood before her, crowned in locks of silver, bright as a full moon and shimmering like starlight.

The woman smiled, and Denavar dropped his guard. "By all the Gods and Goddesses," he breathed. "It's not possible."

The woman stepped towards Ashalea, gently taking her hands. Ashalea sucked in a breath at the touch. At the very real, very alive person standing before her.

"Hello, Ashalea."

The world seemed to close in on itself, folding down into a neat box with room only for two. Ashalea clenched the fingers of the woman, the smooth skin soft and warm beneath her own. She lifted her eyes to the unmistakable similarity of the woman opposite her. There was only one person this could be.

"... Mother?"

Acknowledgements

There aren't enough words to express my gratitude to the wonderful people who have assisted me with this book. Sometimes I wonder if starting my self-publishing journey with a trilogy was a little ambitious, but as I type away today—sun shining, cup of tea within arm's reach—I feel proud and so incredibly joyful to share this book with you, my dear readers.

To my wonderful husband, Jason, if it weren't for your nagging and encouragement, I'd likely still be slogging away and trying to churn through these chapters. Thank you for always believing in me and pushing me to be the best version of myself.

To my family: your encouragement, your love, and your ability to deal with my stress and self-doubt is always appreciated and never forgotten.

To my editor, Aidan Curtis, your advice and friendship help me both as a person and as a writer, and I will never not love the breadcrumb trail of amusing comments during my revisions on the manuscript!

My beautiful beta team, your feedback helped polish this novel and I am so grateful for your time and effort.

To everyone that made this book beautiful inside and out, and whose wonderful friendship has helped me immensely. Special mentions to Erica Timmons for cover design, Julia Scott for the formatting, Emily Johns for the gorgeous illustrations, and Niru Sky for the incredible hardcover artwork!

Special thanks to my bookstagram family for being so supportive and kind. I appreciate you all.

And finally, to my dear readers. Your support, your reviews, your purchases and your kindness—they all make it possible for indie authors to keep writing, keep publishing, keep creating. Thank you so much!

About the Author

Chloe Hodge was born in Adelaide, South Australia, to New Zealand parents, and a Hungarian heritage. In 2017 she completed a Bachelor of Journalism and Professional Writing at the University of South Australia and proceeded to work for the ABC as a radio producer and news reporter, and thereafter a journalist for a technical grape and wine magazine. She is now the owner of small editing business, Chloe's Chapters, and writes Fantasy and Young Adult novels. Her debut novel, *Vengeance Blooms*, Book One of the Guardians of the Grove series, was published in August 2019. The third and final instalment of this trilogy is set to release in 2021.